CELESTE O. NORFLEET

Love
After All

ARABESQUE®

LOVE AFTER ALL

ISBN-13: 978-0-373-83006-0
ISBN-10:   0-373-83006-8

www.kimanipress.com

Printed in U.S.A.

To fate and fortune

Acknowledgments

This is my tenth full-length novel and I'd like to thank the many booksellers and librarians who help keep my dream alive. Your dedication and devotion is unending and I truly appreciate you. I'd also like to thank the many book clubs who have selected my books to read over the years. It is a pleasure to come into your homes and share my imagination. I'd also like to thank my editor, Evette Porter, and my agent, Elaine English, having you on my side keeps me focused and motivated. As always, special thanks to my husband, Charles, my children, Jennifer, Christopher, Prince and Charles. And to my sisters, Amanda and Karen, my brothers, Butch and Garry, and to my mom, Mable E. Johnson, this would not be possible without you all. Lastly, thanks to China, Hattie, Roszine and Steve and to my wonderful in-laws for your continuous love and support. Thank you all from the bottom of my heart.

Prologue

Her rhythm was off. She'd felt it all weekend.

Samantha Lee Taylor knocked twice and waited, then knocked again. There was no reply. She tried the doorknob. The door was unlocked. She opened it and walked inside. Her pulse quickened as she stood in the small vestibule, knowing instinctively that something was wrong. "Eric," she called out. There was no answer. She walked farther inside and found everything exactly in place, exactly as it should be. And a shiver of nerves gripped her.

This couldn't be his apartment, she thought.

Her new boyfriend, Eric Hamilton, a salesman at the computer company where she worked, had stood her up Friday night. She'd called all day Saturday and Sunday, and waited for word from him. He'd never returned her calls. Worry turned to fear and then to suspicion. So here she was on Monday morning, standing in his apartment. Where was he?

"Eric," she called out again as she looked around slowly. "Eric." The apartment was scarcely furnished. She remembered him telling her that it came as is. She walked through the living room to the kitchenette. The tiny refrigerator door and cabinets were all open and empty. She hurried to the next room where she saw that a small bed in the corner was sloppily made. Nearly empty, the room's only furniture was the bed, a chair, a desk in the opposite corner and a small chest of drawers. She walked over to the desk.

A laptop computer, oddly familiar, was the only thing sitting there and it seemed out of place. She lifted the screen and instantly realized that it was *her* personal laptop. She sat down, switched it on and keyed in her password. It was rejected. She tried it once more. Rejected again. The password had obviously been changed. She felt a sudden sinking feeling in the bottom of her stomach. Eric had been on her personal computer and had changed her password. She typed in her back-door command and an instant later the screen saver appeared. He switched computers on purpose, but why?

Seeing the PC gave her pause. Having never been in his apartment before she saw no logical reason for her computer to be there. So why was it? She remembered that a few weeks ago he had made a point of purchasing one exactly like hers. She'd even helped him set it up. Maybe he'd left his at th office and grabbed hers by mistake. As she pondered th situation, she continued to look around as the feeling of bein conned began to sink in.

Samantha slowly walked over to the closet. Opening it, sh got her answer. It was empty. There was no sign of clothe shoes or even hangers. She opened the top dresser drawer. was empty, too. Anxiously, she opened each drawer; eac was empty except for the last one. There she found a phot of the two of them together. Her heart raced and she walke back to the desk and looked down at the computer. As she prepared to turn it off, the phone rang.

She looked around the empty bedroom guiltily, as if she'd been caught in the middle of a police dragnet. She slowly walked over to the phone on the floor and picked it up on the second ring.

She said quickly, "Eric? What's going on, where are—"

"Samantha, get out of there now."

"Who is this?"

"You know who it is, lollipop. Get out of there."

The word *lollipop* stopped her. There was only one person in the world who called her that. "Jefferson?" she asked at hearing her brother's voice for the first time in nearly seven years. "Jefferson, is that you?" Having not heard from him in so long, and now suddenly hearing his voice in the last place she would have expected, stunned her.

"Now!" he repeated more firmly.

A minute later she was on the street walking away from her once-perfect life. She turned as police cars with flashing lights came screeching down the street. As other pedestrians moved toward the sudden police action, she quickly walked away. She removed her jacket, wrapping it around her waist, and tied her silk scarf stylishly around her hair. A few blocks away she hailed a cab, got in and headed back across town to her apartment.

She pulled out her cell phone and saw several messages, none from Eric. She called the one marked Emergency, Please Call. Jillian, her assistant and friend, answered immediately.

"Sam, I've been trying to call you all morning," she said quietly. "Wherever you are, stay there. There's a problem. Eric's not here yet and there are people here looking for him and you, too."

"What do you mean? Who? What people?"

"The police, for one."

"The police!" she said louder than she expected. The cab-driver glanced back in his mirror. She smiled calmly.

"Yeah," Jillian said, whispering now. "They didn't exactly elaborate, but I heard someone say that there was a problem with your company."

"My company? What company? I don't have a company."

"Well, according to them you do. They even showed me letterhead and business cards citing you as the owner of a computer business named Taylor Enterprises. Do you know anything about it?"

"Taylor Enterprises, no, I never heard of it."

"Eric has. Apparently he worked for you at this company."

"He what?" she said, again too loud, drawing the cab-driver's attention once more. He glanced at her through the rearview mirror, then back to the crosstown traffic.

"That's what they said… Eric worked for you. We told them that you were a consulting computer engineer here but they didn't believe us. I overheard one of the police officers mention fraud and embezzlement."

"Fraud and embezzlement… Are you kidding me?" Samantha said in a near whisper, conscious of the cab-driver's attention.

"No, they took the office computers and even your personal computer. Someone said that Eric stole over fifty thousand dollars from the company, with fake invoices. They traced the signature back to an account in your name using a computer here at work. They think you were in on it, too," she said whispering the last part.

"This is crazy. I'm a computer specialist, I do company tech support. I'm not a crook, and if I was going to commit fraud I'd have enough sense not to have the signature traced back to me. That's nuts. I'll be right there to straighten this out."

"No, don't. As I said, the police were in here earlier looking for you. Then about thirty minutes later two other men came looking for Eric. They said that they were from the police fraud division but they looked more like street thugs to me. One had on a bright purple suit and the other had a huge scar on the side of his face. They asked questions about Eric, then about you. I told them that I hadn't seen you in days, but I don't think they bought it."

"I'm not a thief. I didn't steal any money." Like a shattered glass Samantha's mind whirled off in a hundred different directions as memories from her childhood surfaced. "I spent most of my childhood life on the run. I'm not running from this."

"I know that, girl, but you have to, at least for right now," Jillian said supportively. "What about Eric, can you catch up with him at his place? Maybe he can explain this. But if he's involved…"

"Eric's missing."

"Big surprise," Jillian said sarcastically. "I knew he was no good. I overheard one of the police officers say that there was already a warrant out for his arrest from a previous problem."

"I just came from his apartment, it looked like he left in a hurry," she hesitated, seeing the cabdriver glance at her in the rearview mirror again. "The police showed up right after I left."

"Did you find anything?"

"Yeah, my laptop computer was there."

"What? Your laptop, how is that possible? The police just took it away," Jillian said.

"They must have taken Eric's computer. They're exactly the same. Remember, I went with him to buy a new one and even set it up for him? He switched them, I don't even know when."

"I do," Jillian said. "He switched computers last Friday. Something told me that he was up to something when he stopped by late Friday looking for you. You'd just left, I was on my way out and he said he needed to put something on your desk. He had his coat and computer with him when he went into your office."

"You're right, that's probably when he switched computers," Samantha surmised. "I can't believe this. Why?"

"He's a jerk, why else? Hold on, your office phone is ringing," Jillian said. "Maybe that's him."

Samantha waited while Jillian picked up her phone. As she listened to a muffled voice, she looked up at the driver. Apparently his interest in her conversation had long since waned, as he was now stopped at a traffic light, ardently checking out a woman in a midriff and tight jeans walking in front of the cab.

As the driver approached her building she noted two men walking to a car parked out front. One wore a bright purple suit and the other had a scar on his face. The cab slowed to pull over, but she quickly instructed the driver to the take her to building across the street.

"I'm back," Jillian said.

"Was it Eric?" Samantha asked.

"No, stranger than that," she said cautiously. "It was someone else. He said he was a friend of yours, but he didn't want to leave a name or number. He called you lollipop."

"What did he say exactly?"

"Something strange, really strange. He said that when I hear from you, I should tell you wait for the Wizard at Oz." The line went silent as Samantha didn't reply. "Samantha, are you there?"

"Yes, I'm here."

"Do you understand, do you know what he's talking about?"

"Yes. Wait for the Wizard of Oz."

"What does it mean?"

"I don't know exactly. All I know is that I think I have to be scarce for a while. I don't know how long, maybe a few weeks or maybe longer."

"Samantha." Jillian sounded worried.

"Don't worry, I'll be fine. Just do me a favor and don't mention to anyone that we talked, okay?"

"Okay," Jillian said reluctantly. "Is there anything I can do to help? Do you have any money?" She knew Samantha wouldn't ask if it wasn't important.

"There's nothing you can do and I have money saved. I need you to stay as far away as possible from all this."

"Samantha, whatever's going on, please be careful. The two guys that came here didn't look too friendly. I don't know what Eric was mixed up in, but whatever it was sounds serious, so take care," Jillian said.

"I'll call you soon," Samantha promised as the driver stopped the cab and turned off the meter. He told her the charge and began logging in the destination.

As she was looking in her purse for the correct change, she noticed that the two men got into their car but didn't drive away. She knew they were waiting for her.

"Do you have change for a hundred?" she asked the cabdriver.

"Are you kidding me?" he said, looking up in the rear-view mirror.

"Fine, hold the hundred and take me to my bank around the corner so I can get change."

He agreed happily, holding on to the security of the hundred-dollar bill. As he pulled away from the curb, Samantha deliberately spilled change from her purse. Coins fell everywhere. "Oops," she said.

The driver looked up again, seeing that she had ducked down to pick up the coins.

"Which bank?" he asked gruffly as he drove back by the

front of her apartment building. The two men sitting in the car saw only the driver pass by.

Still collecting change, she gave him directions to the closest bank around the corner, knowing that she would walk back to her apartment building and slip in the back door.

Twenty minutes later, two bags in hand, she walked away from her life. Samantha Lee Taylor was now Samantha Lee, and heeding the message, she went into hiding, following the Yellow Brick Road all the way to Oz.

Chapter 1

Over the next four months, Samantha Lee's life was complicated, to say the least. Being conned and betrayed by an ex-boyfriend, avoiding being questioned by the police and hiding out from street thugs had kept her busy, still waiting for word from Oz. In the meantime, she'd been searching for the one person who could return her life to her. She had a score to settle. At the moment, her life was on an even keel. But then again, it was her time; it was after twelve o'clock midnight when everything seemed familiar.

After midnight was the golden hour.

Her father always told her that there were two types of people, predators and decent folk. And that folk coming out after midnight were only looking for one thing—trouble. And more than likely that's what they'd find. He lived by this one truth. And living by this code separated him from the predators. He never purposely targeted an innocent, although the greedy and morally challenged were another story.

Thinking about her father brought back conflicting emotions. Deep inside, she knew that she still loved him, but she also hated what he did with his life. His world had torn her family apart, iced her mother's heart and made her lose faith.

While she was growing up he was her hero. Then he left and the comfortable feeling of family disappeared. Now she merely accepted that he was both hero and villain. Samantha smiled at the stray thought. After midnight was his time, and now it was hers. She now understood what he meant. Her senses were heightened and her instincts were at their sharpest. She ruled the night with complete confidence and control. It was the light of day that often confused matters for her.

"So, how long have you been doing this?"

She looked up into the rearview mirror, then back at the street in front of her. The slightly accented voice startled her momentarily. "Doing what?" she responded guiltily, having been caught slightly off guard. Driving on automatic, she'd let her thoughts wander off and she'd nearly forgotten that she wasn't alone.

"This, driving a cab, how long have you been doing this?" he repeated in a classic Bostonian accent that seemed to give his voice a level of eloquence and charm.

"Not long," Samantha said without eye contact, hoping her short answer would end the prompted chitchat, as it usually did for those who insisted on dragging her into conversation.

"Remarkable, quite remarkable indeed," he said, nodding his apparent approval, then continuing, "You see, I'm a student of the philosophical nature of human behavior. I like to know what makes people do what they do, the will behind the deed so to speak. And I find you, or rather your stated occupation, intriguing—a young woman, quite attractive at that, driving, and all alone at night, remarkable and indeed impressive," she didn't answer. He continued, "I imagine that you would meet all kinds of interesting people, particularly at night."

"At times," she muttered obligingly.

"But then again, it would of course be the solitude that you enjoy most."

"Of course," she moaned inwardly at his persistence.

"How about that?" he said, then paused to chuckle at seemingly nothing in particular. His husky voice cracked with age and then steadied as he repeated, "How about that?"

They drove in silence for a few more blocks until he spoke again. "Are you an aspiring actress or model or writer or something like that?" She glanced up at him and then back at the street as he said. "I only ask because you just don't seem to be the type to do this for a living. So I assume that you're only doing it to raise extra money or as a side job until something better comes along."

"I drive," she answered simply, sticking to her two-word answers.

"Bravo, good for you, well done, and you drive quite well, I might add. You are to be commended."

He sounded too joyous to be believed. She didn't respond.

Moments later, Samantha pulled to a smooth stop at the traffic light beneath a bright overhead streetlamp and picked up the small notebook on the seat beside her. She plucked the pencil from the side holder and jotted down a note to herself. Stray memories, thoughts and ideas often came to her like that. From out of nowhere, an idea would come and she'd write it down for another time. But she found lately she had a dwindling amount of time. And as the hours advanced she could only watch and wait.

The light turned green.

She glanced up momentarily into the rearview mirror at the

shadowed face of the man behind her. He looked away quickly. He'd been staring at her again. He'd been staring at her since he got in. She steadied her eyes on his face, studying the angles as he now kept council with his own reflection in the darkened side window.

Assessing her exposure, she sensed no immediate threat. Returning her gaze to the front, she pulled off.

Misting now, it had rained earlier so tiny droplets of water remained on the windshield, sparkling like diamonds each time they passed beneath a light. She waited until the next streetlamp approached. Looking back again, she took in his features to assess his standing in the food chain. He didn't look predatory, but he was certainly not too respectable to be out after midnight.

She had picked him up at the bus station. He'd caught her eye immediately. Tall, medium build, he stood with a silver-tipped cane at his side. At first he seemed to be looking for someone. She watched as he waited, discounting the cabs in front of her as they piled up and took fares. As soon as it was her turn he stepped up and got into her cab.

He was a plain man with plain features, a moderate nose with full lips reminiscent of his distant African roots; he had a dimpled chin, a cleft, and wore a dark suit that gave him a distinguished air of dignity like that of a funeral director on call.

He was broad and most likely had been a handsome man in his time. He had a generous sprinkle of salt to his pepper hair and carried himself with an air of possibility. A businessman perhaps, but legitimacy was always up for grabs. After all, it was well after midnight and as Daddy always said, trouble.

Samantha nodded to herself absently, knowingly.

"Take a right at the next traffic light," he said.

Samantha looked up in the rearview mirror again and connected with his dark eyes. "Excuse me?"

"Take a right at the next traffic light," he repeated, knowing that he'd obviously interrupted her thoughts again.

She did, easing gently to the corner, looking for oncoming traffic, then turned the corner and slowly accelerated down the one-way street.

"Make a left here and get into the right lane," he said. She did as instructed. "Now pull over right there," she pointed to a darkened office building. "Yes, this is good, right here."

Samantha looked out after her windshield wiper made a quick pass. The murky darkness left a haze of uneasiness as she stopped the cab and shifted to park, leaving the engine running.

"What's the damage?" he asked, leaning forward.

Samantha reached over and released the meter. "Forty-one dollars even." She picked up her log, looked outside again and jotted down the nearest intersection. She grabbed her dispatch scanner and reported in. Something she rarely did but for some reason felt compelled to do now.

"Thank you," the man said as he opened the cab's rear door. He shifted his cane and handed her a one-hundred-dollar bill over the front seat.

Samantha took the money, examining it on instinct. She'd learned the feel of counterfeit paper before she could write her name. The feel was right; the bill was legit. "Do you have anything smaller?" she asked.

"No," he said as he exited. "Keep the change."

A five-dollar tip would have sufficed, a twenty-dollar tip was curious. But a fifty-nine-dollar tip was troublesome. Her gut instinct nudged her cynicism. "Thanks," she said slowly, cautiously. "Do you need a receipt?" she asked just as the door closed soundly.

Slightly hunched over, his cane supporting his weight, he walked with steady even strides. She sat for a while in the darkness and watched as he eventually disappeared across the street, away from the building she'd stopped in front of.

"Hey, you there?" The crackling static broke her focused concentration and ended her line of vision when she reached down and picked up the small wired radio.

"Yes, I'm here," she said in her smooth, deeply feminine voice. She glanced over at the building again. No lights came on—he seemed to have been swallowed by the night. "What do you have for me?" she asked.

"You okay? You never check in after a pickup and drop-off," the dispatcher said through heavy static.

"Yeah, I'm fine," she said, dismissing him but realizing he was right. She never followed the proper procedures. It was mandatory that all night drivers check in as soon as they reached their fare's final destination. She seldom did.

"You sure? You've got your auntie Em a little nervous over here." A new voice chimed into the conversation as her aunt Emily picked up.

"I'm fine," she reiterated. "What do you have for me?"

"I have you off duty. Your shift's over, so click your heels twice, it's time to come on home now, Dorothy."

"On my way, Auntie Em."

Samantha released the side button and tossed the radio on the seat beside her. Samantha's being the only woman on night shift made the dispatcher nervous. Plus, she'd been nearly robbed twice and both times had managed to not only retrieve her cash bag but also drop the perpetrators off at the police precinct across the street from the small cab company.

Each time, the office staff had panicked. But out of twenty-seven cabs on the night shift, she was the only woman and had a perfect record of zero assaults and zero cash loss. But the men she worked with still found it necessary to go out of their way to be almost condescendingly protective.

She shifted gears and pulled away from the curb, then turned off her on-duty light and headed back to the garage.

She let the washers wipe the windshield one last time before turning them off, then rolled down the window and let the fresh sweet clean air into the stuffy cab. She inhaled deeply, filling her lungs with moisture. The smell was exhilarating. Born at midnight, the night held her in perfect safety.

After a quick stop at an all-night diner uptown, she took the expressway back to the garage, a major taboo without a passenger. But she didn't care. If she'd been stopped she'd have done what she always did. Talk her way out of it.

Twenty minutes later she pulled into the cab company depot and rounded the employee lot, seeing that her car was still where she'd parked it. She looked up at the sign as she drove into the garage. Osborn's Cab and Limo Service was painted on a huge white billboard and floodlights made it visible from a mile away.

Clemet Osborn, no longer alive, had owned the small auto garage and was the kind of man everyone came to for a ride. So he made it official and opened the cab company. In the days of the Old West, Clemet Osborn's Cab and Limo Service would have been considered a hole in the wall, a place where anyone, especially of questionable references, could go and rest before moving on. And that's exactly what Samantha was doing now.

She parked her vehicle in the service garage, following standard procedure. She grabbed her cash bag, log, small backpack, brown paper bag, then put on her father's old lucky leather jacket, which she was never without. The night was over as far as she was concerned.

"Well, now, if it isn't Miss Lee returning from the big bad world," Darnell said, looking her up and down when she got out of the car, as if she were the last sip of water in the Sahara

Desert. Her formfitting jeans and oversize sweatshirt made him smile and his mouth salivate. He itched to see what was underneath the bulk she insisted on wearing all the time.

Darnell Griggs, a fellow cabdriver, suffered from a Napoleon complex and was just barely tall enough to reach the steering wheel. He asked her out routinely, and just as routinely she turned him down. Brash and rude, he was a pathetic excuse for a human being, who happened to be married with three kids, living in his mother-in-law's house because he was too lazy to take responsibility and support his family on his own.

He was African-American, the color of bleached paste, who had married a Tootsie Roll-complexioned sister and thought from then on that every woman of paper-bag complexion or darker was fair game. He was so wrong.

Samantha didn't turn around, knowing exactly who it was; she ignored him. He continued as usual. "You look particularly fine this evening. Why don't you let me take you out."

She didn't respond, knowing better. With no makeup, her hair pinned beneath a cap and cheap large Afro wig and her dowdy posture, she knew she was a mess. But it suited her purpose well. Rough and ragged, she avoided attention and did her best to suppress the slightest hint of attractiveness. But apparently Darnell didn't care.

"How about I buy you breakfast?" he said. "I was on my way out, but don't mind hanging around to wait for you," he casually leaned back on the side of her cab.

"No, thanks," Samantha said coolly as she checked the rear seat of the car. She found a gum wrapper, an ink pen, an empty juice bottle and a manila envelope, which she picked up and tucked under her arm while trashing the rest.

"What do you mean, no, thanks? Where you gonna get a better offer? Oh, I see, you waiting on some Prince Charming to come in here and sweep you off your feet. Well, let me tell you something, sweetheart. He ain't coming down here, so you better take what you can get."

Samantha rolled her eyes to the ceiling and shook her head. This was the last thing she needed after just putting in eight hours on the road. With added restraint, she exhaled and walked away.

"Hey, you hear me talking to you?" Darnell said nastily, then grabbed her arm to halt her retreat.

She stopped and looked down at her arm. His fingers, pale and clenched, were wrapped tightly around the arm of her leather jacket. She looked him in the eye. He let go and backed off instantly, looking around quickly, knowing that there were any number of men in the garage ready and willing to step to anyone who harassed her.

"You still think you too good for me, huh?" Darnell said, sneering nastily as he always did when he didn't get his way, which was more often than he wanted to admit.

"Yeah, something like that," she answered plainly, barely focusing on his comments as she continued to walk away. Ignoring Darnell was the only thing known to deflate his oversized ego.

"You know it's because of me that you even got this gig. One word from me and you're gone," he threatened openly. Being Clemet Osborn's son-in-law gave him a false sense of power.

"That's fine with me," Samantha said easily.

"What, you think I wouldn't fire you?"

"Give it your best shot," she said, calling his bluff, knowing that he didn't have any power to hire or fire anyone.

"You're gonna see me in a different light one of these days, Miss Samantha Lee," he hissed. "You're gonna come to me begging me to take you out."

Sexual harassment on the job was tolerable at times, although if Darnell ever became a real threat she knew she had options. There were plenty of men who saw her as either a hardworking, no-nonsense coworker, or had placed her in the younger-sister category and become instantly protective. But she had always preferred to handle her own business her own way. She hadn't reached that point yet with Darnell, but he was sure 'nough getting close.

She continued walking through the garage tossing her arm up, waving at cabbies as they entered and left. Then she stopped by Deacon Payne's alley briefly to get a quick run-down on the day.

Deacon was an ex-con who had been rehabilitated and been living on the straight and narrow for over ten years. He had been a gambler with a temper who'd served three years for assault and another three for seriously chastising another inmate for being a stool pigeon to a guard.

The moment Samantha met him four months ago, she felt an instant kindred spirit. Of the men who worked at Osborn's Cab and Limo Service—most on their second chance—he was her favorite. He reminded her of her father and her hope that one day he would have settled down and ended his long career on the other side of the law.

"Hey, Sammy," Deacon said as he looked up on seeing her approach. She was typically rumpled and disheveled; her appearance, truly streetworthy, made a very pronounced *do not approach* statement, but he knew that she was a diamond beneath the tattered clothes, Negro League baseball cap and ill-fitting oversize jacket.

Samantha smiled brightly as soon as she saw him. Few men were given latitude to call her Sammy; Deacon was the only one she could remember in a long time. Covered in a fine sheet of oil and grease, he was bent over an open hood, arm deep in the belly of a cab's engine carriage.

"Little man giving you trouble?" he asked, spying Darnell glaring at her from across the garage.

Samantha looked over to where Darnell had retreated to lick his wounds and solicit one of the women from the front office. "Nothing I can't handle."

"I'd be happy to tap his brakes or slam a hood down on his hands for you."

Samantha chuckled, humored by the extreme nature of Deacon's idea of handling a problem. "No, thanks. I appreciate the offer, but he's all wind, no substance."

"Yeah, I got that, but if you need…" He shrugged and chuckled to himself. She joined in the private joke. "So what's up? I heard you had a little problem out there."

"Really, where'd you hear that?" she asked, leaning her back against the front grille as he continued to work on the engine, knowing of course that gossip flowed through the garage quicker and thicker than engine oil. She knew he had a way of getting information that rivaled most intelligence agencies.

Deacon laughed and shrugged with an innocent look, which was difficult since he was the size of a grizzly bear and oftentimes thought to be just as mean.

Samantha shook her head and waggled her finger at him, chastising him as she would a child. "You know better than to listen to these hyenas when they start chattering."

He smiled, showing every one of his big, white, straight teeth. "Sometimes even a chattering hyena can get it right. You okay?" he asked, nodding then standing up straight. At six foot seven, he instantly dwarfed her average-size frame.

"Don't I look all right?" she asked, then placed the envelope intended for the lost-and-found bin on the car's front fender along with the brown paper bag. She opened her arms wide and dropped her backpack from her shoulder to her hand.

"Yeah, you look just fine. Make sure you keep it that way." He reached up and touched her nose in a manner that reminded her of her father again.

"Before I forget, I picked this up for you," she said, handing him the brown paper bag.

"What's this?" he asked, then took the bag and opened it. He stuck his nose in as soon as he smelled the sweet aroma wafting out. "Oh, man, this is perfect, I was just thinking about stopping by and picking up a couple of these." He dipped his face deeper into the bag, then glanced up at her. The look on his face, a smile as bright and wide as sunshine, was pure heavenly delight. "You read my mind."

"There're four in there, so pace yourself," she joked.

Deacon laughed, as they both knew that he would devour all four sticky buns as soon as he had the opportunity. "Thanks, Sammy," he said, hugging her dearly.

"You're very welcome, anytime."

"I'm a save this for my next break," he added after taking one last quick whiff.

"Good idea. So what's going on around here?" she asked casually, looking around the garage. A friendly card game was going on across the room, and several drivers a few feet in the opposite direction were standing around laughing and talking as a third driver vacuumed out the backseat of his cab.

"Nothing much," Deacon said, taking one last look, then putting his brown paper bag on the high counter behind him.

Samantha, still looking around, spotted a man she didn't recognize standing off by himself across the room, reading a newspaper. New faces always caught her attention. He was dark, medium height with a scruffy beard and had a cigarette tucked behind his ear. His eyes were hooded and the newspaper was positioned over his face, yet she could tell that he was staring in their direction.

"Quiet, huh?" she asked.

"Yep, quiet just the way I like it," Deacon said, smiling and wiping his hands on the already soiled rag in his pocket.

She glanced back at the man with the cigarette. Her gut instinct warned her off instantly. "You sure?" she asked, nodding to the man watching them.

Deacon picked up a hubcap and glanced in its reflection. The man with the cigarette behind his ear immediately caught his attention. He knew that was who Samantha meant. "Name's Kareem. He just got out. He did a nickel and a few for a B and E contract."

"Five years for breaking and entering sounds pretty lenient."

"He knows people."

"Apparently," she muttered, turning her back to him.

"Word is he was also up for a deuce and a tre on the back end of the nickel, something about breaking a couple of noses and a few ribs in a fight with two other inmates."

"Sounds like he doesn't play well with others."

"Self-control issues. I can relate."

The lingo they spoke was a mixture of street and prison yard made up of codes and ciphered cryptograms. But they understood. "Lesson learned?" she asked.

"The line thinks so."

She snickered, shaking her head knowingly with part pity, part annoyance. "The parole board would let the devil go free in heaven."

"True that, but second chances and all, I guess he's straight for the time being. He's got to do the check-in thing. Why, you worried about something?" Deacon asked, sparing another glace across the room.

"Nah, just being thorough, that's all," she said easily while leaning back to stretch her stiff muscles from the long shift. "I like to know who I'm working with, you know that."

"You know that I got your back, Sammy," Deacon said. They exchanged a knowing look that could only have passed between family. Deacon was an after-midnight person—at least, he had been at one time. And the moment they had met she knew it instantly. It was a look in the eye, a nonverbal communication that announced the presence of a kindred soul. You never con family.

Samantha exhaled loudly. "All right, I'm out."

Deacon nodded. "Take care."

"Always," she walked over to the bulletin board with new listings for the week. The man with the cigarette came up behind her. She turned cautiously and looked up into his dark eyes.

"Hey," he said, nodding. She didn't respond but instead nodded in return. They stood side by side for a few minutes until he spoke again. "Word is we have a mutual friend."

"Is that right?" she asked, not particularly interested.

"Yeah," he said. She didn't reply. "He said that if I bump into you I should give you a message."

She turned, slightly more interested. "Who exactly is this friend?"

"Jefferson."

"Sorry, never heard of him," she said flatly.

Kareem chuckled. "He said you'd act dumb, lollipop."

"What did you just call me?" she asked calmly.

"I see I got your attention. Good," he said. "Our mutual friend said to tell you that a game is in play."

The expression instantly sank her heart. Game in play was always her father's term for working a con. "Is that it?" she asked.

"No, he needs a favor."

"What is it?" she asked coldly.

"You'll be heading to L.A. soon."

"L.A., as in Los Angeles?" she questioned, feeling her heart skip a beat. L.A. meant California, and California meant flying. Something she avoided like the plague.

"Yeah," he said, looking at her strangely, seeing her apprehensive reaction. "He said that he needs you to play a computer game for him and that he'll have a friend waiting to meet you. He also wants you to check this out." He handed her a small disc. She took it and slipped it into her backpack. "Says that you should do what comes natural and he'll text you on this." He reached into his pocket and pulled out a small thin cell phone. "Here," he offered.

She looked at the phone as if it were a poisonous snake. "Is that all?" she said, finally taking the phone.

"Yeah, that's it," Kareem said, then turned, seeing Deacon looking at them together. "Have a nice day."

"Hey, Sammy," Deacon said as he approached the two standing side by side. "You forgot this." He held out the manila envelope from the back of her cab. Then, seeing the hesitation on her face, he turned to watch Kareem as he quickly got into a cab and drove off. "What did he want?"

"Nothing, just talking, shooting the breeze," she said playfully not wanting to alarm Deacon. "Thanks." She took the envelope. "Take care." She smiled easily.

"Yeah, you, too," he said, not believing her nonchalance and fully intending to keep an eye on Kareem just in case.

The main office was empty except for Emily Osborn, a Bible-toting pastor of the All Saints Baptist Church four short blocks away and a friend of Samantha's family since she was a child. Her husband, Clemet Osborn, had suddenly died of a heart attack years ago and she took over running the company. She was considered the mother hen and kept a tight rein on all her chicks. Her special chick was Dorothy, her pet name for Samantha since she was a child.

Emily preferred to work at night and when she'd been informed that Samantha was coming for a while she was delighted. So as soon as Samantha showed up, she put her to work. The rule was, no one hung around the garage without working. So, for the past four months Samantha drove a cab and waited.

"You okay, sweetie?" Emily eyed Samantha, scrutinizing her face for the slightest blemish.

"Right as rain, Auntie Em," Samantha said, handing her the cash bag and the log sheets from her clipboard.

Emily took the offered items, tossed them on the desk and continued her inspection. "You sure?"

"I'm sure. What's new?" she asked hopefully.

"Not a thing, same old, same old." She paused and grimaced. "You sure you're okay? You sounded a bit distracted earlier tonight and now you look like you've just seen a ghost."

"I'm just tired. But I got my ruby slippers on and I'm going to click my tired butt on home."

Emily laughed, loud and joyous. She loved the way they talked the Oz talk as they always did. It was like a secret handshake in a secret club. At one time Darnell tried to get into the act by declaring himself the Wizard, but that didn't last long. He soon gave up and found his place back in Munchkin Land.

"You do just that. Good night, Dorothy."

"See you later, Auntie Em." Samantha turned to leave. but remembered the envelope she carried. "Oh, I almost forgot, I think my last fare left this in the back seat of the cab. He might call in for it." She handed the envelope to Emily and left the office.

As soon as she stepped out of the garage she looked upward, letting the slight drizzle dampen her face. She walked over to her car and pushed the alarm release, but stopped when she heard her name being called behind her. She turned. Emily was hurrying across the parking lot carrying a "What would Jesus do" umbrella.

"Sammy, this is addressed to you," she said breathlessly, holding the envelope out beneath the shelter of her umbrella.

"What?"

"That's what it says." She turned it over and read the name aloud. "To Samantha Lee Taylor."

Samantha took the envelope cautiously and looked around the empty parking lot. Suddenly she felt vulnerable, but she had no intention of getting Emily involved. "Oh, that's right, thanks, Emily, I must have forgotten and left it in the back of my cab by mistake." Proficient at lying as Samantha was, this one was adequate to placate Emily's curiosity.

"You sure?" Emily asked.

"Yeah, my head's all over the place. I think I might be coming down with a cold or something. I completely forgot it was mine." Samantha said, smiling happily as she casually glanced around the immediate area again.

"All right, sweetie, you drive careful out here. There are a lot of crazies on the road that are trying their best to meet my Lord sooner than expected."

"I know," Samantha said, knowing Emily's "dangers-of-the-world" speech by heart. "I'll be careful. Good night."

Emily turned and headed back to the garage. "Emily," Samantha said. Emily turned around as Samantha continued. "Thank you for everything you've done for me. You've given me a home and a family and I'll never forget your kindness."

"Sweetie, you're like a daughter to me, you know that. And as soon as that package arrived for you from overseas, I knew to expect you. But Lord, I never expected to see you looking so despondent. When you came in four months ago, I knew you needed this place. It might be old and a long way from being perfect, but it's shelter and a dry port in a storm."

"Yes, it is," Samantha said. "Thank you."

"Don't thank me. The door is always open to anyone in need as long as they're willing to work."

Samantha nodded. It was a well-known fact that cabbies

came and went at Oz all the time. Not many stayed longer than a few months, and like her, some were waiting, some were in transit and some just needed a place to call home for a while. And as they left, there was always a new face to replace them.

"You have to go now, don't you?"

Samantha nodded. "Yes, I think so."

"The Lord told me that you needed to be here for however long it takes. Trust him. He'll light your path."

Samantha smiled and nodded her appreciation. "I wish I had your faith, Auntie Em."

"I'm a God-fearing woman, but I wasn't always as you see me. If or when you need me, call. You'd be surprised at the folks I still call family." Samantha nodded soberly. "And remember, we're born into a family, but family isn't always just by blood. I have a friend who I haven't seen in near thirty years, but in my heart she's still my sister, my family, and you never turn your back on family, no matter what the cause. Family is forever."

Samantha knew that to be true. It was something her mother and father always said: *Family is forever.* And being raised on that mantra, she knew that when trouble came, her family would be there for her. "Thank you, I'll remember that."

Emily nodded her assurance. "Be safe and remember, there's no place like home."

"I'll remember. 'Bye, Auntie Em," Samantha said softly as she looked after Emily, seeing that she got back into the garage safely. She spared one last thorough look around, then turned and got in her car and pressed the lock down securely.

She read the name on the back of the envelope again, printed small and in the lower corner. With trembling fingers she opened the envelope and read the note inside. It was concise and to the point, telling her exactly what she needed to do to find Eric. It was signed Lincoln. She tipped the envelope over and pulled out a first-class ticket and read the date, time and destination.

She looked up slowly, then without moving her head glanced around the immediate area. At one in the morning it was nearly deserted. She glanced over to the police precinct across the street from the cab company.

The location was an unlikely choice for someone trying to be invisible or disappear, but she remembered her father's words well: "Hide in plain sight. No one ever looks in their own backyard."

A few uniformed police officers stood outside talking. She replaced the contents of the envelope, stuffed it in her backpack, then started the car and pulled off slowly as if nothing was wrong, waving casually. The two officers returned her gesture as a third joined them and they walked into the building together.

Sixty minutes later, after stopping at her rented apartment for her overseas package and four ATMs, she parked her car in the bus terminal overnight parking lot. She signed her name on the back of her car-registration form, jotted a quick note and stuffed both in the glove compartment. She hurried through the terminal, purchased a one-way ticket and begged a blank envelope from the information desk. She addressed the envelope, dropped her car and apartment keys inside, sealed and mailed it, then hopped onto the next departing bus headed west.

Her cell phone rang. After reading the quick text message, she eased back into the seat, closed her eyes and waited for the next move.

Chapter 2

The effect of working double-digit hours seven days a week had finally taken a toll on him. He was exhausted. He felt empty inside, no excitement, no joy, just empty. And now, after a particularly stressful day, there was finally a moment of peace as Jackson Daley sat in his office chair and swiveled around to face the window behind his desk, smooth jazz playing softly in the background.

He was about to take a well-deserved break, a long weekend off, no work, no radio and no family, completely alone and devoid of drama. He intended to take either his plane out of its long hiatus or his boat down the coast and just relax for a few days. He sighed deeply, savoring the idea, but then his thoughts crowded with business again.

He glanced at his watch, then out at the view.

It was dark and the glittering lights of Los Angeles shone and reflected across the city like tiny diamonds tossed out and scattered on black velvet. He loved the night, and from twenty-five stories up the cityscape view was spectacular. Looking out at the impressive skyline often stilled his thoughts. But nothing short of a miracle could do that tonight.

True, he lived a charmed life, one of affluence, money and power. But with affluence and power came responsibility, and his was more than most. With work as his only outlet, the boredom of life was his future—tame, safe and monotonous at best. He feared following in his father's footsteps, a slave to the boredom of excess.

He was the oldest son of divorced couple Rachel and Marcus Daley, second-generation media entrepreneurs. His grandfather, deceased founder of Daley Communications, was in his time a pioneer in the African-American broadcast industry. Over sixty-five years in the business, the Daley family owned more than eighty-five broadcast stations. Their satellite and base of operations were in this twenty-five-story building in the heart of L.A., which was also the main radio station that broadcast in syndication nationally.

When his grandfather died, he left the majority of stock to his daughter-in-law and not to his disinterested playboy son, Marcus, causing their teetering marriage to deteriorate instantly. Their subsequent bitter divorce had torn the family and business apart even more, and Jackson was hard pressed to bring it together.

Host of a nightly radio talk show, Jackson also served as vice president and general manager of the broadcast division of Daley Communications. His father was at the moment president and CEO. And since the death of his mother six months ago, the hierarchy of control wavered between the two, causing an already deep rift to expand even further.

Rachel, like her father-in-law, overlooked Marcus and left Jackson with the majority of stock control, which sent Marcus storming into court to contest the will and regain complete control of what was once his father's company. The bitter litigation had leaked out to the media, creating not only nervous board members but months of newspaper gossip and fabricated speculations. The once-admired Daley family name had become tabloid fodder.

So at the request of his sister, the company's public relations director, Jessica Daley, Jackson once again asked for a meeting with his father to hopefully settle matters at least publicly. But dreading the inevitable, Jackson knew what was coming. The discussion they'd had a hundred times or more would be rehashed. He looked at his watch. It was time.

He walked to his father's office on the other side of the building, knocked, then walked in without waiting for a response. He glanced around the room. Exaggeratedly decorated along the lines of big and obnoxious, the huge space and overly elaborate furniture nearly dwarfed his more than six-foot frame. His father's taste ran toward the overstated.

Without looking up, Marcus Daley, sitting behind his ornate desk, began speaking. "I hope you've come to tell me that you've reconsidered my suggestion."

"Your what?" Jackson asked, taken off guard by the left-field question. Then he remembered a conversation he'd had with his father earlier in the week about announcing an engagement between his associate, George Cooperman's oldest daughter, Shauna, and himself.

They'd dated, at his father's prompting, for three weeks the year before. But after the fourth date she wanted to announce their pre-engagement minus an actual proposal from him. Their relationship, strained from the beginning, continued to be just as stressful and bizarre. When he realized that Shauna was vain, arrogant, shallow and jealous, he knew that she wasn't the woman for him. Convincing her took some doing but he finally detached himself from her clingy tentacles and moved on. She still hadn't.

So, since his father's suggestion of a possible engagement was absurd, he didn't even bother considering it. Just because the woman had a thing for him and their fathers were doing business together didn't mean that he was part of the deal. The Middle Ages concept and his father's incessant prompting did nothing to change his mind. "No, not even close," Jackson finally said.

"Shauna Cooperman is a perfect match." Marcus looked up at his son for the first time since he'd entered. "She's worth over thirty million dollars in her own right, not to mention her stock options and her inheritance."

"I don't intend to marry for money," Jackson said, knowing that his father had married his mother for her wealth. Apparently strained from the beginning, their tumultuous affair-ridden relationship lasted for years for no other reason than public appearance. When Marcus, after learning of his wife's terminal illness, took control of the board with a no-confidence vote and ousted her as president and CEO, it nearly destroyed her.

Her sweet revenge was to leave all her shares to Jackson in her will, securing him as head of the company, knowing that he would never sell out and would continue to keep it in the family. She'd long ago taught him that all the money in the world would never buy happiness, and she was an example of that fact.

Marcus stopped writing for a second, feeling the sting of his son's words. "Money is power. You need to respect that and learn to use both wiser."

"Like you?" Jackson asked, then watched as his father continued writing again. "Look, I didn't come here to discuss the women in my life."

"There are no women in your life." Marcus hit solid and smirked. "So I suggest you reconsider. It would be a sweet PR piece and we could use all the positive press we can get," he continued. "A joint effort, a business venture and partnership between companies and families. I can see the headlines now. We'd get double exposure with one paragraph added to the press release, a complete and full partnership."

"No."

Marcus looked up at his son. He saw the handsome reflection of his own face from years past. Then he looked into his son's eyes, seeing his late wife. Pale green and penetrating, mesmerizing to the point of hypnotic, his son's eyes, like his wife's, seemed to pierce right through him, seeing and knowing everything.

Initially, they were reason he had been so attracted to her. Her beautifully captivating eyes had fascinated him the instant he saw her. She was mesmerizing and he fell instantly in love. Yet over the years, he grew to despise that knowing look, and now he was again looking into the same eyes. Marcus glanced away, refocusing on the papers he'd been reviewing.

In truth, he needed this marriage as much as he needed the business venture. He didn't trust George Cooperman, and a union between Jackson and Shauna would guarantee that he wouldn't be double-crossed.

"There will be no business venture with George Cooperman, particularly not now. The man has three separate indictments and one pending," Jackson said adamantly. "Do you really think that's all he wants? Cooperman goes through companies like tissue. He owns cable conglomerates all over the country. What does he want us for?"

"Oh, there'll be a business venture all right. George Cooperman and I have it all outlined. He has a company to sell and we're in the market to purchase. Everything is already set up.

He's even introduced me to his moneyman. He's a reputable broker handling the whole thing. We're in final negotiation on the details now."

"You still don't get it. Cooperman doesn't just want to sell you a company, he wants to take over *this* company. He always has. It's what he does. He finds a way in, gobbles up stock, then drives the interest down so that he can tear the company apart from the inside. Then he sells it off like a Monopoly game board. It's not a business venture he's after. If he gets his foot in the door it's a takeover, and I'm not going to let that happen. We owe it to—"

"To whom, my father, your mother?" Marcus asked as the two men glared at each other. "This is my company now, not yours. I decide what happens with it."

"That'll be up to the board to decide next week."

"Having the majority share doesn't automatically make you chairman," Marcus warned.

"It doesn't preclude it."

"This purchase will position me to retain control. Once the board sees my new vision—"

"It'll be too late by then."

"I know what I'm doing," Marcus stated firmly.

"You can't buy this company," Jackson said.

"Watch me."

"You don't have the capital."

Marcus smiled. "I'm getting the money."

"How? From whom, the banks, Cooperman?" Jackson asked.

Marcus chuckled at his inside joke. He had everything planned down to the last detail. He'd already made twenty thousand dollars in profit with no risk and was about to double his stake to the sum of fifty thousand dollars on the same gamble. He needed cash and was making it, quick and easy.

In his mind this was war, the same war he'd fought with

his father and his late wife. His father had controlled the company and doled out his life to him like a miser. Then his wife had controlled everything, only because she had the money when they were desperate because of a previous attempted Cooperman takeover bid. She'd saved the company, and in gratitude for his father's sake he'd married her.

"The proposed deal won't be approved," Jackson said. "Cooperman will never sit on the board."

"Believe me, it'll be approved. This deal is too sweet to pass up and you need to seriously think about a personal union with Shauna before it goes through."

"There's nothing to think about, it's not gonna happen," Jackson reiterated firmly. "Shauna has serious issues. She broke into my house several times and stalked me for nearly three months after we split up. I had to threaten her with a publicly released restraining order to back her off."

"She's a woman who needs love."

"She's a woman who needs shock treatment."

"Consider it. I'd like to make an official public announcement about the business venture during my acceptance speech for the National Association of Black-Owned Broadcasters awards ceremony and dinner," Marcus said instructively, knowing already that he'd be receiving the Lifetime Achievement Award.

"Have you any idea who you're talking to?"

Marcus looked up. "Not a very astute question, Jackson. You're my son."

"At thirty-one, I believe I can find my own bride. And she, whoever she is, will certainly not be part of a business deal to solidify a partnership or in serious need of psychotherapy."

"Consider it," Marcus said stubbornly as he picked up a magazine next to the papers he was reviewing and tossed it across the desk. Then he lowered his head and went back to work.

"What's this?" Jackson asked, seeing the magazine was *Black Enterprise* and his father's smiling face was on the cover.

"Check it out. There's a favorable article in there about the company for once. Your sister handled it, and it's pretty good."

Jackson signed heavily; dictatorial commands and then avoidance were his father's two favorite means of communication. "I didn't come here tonight to argue. I just came to remind you that tonight's my last on-air show," Jackson said, ignoring the magazine. "I'll be taking a few days off to handle some personal business. If you need to contact me I'll be on my cell. I'll see you next week." He turned to leave, then stopped.

Marcus looked up again. "So you're still going through with this, huh?" he said, still annoyed by the decision.

"Yes," Jackson said, having informed his father four weeks earlier of his decision to leave the show.

Jackson, with his unique skills and the smooth silk of his deep, chocolate-melting voice sent the ratings soaring along with the profits. His nightly radio show, *Love After Midnight,* was syndicated in more than forty urban markets and went out to over almost every major city in the nation. With more than twenty million listeners a week, he had a faithful following that made even celebrities drool.

When he'd informed his father that he was ending his five-year run as DJ Love, Marcus nearly blew a fuse. And since their relations had been strained from as far back as Jackson could remember, Marcus's reaction was expected.

"Remind me again why you're doing this?" Marcus said.

"I need to take care of some personal business," Jackson said, turning to face his father again.

"Personal business, what the devil does that mean?" Marcus said tightly, obviously still furious about Jackson's decision to end one of the most popular and profitable radio talk shows in the lineup.

"It means that I have to take care of some personal business and that as of tonight I will no longer handle both on-air and management responsibilities. Next week I'll be refocusing and redirecting all my time and energy solely to the business side of Daley Communications."

"And you're taking time off for that?" Marcus asked. Jackson didn't even bother nodding. "Well, how long is this *personal business* going to take? We have a real business to run, not to mention that I have this cable network deal working, and you need to prepare for the FCC renewal contract next week," Marcus said tensely. The pitch in his voice was that of worry and concern, not for his son but for the business deal.

"I should be back in plenty of time," Jackson said, feeling his anger rise to equal that of his father's.

"Should?"

"Yes, should."

"You're doing this out of spite, aren't you?" Marcus said, finally leaning back from the desk and relaxing in the padded chair.

Jackson saw the fierce anger in his father's eyes as Marcus threw his fountain pen on the desk beside the magazine he'd tossed earlier. Suddenly, the man he hoped to reconcile with one day disappeared. "You realize of course the midnight drive time is gonna plummet to nothing. And what about your segment, *Love After Midnight,* have you even considered that?"

"Of course I have. Everything's already taken care of."

"Meaning?"

"Meaning that I've made other arrangements."

Marcus snorted and sucked his teeth. "You've made other arrangements," he repeated. "You don't own this company yet, boy, you answer to me. I'm still the CEO and majority share-holder. This is my tenure. I don't give a damn what your mother put in her will, this is my company and it always will be. My father started it, but it was my dream, my idea from the beginning until he took it over." The angry tone in his usually smooth voice bellowed throughout the room.

Feared by most of his employees and despised by the others, Marcus raged as Jackson's calm demeanor never wavered. He was used to his father's dictatorial tirades. A bully and tyrant, he did his best to intimidate those around him. In most respects it was either his way or no way. And if you didn't do what he suggested, there'd be hell to pay.

"And while we're on the subject," Marcus continued as he slammed his reading glasses down, sending them spinning across the glossy surface of his desk, "about this lawsuit…" he began as Jackson turned and walked away "…come back here, I'm talking to you…"

When the discussion got around to the lawsuit, Jackson always walked out. He went back to his office and closed the door soundly. The strained relationship with his father still took its toll on him. He stood at the window as the music continued to play softly in the background.

His vision was to revitalize Daley Communications, but to do that he needed complete control, and his father would never relinquish control easily.

Rationalizing their differences only made their similarities more distinct. They were too much alike, both strong willed, determined and obstinate. After a few minutes, Jackson walked over to his desk and sat down, seeing that a manila envelope was now sitting on top of his keyboard. Knowing that it hadn't been there before, he picked it up and opened it.

Moments later he stood looking down at the eight duplicate papers on his desk, fanned and spread out like an accordion. He glanced from paper to paper, examining each in detail as if to rearrange the words to give them a more acceptable meaning.

But facts were facts, and although unstated, the message was loud and clear. Threats, extortion, blackmail, call it what you will. He didn't like it, and he was determined to get to the bottom of it. He stuffed the papers back inside the envelope.

Fury drove him as he stormed to the receptionist's desk. "Where did this come from?" he bellowed, startling her to physically jump from her seat.

An office temp, the mealymouthed woman with thick glasses and a modernized version of a beehive hairstyle, nearly fainted. She looked up at Jackson, seeing the rage on his face, and gasped for air. She held her hand to her chest while her eyes weakened and watered.

Jackson instantly regretted his impulsive action. "I'm sorry," he said quickly, seeing the woman's obvious distress. He offered her a glass of water and suggested that she take a few minutes in the ladies' room to gather herself. When she returned, still on shaky legs, Jackson calmly asked her where the package had come from.

"I d-don't know," she barely stammered out. "It was here when I returned from the ladies' room earlier. I was just about to leave for the night when I saw it sitting there on the counter. Since it apparently arrived so late and there was no return address, I assumed it was an interoffice package or something you'd been expecting, so I took it right into your office."

Jackson nodded and thanked her for her assistance. He said good-night and again apologized for his outburst. As soon as he got back to his office he closed the door and opened the package again. Everything was there just as he'd seen it earlier, his entire family business on the verge of collapse. If this was true and it ever got out, there was no telling what damage it could do.

He spilled the contents of the package out onto his desk again and shuffled through them, methodically separating items in an order of degree of damage, eight items total, all potentially detrimental. Of course, there had been other attempts to extort money, but none of them even came close to the specifically noted allegations on the eight pages lying on his desk.

He picked up and read the enclosed letter again. It was detailed and poignant and offered him a single option—one small favor in exchange for the original documents or read about them in the newspapers.

He picked up the first-class plane ticket and read the date, time and destination. He looked at the calendar on his desk. According to the note, he was scheduled to leave that night, giving him no time to initiate damage control.

He looked at his watch, then at the spread of documents. Did he have a choice? Secrets clung to his family like static in a dryer. His grandfather founded the business on the backs of others as speculation of fraud and deception swirled around him constantly.

Cleaning up behind his family had become a recurring theme in his life. Scandal after scandal had kept them on the front pages of the newspapers for years. His grandfather's shady past, his father's numerous and not-so-secret affairs, and now his mother's secret to have him search for a man from her past.

It was her last request to find a man named Robert Taylor. But he had refused. She asked him again, and he refused again. Then two days later she died and the guilt of his refusal had eaten at him ever since.

For some reason completely obscure to him, she needed to find this man, and now he felt obligated to fulfill her last wish. He had no idea who Taylor was or what his relationship to his mother was, but he intended to find out. But first he needed to continue with what he'd been doing for what seemed years, plugging holes like a cheap plumber.

In hindsight, he always knew that there was something more going on. He should have followed his instincts. His grandfather knew, his mother knew. She had to. Why else would she have done what she did? Knowing of course that it would infuriate his father, she'd had the last laugh. And all his affairs and secret rendezvous came down to this.

He placed the papers back in the envelope and sealed it securely. He turned back to the night sky. So much for a few days of rest and relaxation. Somewhere out there, someone knew secrets that could ruin his family and his future. His phone rang. He turned quickly, then picked it up cautiously. "Yeah."

"Hey, Jackson, get a move on. It's your last show, you don't want to be late, do you?" Carla, his producer, said jokingly. "It would be kind of hard to *Love After Midnight* if you're not here."

Hearing his producer's voice centered his wayward thoughts. He had a job to complete, and after that he intended to take care of this other problem. "I'm on my way," he said. He placed the envelope in his briefcase, gathering a few other documents, then walked out of the office and took the elevator down twenty-four stories to the studio. It was almost seven o'clock and his radio show, *Love After Midnight*, was about to begin.

This was the one part of his job that he truly enjoyed. He'd fallen into the position by accident a few years ago when he was forced to go on air to replace a drunken disc jockey. He'd received such rave reviews that he took over the spot permanently. Having grown up in the business and having been a DJ in his teens and an on-air personality in college, he comfortably knew his way around a studio. The ratings went through the roof. And he'd found himself leading the nighttime slot ever since.

So, even after a full day's work in the upstairs offices, he would walk into the dark closed studio and don his on-air persona, DJ Love, and forget his troubles by doing the number-one-rated show in its drive time.

Jackson's degrees in journalism and psychology prepared him, but even so, the resounding onslaught of popularity was staggering. As DJ Love he invited noted guest psychologists and psychoanalysts to call in to give more professional responses, but it was his informal dispensing of commonsense reasoning that sent the ratings soaring.

Jackson, under his DJ Love persona, never conceded to personal appearances. He preferred to remain anonymous. Once rumor spread that he would be at a particular function, the women came out in droves. Hundreds, thousands came, drawn like moths to a burning flame by that voice on the radio. His absence only increased his popularity.

Unfortunately, Jackson had to give it up. Tonight, he sat down in the solitary booth, adjusted his earphones and maneuvered the microphone. Carla waved from the side booth, nodding to her countdown. Moments later the On-Air light went on and at seven o'clock that night DJ Love began his last show.

As he played soft jazz with topical conversation and phone-in conversations and requests, DJ Love's sensuous voice flowed through the radio airwaves like liquid lava. Hot, steamy and burning, he scorched everything and everyone in his path as he melted the wires the way he melted the hearts of millions of listeners syndicated all over the country.

His considerable talent and skills had been honed a long time ago. Mixing sensuality and playful provocative banter was his specialty. Joking, teasing and toying, he took his listeners along on a wondrous journey that led to somewhere north of ecstasy and south of rapture to a place after midnight called Nirvana's paradise.

Perfectly positioned in a drive time from seven to just after midnight, he was every woman's nightly fantasy and every erotic dreamer's star.

His dedicated listeners' demographics ranged from sixteen to sixty. And personal Web sites and blogs popped up weekly, praising his skills. When he did phone interviews, which was seldom, lines were jammed as even popular musicians and celebrities waited to come on his show.

Tonight was no different. The phones were lit up like the NYC Rockefeller Center Christmas tree. And since early that morning, listeners had been recording messages to say a personal thanks and goodbye to DJ Love.

Like a poet and statesman, DJ Love had always spoken the truth, touting advice and wisdom about finding and keeping a good relationship, being true to yourself, and seeking self-respect. His show centered on dating and the single life with such topics as the ideal date, how to impress the opposite sex, the morning after and finding perfection in an ordinary world. For women he was a godsend, for men he was the ultimate answer. But tonight it would all come to an end.

As Jackson took another call, he looked up and waved, seeing his sister, Jessie, enter the production room. She returned his wave as the caller asked questions about the new show he was producing. He promised someone just as insightful and entertaining. The board lit up all over again.

Getting the nod from Carla, he switched a small lever on the control panel in front of him and welcomed Dr. Terrence Russell to the show. Terrence was DJ Love's replacement. The two men talked briefly about Terrence's background and his vision for the show, then joked as Terrence answered a few listener calls from his location in New York.

Jackson motioned for Jessie to come into the main taping

booth. Four years his junior and always stern and formidable, she recently had begun acting more like his mother than usual.

Jessica Daley, the public relations director, stood at the plate-glass window and watched the last few minutes of Jackson's farewell show. The tearful goodbyes of the call-in listeners had the phone lines tied up for days, even though she'd added an additional ten phones with twenty lines each. It didn't matter. In syndication heaven, the pleas for him to stay had flowed from coast to coast in nonstop mode since the minute word got out that he was leaving his talk show.

Jessie quietly opened the glass door and tiptoed into the inner studio, taking a seat across from her brother and adjusting the large microphone away from her face. She listened as Terrence signed off and several devoted fans expressed deep sorrow at DJ Love's leaving. This was tearfully echoed by numerous others as Jackson gave listeners an open mike to express their appreciation.

Jackson was talking with a listener who vowed her unwavering support and promised to continue listening and waiting for him to return. As he cut to a commercial, Jessie began applauding.

"Hey, Jess," Jackson said, removing the headphones and moving the microphone from in front of his mouth. "How are you? What's up?"

"What's up! I'll tell you what's up. This break of yours can't come soon enough. You look horrible," she said, seeing the threat of dark circles under his eyes.

"Thanks," he said sarcastically, knowing the loving sibling bond they'd shared all their lives.

"No, seriously, I mean it, you look like you're completely exhausted, like you haven't had a good night's sleep in months, let alone gotten out and just relaxed and had some fun."

"I haven't," he said truthfully.

"It shows," she said as Jackson shook his head, knowing his sister's penchant for complete honesty. "Jackson, taking over mother's responsibilities when she got sick and then keeping it after she died, plus doing your own job and the nightly talk show, is just too much. You must be completely wiped out. I'm worried about you."

"I'll be fine," he assured her nonchalantly.

"No, really, I'm seriously worried about you," she reiterated more firmly.

"I'm fine," he said again, this time more convincingly.

"You don't look fine."

"So what are you doing here this late?" he asked, dropping the subject. "Shouldn't you be out partying or whatever it is that PR people do at midnight?"

"I thought I'd spend some time with my big brother and attend his farewell show." She paused. "They're really gonna miss you, you know," she said as the phone lines continued to light up on the computerized phone console.

"Yeah, for the next three days at least. You know how fickle this business is."

"Yeah, I know, but as PR director I can tell you mail has been flooding in for weeks and the phones have been ringing off the hook. There are thousands of calls coming in every day. Most have questions about when or if you're coming back and if not where you will be going. I actually had to add additional lines just to handle it."

"I'm sure you handled it."

"As I always do," she said, lacking modesty. "Are you ready for this next move?"

Jackson thought for a moment, then smiled. "Yeah, I am. It's time."

Jessie nodded, agreeing. "I think so, too. So what are you gonna do until the official announcement next week?"

"Take some time off, rest, maybe travel a bit, take the plane out and head up the shoreline or take the boat and do a little fishing down the coast," he said, speculating.

"You, fishing, that's new. And as for traveling a bit, your plane is probably completely rusted over and that boat of yours surely has termites since it hasn't been in the water for at least two years." She paused a moment and considered. "Okay, give, so what's the big secret? What are you really doing, what do you have planned?"

"Nothing, actually, just what I said, take care of a little business, then rest and relax."

"What kind of business?"

"Personal business," he said.

"Such as?" she prompted with no intention of letting the conversation go that easily.

"Such as personal business," Jackson repeated, not wanting to tell his sister about their mother's last request of him to find another man for her or about the package he'd received.

Jessie smiled, knowing that there was no getting around him at times. "Anything I can help with?" she asked with sisterly concern.

"No, not this time. Don't worry, I got this."

"By that sly look on your face I'd say that there was a woman involved, but you haven't exactly been burning up the social scene lately. To tell you the truth, I have no idea how you give such great advice to your listeners when you haven't been out on a date in almost a year."

"Dating is tricky," he confessed.

"You're preaching to the choir on that one," Jessie said. "But I remember hearing your show last night. I think it was called, 'The Making of a Fantasy.' I was stunned. The advice you gave was seriously on target. You actually made me want to get out there and find my soul mate."

Jackson smiled proudly.

"Don't look so smug," she added. "You should take your own advice and get out there yourself."

"I'm too busy at the moment," he confessed.

"Too busy for a fantasy, for love. Mom would have hated hearing you say something like that."

"She would have understood."

Jessie nodded. "Yeah, she probably would have, up to a point. But she would never have agreed with work precluding having a life and you know that."

They smiled, each remembering their mother fondly. Then for no particular reason they started chuckling. "Did she ever talk to you about things?" Jackson asked.

"What kind of things?" she asked.

"Personal things," he said.

"For instance…" she prompted.

"For instance, she lived on the East Coast, right?" Jessie nodded. "Her family, did she ever mention anything about them?"

"Are you getting sentimental?"

"No, just curious. Did she?"

"Yeah, we talked about family sometimes."

"She never talked to me about them."

"You were busy."

"Doing what?" he asked, seriously not knowing.

"Jackson, you've worked steadily since you were fourteen years old. Then after college you did everything to avoid this business, even being a cop for a while. But it's in your blood. Now you live and breathe this business. I'm surprised you even remember me. I guess it's no wonder you don't have a life now, you never had one before."

"There's nothing wrong with wanting to succeed."

"Of course not, but there is a balance. You spout remedies

for the single life after midnight and never take your own advice. I'll tell you what, after last night's show, 'The Making of a Fantasy,' go out this weekend, find a fantasy. Better yet, I have an idea, why don't I fix you up with—"

"Don't even think about finishing that statement," Jackson warned firmly. Then seeing Carla raise her hand to get his attention that the commercial was almost finished, he replaced the mic and headphones.

"Are you sure?" she asked playfully. Jackson gave her a firmer look. Jessie chuckled. "Okay, okay, I get it. No fix-ups."

"Thank you."

Jessie nodded with assured trust as Jackson looked up at the clock. It was almost time to end the show. The commercial and promo ended and Jackson returned to the air, said his final goodbye, then motioned to Carla to cue up the promo for the replacing segment.

At one o'clock, the show ended.

Jackson looked up at his producer. She nodded. Seconds later the On-Air light on his panel went out. He removed the headset and pushed back from the counter. It was over. He stood, stretched and gathered his half-filled water bottle. As he turned, a parade of coworkers came into the booth carrying a cake, glasses and several bottles of champagne. Jackson looked over to his sister. She smiled, having apparently known all about the celebration.

Singing two tone-deaf verses of "For He's a Jolly Good Fellow," his coworkers made him sit, listen and enjoy. Jackson turned away, embarrassed by the torturous performance. His hope to slip out quietly had evidently gone up in smoke. So, for the next forty minutes he listened to wisecracks, jabs and jokes about everything from his once bad-boy image to his DJ Love persona to his wealthy family.

Three bottles of champagne and half a cake later, he said

his final farewells. He gathered his briefcase and slipped out the side door, leaving virtually unnoticed. As soon as he walked to the front lobby he spotted his father and the two night security men standing at the main receptionist's desk. No one spoke as Jackson walked toward them.

Both guards, senior in the position, recognized the moment and nodded to each other. They grabbed their computerized security checklists and glanced at their watches. Though it was clearly too early to make rounds they still made themselves scarce, nodding respectfully to Marcus as they left.

As Jackson approached, the guards shook his hand. Then after a brief conversation he told them to stop by the booth for cake, and they readily accepted. As the two guards walked away, Jackson turned to his father who had turned to watch the friendly interaction.

"You really understand them, don't you?"

"Who?" Jackson asked.

"Them, the employees. They work for us."

"They work *with* us and we work *with* them."

"Yeah," Marcus said, obviously not contemplating the subtle difference.

"Were you waiting for me?" Jackson asked, his voice echoing in the large space.

"I have an appointment coming in," Marcus said.

"This late? Who's the appointment with?" Jackson asked.

"You still leaving, huh?" Marcus responded, not bothering to answer the question. Jackson walked over to the receptionist's counter and placed his briefcase on the floor and the envelope on the counter.

"Yes," Jackson said, now standing beside his father.

Marcus snorted and sucked his teeth, something he did whenever he found himself head-to-head with his son, which was often. Since taking over as division head, Jackson had battled his father on every front. Old ideas versus new ideas. They didn't agree on anything, the latest dispute being the proposed partnership between Daley Communications and Cooperman Enterprises. Jackson slid the manila envelope across the counter to his father.

"What's this?" Marcus asked.

"Open it."

Marcus opened the envelope and quickly read through the eight pages. His eyes grew wide in shock as he flipped through each. "What is this?" he asked again.

"You tell me."

"Are these the originals?"

"I doubt it. Do you recognize them?"

"Where did you get this?" He looked up at his son for the first time since they'd stood at the counter.

"Is it true?" Jackson stared at his father as if seeing him for the first time. Marcus turned to him, and their eyes met. Marcus quickly looked away, averting his son's accusatory stare. Usually a man of many words, he fell uncharacteristically silent. "It is true, isn't it?" Jackson surmised.

"Where did you get this?" Marcus repeated in nearly a whisper.

"It was a gift. Someone left it upstairs at the executive suite reception desk earlier this evening."

"Who?"

"He didn't stick around, obviously."

"And you didn't say anything earlier."

"Like what?"

Marcus didn't answer. He looked at the eight pages again and began flipping through and shaking his head steadily. "So this time you're taking off, this personal time—"

"Had nothing to do with this at the time," Jackson said.

"And now?" Marcus asked.

"Now it does? I need to take care of this, obviously."

"Obviously," Marcus repeated.

"Is there something you want to tell me?" Jackson asked.

"I, we…" he began, then paused and looked over to his son. "If any of this ever got out, we'd be ruined," he said, quietly pulling out a crisp white handkerchief and dabbing his brow. Breathlessly, he continued, his voice monotone, subdued. "Everything we ever worked for, everything we have, it'll all be gone."

"I realize that," Jackson said.

"Look, I know that you and I have had our differences and maybe some of that is my fault. You don't agree with my vision of the future of this company, and that's fine. But if this gets out…" He paused again. "Do what you have to do, get this finished."

"I intend to," Jackson said firmly.

"Do you need any help?" Marcus asked as he awkwardly stuffed the papers into the envelope then slid the package back to his son.

"No, I'll handle it. The fewer that know about this, the better," he said as he pressed the button on his key chain. Both men turned on seeing headlights outside. Then almost instantly a car pulled up. After a few minutes a man, got out and approached the building. "Your appointment?" Jackson asked.

Marcus nodded. "Yes." He reached over behind the receptionist's desk and pressed a button releasing the night security lock on the front door.

Jackson walked out just as his father's appointment entered. Both men nodded a cordial greeting and left it at that. Jackson shook his head knowingly. He could feel trouble brewing.

He got into his car and headed toward the expressway. He took a deep breath and sighed. He was so weary of pulling his father's butt out of the fire. But maybe this was a good thing. For so long he had played it safe, done the right thing and always what was expected. This small departure from the norm might be just what he needed for him to feel alive again.

He worked sixteen hours a day, seven days a week. He went from college to grad school to work and ultimately focused all his attention on the development of Daley Communications. Everything he did was of direct benefit to increasing the company's bottom line. Unfortunately, somewhere along the line he had forgotten what it felt like to live.

Something his mother had always warned him never to do. *His mother.* His thoughts rest with the promise he'd made her before she died. He'd put it off intentionally for six months, and just when he was ready to fulfill it he had to put it on hold again.

A determined grimace pulled across his face. His intention was to clean this mess up as soon as possible with as little exposure as possible. He looked at his watch; it was well after midnight.

Chapter 3

It was a fool's errand and Jackson, exhausted and infuriated, hated wasting his time. A day of travel and a day of waiting for someone who hadn't shown up had put him in a foul mood. This was obviously some kind of game. One he was already tired of playing.

But the documents were real enough, of that much he was sure. Witnessing his father's expression at seeing them told him that they were genuine. The question was, what to do now? He ruled out calling the police since exposure was a major concern and the lack of integrity ran rampant—selling stories to tabloids was everyone's part-time job.

He considered hiring a private detective, but again trust was an issue and the lack of privacy and the bad publicity would only add to the already escalating dilemma. Eventually, only one logical answer came to mind—he needed to take care of this personally and that meant waiting to be contacted again, but this time on his terms.

Mulling over his decision, he walked into the airport's first-class lounge and looked around. Several businessmen were seated at the bar talking among themselves, as were two women in the corner. There was a man offering a drink to a woman seated alone by the window, and there were three or four others apparently also traveling alone, sitting around, sipping drinks or speaking quietly on cell phones, one talking loudly about a failed business deal. Tired and ragged, he was midway through a forty-eight-hour coast-to-coast turnaround.

Jackson had taken the red-eye from Los Angeles to New York, then the first available flight back, taking him through Chicago with a two-hour layover. His flight had just landed, and with hours to kill he decided to grab a drink and a bite to eat.

Jackson walked down the length of the bar and took a seat on the last stool. He glanced around again just in time to witness a man slam away angrily after apparently approaching the woman by the window.

The bartender walked over and placed a small square napkin on the glossy polished counter in front of him. The man nodded briefly in a combined gesture of greeting and asking for his drink order.

Jackson acknowledged with a nod and ordered a beer on tap and a menu. As the bartender grabbed a chilled glass and pulled the level down, nearly foam-free dark amber liquid poured out and filled the glass. He glanced up briefly, then back at the brew just topping the mug. Smiling and shaking his head, the bartender released the lever and set the beer in front of Jackson, picking up the twenty-dollar bill sitting on the counter beside the napkin.

He walked away, headed for the cash register, but paused long enough to take an order and fill a long-stemmed wineglass with a dark burgundy wine.

As he brought the change back to Jackson he leaned over the bar, smiling while nodding his head across the room. Jackson turned slightly toward the direction the bartender nodded. The man he'd seen and heard earlier was still talking loudly on the phone. Then he ordered a glass of burgundy and walked over to a woman sitting alone by the glass window.

"Watch this," the bartender said, chuckling to himself.

There was a brief interaction as the man placed a third drink on the small table, then uninvited sat down in the empty seat across from her.

Jackson couldn't hear what they were saying, but it was obvious that the man was interested and the woman wasn't. Seemingly stuck-up or haughty, she smiled politely, then shook her head and turned back to the window. Apparently undaunted, the man got louder as the woman's demeanor remained steadily aloof.

"She's been shooting them down ever since she walked in here," the bartender quipped quietly. Jackson shifted the change back across the counter and nodded.

Understanding, and accepting the generous tip, the bartender smiled happily. "Thanks," he collected the change and dropped it into the tip jar behind him, then headed back to the other end of the bar as a loud group of travelers walked in.

Jackson took a few sips of his beer and casually looked around the now crowded room. He turned, seeing that the bartender continued to watch across the room. The man still trying to talk to the woman at the window gulped the last of his beer and became more adamant about his intentions. The woman never turned back to him. Then he reached across the table and roughly grabbed her. She resisted, jerking away.

In an instant, Jackson got up and walked over.

He gently touched the woman on the shoulder and leaned down to her ear and spoke loud enough for the man across the table to hear. "Sorry I'm late, sweetheart, traffic is miserable out there." Then he looked up questioningly to the apparently intoxicated man across the table as he quickly let go of her arm.

"That's okay, darling," she said, instantly going along with Jackson's ploy. "This gentleman was kind enough to keep me company until you got here. Thank you, sir," she added pointedly and the man stood, muttering a few incoherent words, and walked out.

"Are you okay?" Jackson asked as he continued to lean close but this time he spoke more quietly in her ear.

The woman glanced to the side without looking up at him. A gentle wisp of loose hair dropped against her shoulder. "Yes, thank you, I appreciate your assistance," she said then glanced at her diamond watch, gathered her belongings and as smooth as silk stood and walked out of the room without a single look back.

Jackson watched her walk away until she disappeared into the thickness of the flowing crowd of airport foot traffic. He half smiled. Her long lean legs and the sweet sway of her hips were beauty to behold. She was something else, all business and all gorgeous, and now she was a fantasy. And given the time, he might have attempted to talk to her himself, but her prompt departure took care of that idea.

Although he never actually saw her face, he imagined she was attractive. Her body alone had him itching. But the obvious don't-touch signals were blaring, too. Her hair was pulled back severely in a tight braid, she kept to herself, sitting alone, not talking to anyone, and she didn't make direct eye contact, all signs that she didn't want to be bothered.

Jackson turned back to the bar, seeing that his seat and most of the bar's counter had been usurped by the large crowd of travelers. He sat down at the now-vacant table. A few minutes later the bartender brought over another beer and cleared away the untouched wineglasses.

"Nicely done, smooth, you could be a professional," the bartender said, wiping the table with a clean white towel and placing the glass of beer in front of him. Jackson put his hand into his pocket and pulled out another twenty. "Nope, you just saved me a lot of potential aggravation," the bartender said. "It's on the house, enjoy. Here's a menu. Let me know when you're ready to order."

Jackson nodded his thanks and relaxed back, opening his menu but still thinking about the woman who had just walked out of his life. What he saw of her was attractive and he didn't necessarily blame any man who felt bold and brave enough to approach her, but she obviously wasn't interested.

He smiled at the possibility without realizing it. It had been a while since his last relationship. Maybe now that his workload had lightened he'd consider Jessie's offer. He chuckled to himself, knowing of course that he wouldn't.

The scent of the woman's delicate perfume still wafted in the air. He inhaled deeply and again smiled at nothing in particular as his phone rang. He looked at the displayed number; it was his father again for the millionth time.

In actuality Marcus had called at least fifty times since Jackson left Los Angeles two days ago. Having not responded to any of his calls, Jackson knew that his father was desperate, yet he still seriously considered tossing his cell phone out the window.

"Where have you been? I've called you a dozen times. Did you get the originals?" The voice on the other end, obviously stressed, asked immediately not bothering with greetings and pleasantries.

"No," Jackson said, hearing the disgusted sound of his

father's exaggerated exhale. "The contact never showed up." Marcus sighed heavily a second time. It was obvious that he wasn't pleased, but then few things pleased him lately.

"What do you mean he didn't show up? You've been gone for two days already. What happened?" Marcus asked.

"I can't go into that right now. Suffice it to say I followed his instructions, went to the hotel to meet him, but he didn't show up," Jackson said as he looked around the area, seeing that more customers had entered the bar and the small space was getting crowded. "We'll have to talk about this when I get back. My flight's about to take off."

"Your flight? What flight? You can't leave. You need to go back to that hotel and wait until he contacts you. Stay as long as it takes," Marcus demanded. "You can't just walk away and leave. We need those original documents."

"Yes, I realize that, but I waited for twenty-four hours. That's enough patience. If this person wants payment he's going to have to contact me again."

"Those documents could ruin this company, and you decide that a few more days aren't worth your time?"

"I didn't say that. Apparently, whoever this person is wants to play games, but if he wants payment he's going to have to meet me face-to-face. I'm through playing his game."

"And what about the company? If word gets out—"

"The company will be fine."

"My reputation is on the line."

"You should have considered that before you started all this."

"It's well and good for you to say that now that you've enjoyed the bounty that my actions provided. I did it for us, for this company, for you."

"You did it for yourself."

"That's your mother talking," Marcus declared.

"Don't bring her into this, she has nothing to do with it."

"Be that as it may, she was right there by my side every step of the way."

"I won't get into this with you right now. It's his move, we'll just have to wait to see what happens next."

"We can't afford to just sit around and wait."

"Correction, *you* can't afford to wait. I can."

Jackson closed his cell phone and put it in his shirt pocket. He took a deep breath and turned to look out the window.

As always, their conversation had ended abruptly. Jackson took a sip of his beer. He looked back over to the bar. A different bartender was there, laughing and talking to a few patrons at the counter.

The perfumed-scented air, now completely faded and obscured by cigarette smoke, had dissipated, but Jackson smiled remembering the woman who had sat at the table. She, whoever she was, was the one bright moment in an otherwise disappointing and dismal trip, and now he was more than glad to be headed back home.

Transformed, she was the profiled epitome of executive style. Samantha, now completely reinvented in a stylish Suzi White business suit, four-inch Manolo Blahnik heels and designer reading glasses, sat in her first-class seat with the latest editions of *Architectural Digest* magazine and *Computer Today* on her lap. She flipped through the pages as her thoughts centered on her task. She steeled her courage as she focused on what she needed to do. Patiently, she waited for her part to begin.

As she glanced around the cabin, she remembered her last experience in first-class. It involved her brother, a banker, a baseball player, his agent and a large endowment to her education fund, which was eventually paid in full, compliments of her brother, who had simply asked her to do him a favor and she did.

The thought immediately made her smile. Where her father had mastered the jaunty carefree life of the con, her half brother, Jefferson, seven years her senior, had achieved flawless perfection. Like a Hollywood mogul, he directed, produced and wrote everything from start to finish. Every character and mark played right into his hands. And like a chess master he was twenty-five moves ahead before anyone even sat down to play.

And as with his skill, everything worked in timely fashion, perfect precision, and everyone walked away either richer, wiser or wishing that they'd never gotten up that morning. But no one complained. How could they? Greed had a way of making a point.

That was the last time she saw her brother. She heard that he had retired and was off to places unknown, doing exactly what we enjoyed doing.

But that was her old life; she hadn't seen him in years and certainly hadn't played the game in years. At a certain point she realized that the risk wasn't worth her freedom and definitely not worth her life. Her father took that chance each time he walked out the door on another one of his jobs. Robert Taylor knew, as they all did, that there was always a chance that he wouldn't come home.

Then it happened. A long con, it was a simple job, a quick switch and grab with a major payoff. Unfortunately, a member of his crew got greedy and went beyond the anticipated plan. That mistake cost the guy his life, and cost Robert fifteen years of his life. One member of the crew got away and her father never exposed him. Robert might have been undependable and conflicted, but he was also loyal. He'd never betray his crew, no matter what the circumstances. So he went to prison and so did his secret, leaving her and her mother with nothing.

Unfortunately, Robert's imprisonment eventually led to her meeting her ex-boyfriend, Eric. She was signing off on some paperwork at her father's attorney's office after work one day. A man grabbed her purse and Eric, stepping in, retrieved it and chased him off. He saved her.

At the time she wasn't sure if he'd followed her or not. He said that he hadn't and just happened to see her leave the building at the last second, but now she knew that was a lie. But at the time she accepted his explanation and his offered friendship. He was a friendly face and had a smile that was infectious.

He seemed perfect, tall, dark and handsome, and he treated her like a princess. He was the first man she trusted to tell the truth about her family. Being that they were coworkers, she didn't want him surprised or embarrassed if anyone ever saw them together and knew who her father was. She told him just about everything about her family and he was okay with it. He accepted that her father was in prison and he even tried to convince her to visit Robert. But she never did.

That seemed to disappoint him. It wasn't until later that she figured it out. Their meeting, their romance, their love, was all one big con to get her to trust him and to get her to see her brother. The only thing he ever wanted was what her brother knew about the business.

When it became obvious that she wasn't going to be pressured into visiting her father or telling him how to contact her brother, Eric broke into her office, used her computer and stole money from their employer to pay off a con gone bad.

He used her and she let him. The only saving grace was that she'd never contacted her father or told Eric how to find Jefferson like he wanted her to do. But as her mother said, family is forever and you never betray that. He tried everything to persuade her to make contact, but she had always adamantly refused. That was the one good thing she'd done.

Now, seated at the window, Samantha looked out and watched the airport handlers load the last luggage cart and make final preparations for the plane's departure. Her thoughts wandered to the path before her now. Jefferson's message said that a friend of his would contact her. Not knowing who it was, she reminded herself that she needed to be open to anything.

Like Kareem in the cab company, Jefferson had many friends.

"Excuse me," he said, interrupting her wayward thoughts. As she looked up, he smiled, his eyes dancing. "I think you're in my seat," Jackson said as he looked up at the small metal tab above the seats, then at the boarding pass in his hand. "I believe I have the window."

Samantha nodded, removed her reading glasses and sized him up quickly. To say that he was attractive was a stark understatement. The man was gorgeous. His face was as smooth as mocha silk with just enough evening shadow on his chin to make him look dangerous and sexy. His lips were strong, full and firm, the kind that could kiss a woman into submission.

His dark, wavy hair was cut short, with half sideburns that stopped short of his chiseled jaw and firm chin. Tall, with broad shoulders, he was exceptionally built. But it was his eyes that gave her pause. Framed by thick dark lashes, his eyes, exquisitely divine, shot right into her the very instant she looked up at him, mesmerizing her to silence.

She smiled, numb. He tilted his head downward as if to increase the intensity as his eyes brightened knowingly. They were luminously breathtaking and she suspected he'd been told that more than a time or two.

"Is that right?" she finally said as she pulled out her boarding pass and checked the seat number and the armrest number. "It appears you're correct."

"Do you mind? I'd prefer the window seat," he said.

"Not at all," she said, then stood and moved to step back into the aisle.

Jackson, who had begun storing his bag in the overhead compartment, stepped aside and right into her path. Their bodies connected against the back of the seat in front of them and pressed closer as another passenger passed behind them. The maneuver was completely innocent but extremely sexually suggestive.

Their eyes locked as she looked up and he looked down.

"Thank you," he said provocatively, leaving it up to her to know what he was thanking her for. He smiled, grabbed his briefcase, then ducked his head and moved to the window seat and sat down.

His gold Rolex gleamed as she inhaled the scent of his expensive cologne. "My pleasure," she responded as she sat down in the aisle seat and placed the magazines back on her lap and continued flipping through the pages.

Jackson looked around the immediate first-class area. "Looks like we've got most of first-class all to ourselves, at least for the next few hours," he said as he glanced at her legs and then at the name of the magazine she had on her lap. She nodded but didn't speak, then obligatorily glanced around the first-class cabin also. He watched the smooth perfect softness of her caramel skin as she turned, noting also the single two-carat diamond stud earring.

Jackson smiled as he took the opportunity to observe her more closely. He'd seen her before, of course. She'd been in the airport's first-class lounge sitting alone nursing what looked like a glass of white wine as two others that hadn't been touched sat across from her.

Now, seeing her face-to-face, he changed his assessment of her. She wasn't stuck-up or haughty, she was something more. Attractive, yes, she was definitely an attractive woman, elegant and glamorously styled. She was impeccably dressed with the knowing air of a boardroom executive. But then there was something else behind her aloof coolness, an attitude definitely, but something more elusive. He was intrigued.

Finding a woman with money and power was relatively easy in his circle. They were a dime a dozen. They moved awkwardly in an affluently graced society that had groomed them for perfection since birth. But finding a woman with that certain something and who moved with the ease of assured confidence by her own making was something else completely. The difference, subtle to most, was blaringly obvious to him.

They sat side by side in silence as a continuing flow of passengers began to enter the plane and take their seats farther back. Preoccupied, Jackson rested his head back on the cushioned headrest and relaxed. The stress of the past few days had worn him down. He was glad to be headed back home. That is, until his phone rang. He pulled it out and looked at the number. He closed his eyes and exhaled. It was his father again and he wasn't in the mood to deal with that. "Damn," he said tightly, then turned off the phone and put it away.

"Are you okay?" Samantha asked, witnessing his tense reaction.

He turned to her. "Yeah, sorry about that. Business," Jackson said to Samantha, seeing that she had stopped flipping through the magazine. "I didn't mean to get so loud."

"It wasn't loud," she said, half smiling. "Sounds like trouble brewing."

"Trouble is always brewing, but then life is trouble."

"At times, true," she turned to look directly at him. "Look, I know this is going to sound like a come-on, but honestly it's not. You look familiar. Have we met before?"

"A come-on?" he asked, lightening his mood.

"You know what I mean. A pickup line."

"And are you picking me up?" he asked hopefully.

"No, sorry, I'm just curious, I know I recognize your voice. I just can't seem to place you."

"Well, as a matter of fact we did meet briefly," he said. "I was in the first-class lounge an hour or so ago when…"

"Oh, yes, of course, it was you, my knight in shining armor," she smiled and his attraction was complete. "Thank you again, that was very kind of you. A lot of people these days would prefer not to get involved."

"Don't mention it. My sister has the same problem when she travels. She can take care of herself, but I hope someone might be there if ever she needs."

"It is a different world and I seem to attract a lot of complications lately," she said.

"I have to confess, truth be told I considered coming over, as well, but thought better of it after I saw you shoot down the other men who approached you."

"I wasn't that bad, was I?"

"Not at all," he said with obvious facetiousness. "Jackson, Jackson Daley," he said, holding his hand out to shake.

Samantha looked over to the offered hand. "Samantha," she said, leaving out her last name. He shook her hand, smiling warmly.

"Samantha," he nodded. "Nice name, different, it suits you. Do your friends call you Sammy?"

"No. Do your friends call you Jackie?"

He chuckled. "Touché. It's a pleasure meeting you, Samantha, no last name."

"Same here, Jackson, Jackson Daley," she said.

He chuckled again. "So, are you a computer specialist or an architect?" he asked, glancing, then pointing down to the magazines on her lap.

Samantha had stopped turning the pages. "Actually, I…" She paused a second and smiled. "I put things together from time to time," she said cryptically as the plane's engines began to hum louder and the attendant closed the front hatch and secured it. Samantha glanced around Jackson and out the window nervously, seeing that the plane was getting ready to back away from the gate tunnel.

Jackson smiled at her vague answer as he glanced down at her left hand, noting the distinct absence of ring or ring shadow and tan line. He looked into her eyes as she glanced out the window, seeing and recognizing her nervousness. "Do you fly often?" he asked casually as he placed his briefcase under the seat in front of him while purposely blocking her view of the plane preparing for takeoff.

"No," she said tightly, leaning back. "I prefer to take trains."

"How fortunate that you didn't this time or we might never have met," he said as he leaned back up and noticed the now-strained expression on her face. "Are you okay?" he asked.

She nodded slowly. "Just a little anxious. Actually, just a lot anxious."

"Flying?" he asked. She nodded briefly as other passengers settled themselves and began talking excitedly. She watched as the flight attendants walked down the aisle checking and securing the overhead compartments. "Try not to think about it."

The engine roared louder. "Impossible," she muttered.

"Statistics say that flying is by far the safest mode of transportation."

"Statistics? You have to be kidding me. A million-ton metal cylinder filled with passengers riding on a thin air current doesn't exactly fill me with reassurance."

"Aerodynamics, planes fly between streams of air and ride the currents. It's perfectly safe and perfectly natural. Birds do it all the time."

She looked over to him. "No offense, but that doesn't help. Birds don't weigh a few million tons," she said, exaggerating.

He smiled, then chuckled with ease. "When you think about it, it works."

"No offense again, but, I prefer not to think about it if you don't mind," she said tensely.

He smiled again, enjoying her remarks. "Anything I can do to help?" he offered with sincerity.

"No, thanks." She laid her head back and closed her eyes, taking a deep breath and exhaling slowly.

"I gather you're not much of an airplane talker then," he said after a moment's silence. When she didn't respond, he continued, "Personally, I enjoy flying, particularly after midnight, the red-eye. It relaxes me. A few hours through the night and you're there at your destination."

She nodded absently, focused more on the accelerating engine noise than what he was saying. "So, are you traveling on business or running away from an old boyfriend?" he asked jokingly.

Barely registering, she shook her head. "Neither."

The engine sounded again and the plane began to move away from the boarding tunnel. Samantha's eyes popped open. As the plane rolled backward, an attractive young flight attendant walked over. She smiled and checked their seat belts. She looked directly into Jackson's lap and smiled brighter, asking if there was anything she could do for him. He declined her open offer. Then she smiled obligingly at Samantha, knowing that her open display of attraction was too obvious.

Samantha gripped the armrest tighter in anticipation.

"It'll be over with soon. Takeoff is always the worst. It's the whole expectation thing," Jackson said softly in her ear. "Try not to think about it. Distract yourself."

She nodded absently, taking his advice. "Okay."

The plane continued to taxi to the runway. As the engines roared louder, Jackson sensed Samantha's tense reaction. She gripped the armrest tighter, closed her eyes and held her breath. The plane began to roll faster down the runway, preparing for liftoff. Samantha tensed even more.

"Kiss me," she said breathlessly, completely out of the blue.

Jackson looked over to her. The odd request took him completely off guard. "Excuse me? I don't think I heard you correctly. Did you just say—"

"Yes, you heard me correctly, kiss me now," she repeated more firmly.

Jackson smiled at his reaction. The impulse hit him before he stopped to consider his actions. Samantha loosened her seat belt, leaned over to him, braided her hands behind his neck and pulled him to her mouth. She kissed him hard, long and thorough. Surprised at first, he hesitated. Then within seconds he returned her kiss with equal passion and verve. He released the armrest between them and reached out to hold her more firmly.

Intertwining them as one, the kiss continued as the plane climbed higher and higher. By the time it had reached its primary cruising altitude their kiss had turned into a passionate embrace. When the captain's voice came over the speaker Samantha leaned back and touched her finger to his lips to wipe the soft smear of coral lipstick from his mouth. Jackson smiled, licking his lips, still tasting her and still slightly in shock.

"I can't believe I just did that," she whispered, completely mortified.

"Wow. That was…"

"I'm so sorry about that," she said, apologizing as she leaned back and tightened her seat belt again. "That was a mistake."

"No, really, please. No apology necessary."

"This is so embarrassing. I can't believe I just did that," she repeated as Jackson chuckled softly. "Look, I assure you I'm not a wack job or some psychotic lunatic. It's just that when you suggested a distraction I remembered reading somewhere in a magazine that kissing done well was the ultimate distraction."

"Did it work?" he asked with complete assurance.

"I think you know the answer to that."

She looked over to him for the first time since the kiss. He smiled. She smiled and added a slight blush.

"Thank you," she whispered.

"My pleasure, I assure you. And anytime I can be of service again, don't hesitate to call on me," he reached into his pocket and pulled out a Daley Communications business card.

Taking his card, she nodded. "I'll remember that."

Jackson watched as Samantha took a deep breath, then closed her eyes and laid her head back on the headrest. He smiled. Seeing her relax and at ease, at least for now, made him feel good for some reason. This was by far the best flight he'd ever experienced. He reached down and opened his briefcase and pulled out a small laptop computer. After another quick glance at Samantha, he turned on his overhead light and within minutes forced concentration.

But instead, his focus was edged and lapsed several times because of inner distractions. The last forty-eight hours had been frustrating. The mysterious package with enough evidence to ruin and potentially destroy his family and business, flying coast to coast to meet someone who never showed and the constant battle with his father had drained him. The only bright spot was... As he looked over at Samantha, he smiled and centered his thoughts. Moments later he was completely engrossed in business.

Her eyes closed, Samantha's mind whirled in circles. What was wrong with her?

This man must think that she was nuts.

What was she thinking? Hell, if a complete stranger were to suddenly say kiss me and then proceed to kiss her she would surely have thought he was nuts. That is, after she finished breaking his legs and his neck. She was completely mortified. Then she remembered what he'd said earlier about her running away from an old boyfriend. Was it possible that he knew something?

The suspicious side of her nature instantly came out. Maybe it was all a setup. Who better to know that she hated flying and only flew after midnight than her ex-boyfriend, Eric? They'd had numerous conversations about her flying out to visit her father and each time she refused. Of course, it was a setup.

The sudden act of chivalry, the ease with which he'd dispatched the man in the bar, the coincidence of sitting side by side in first-class, it was all beginning to look too planned, too real and too familiar. And come to think of it, she'd met Eric the same way.

Had she not learned anything during all the years with her father and then hanging around with her brother? This was the classical pickup and she fell for it. First, the rescue from the apparently intoxicated man in the lounge, and now her rescuer here on the plane—the coincidence had setup written all over it. True, she hated flying. True, she was nearly petrified when it came to takeoff. And true, she did read that kissing, when done right, was the ultimate distraction. And Mr. Jackson Daley definitely knew how to do it right.

He'd held her firm but not too tight and his lips were soft and gentle but purposeful. Although she'd planned on a simple kiss, closed mouth, lips pressed to lips, what had began as completely innocent turned quickly into heated passion, desire and hunger. His mouth had opened and she touched his lips with her tongue. After that, a whirlwind of instincts took over.

The last man she kissed, over three months ago, was Eric and there was no comparison. Eric kissed like a soggy plunger and Jackson kissed as if he had invented the concept. He obviously knew how to curl toes and weaken knees. When he wrapped his one arm around her body and drew her close as the other hand drifted to her waist and down her thigh, she nearly jumped into his lap.

Then the thought hit her. If his kisses were that passionate, then making love to him had to be—she paused and smiled—mind blowing. The visual stimulus was intense.

She slyly glanced over to Jackson as he continued typing and reading and doing whatever it was that he was doing. Apparently he was completely engrossed. The plane could have fallen fifty feet and he wouldn't have noticed. Or would he? Maybe it was all an act? she questioned mentally.

What was wrong with her? The last few months she'd been driving herself nuts. Second-guessing and questioning everything and everyone was driving her crazy as her innately suspicious nature constantly emerged. She had no idea how her father, her brother or anyone else did it. How do you trust anyone when you've learned all your life never to trust?

She inhaled deeply, smelling the spiced scent of his expensive cologne. Then she tensed inwardly at the thought of his arms wrapped around her just a few minutes earlier. Maybe she was wrong. Maybe, just maybe, he was exactly as he appeared, a nice guy who just happened to be in the right place at the right time.

Confused and jumbled, she wasn't sure if it was still nerves at flying or the fact that Jackson, Jackson Daley had just kissed her senseless.

Suddenly a flash of heat hit her and the vented air around her steamed up and certain body parts began to hum as the image of their intertwined bodies sent a flash of fire through her. She needed air. But traveling at an altitude of over twenty thousand feet above the earth wasn't exactly conducive to stepping out and getting a breath of fresh air. So as discreetly as possible, she grabbed her purse and headed to the small lavatory four seats back to regroup with a cool towel.

Two hours into the flight Jackson looked up from his computer screen. It was dark inside the cabin. The lights had been dimmed low and a calm hushed silence surrounded him. This was the time he enjoyed the most. The stillness of the moment always helped him think.

He glanced out the small window. The full moon, completely obscured, reflected its moody luminescent glow onto the wafting clouds below. They were over land but he had no idea where. He did know that they were very close to their destination.

He looked over to Samantha's seat. She was gone. He remembered looking over at her a few times earlier. She was sitting beside him quietly, her eyes still closed. He knew that she wasn't asleep. The stilled calmness of her breathing was slowed and patient. She was thinking.

Her face, smooth and silky, was the color of honey on a summer day. A slight hint of pink brushed her high cheeks and a soft reapplied coral tint covered her sensually full lips. The lips and mouth he remembered well, too well. A sly smile pulled his mouth wide and lit up across his face as the memory of their mouths pressed together sent a quiver down his chest, into his stomach and lower still. His body instantly reacted to the memory.

He had glanced down at her legs several times. Her suit skirt was just short enough for teasing interest without being overtly obvious.

Samantha had done in ten minutes what the average woman couldn't do in ten months. She'd made him want her.

His smile broadened; there was no way that an airplane's takeoff would ever be the same for him again.

Women went after him constantly. His position, his money, his looks had always gotten him noticed. And being a red-blooded man, he enjoyed their generously offered favors. So, seldom did he actually have to pursue a woman. But it appeared that Samantha might be one of the rare few who wasn't particularly impressed by his assets. He liked that.

Kiss me, kiss me now.

Jackson smiled at the vivid memory and her breathless request as it echoed in his mind. She was bold and brazen and completely unpredictable. He liked that, too. No second thoughts, no doubts and no regrets. Well, maybe a few. He smiled again and chuckled softly at her prompt apology. Yet without question she handled herself and those around her with a casual distance that captured his interest and then begged to be explored. She seemed confident and self-assured with a decisive swirl of power surging just below the surface. Unrestrained and without inhibitions, she was the kind of woman any man with half a brain wanted to know.

Seconds later, an occurrence dawned on him. Any man. Surely there had to be a man somewhere. There was no way a woman like her could be unattached for any length of time. Not really knowing anything about her, he suddenly found himself envying the man in her life.

Then with renewed interest he looked around the empty first-class area. The attendant, noticing him, walked over immediately.

"May I get you something, Mr. Daley? Champagne, wine or perhaps something to eat? We have a variety of meals and snacks available."

Jackson continued to look around for Samantha. "Uh, sure, coffee, black with one sugar."

"Is there anything else I can offer you?" she propositioned suggestively, letting her long auburn curls trickle down her shoulder as she leaned over, displaying her very obvious swell of double-D-endowed silicone. Emerald-green eyes flared bright as her fair skin flushed. "Something off the menu perhaps?" she offered.

"No, thanks," Jackson said, having gotten her overt proposition and politely turning her down.

She nodded. "One coffee, black, one sugar, coming right up," she handed him a small menu. "Just in case you change your mind, we also have a full menu, a delicious fresh fruit or Waldorf salad or a chicken salad on croissant."

"No, just the coffee, thank you," he said. She nodded, slightly disappointed, and turned to walk away. "Excuse me." She turned again, smiling hopefully. "Where did, uh…" He paused, remembering that Samantha hadn't given him her last name. "The woman who was sitting here go?"

"Ms. Lee has taken a seat a few rows back."

Jackson nodded and turned, glancing back, but he didn't see her immediately. The first-class seats were too high and heavily padded. "Thanks."

"Sure, anything else?" the attendant asked. He declined and she continued down the aisle, taking additional drink orders.

Tempted, he considered getting up and joining Samantha but thought better of it. She had definitely aroused his interest, but he decided to bide his time. He looked down at his computer screen and began reviewing his FCC proposal. Moments later, he closed the lid and glanced out the side window. When he turned back around, Samantha was sitting down beside him again. "Welcome back," he said.

"Thanks."

"You missed me, of course," he joked.

"Of course," she said, jokingly agreeing with him. A few

minutes later the attendant arrived with a cup of coffee and a glass of white wine.

Jackson accepted his hot coffee from the attendant and she placed a glass of white wine in front of Samantha. She asked if there was anything else. Both replied no.

Samantha sipped the wine. "You looked very intense earlier," she began. His confused look made her clarify. "Your work, I didn't want to disturb you when I returned."

"Business," he offered.

She nodded. "I assumed as much." A comfortable silence drifted between them as she sipped her wine.

"Okay," Jackson began after glancing at his watch. "We've got at best another twenty or thirty minutes, depending on the tailwind."

"Twenty or thirty minutes for what?" Samantha asked.

"To cut to the chase and get the preliminaries out of the way," he said. Samantha began laughing. "You think I'm joking?"

Samantha looked over to him for the first time since sitting down again. She paused to consider her answer. "No, on the contrary, I believe you're very serious."

"And you know this how?" he asked.

"Because you're attracted to me," she answered simply.

Jackson laughed at her unequivocal bravado. "Exactly, and you're attracted to me. So we can dance around this or we can own up to it and cut out the unnecessary chitchat."

"Kind of get to the point," she said. He nodded. "I see," she offered.

"Exactly. I'll start. I'm single. I live on the beach in Malibu. I have a good job in broadcasting. I come from a good family, I'm comfortably well-off and I've had all my shots."

Samantha laughed at Jackson's last remark. "Sounds like I should be impressed."

"Are you?"

"Of course," she lied playfully.

"Good."

Before he could continue, turbulence interrupted them. Samantha quickly grabbed the wineglass before it spilled on the small tray. "That was fun," she joked cautiously, then picked up the glass and sipped her wine quickly.

"Are you okay?" he asked.

She nodded and smiled weakly. "So, Jackson, Jackson Daley, what exactly do you do in broadcasting? Is it radio, television, cable or satellite?"

"Radio primarily, satellite hopefully. We're diversifying as soon as FCC regulations are renewed and approved."

"Sounds interesting," she said.

"So, Samantha, what do you do besides put things together?"

"I'm a consultant."

He smiled. "That's a great word, consultant. It can mean anything from selling brushes door to door to unemployed bricklayer."

"I'm somewhere between the two."

"That covers a lot of territory."

"Yes, it does."

"Ah, so you're a woman of mystery."

"I work with computers," she said, relenting.

"Everybody works with computers," he said of her obvious remark.

"You know, you're right," she agreed smiling.

"Okay," he said, deciding to drop the line of questioning. "I assume you don't live on the West Coast?"

"No, I don't," she told him, not specifying the exact location.

"And you're going to L.A. on business?"

"Yes."

"How long are you staying?"

"Not long."

"Maybe we'll run into each other."

"Maybe," she said.

They slipped into a comfortable silence as the attendant stopped by to offer her services and retrieve the coffee cup and still nearly full wineglass. Jackson joked with the attendant. She giggled joyfully and then continued retrieving trash from the other passengers in first-class.

"You have a very distinct voice, gentle, smooth. You must be perfect for radio. Are you on the air?"

"I have done on air from time to time, in college," he said, purposely omitting that up until two days ago he was DJ Love. "Do you know much about broadcasting?"

"No, but it sounds interesting. Tell me about it."

They talked for the next thirty minutes, interrupted only by occasional turbulence and an announcement from the captain. By the time they were preparing to land Jackson realized that he had dominated the entire conversation. Samantha knew just about everything there was to know about him and broadcasting, but he still knew next to nothing about her.

He had asked questions of her background and her career, but she was evasive and turned the conversation and questions back to him, the last topic of which was the magazines in her lap and whether or not she was in the architectural or computer fields. Not completely to his surprise, she avoided the question and he still had no idea exactly what she did for a living since she still hadn't giving him a definitive answer one way or the other.

"Once again, not an answer."

She smiled passively.

"So tell me, Samantha, are you always this evasive?"

"Evasive? Me?" she questioned.

"Yes, you have the art of avoiding answers to questions

down to a science. You know just about everything there is to know about me and I know next to nothing about you."

She smiled. "Not true. For instance, I don't know your favorite color or your favorite song or the name of the first girl you kissed."

"Purple, 'Hearts Afire' by Earth Wind and Fire, Claire Hathaway in the hallway after third period biology class and nice try, illustrating my point exactly, evasive. You still haven't answered my question."

"You know plenty about me," she affirmed.

"For instance?" he suggested.

"You know that I'm a very private person."

"And that's about it."

"That's pretty much all there is," she assured him.

"I know that you have an interesting accent."

Samantha froze, then grimaced. She hadn't been aware that she was using an accent. *Mistake,* she chastised herself. She had to be more careful, particularly since she had no idea who she was meeting and how many other people were involved. She looked over at Jackson. His innocent bewilderment surprised her.

"Did I say something wrong?" he asked.

"No, not at all, I was just thinking. It's curious that we met in the first-class lounge and also just happen to be side by side in first-class on the same flight with the same destination. Awfully big coincidence."

"You sound suspicious."

"It's my nature."

"Aha, you have a suspicious nature. A clue, so that would make you either in law enforcement or part of the criminal element on the other side." He smiled jokingly and chuckled at the absurdity.

"Guilty. I'm part of the criminal element on the other side," she said, tongue firmly in cheek, then joined his laughter.

He nodded. "A criminal element, excellent. I've always been attracted to dangerous women."

"Do I look dangerous to you?"

He took the opportunity to peruse her face and body thoroughly. "Yes, you do, very dangerous with a criminal mind."

"I'd say that you were more attracted to the criminal body, but…" She paused to glance down at his body with appreciative enjoyment. "I must admit, the broadcast body is quite attractive, as well."

Jackson laughed louder this time, humored by her intuitiveness and overly suggestive comment. She knew exactly where this playful conversation was going and even led the way. Bold and audacious, he had definitely enjoyed this flight and there was no way he wanted it to end when the plane landed.

"That said, dinner?" he asked.

"What about it?" she asked, already knowing.

"Have dinner with me this evening," he specified.

"Why?"

"I don't want to eat alone."

"I'm not available this evening."

"Then have dinner with me this afternoon."

She smiled, actually considering his invitation. But business was business and she needed to stay focused. "You are charming," she said. He nodded, accepting the compliment. "But another time, perhaps."

"I'm gonna hold you to that," he promised.

Moments later, the captain's voice came over the speaker informing the passengers that they were preparing to land at LAX. The attendants walked through the cabin checking for down trays and loose seat belts. With everything in order, Samantha rested her head back and exhaled slowly.

Jackson leaned over and asked, "How are you at landings?"

seeing that the sound of landing gear and machinery opening tensed her.

Samantha took a deep breath then exhaled slowly. "Okay-ish."

He leaned closer. "Well, if you need another distraction, I can think of something a bit more involved."

She laughed and momentarily forgot all about the plane landing.

Ten minutes later the flight was over and they stood talking in the waiting area, neither one wanting their time to end. "Well," she began, "thanks for the conversation. It was nice meeting you, Jackson, Jackson Daley." She turned and started to walk away.

"What, that's it?" he said. She turned to him. "You're just going to kiss me, use me and walk off like that?"

She smiled and stepped back. "What would you suggest?" He smiled, then chuckled. "Never mind," she decided as they laughed together.

"I really enjoyed this," Jackson said, stalling.

Samantha nodded. "Yeah, me, too. Take care," she added as she stepped to walk away once more.

"So I think maybe we can get together again," he quickly said.

"You think so?" she asked.

He nodded, seeming to calculate their time together. "Definitely, although I don't have anyone in my life at the moment and I'm not looking for anyone." He paused.

"Ditto, I don't have anyone in my life at the moment, either, and I'm not looking for anyone."

"Good. With that said, we should have dinner or lunch or breakfast."

"Didn't we already cover this?"

Jackson smiled the drop-dead, toe-curling smile that seemed to buckle her knees. "You said another time, and this—" he paused, glancing at his watch "—is another time," they said in unison.

"Cute," she said, unable to not smile at his gentle persistence. "Very cute."

"Is that all?" he asked.

She inhaled, then exhaled with added exaggeration, knowing that this wasn't a good idea. But temptation pressed her. "Is this you being charming again?" she asked. Jackson laughed. Nodding, she joined in. "I'll take that as a yes. So this dinner or lunch or breakfast, are you talking right now, here at the airport?"

"No, I was thinking more like someplace in town," she didn't reply. "Los Angeles is famous for its unique cuisine and diverse restaurants. It would be a shame to fly all the way out here and not sample the local delights."

"You think so, huh?"

"I know so," he assured her. "You mentioned that you were busy this afternoon, so how about a late dinner?"

She paused a moment. The package she received at the cab company promised Eric's whereabouts and instructed her to take a flight out of Chicago to Los Angeles then wait. She had no idea when her mysterious benefactor would contact her; and sitting around her hotel room all night and all morning. afternoon and evening waiting was the last thing she wanted to do. A distraction would get her mind off her anxiousness. "Okay, a late dinner sounds wonderful."

Jackson was pleasantly surprised. "Great. Dinner it is. Where are you staying?"

"The Beverly Wilshire Hotel."

"I'll meet you in the lobby at eight o'clock."

She nodded. "Perfect."

"Do you have a ride to the hotel?" he asked.

"I'll catch a cab."

"Are you sure? I'll be happy to escort you."

"No, not necessary. I'll see you at eight. 'Bye."

Jackson nodded and watched her walk away.

The soft sway of her hips reminded him of the first time he had watched her walk away. His already bursting smile broadened as he focused on the snug pull of her skirt and how it accentuated the sweet heart shape of her rear. Unable to look away, he watched the gentle sway with each step. A leg man, he let his eyes drift down. In sheer stockings the firm muscles of her legs were heaven, and the four-inch heels accentuated every curve.

If this was any indication of their evening together, he couldn't wait to see where this would lead. With one possible destination in mind, he hoped for the best.

Unconsciously he licked his lips. He had no idea how long she was in town, but he intended to see her as much as possible.

There was a passion about her that excited him. It was a certain something that he hadn't seen before, and whatever that something was, he wanted more.

Chapter 4

As soon as the cab dropped her off, Samantha entered the lobby of the Beverly Wilshire Hotel. She paused and glanced around. Behind dark sunglasses she looked at the faces of the people standing around. At almost five o'clock in the morning the lobby was empty with only a few hotel employees milling about, cleaning or talking among themselves. Several of them looked up as she entered, and smiled a greeting.

She nodded amiably, knowing that looks were deceiving.

The envelope from the back of the cab was from someone named Lincoln. She had no idea if the person was male or female. All she knew was that Lincoln claimed to know where Eric was and had sent her a first-class ticket to L.A.

She was greeted by a doorman, who took her luggage and escorted her to the front desk, where a pleasant-looking woman yawned wide and long, then smiled, politely excusing herself.

Following instructions, Samantha asked for messages at

the front desk. There was an envelope waiting for her along with a key card to an upstairs suite. The front-desk clerk told her that she'd already been checked in. Samantha stepped aside, opened the envelope and read the note, which informed her that she would be contacted later on that night. She walked away from the desk and headed toward the elevators but stopped when her name was called by the front-desk clerk.

"Excuse me, Ms. Lee, one more thing." Samantha turned, seeing the clerk hurrying behind her with a large bouquet of flowers. "These are also for you."

"Are you sure?" she asked, slightly skeptical.

"Yes ma'am, they were delivered for a Samantha, but unfortunately the florist didn't send a last name. They just arrived a few minutes before you came in with a note that you would be checking in this morning. Since we don't have any other guests named Samantha, and you hadn't arrived yet, we were just about to send them back, but then when you asked for your messages…"

"Yes, thank you," she said, taking the flowers and continuing to the bank of elevators. She pushed the button and the doors opened immediately. She stepped inside, pressed for the ninth floor and leaned back against the mirrored wall. The smooth ride gave her time to reflect. She had no idea what to expect next, and whatever was waiting for her she hoped she was ready.

When the doors opened, she walked down the deserted hall to suite 915. She stood at the door and waited a few seconds before proceeding. Then she slid the key card through the slot, opened the door and walked inside.

After a quick look around, satisfied that she was alone, she sat down on the side of the bed, picked up the phone and called down to the front desk. Identifying her room number, she asked for confirmation of the name on the registration, who made the reservations, when and how the room was charged and to what account. Everything came back in her name. And the room was charged to an open account by an overseas bank credit card.

She pulled out her laptop computer, plugged it in and began her search. She found a back-door file into the hotel's registration system and confirmed what she was told over the phone. Everything, as far as the hotel was concerned, was in the name of Samantha Lee, and there was no Lincoln or Jefferson Taylor registered in the past six or the next three months.

She dug deeper but found nothing she didn't already know. Someone had gone to a lot of trouble to cover their tracks, and whoever set this up had done a very thorough job. They had manipulated both her and the system, and she didn't like being manipulated.

For every lead she uncovered, there was an abrupt end, as if someone knew she'd be looking. And for every question she had, more occurred to her. Who was Lincoln? How did he know where to find her? How did Jefferson know about his package? Were they working together?

A half hour later, as dawn began to creep over the boxed horizon, she was right back where she started. Frustrated, she lay back on the bed, exhausted, realizing just how tired she was. Two buses, one train and a flight halfway across the country could do that.

As instructed, she'd followed the directions exactly and seven hours ago had arrived in Chicago to catch a nearly five-hour flight to Los Angeles to meet someone named Lincoln and hopefully get her life back.

The thought of her life before and her life now swam bitterly in her mind. Was it that much different? Soon after her mother had died she had separated herself from her family and decided to live her life solo. Her emotions were severed and she took life with no regrets and no expectations. That is, until Eric.

He changed everything. He made her feel, and for the first time in a long while she came out of her shell to enjoy life. Then he betrayed her and left her with nothing, exactly as her father did to her mother.

After a hot shower, she changed her clothes then climbed into the comfortable bed and closed her eyes. But sleep didn't come as easily as she expected. To her surprise Jackson Daley came to mind and again she wondered if he was part of this. He was charming and funny and had a way of making her feel at ease, which was exactly what a con man could do.

But maybe she was reading too much into their meeting. After all, not everyone in the world was out for the con. There were honest people out there. And there were people who were genuinely kind and good. The trouble was, she knew too few.

In retrospect, she had lived an isolated life straddling and dancing along that imaginary line between trust and deceit. She expected the worst and was seldom disappointed. Of course, she was definitely no angel, but the dark predatory world of after midnight never drew her in, either, not like it had drawn and eventually consumed her father. He never could walk away, even when it meant losing his family— losing her.

He was skilled and focused, an expert in his chosen profession, with the commitment and charm of a true master, but not the attitude. Cons and swindles, marks and patsies were his life. From depravity, decadence and greed, his marks gave willingly, usually ill-gotten gains, and he took graciously, but only from the deserving, never from the disadvantaged.

There was honor in the taking and it wasn't all about the

money. Going after those who'd binged from the less fortunate gave him particular pleasure. They took and then he took
from them. And the inability for recrimination delighted him.
Payback was never an option, particularly when the mark had
to also admit wrongdoing. Conning was the ultimate win-win.
You can't point the finger when you're just as wrong.

When she was a child he was her Robin Hood and the
world was her Sherwood Forest. His Merry Men were her
family, and life was good. She lived everywhere and nowhere,
learning all she could from those around her. Then her father
had walked away to a different life and left her and her mother
with nothing. But that was then.

A sad feeling of loss washed over her as she refocused.
She'd been thinking about Robert Taylor a lot lately. She
missed him more than she thought. The last time she saw him,
he was walking out the door, promising to return soon. He
never did. She was angry then, and now it was too late.

For over fifteen years, and all her adult life, they had been
separated by barbed wire, automatic weapons and prison bars.
Then, when she'd heard through the ever-persistent grapevine
that he was being paroled within the next few months, she'd
had mixed feelings. But now it was too late. He was gone,
leaving her with only memories.

She wished him the best and like her forever-faithful
mother, she still loved him. No blame, no fault, because ultimately he'd done what fathers were supposed to do, he'd
taught her how to survive.

And up until recently she'd done just that.

Unfortunately he'd done his job too well. Her half brother,
Jefferson Taylor, had followed in their father's footsteps. And
he had exceeded all expectations. Rumor had it that after Jefferson's last extremely successful endeavor, he had apparently
cut his losses and walked away, retired to a home somewhere

in New Mexico, Arizona or maybe Crete or the south of France. No one really knew for sure.

Tall, dark and handsome, Jefferson had been her idol. She adored him. He was perfect as far as she was concerned. And now the fact that he'd gotten out of the life only endeared him to her. Unlike their father, he knew when to walk away, and did. But the two men she most depended on in her life were out of reach and she needed to depend on herself.

She smiled leisurely as thoughts of Jackson weaved through her mind again. She drifted off to sleep with that same smile.

At ten minutes to eight, Jackson walked into the Beverly Wilshire Hotel and looked around the expansive lobby. Impressive was an understatement. He headed to the courtesy phone and called the operator, asking for…

It hit him, Samantha had never given him her last name. Then he remembered that the flight attendant had referred to her as Ms. Lee when he asked where she was. He asked to be connected to a hotel guest named Samantha Lee. When she picked up, he smiled.

"It's eight o'clock," he said smoothly.

"Who is this?" Samantha asked cautiously, her voice husky from her short nap.

"Don't tell me that you've forgotten me already?"

"Jackson?" she asked, slightly confused. There was no way she'd been asleep for twelve hours straight. She was tired, but not that tired. She looked over at the clock on the nightstand. It was eight o'clock in the morning. She'd been asleep for only two hours.

"Did I mention that I was also impatient?"

"No, I guess you left that one out," she said.

"It's eight o'clock and I'm downstairs in the lobby."

"The suggestion was dinner at 8:00 p.m.," she said, emphasizing the last word.

"I couldn't wait. May I come up?"

"I'm not dressed."

"Don't go to any trouble on my account," he said suggestively.

"I'm in bed, you know, jet lag and all."

"In that case, may I come up and join you?" He heard lightness in her sigh and knew that she was smiling even through the receiver.

"Give me twenty minutes, I'll be right down."

Jackson hung up the lobby phone and smiled as if he'd just won the million-dollar lottery. He had no idea what he was doing, but for some reason he couldn't stop himself. After leaving the airport he'd gone home, showered, changed clothes and was standing out on his deck overlooking the beach and water when an uncontrollable urge steered him back into the city. As if on automatic, he drove directly to the Beverly Wilshire Hotel.

Even though she didn't wear a wedding band, he had no idea if she was married, engaged or even in a relationship. Her not looking for anyone didn't necessarily stipulate. All he knew for sure was that he wanted to see Samantha again, and tonight wasn't soon enough.

Maybe it was the fantasy idea Jessie had planted in his subconscious or maybe it was just a crazy whim, but either way, he wanted to spend time with Samantha, and the sooner, the better.

Her subdued energy and her passion intrigued him. And of all the women he'd known, she was by far the most exciting.

He walked over to the lobby newsstand and glanced over the assortment of newspapers and magazines stacked and piled across the small counter. He chose a *Black Enterprise* magazine, paid for it, then sat down on one of the overstuffed lobby sofas and flipped through the pages leisurely. The inside cover showed the standard PR as usual. Daley Communications was a staple in the African-American community.

It was his mother's idea to have a full page ad in the magazine every quarter. It was the one thing that hadn't changed even after her death months ago. Jessie made sure of that.

Although it was a fact that his grandfather had started the company over sixty-five years ago, it was his mother's vision and her ingenuity twenty years ago that really made the company. When that company was stagnant and in danger of extinction, it was also her money that saved it and eventually turned it into the conglomerate it was today.

Jackson continued turning pages. He paused when he saw the photo. There it was, his father's smiling face as close to genuine as he could get. To the world he was a genius with a vision for the future, but to Jackson he was a user who usurped ideas and took all the credit.

"Women. It takes them forever to get ready."

Jackson looked up, and saw an elderly gentleman sitting on the sofa across from him, dressed in the typical tourist outfit. He even had a camera around his neck and a fanny pack secured around his waist.

Jackson nodded.

"I see we have the same taste in literature," he said, tilting his magazine up to show that he also had a copy of *Black Enterprise.* "Very informative."

"Yes, it is," Jackson said as he continued flipping through the pages.

"So," the man continued, "are you here on your honeymoon?"

Jackson half chuckled. "No, nothing like that, just hanging out for the day."

"Ah, I see, got the day off, nice, nice indeed," the man said, nodding. "So, is California home for you?"

"Yes, born and raised."

"Nice place. A bit more sun than I'm used to, but no complaints. As a matter of fact, I could get used to this weather, better than back East. It was near freezing when I left."

"Yeah, I was in Chicago earlier. It was a bit chilly."

"I heard that," the man said and he looked at his watch, then at the bank of elevators. He was obviously sitting in the lobby killing time and waiting for someone to arrive.

"So, what do you do?" he asked.

"I work in broadcasting," Jackson said.

"Television?"

"No, radio," Jackson corrected.

"Nice, nice indeed," he said glancing at his watch again. "Me, I'm retired. Yes, sir, worked all my life now it's my turn to just sit back and relax."

"Sounds good." Jackson said.

"Been doing some traveling lately," the man added. Jackson nodded obligingly. He continued, "Read about these places all my life and thought that this was the perfect time to check them out. Las Vegas, now, *there's* a place to go."

Jackson listened as the man continued talking about his recent travels and the extended list of places he intended to go.

Samantha sighed heavily. As soon as she'd agreed to meet him she hesitated. It wasn't that she didn't want to see Jackson again, it was that she did. What was she doing? She posed the question rhetorically. What comes natural, she answered instantly, exactly what Jefferson said to do.

But nothing about this was natural. There was no way she'd agree to go out with a man after meeting him just hours earlier. And even as she dressed, the usual myriad of doubts haunted her. Suddenly, the scent of fresh flowers got her attention. She'd forgotten all about them. She walked over and plucked a small envelope from one of the stems.

She opened and read the card aloud, "Welcome to L.A., Looking forward to the next few days, J. Daley." She smiled, then leaned in and smelled the heavenly scent. All of a sudden, meeting Jackson seemed natural.

What was it about him that tempted her so?

He was attractive, certainly. There was no denying that fact. Beneath the cool exterior of his Armani business suit he was certainly built like a bronze statue with a body that had to be deliciously lickable. But it was his eyes that astonished her. Piercing and intense, they were stunning amber starbursts washed in pale green sunlight, and when he looked at her she felt her whole life exposed, but not in a bad way. It was as if he saw her for who and what she was and still wanted to be with her.

The disqualifying truth of her family always made her edgy. There always seemed to be a ticking time bomb ready to explode as soon as she met someone. The closer they got, the more anxious she became, knowing that the truth would inevitably come out and she wasn't going to lie. If they weren't in the business, they didn't understand those who were. And judgments, justified or not, were something she refused to accept. She loved her family, warts and all, and accepting her meant accepting them.

She looked at her reflection in the mirror as she styled her hair and applied a soft tint to her lips and cheeks. Act natural, she reminded herself, then grabbed her hat and purse and left the room.

A moment alone in the elevator gave her time to regroup. She took a deep breath and heard her father's words reminding her that no matter what the situation, she should always be proud of who she was and where she came from. As others cheated, lied and stole behind boardroom doors and political parties, it was his honor to give them a taste of their own medicine. He believed it, but she didn't. Two wrongs didn't make a right.

Two minutes later she walked through the lobby and saw Jackson sitting and talking with another man. She smiled, seeing him before he saw her. Out of his tailored business suit, he'd changed to a more casual polo shirt and slacks. Either way, he was still gorgeous.

He stood, seeing her as she walked over to the lobby seating. "Wow, you look fantastic," he said as soon as she approached. His eyes lit up bright and wide. He stared at her face. She looked different since earlier that morning. Instead of her hair pulled back in a tight bun, she wore loose curls that gently danced on her shoulders. She wore hoop earrings and a simple chain around her neck. His eyes drifted down her lean body, taking in the slim firmness of her simple sundress and the strappy high-heel sandals with a matching purse. She had dark sunglasses and a wide-brimmed hat in her hand.

"Thanks, so do you."

"Come on, let's get out of here," he said, not wanting to waste a single moment of the time they had together.

He glanced at the older gentleman he'd been talking with. They each nodded a parting salutation, and then Jackson took Samantha's hand.

"So where exactly are we going?" she asked, not moving.

He turned. "This is California, sweetheart, we're going to the beach, of course."

"Of course," she said as he squeezed her hand gently and whisked her away.

Moments later they were sitting in his sports convertible, a Mercedes-Benz SLR McLaren, driving along the Pacific Coast Highway, the ocean on one side and the hilly knolls of Malibu canyons on the other. The low steady resonance of the engine mixed with the smooth jazz on the radio added to her enjoyment. She rested her head back on the headrest, allowing the bright sun, the salted air, the warm breeze to blow through her hair and on her face. She felt invigorated.

"So," she began after nearly fifteen minutes of silence, "this is what Californians do on a weekday instead of grinding the stone—ride up and down the coastal highway, jamming traffic." They slowed, hitting a patch of congested highway thickened with more traffic. They eventually came to a complete stop.

"Looks that way."

"Impromptu parking lot?" she asked jokingly.

"Yeah, something like that," he responded, glancing up in the rearview mirror as someone a few cars back decided that blowing his horn would make a major difference. "Why do people do that?" he asked rhetorically.

"Do what?" she asked.

"Blow the horn. Traffic isn't going to move any faster. Impatiently blowing the horn does nothing but irritate the drivers around them."

"True," she agreed. "I guess it makes them feel like they're doing something, you know, in control of the situation, even if it's just an illusion."

With all the cars around him completely stopped, Jackson took a moment to look over at her. He smiled and nodded his head, obviously impressed. "That's pretty insightful of you. What do you do, drive around the city all day figuring these things out?"

"Sometimes, yeah, but that's only my part-time job. Truth is, I rather like driving in traffic. Actually, I find it peaceful."

"Well, welcome to California, then. You're gonna love it here, so if by chance you're in the market for a new home…"

"Are you trying to sell me one?"

Jackson chuckled, and she joined in. "Nah, seriously, traffic isn't always this bad," he said.

"So this is home for you, I gather?" she asked.

"Yes, I was born and raised right here in Los Angeles."

"Sounds like you really love it."

"I do," he paused a second, then continued. "You can find anything and everything you can imagine just by going a few miles in any direction. It's beautifully diverse. Los Angeles, like most cities, is basically broken up into smaller cultural and/or economical subdivisions, but of course it's most populated right in the heart of the city."

She glanced over at the view on the other side of the highway. "And the infamous L.A. beaches?"

"Oh, we have plenty of them. The coastline is miles and miles long. So actually there aren't just a few beaches, there are dozens and dozens."

"So where exactly are we going?" she asked as traffic cleared and they passed a sign stating that they were north on the Pacific Coast Highway and nearing west on Interstate 10.

"A nice little spot I know just up the coast a bit more. I think you're gonna like it." Samantha nodded as an unexpected yawn caught her off guard, and she reached up and covered her mouth. "Tired, still jet-lagged?" he asked, glancing over to her.

"A little," she sighed then laid her head back on the comfortable leather and closed her eyes behind the dark sunglasses as she dipped her wide-brimmed hat against the wind.

"Lie back, relax, take a nap, we'll be there soon." She nodded as they fell into an easy silence. Jackson drove and Samantha did exactly as he suggested. He glanced over to her from time to time, seeing the sweet perfection of her contented smile. She was a different woman from the person on the plane just hours earlier, and he decided that he liked this Samantha just as much.

A few more miles down the road he steered the car off the highway and through a complex of large office buildings and then through a small township where dozens of storefront restaurants and trendy boutiques lined both sides of the street. He continued farther, driving upward, as if to reach the top of a hill.

The winding turns seemed more dramatic than they actually were as he easily handled the road and maneuvered through traffic with ease. He passed a small garden plaza and drove a few more blocks, coming to another smaller collection of stores and boutiques.

Moments later, he pulled into a graveled parking lot and turned off the engine. He looked over at her. She opened her eyes, hearing that the engine had gone silent and feeling that the car had stopped. Meeting his pale eyes, she turned to him. They smiled politely. "Nice rest?" he asked.

"Yes, it was wonderful. I can't believe I dozed off like that. She looked at her watch. They'd driven over an hour and a half from Los Angeles. "Are we—" she stopped when she started looking around "—there yet?" Her mouth dropped open at the breathtaking sight in front of her. Touching the wide brim of her hat, she looked up.

The quaint building several stories high and seemingly surrounded by a barrage of blossoming orange trees looked more like someone's old grandmother's house than the restaurant and inn it professed itself to be. The antique sign out front, weathered and distressed, called it an authentic beach bungalow, but this was nothing like the one-room bungalows she'd seen on television and in the movies.

It had a wraparound porch with white high-back wooden rocking chairs neatly spaced apart, gingerbread accents and probably hundreds of thousands of colorful flowers scattered along the edging in the front yard and around the sides, giving the inn a homey, comfortable look and feel. She liked it instantly.

"What do you think of the old place?"

"It's so charming," she said exuberantly.

Jackson got out of the car. He walked around to the side and opened the door for her. "This is the real beauty of California," he said. She stepped out and tossed her hat in the backseat, then turned and looked up at the bright white building with the large black shutters and overflowing flower boxes.

"I like it," she said as she walked toward the entrance gate, then stopped and took the time to look around. Jackson followed, enjoying the newness of her wonder. She started toward the narrow path leading to the front door but he stopped her.

"Wait, I want to show you something first, this way."

He led, she followed. They walked down a slate-stone path leading through trees and bushes circling around to the side. Although the front seemed small and quaint, the building was actually quite huge and much larger than she imagined. After they passed a grouping of citrus trees they came to a narrow clearing.

"Careful, we're perched right on a hillside overlooking the surf. The cliff stops and gravity begins," Jackson said, holding Samantha's waist and helping her climb a small mound. "This way," he said, taking her hand. Then he moved aside as Samantha stepped forward, giving her the first unobstructed view.

It was as if they stood at the edge of the world. All she could see was the skyline in front of her. Located high on a hill, the inn overlooked the ocean as the grassy knoll came to an abrupt end at a drop of more than fifty feet and an outlay of bleached white sand and then presumably the Pacific Ocean.

"Wait, where are we?" she asked again, continuing to look around in amazement.

"Not exactly Kansas anymore, is it, Dorothy?"

She turned to him quickly, stunned by his statement. "What did you say?" she asked, her eyes wide with trepidation. Her heart suddenly skipped a beat, then did double time to catch up.

"Kansas, you know, Dorothy, the *Wizard of Oz,*" he said, hoping for some sign of recognition instead of the anxious expression on her face. "Never mind, it was a bad joke."

Samantha relaxed, realizing Jackson's innocent joke was just a coincidence but that it had still hit too close to home. "Yeah, I know, I get it, Munchkins, Yellow Brick Road." She half smiled, then turned back to the view. "You're right, it's definitely not Kansas."

"Is that where you're from?" he guessed.

"It's fantastic, beautiful," she said and began walking toward the waist-high railing to get a better look at the view. "I can't believe the view, everywhere you look. It's breathtaking."

"That's Malibu. It's a unique location. It has canyons, mesas and beaches, with both ocean and mountains surrounding the entire area."

"Wow," she whispered, entranced by the sight. She inched closer for a better view.

"Careful," Jackson warned, taking her hand gently and holding her firm. "We're right on the edge."

"Don't worry, I've been on the edge all my life," she said offhandedly, then instantly thought better of the remark.

Jackson didn't reply, but she knew that she'd only piqued his curiosity even more.

They stood side by side looking out at the bustle of traffic directly below and the peaceful serenity of the view from the distance. Like two different worlds, the contrast was remarkable. One side was chaotic and the other was calm, a battle of two worlds not unlike her own inner struggle.

"Come on," he said. "Let's get something to eat."

She nodded her agreement, but still reluctantly turned to follow him. Walking away from something so wonderful was hard. She wondered how hard it would be to walk away from Jackson when the time came.

Chapter 5

As soon as they entered the small inn, Jackson was welcomed personally by the owner, Mr. Perry, a sixties actor in black exportation films who'd parlayed his meager salary into beachfront real estate and become an instant success. Jackson was treated like royalty, as Mr. Perry escorted them through the main dining hall and directly to their table.

Privately seated on the outside terrace, they enjoyed the spectacular view as they ate. Without waiting for them to order, Mr. Perry offered a full breakfast consisting of hot tea, lattes, fresh fruit, cheese and sliced bread with scrambled eggs, bacon, wheat toast, powdered waffles and croissants with homemade preserves.

The meal was delicious and they chatted easily about Malibu and California.

Samantha looked around as she sipped the last of her tea.

"This certainly wasn't what I expected my day to be like when I got on the plane last night."

"Is that a good thing or a bad thing?" he asked.

She smiled. "A very good thing. Thank you for a wonderful morning and afternoon."

"Whoa, the day isn't over yet, I hope, unless of course you already have plans for the rest of the afternoon."

"No, no plans."

"Good," he said happily, relieved.

"What do you have in mind?" she asked.

"I thought maybe we'd stop at a few of the small vineyards up the coast."

"Vineyards?" she questioned. He nodded. "Sounds perfect, I've never seen a real vineyard before."

"Then you're in for a treat."

Their waiter came and removed the dishes. Moments later, Mr. Perry arrived with two champagne mimosas. He stayed a few minutes to offer polite conversation, then just as quickly exited. "He seems really nice," she said. Jackson nodded. "I still can't believe he owns all this. Do you come here often?"

"Often enough, I suppose," Jackson said cryptically.

"So, Jackson, Jackson Daley, is this your hot spot?"

"My what?"

"You know, your hot spot. The place where guys go when they think they might get lucky."

Jackson burst out laughing. "Where in the world did you hear that?"

"My brother told me about hot spots years ago. He warned me never to trust a man who takes you to his hot spot the first time out together. He said that the guy only wants one thing."

"I've never heard that term before." She nodded. "And your

brother told you this?" She nodded again. "Let me guess, you worshipped him and everything he said was the absolute truth."

It was her time to laugh. "Yeah, something like that."

"You're close with your family, then?" he asked, expecting her to say yes. Instead, the easy laughter that had slipped out just seconds earlier quickly ceased and the bright smile that followed tightened as she looked away.

"No, not anymore."

"I'm sorry, I didn't mean to bring up uncomfortable memories."

"Memories," she nearly whispered. "They're always with us, can't run away from them no matter how hard we try."

"Like family," he confirmed.

"Yeah," she agreed. "Like family."

Jackson held his glass up. "To good memories to come."

"I'll drink to that. Cheers," she said, clinking her glass to his. They sipped the mimosas as Jackson began chuckling again. "What?" she asked.

"Hot spots, huh?" Jackson said. She nodded. "I think I'd better look into that," he added looking into her sparkling eyes. The warm citrus-scented breeze enveloped them as they sipped their drinks, letting the conversation lapse, leaving them simply sitting and smiling.

"What?" she asked, seeing him staring at her.

"Not to get too personal, but you're not from Chicago, either, are you?"

"Am I not? What makes you say that?" she asked.

"A hunch. Call me highly intuitive. As a matter of fact, I'd say that you were more probably from New York or New England."

"You think so, huh?" she asked. He nodded. "Sounds like you've really been thinking about this."

"I have."

"Maybe you should consider getting a hobby."

He chuckled. "You kind of made an impression on me. Not something easily achieved—very few women can do that."

"Given the limited time," she offered.

"Given any amount of time," he replied.

"I'm flattered," she said awkwardly, then took a deep breath and changed the subject. "So, a disc jockey?"

"Excuse me?" he asked.

"In college, you said that you were an on-air personality, a disc jockey, right? I'm curious, how exactly does that work?"

"Nope, not this time. It's been all about me for the past hour and a half, not to mention nearly four hours on the plane. Tell me something about you," he said.

"And ruin the fantasy?" she said.

"Fantasy?" he asked.

"Of course. Isn't that what this is?" she said.

"And everybody needs a fantasy, right?" he surmised, recalling his show topic a few nights ago.

"Except for me. My life is complicated enough, believe me. I don't have time for fantasies," Samantha said.

"Maybe you just haven't found the right one."

"Maybe…"

"Interested?" he asked.

"So exactly where does this fantasy lead?"

"I guess that would depend on…" he prompted.

"On how far we want the fantasy to go," she said.

"Exactly," he confirmed.

"Exactly," she added.

"Okay, fair enough."

She nodded.

He continued, "So as part of the fantasy, answer the question, tell me about yourself."

"There's not much to tell."

"There's no getting around your guard, is there? I ask questions and you maneuver around them, quite skillfully, I'd say."

"I'm not that evasive, am I?" she asked already knowing the answer. Then she paused and decided to open up a little. After all, she had no intention of seeing him after today. "Okay, what do you want to know?"

"Tell me something about your family."

She frowned and looked away again. "I don't talk about my family anymore."

"The word *anymore* implies that you did at least once talk about them. What happened?"

"I opened up to someone once and it didn't work out," she said, easing away the uncomfortable feeling and taking a deep breath. "What's left of my family and I went our separate ways a long time ago. We didn't agree on career paths. My mom died and my father and I never—" She stopped and looked at him briefly, then back to the view.

"Thank you," he said softly.

"For what?"

"For trusting me just a little bit, I know that was difficult for you."

Samantha smiled, feeling an opening in her heart expand. She watched as Mr. Perry returned to offer more beverages. He and Jackson talked and joked briefly while she looked on.

Jackson had a comfortable way about him that had put her at ease the moment they met. His voice was gentle and caring and she could easily imagine people telling him all kinds of secrets. She nearly did. He was right, she did trust him, at least enough to even consider discussing her fractured family.

As soon as Mr. Perry left, Jackson reached across the table and took her hand. "Now tell me about you."

"I don't want to bore you."

"I don't bore easily, try me."

"I don't want to scare you."

"I don't scare easily, try me."

"Okay, let's see…about me," she said, then paused to consider the truth. "My life is complicated at the moment."

"Your life or you?"

"Both. I grew up kind of nomadic, all over the place. My parents separated when I was young. I lived with my father, then my mother. I got into computers and other things."

"Such as?"

"Trouble," she said hesitantly. He nodded. "I stuck with computers. They were the one stable thing I could easily control. And that's pretty much everything," she said, giving him just enough while keeping the details as vague as possible.

"What company do you work for now?"

"I consult with a small computer company by logging in from wherever I am, whenever I'm needed. I write programs and detail systems, although I primarily specialize in high-end servers to correct glitches in internal systems before they corrupt the mainframe system."

"You're a computer systems troubleshooter?" he asked.

"Put simply, yes."

"Impressive. So you're smart, beautiful, complicated, and you know computers."

"I'm not just a pretty face," she joked.

"So why not work in a single company? I'm sure your services are well in demand. I know when our computers need work, the systems specialist charges a near fortune."

"Been there, done that. I don't have the disposition for the corporate world anymore."

"Hence, you consult."

"Yeah, my terms, my time."

"While still making you nomadic, moving from company to company, coming and going as you please. Interesting."

"Yeah, I guess so. I never thought of it that way."

"Are you happy?"

"At the moment I'm ecstatic."

"No, I meant working as a consultant, are you happy?"

"For the most part, yes, I enjoy the challenge. There are good days and bad days and even exceptional days, like most jobs." He nodded his understanding. "So what else do you want to know about me?"

"Your business out here, is it going to take a while?"

"I assume your question is for obvious reasons," she asked, prompting his intentions.

He nodded, smiling shyly. "Yes."

"Actually, I don't know. I have a meeting soon, I don't know when exactly. Hopefully I'll find who I'm looking for then."

"You misplaced someone."

"I'm looking for someone, yes."

"That's interesting, I was back East looking for someone."

"Did you find her?"

"You assume that it's a woman."

"Bad assumption. Did you find him?"

"No, and I have no idea if it's a man or a woman."

"Sounds mysterious."

Jackson shook his head. He wasn't about to get into details. "Let's just say that this person has something I'm interested in buying."

"You're a collector?"

"In this instance, yes. And who is this mysterious person you came looking for? A man, no doubt."

"What makes you say that?"

"Call it an educated guess. Who is he, family, friend?"

"An old friend."

"And I suppose that would make me…"

"A new friend," she answered before he did.

"I see. Well," he picked up his glass of water, "here's to us both finding what we're looking for."

Samantha picked up her glass and gently touched it to his. "Cheers."

The moment went silent as she looked down over the cliff to the horizon across the way. The sun was dutifully suspended above them, and a haze covered the crystal-clear blue sky. "It's really beautiful here."

"Yes, it is," he said staring at her and wondering.

"Tell me something," she said after a brief pause. "If you could do everything all over again, I mean, from the beginning, clean slate, would you?"

"What do you mean, this, us, together right now?"

"No, I mean everything, your whole life. If you could go back and follow your dreams, your real dreams, would you?"

"You mean live the life I want?"

"Yeah, totally change everything."

He thought a second, then answered. "Probably not."

"Really, why not?" she asked curiously.

"Consequences."

She looked questioning. "Okay, but what about the bad times, the heartbreak, the tragedy and the pain? You'd never have to experience any of that."

He continued, "Our experiences are what make us who we are, the good, the bad and the ugly. Love and joy would be meaningless without heartbreak and pain."

"So what exactly are we doing, Jackson?" she asked.

"We're getting to know one another."

"Why?" she asked.

"Why not?"

"Well, for obvious reasons, one being that I'll be leaving

in a few days, so if this is about getting me into bed you're taking a long time to get to the point."

Jackson nearly choked on his water. "You don't pull any punches, do you?"

"No, I live life for the moment, no time for anything else."

"And what moment is this?" he asked.

"What else do you want to know about me?"

"What you look like waking up in the morning after making love all night," he boldly said, interested in her reaction.

She smiled slyly. "Is that right?" He nodded, focusing his eyes on hers. "I guess there's only one way to find out," she leaned across the table and kissed his lips gently. "Your place or mine?"

Samantha sighed gently as she waited for his reply. The answer to a question that they both knew was in the offing since she'd kissed him on the plane. Everything they did, every word they said and every breath they took was leading to this one moment in time. She knew it and he knew it. His eyes, exotic and hypnotically beautiful, seemed to pierce right through her. But she met his stare brazenly and boldly without wavering.

A slow easy smile pulled at the corner of his lips, then crept wide in pleasure. Meeting on a four-hour flight, strangers, both—it was the perfect fantasy come true. He looked at her as if she were the only person on earth, then answered, "Neither."

Chapter 6

The compromise was simple. They got a room at the inn.

Bungalow number twelve.

While Jackson made arrangements at the front desk, Samantha walked around behind to the back of the restaurant and stood looking out at the blue water and brightening day. The troubling cares of her world began to melt away as she watched the distant waves gently lap the shore. This wasn't what she'd intended, but it was what she wanted.

"I thought you'd changed your mind and left me," Jackson said as he approached, walking up behind her. He rested his hands on the railing and looked out.

Samantha turned, "Never. I just wanted to see the view once more." She stood by his side, then reached down and intertwined their pinkies. A few minutes passed as they just stood looking out.

"We don't have to do this," Jackson said, still looking out at the ocean.

"Ready?" she asked, turning to him and slipping her hand in his. He took her in his arms and kissed her. Soft and sweet, his mouth opened to hers and she diligently responded. When the kiss ended they smiled, feeling the warmth of their yearning surround them.

"This way," he said. They walked back toward the front of the building, entered the inn and climbed the stairs to the second level. Jackson opened the door to the last room on the left and Samantha peeked inside. The room instantly took her breath away. Small but nicely designed, it was quaint and just as she expected.

Her eyes bounded in every direction, seeing the sweetest explosion of poppies, primroses and hydrangeas greeting them. Red, purple, blue and orange, the frills and twills of paisley and lace oozed from every crevice.

There was a large picture window and a sitting area in front with a view of the ocean that was spectacular. The bed, she presumed king-size, was canopy style, with sheer panels draped down, covering three sides and took up most of the floor space. Obviously the quiet, secluded inn's guests spent most of their time occupied inside.

Elaborately designed, the room was decorated in an eclectic Mediterranean style reminiscent of Casablanca. It was a desert oasis, a Moroccan boudoir and a Mount Olympus retreat all rolled into one.

"Feeling exotic?" she asked jokingly.

Jackson took her hand. "Second thoughts?" he asked, mistaking her pause at the doorway for hesitation.

"Not at all…you?" she retorted looking up into his heavenly eyes.

He shook his head. "Not a chance."

A knowing smile on both of their faces turned quickly to mild but deliberate laughter. The would-be awkward moment dissipated before it even appeared. This was going to happen. In a few minutes they were going to be naked and wrapped in each other's arms. And the image warmed her.

Suddenly the semantics of the moment occurred to her. She preferred to be on top. Would he? She liked undressing herself, needed a private moment in the bathroom before, and preferred to have the lights off and curtains drawn. Would he? Condoms, she didn't have any, did he?

"Do you have ah, um…"

"Yes, several."

An anticipatory smile crossed her full lips. This was going to happen and she intended to enjoy every succulent moment of it and him. She walked in. He followed.

But before she could take three steps into the room, the door closed; he grabbed her hand and drew her back. She slammed into solidness, nearly taking her breath away. He instantly wrapped his arm around her waist and drew her closer to his hard body. Just inches away, he paused, searching her face for any sign of uncertainty. Instead, she smiled and that was all he needed to see.

"Where have you been all my life?" he muttered.

His mouth, hot and wanting, immediately clamped onto hers, demanding and promising an afternoon of pure heavenly delight. His one hand held her slim waist tight against his body as the other grasped her at the nape of her neck. He combed his fingers through her hair, then held her in place, escalating the passion of the embrace and stilling her to his mouth.

Samantha, reeling in the power of his kiss, held her arms to her sides and allowed him to master the moment. He did with an intoxicating fierceness that made her want him even more. Then slowly she maneuvered to wrap her arms around his neck. Holding him felt so right. Kissing him felt divine, even better than she remembered.

Wanting the kiss to last a lifetime, she tilted her head to savor as much of him as possible. Deepening, the kiss continued, consuming both of them, leading to breathless anticipation.

When their lips finally parted, they were both dazed and nearly panting. Looking into each other's eyes, they smiled with giddy desire seconds before their lips met again. Feverishly and hungrily eating and savoring the taste of each other's mouths, they succumbed to the ignited passion. Her heart pounded in a rhythmic beat she hadn't heard in a long time. She was alive again and it felt so good.

Her body tingled, her thoughts muddled, her senses were on fire and her heart pounded like a drum. She was lost, blinded by her desire and overcome by the longing they shared as her passion intensified and she felt a swell of hunger poised, ready to explode.

Then their lips parted.

They held on to each other, rendered breathless by the consuming passion. "I love kissing you," Jackson said.

"Yeah, me, too," she replied, winded.

He leaned in to continue.

"Wait," she said, pulling back a little to catch her breath. "I need to go—" She didn't finish as she started looking around the room for what might be the bathroom door. She saw a partially open door and what appeared to be a cast-iron lion-claw tub. She pointed and backed away as his hand still rested on her waist. He finally released her. "I'll be right back," she promised.

Jackson nodded, then shook his head in amazement as she retreated. As the bathroom door closed behind her, he turned and walked over to the large picture window. His composure was waning fast. The effect she had on him was unbelievable.

Known for his discipline and restraint, he teetered on the edge of losing all control. He couldn't think. She'd clouded his mind and all he could think about was being with her—like a teenager out on a first date. His palms were moist and his heart raced nonstop.

He stood at the picture window. In the stillness, he focused on the thin, sheer curtain surrounding the window, then looked beyond to the view in the distance. Mountainous terrain on one side sloped down, meeting the ocean on the other, diametrically opposite but yet the same. Not unlike Samantha and himself. He turned to the bathroom door. Hearing the water running, he turned back to the view.

As the morning receded and the sun anchored directly above, the meaning of their time together became clear. The last few hours with Samantha had completely staggered him. She brought an unexpected zeal into his life, a joy he'd forgotten, something he hadn't experienced in years. Her sense of freedom and spontaneity drew him in.

He laughed and talked and joked and just enjoyed being with her. She had an energy that intensified his pleasure, taking him to a new place, and he wanted more. He was happy, and gorged himself on her limitless spirit. Realizing that just a onetime fantasy wouldn't be enough, he decided that he needed to extend their stay.

This was so unlike him. He was always so focused and deliberate. And when it came to women and making love, he was extremely discerning. But here he was, nonetheless, about to make love to a woman he'd met on a plane just a few hours earlier. The suddenness and reality of his actions excited him even more. If it were anyone else but Samantha, he would have politely excused himself and then just walked out the door. But it was Samantha and there was no way he was going to budge from this spot.

He turned again, looking back at the closed door across the room. Anticipation stirred his body to react and his imagination to soar. He sighed heavily, shaking his head, then walked over and picked up the signature champagne bottle that he'd had delivered to the room and examined the label: Louis Roederer 1999 Cristal Brut.

Approving, he unfurled the foil and removed the wire, then gently popped the cork. He poured the luxurious pale golden libation into glasses and turned on the radio beside the bed. Soft music instantly flowed through the room. He pulled three condoms he'd purchased downstairs from his pocket and tossed them on the side table.

Seeing them lying there made everything real. He was about to make love to a woman he had met less than ten hours ago. Given his usual near-prudent personality, this was totally out of character, but there was something about being with Samantha that made it feel right.

Although solicited and propositioned on a regular basis, he never took advantage of the many offers. Power and position came with responsibility and he took that responsibility very seriously. He usually got to know a woman before being with her physically. But the suddenness of the moment and the excitement of the fantasy that drew them together was overwhelming. He turned back to the window.

Samantha had secrets, and he had learned just recently how dangerous secrets could be. His grandfather and father had secrets, his mother had had secrets and now Samantha Lee was his secret.

Samantha leaned back against the closed door. She inhaled deeply and released a slow, deliberate breath as she put her head back, closed her eyes and smiled, her thoughts spinning in wild disarray. The energy and excitement of the moment had thrilled her. Everything was happening so fast, too fast. She had no idea what she was doing, but she liked it. A few seconds later, she opened her eyes and looked around.

Scattered vases of fresh flowers, baskets of large fernlike palms and golden accents against deep purple and pink paisley walls surrounded her. The hodgepodge of jumbled tackiness worked in the small space. The exotic motif of the bedroom had continued into the bathroom. Rich in deep purples, gold, orange and magenta, it was a beautifully designed oasis. She walked over to the sink and turned on the faucets, letting water run into the shell-shaped sink. She watched as the clear liquid circled and poured down into the drain. Then she looked up at her reflection in the mirror. Her dark eyes shone clear and vibrant.

She needed to gather herself. Granted, she was no virgin, but this was a long time coming. It felt good to be wanted and desired, even if it was just for one moment and only a fantasy.

She intended to fulfill every desire as her imagination began to sift through the possibilities. He was built for loving. Every inch of his hard body was a delight. She shuddered as a flash of heat burned through her. Then she turned, hearing the sound of a cork popping in the next room.

She dropped a thick white hand towel into the sink and let the cool water soak the fibers. She squeezed the towel dry and dotted the cooled moistness on her neck. A few deep breaths and she was calm.

She removed her jacket and looked at herself in the waist-high mirror. She turned sideways seeing the trimmed silhouette of her profile. She wasn't particularly tall but she was nicely endowed with measurements any woman would be proud of. She reached up and fluffed the loose curls around her face, letting them tumble neatly onto her shoulders.

Fairly certain that she was at least presentable, she grabbed her purse from the countertop and pulled her lipstick out, then decided against freshening it, knowing that it would just be smudged anyway. Then, as she watched the coral tint retract into the tube, a shiver of doubt twisted through her. She was about to make love to a complete stranger for no other reason than the fact that she was attracted to him and that opportunity had presented itself.

A fantasy, they'd called it. This was as they'd agreed, a fantasy, and fantasies can't be censored. She smiled as the liberating moment seemed to quash her doubts and renew her excitement.

The man waiting for her on the other side of the door was a dream—no, a fantasy. He was handsome, hot and sexy and the thought of making love with him made her body burn.

She took one last glance at herself in the mirror, smiled and nodded. "Let the fantasy begin."

She opened the door and looked around. Jackson was standing at the window with his back to her. He seemed to be so intently looking outside that he didn't realize she'd returned. She stood a moment and watched him. His shoulders were broad and strong and the soft sway of his knit shirt was tucked neatly into his slacks. He looked every bit the fantasy.

"Hey, are you ready for me?" Samantha asked seductively as she waited in the doorway.

Jackson turned and smiled, seeing her standing there. She was too beautiful for words. Still wearing the sundress, she had removed the jacket, exposing the sweet cinnamon of her shoulders and deep, hallow plunge of her cleavage. "Definitely," he finally replied through the sudden dryness in his mouth. "Since the moment I saw you."

"Is that right?" she said, interested. He nodded as he watched her walk slowly toward the bed, then stop at the swayed curve of the bedpost. "So you knew this was going to happen—*we* were going to happen."

"Let's just say I was highly optimistic."

"That confident, huh?" she asked.

"No, just hopeful," he said almost shyly as he picked up the two glasses of champagne.

She returned his smile, then bit at her lower lip and motioned with her finger. "Come here," she said softly.

Jackson walked over and stood toe to toe, looking down into her deep dark eyes. He surrendered instantly. Who she was or what she was doing here didn't matter. He was falling for her and it felt good. The sweetness of her smile and the gentleness of her voice softened him. All of a sudden, the hidden secrets disappeared. The only thing that mattered at this moment was that he wanted her and she wanted him.

"No strings," she warned, making sure that they understood each other's intent.

"No strings," he repeated.

"Live, then let go," she added.

He nodded agreeing. "Live, then let go."

She took the offered champagne. "To fantasies," she said.

"To fantasies that come true," he added as their glasses clinked and they each took a small sip. She handed the glass back to him and he set them both down on the bench at the foot of the bed.

She reached up and touched his silk knit shirt. Spreading her fingers, she fanned her hands wide across his chest, feeling the solid firmness of his body. It had been a long time since she'd touched a man like this. It felt good. He felt good. "So tell me about this wanton fantasy of yours," she said, rising up to whisper close to his ear.

"I meet a woman on a plane…" he began, his deep voice resonating seductively sexy, sending a fire burning straight through the core of her body.

"And...?" she prompted boldly.

"And we talk and we realize that we have a lot in common," he continued. "And the attraction is mutual."

With deliberate agility she slid her hands down the length of his arms, feeling the muscles tense and tighten beneath her touch. His reaction prompted her further. She pulled the hem of his shirt from his pants and up over his head. As she dropped it onto the end of the sleigh bed, she glanced down the front of him and smiled. He was just as gorgeous as she imagined.

"There's an early-morning rendezvous at a...a..."

She leaned in and kissed his chest. He groaned his approval. "Yes, tell me more. What else happens?" she asked, continuing to tease his body with her mouth and hands.

She laid her hands on his chest, following the shape and form and letting her fingers embrace the tiny scattered hairs. She heard a second slow groan. His burning skin, warm to the touch, sparked with terra-cotta tints as she teasingly scratched her nails down his chest. He was perfect. Not too muscled, not too bulgy, not too overdone, he was just right. She continued gently scratching down to the hard impact of his stomach, feeling the quiver of her own and the tenseness of his reaction.

His body shuddered, making her smile, delighted by the reaction. His jaw tightened in restraint and his breath quickened. She caressed the places her nails had raked, then kissed the dullness, sending another shudder through him.

He refocused to clear his thoughts. "Then we arrive at an out-of-the-way inn by the beach and..."

"And..." she repeated as she moved closer still, kissing his chest and shoulders, each time waiting for the soft moan of longing to escape from the deep recesses of his throat. She continued kissing a trail of passion from his chest to his shoulders and up to his neck. As she reached up, the silk fabric stretched across her breasts brushed against him and a sharp intake sounded and sizzled. Nuzzling closer she arched and pressed forward and felt the tenseness of his body pull tight in restraint.

"There's champagne and soft music and…"

"Yes, what happens next?" she asked, taunting his resolve by rubbing up against him.

"…and…" he muttered, breathing deeply.

"And?" she asked patiently.

"…and then we make love."

"I like it," she said approvingly. Within seconds the loose dam broke and in an instant he wrapped his hands around her waist and drew her body even closer. She gasped at the suddenness of his passion. The simmering heat exploded and a fury of kisses rained down on her body as the burning hunger erupted in a blaze. His open mouth sealed to hers and she accepted his offering. A breathless rush of focused passion poured from the rapturous moment as each partook in the surging pleasure.

In a heaving, panting blur, hands and arms flailed and hungry kisses reached a pinnacled intensity. She molded her body to his and he arched forward, taking all of her. They held nothing back as the blurred ravage of kisses continued. The rage of unrestrained passion burst as breathless and winded they came to a halt still wrapped in each other's arms.

A brief silent moment passed.

She looked up into his soft eyes and smiled. His hands came up to her sides and gently caressed her arms and shoulders, kneading small circles with his fingers. She tilted her head involuntarily and he dipped his mouth to her neck. She rolled her head back, giving him full access, and he graciously accepted her invitation.

Holding his one hand firmly on the small of her back, he

leaned in, taking her off balance as he held her confidently and securely. She wrapped her hand around his waist and allowed him to ravish her body. Masterfully, he sparked the burning flame as she relaxed back, giving him full access.

He dipped down farther, planting tiny kisses, nibbling down her neck and across her shoulder. Crossing to the opposite side of her body, he continued the onslaught, finding a new passion as his tongue licked into the wanton crevice between her breasts. Her arms weakened as he held her back securely, preventing her from falling.

Trust wasn't easy as she, timid at first, finally gave in without qualms. She relaxed in his arms and let him lead. She was always in control, always on top—this trusting feeling was foreign, but she liked it. The weightless dip was completely beyond her control. Dipping down, she lay in his arms completely vulnerable. Her mind soared in wonderment of the moment. She trusted him not to let her fall. Monumental at the least, it was the first time she'd ever felt the freedom of complete trust.

He slowly released her to stand up in one smooth motion. She found her legs feeble and weak. Steadying herself, she looked up into his smiling eyes, seeing the passion and the smoldering earnestness proceed to a seductive taunt. His hands rested gently on her hips. She turned. Taking his cue, he unzipped her dress and eased it from her body. Seeing her bare back, he placed his hands on her shoulders and began massaging her neck and shoulders with firm gentleness.

She moaned her pleasure, feeling the weight of her troubles lift away as she stood before him.

His lips touched her neck as his hands came to rest on her waist. Tiny kisses traced a burning path across her shoulders and up her neck. She reached for his hands and placed them to cup her breasts. He covered her and she nearly lost all senses. The divine feel of his hands on her was ecstasy.

"You take my breath away," he said, whispering behind her drawing her back closer to his body. She felt his hardness instantly, then turned within his embrace and looked up into his heavenly eyes. He looked down the length of her body, seeing the perfection he wanted. Her taut nipples reached out to him. And he, helpless to deny, leaned down and kissed each of the sweet brown orbs, licking the hardened pebbles and sending the blazing fire deeper into her body.

She backed him against the bed, intending for him to sit. He did as he reached out to draw her in, tucked neatly between his legs. He wrapped his arms around her waist and held on, his face pressed perfectly between the sweet swell of her ample breasts. He slid his hands down her back to rest firmly on her rear still covered by the white silk Lycra-and-lace panties.

He looked up at her. "This, you and I, was a long time coming."

"You think so, huh?"

He nodded and whispered, "I know so. I've been waiting for you." The complete assurance of his words and the sincerity in his eyes overwhelmed her. She took comfort knowing that this was right, and for the first time in a long while she savored the moment as an easy smile broke free.

She leaned back and tucked his face between her hands and stroked his lips with her thumbs, then moved to within inches of his mouth. "Kiss me," she commanded sweetly. He did. With slow, deliberate, devouring presence he tasted her lips, sucking her tongue and loving the sweet nectar of her mouth.

In return, she melted easily into his embrace as their lips met and the kiss sealed the promise. There was no fear, no hesitation, no trepidation. This was all she ever wanted, to be with a man who cherished her even if it was only for a short time. In their sweet repose, the gentle, tender kiss continued slowly, effortless and deliberate as burning passion consumed them both.

He lazily kissed her neck, her shoulders, down her arm to her stomach and around her waist and along the elastic trim of her panties. Turning her around, he continued kissing her body, then held her in place as his hand gently massaged her shoulders, her back, and the firm round of her buttocks. She arched back, stimulated by his touch. She felt the heat of his mouth as he kissed the tiny tattoo just at the base of her spine.

"I like this," he said, his voice husky with desire. She felt his finger trace the outline, then his mouth return to lovingly caress her body. Her legs weakened as he held her steady.

She turned to him and looked into his eyes.

Descending needfully, she reached for his belt and loosened it along with the clasp of his pants. A thickness instantly protruded, giving evidence of his arousal.

She inched closer, climbing up onto the bed, straddling his body. He held her in place as he cupped her breasts, and his mouth suckled the object of his desire. She arched her head back and held on to his shoulders as he savored the delight of full access.

Teasing and tormenting, her thoughts whirled in his fantasy. She held tight, clinging to the urgency of the moment. He kissed her fully and completely, leaving no doubt as to his intention. Hard and demanding, the kiss devoured each of them. With fierceness beyond their expectations they savored the rapture and fulfilled the dream. The fantasy had come alive. When the kiss ended she looked into his eyes, smiling.

"Make love to me," she whispered.

He nodded.

She slid around him and lay down on the bed, watching him stand and remove his pants. She lay back, cushioned by the thick headboard of pillows. He sat down and placed his hand on her stomach. She quivered. His fingers spread wide, teasing the lace trim on her panties. She bit her lower lip in anticipation.

He leaned down and kissed the tips of her nipples, sending a throaty moan through her body. As his tongue traced the darkened orb, she gasped and sighed slowly. She cupped his neck and he kissed and licked his way lower and lower until he came to the treasure he sought.

With stealthy agility, he pulled the elastic band down and ran his fingers over the tiny curled hairs. She gasped again, louder, stronger, fuller. She reached for him but he denied her, instead continuing to focus on his newfound treasure.

He touched everywhere, stroking her masterfully, sending a blinding fire over every inch of her skin. The thrill of his hands was mind-blowing. She closed her eyes and reveled in the sensual sensation. His mouth came to her stomach, kissing and licking the sides just below the sweet mounds of her breasts.

She arched her back as the swelled fullness begged to be tended. He did, kissing the full underpart of her breast while his fingers continued the assault on his treasure. The ecstasy of the moment left her breathless as his ravaging fingers sent her on a ride straight through the center of the universe. Her heart raced as she opened her eyes to see him looking down at her.

"Come inside," she beckoned.

He reached over and grabbed one of the three packages on the nightstand, covered himself and moved above her. She opened up to him and he gave himself to her in one smooth burst of desire. Planted firmly, he rocked up, sending a thrill through both of them, then eased back slowly. The rhythm increased as she bit her nails into his back and held on tight.

Meeting power for power, they danced as his mouth came down and captured hers. Kissing, tasting, sucking, their tongues intertwined and their lips, swollen from passion, yearned for more. Wild and furious, the tension built, accelerating at full force beyond what either of them had expected. The pinnacle, ever within reach, delayed driving them further, into a raging inferno of passion. Then, in one blinding moment of ecstasy, they erupted.

He poured his life into her and she held tight, accepting all of him. Their bodies, taut and tight, pulled against the one thing they couldn't deny. The hunger of their physical attraction had brought them to this moment, but the power of their hearts united had taken them all the way.

This was more than a onetime fantasy.

He dropped to her side, pulling her on top of him. She lay comfortably sprawled over him, fitting her body to his perfectly. They lay in silence as the music still played around them and the traffic still flowed outside and the world still turned on its axis. As their beating hearts returned to normal and their breathing subsided, he reached up, encircling her with his arm and holding her firmly in place. She smiled. "That was..." she began in a whisper, but didn't finish as he answered.

"...yes, it was," he relayed raggedly, stroking her arm and back dreamingly.

The accepted serene tranquility of the moment silenced them as neither one attempted to speak again. Their bodies and their hearts had spoken and the need for something audible was nonexistent. Later, they faded off to sleep, only to wake again and begin the rapture once more. She, on top this time, gave new meaning to riding all the way to the stars.

As they met their rapture once again they stared into each other's eyes knowing that this wasn't the end, it was only the beginning.

The thought that this was a onetime thing, a meaningless interlude between consenting adults, seemed to fade away. It was more and they knew it.

Chapter 7

Showered and dressed once more, Samantha sat on the side of the bed in her hotel suite and shook her head, still astonished by her actions as she confessed to her best friend.

"I still can't believe I just did that," Samantha repeated a fourth time as she listened to Jillian chuckle through the phone. "This isn't funny," she insisted almost virtuously. "It was a mistake, a huge mistake. I came out here for two things, to help Jefferson and to find and confront Eric, and instead I wound up in bed with a perfect stranger all afternoon and most of the evening my first day here. And on top of that, I know I missed my connection with Lincoln. Now what am I supposed to do? I can't believe I did that," she repeated.

Jillian Cooke had known Samantha since their freshman year in college. They were roommates who'd despised each other at first sight. Then, brought together by a cheating two-timing boyfriend, they'd commiserated and bonded, consoling each other through school drama, boyfriend drama, ex-fiancé drama and numerous personal crises to become almost sisters.

So at three o'clock in the morning when Samantha called Jillian, it wasn't at all surprising. They often talked into the late hours of the night. And since Jillian knew all about Samantha's family and her recent troubles, including the reason she was in L.A., calling her to bemoan was only natural.

Sounding like a snorkeling hyena, Jillian yawned and chuckled at the same time. "Do you know that for sure? Did he call or leave a message or something like that?"

"No, but that's beside the point. I was distracted and I blew it. It was completely unprofessional."

"That's because you're not a professional. Samantha, from everything you've told me about your brother, it seems to me that he asked you to do this for a reason. He trusts you to be *yourself* and not a professional. Didn't he tell you to do what came natural?"

"Sleeping with a man I met on a plane several hours earlier is definitely not natural for me. I would never have done anything like that."

"And yet you just did."

Samantha groaned. "Don't remind me."

"And about this Lincoln guy, he'll show up again. Jerks like that always do. Just be patient. And in the meantime, tell me about this perfect stranger. Exactly how was he?"

"Jillian," Samantha said, not at all astonished by her friend's curiosity, "I am not going to tell you stuff like that."

"Why not? I'd tell you."

"You probably would," Samantha said, knowing her friend too well. "But all that aside, he was just a guy who happened to be in the right place at the right time, a perfect stranger."

"Perfect, huh?" Jillian said, catching her friend's subtle inflection on the word *perfect*.

"Stop reading into this. A complete stranger, okay? Not perfect. I slept with a complete stranger. Either way, I can't believe I did it."

"Look, how long have we known each other?"

"What does that have to do with anything?"

"Just answer the question."

"Since our freshman year at college," Samantha said.

"Exactly, and in all that time I've sat back and seen your life stuck on perpetual boredom. I say it's about time you shook things up a bit. So Sam, why are you beating yourself up about this?" Jillian asked. "It's been over three months since you've said more than five words to any one man at any single time, and I know it's been a lot longer since you were intimate with a man, so if you ask me, I say it was about time. And so what if he was a perfect, or rather, complete stranger? He was a man, and believe it or not, having a man around every now and then is a good thing."

"Don't try to rationalize it, Jillian. The only good thing is that he has no idea who I really am, or anything else about me. I snuck out of there a few hours ago, caught a cab and came back here to the hotel. I don't expect I'll ever see him again."

"For you to feel this guilty, I sure hope that he was worth it." Jillian paused. "Well, tell me, was he?" she asked boldly.

"I don't kiss and tell, you know that," Samantha said calmly.

"Come on, it's a valid question," Jillian said. "How was he?"

Although the two friends seldom interfered in each other's personal lives to the extreme, Jillian knew Samantha's hesitation. Opening up was hard for her, particularly when it came to her feelings. But slowly she'd seen her friend open up and in the past few months she'd been more open than ever as

Jillian became her confidante and sole connection to a world that she was forced to leave behind.

Also a computer engineer, Jillian had quit the company they'd both worked at after learning that the company had committed more fraud than Eric. Now together, they had started their own company.

As such, Jillian sent electronic diagnostics and Samantha would access them from her computer, connect, locate and then fix the problem as if they were right there together in the same room. It was the perfect solution for both of them as the new arrangement worked like a charm.

To the outside world, Cooke and Taylor Computers was a thriving business that could successfully fix and restore any computer problem in a matter of a few days. Defining their roles, Samantha became the silent partner and Jillian took the visible lead.

"Oh, come on, you can tell me," Jillian said as Samantha remained silent to her last plea. "Who am I gonna tell? It's not like I meet a lot of people sitting in my home office deciphering computer code all day." Jillian paused again for a reply. "Oh, no, was he that bad?" she finally moaned, realizing the sad possibility.

Samantha sighed, shaking her head remembering Jackson and their third time together. She exhaled slowly, smiling. "On the contrary, the man had my toes curling every two minutes. He was…" She paused again. "Unbelievable, insatiable, creative. He had me nearly screaming my head off."

"Say what?" Jillian intoned with delight as they giggled like two schoolgirls at recess. "Go, girl, you finally got your groove on, good for you," Jillian singsonged with chanting humor. "It's about time. Finally you can have some kind of life again. This whole giving up on the men in your life is just not right," she added.

"I gave up for good reason, or have you forgotten my Eric drama?"

"Hardly, but he was just one man—stupid, foolish, a jerk, brainless, a twit, a moron."

Samantha smiled again as Jillian's added descriptions and her talent for exaggerating always had a way of making her feel better. "You're preaching to the choir on that one. But all in all, I gave up for good reason," Samantha said.

"I know," Jillian said softly, knowing the pain of her friend's past and the suffering she'd experienced growing up.

Samantha stilled. On some level she knew Jillian was right. She'd lost faith in men a long time ago and Eric only reinforced her decision. Then the thought of Jackson weaved through her mind. "And one incredible night doesn't change anything. Trust is hard for me."

"Yet you meet a man on a plane, a perfect stranger—sorry, a complete stranger—you have him drive you to who knows where, you make love with him for hours on end, and then you fall asleep in his arms. Excuse me, but that sounds like a whole lot of trust going on to me," Jillian said.

"It wasn't exactly like that. He…I…we…it wasn't like that," she repeated, trying to convince herself as she failed miserably at convincing her friend. "It was all just a fantasy."

"Call it what you want, you made a connection, girl, and by what you just told me, so did he," Jillian said.

"No, it was just a fantasy, a one-night stand, that's it. I have no intention of repeating it."

"That sounds familiar."

"What?"

"Doing that thing you do."

"What thing I do? Okay, let's hear it," Samantha said, knowing what was coming next.

"It's all Robert Taylor's fault," Jillian began.

"Because it is," she insisted.

"You don't know that. All you know is what your mother told you and she was a tad on the bitter side."

"I know you're not defending him now," Samantha said.

"No, of course not. All I'm saying is that for the ten years that I've know you, you've held a grudge against a man that you haven't seen since you were a lad. Every man you meet has to deal with the Robert Taylor curse and they don't even know it. Isn't it time to let it go?"

Samantha didn't respond. She considered Jillian's comment. Then just as she was about to speak, a heavy knock on the door startled her. She turned, then looked at her watch. It was twelve-forty-five in the morning. "There's someone at the door. I have to call you back, take care." She hung up quickly.

The knock sounded a second time as Samantha slowly walked over to the door. "Who is it?" she asked with her hand on the knob.

"Ms. Lee?"

"Yes," she responded.

"It's the bellman from downstairs. Sorry to disturb you, ma'am, but I have a note for you. It was delivered to the front desk a few minutes ago and asked to be hand delivered. It's marked extremely urgent."

Samantha opened the door cautiously. Then, seeing a pimple-faced teen with a silly grin and a uniform a size too big, she relaxed. He held out a sealed envelope. Samantha took it and looked it over. The young man waited uneasily, shifting from foot to foot.

"Oh, right, of course, just a minute," Samantha said and she stepped away, grabbed her purse and handed him a generous tip.

"Thanks, good night," he said, now overly exuberant as he shoved the bill into his pocket, smiled wide, tipped his hat, then turned and headed back down the hall to the elevators.

Samantha stepped out farther into the hall and glanced both ways down the empty corridor. The eerie emptiness of the repetitive doors gave her a disturbing sense of vertigo. Seeing no one around, she went back into her room and closed the door.

She walked over to the bed and opened the envelope carefully. Small and neatly printed, the handwriting was the same as before. She read the short message, then read it again.

Ms. Taylor, I'm delighted that you and Mr. Daley hit it off so well this afternoon. It will make the next days that much more successful. Lincoln.

A chill shivered down her back. The words *hit it off so well* stuck out instantly. She read the message again, this time aloud. Hearing the words out loud drove home the message. The explicitness of the note regarding her day spent with Jackson was well understood. Either she had been followed or Jackson was Lincoln, or at the very least was working was with him.

Her heart began pounding. She tossed the note on the bed, grabbed the suitcase and tossed it on the bed beside the note. In a blurred rush she swung open the closet door and began gathering her clothes and tossing them into the open suitcase. She hurried into the bathroom collected her things from the counter, then headed toward the bed.

As soon as she dropped her toiletries into the bag, there was another knock at the door. She stopped and turned to the door. "Who is it?"

"It's Jackson. Open the door, Samantha."

Jackson's voice was tight and demanding. Samantha looked around the room anxiously. "Jackson, I'm busy right now."

"Open the door, Samantha," he repeated.

She walked over and opened the door. "What are you doing here?"

"You can stop playing games," he said as he walked past her and stood in the center of the room, his back to her.

"What are you doing here?" she repeated.

He noticed the half-packed suitcase on the bed and turned to her. "Leaving so soon? You haven't even been paid yet," he said, pulling out his checkbook.

"Excuse me?" she said, appalled by his implication.

"But then I guess in your kind of work you'd prefer cash," he added.

"If you're implying what I think you're implying…" she said, finally slamming the door of the suite closed.

"Don't flatter yourself, Ms. Lee," he quipped as he began riffling through the cash in his wallet. "I'm only here to finish our business."

"You need to leave, now," she demanded, aggravated with herself that she had misjudged him so completely.

"Not until we settle our business," he assured her firmly.

"Our business? What business? I have no idea what you're talking about," she said, then paused, realizing that she'd been conned again and he was obviously Lincoln. "Oh, I get it, it was you all along." She stopped and shook her head, disappointed. "Fine, if it's money you want I'll pay you."

"What?" Jackson asked, stunned as he watched her storm over to her purse and toss cash on the bed for him.

"You heard me," she said. "Take it, that's all I have right now."

"What are you talking about?" he asked, seeing the money on the bed.

"There's only a few thousand dollars there. If it's not enough I'll get more…"

"Look, I'm paying blackmail, so just give me the originals and let's end this charade now…" he demanded at the same time she was talking.

"I can't believe that I fell for this again. I hope you and Eric had a good laugh on my behalf. Just give me the information and get out…" she continued, ignoring him as he spoke.

Then, at the same time they stopped and looked at each other as if they were both crazy as each finally realized what the other had said.

"Wait, did you say blackmail?" she said finally hearing him. "What are you talking about?"

"I don't get it, why make love to me all afternoon and half the night if all you wanted is the money? Why the games? Why not just name your price?"

"Games," Samantha said, then chuckled. "Oh, please, you send me a ticket and get me all the way out here saying that you can help me find him and you say that *I'm* playing games?"

"I didn't send you anything. You arranged for this meeting, you have the documents. I want them. Just name your price so we can get this over with."

"I didn't arrange anything. You got me here. There's your note," she said, motioning to the note she'd dropped on the bed earlier. "Do you know where he is or not?"

"Where who is?" Jackson said, sparing a quick glance at the note.

"Eric," she spat out.

"I should have known you were just too good to be true. You pretended to be everything I wanted in a woman. I bet that you had me pegged from the beginning. In the bar, I can't believe I fell for the damsel-in-distress act," he said as she began shaking her head, denying everything. "I was actually falling for you," he said, chuckling in disbelief.

"Just tell me where he is and go," she said.

"Lady, you were wrong on the plane. You are nuts."

She smiled and seemed to relax. "You blew it, all this work for nothing. So, what are you, the roper or the lure?"

"The what or the what?"

"Oh, come on now, the jig is up. You've been caught. But I'll give you your props, you were good, very good. I almost bought it. The kiss on the plane was brilliant, the restaurant, the drive to the inn, all perfectly executed. Congratulations, you got me," she walked around and continued tossing things into her suitcase.

"*You* kissed *me*," he reminded her.

"You're right, I did, bravo." She slammed and locked the case, then began applauding. "End of con. The shill in the first-class lounge at the airport was a bit over the top. But playing a man against the wall is always tricky. You have guts. I'm impressed and that's not easy to do."

"Oh, come on, Samantha," he said firmly. "The game is over. I got your note."

"My note? What note, what are you talking about?"

He reached into his pants pocket and pulled out a familiar envelope and handed it to her.

She looked at it without touching it, already guessing what it said. "When did you get that?"

"At the inn where you left it for me an hour and a half ago, so as you can see, there's no need to continue with this, just tell me how much you want," he repeated plainly as he stood in the center of the suite with his checkbook in one hand and cash in the other.

She looked into his eyes and read the expression. Either he was the most brilliant inside man in the history of the con or he actually had no idea what she was talking about. The sudden thought of being trapped hit her. "You need to leave now," she said and grabbed her suitcase and bolted for the door.

"Wait," Jackson said, quickly cutting her off before she reached the exit. "You obviously know what's going on, or at least have some idea, so tell me."

Samantha shook her head. "I'm out of here." She side-stepped him and opened the door as he turned to follow.

"Good evening, or rather, good morning."

Samantha stopped. Her mouth dropped wide open as a man stood directly in her path. Jackson stopped right behind her as both stood looking at an elderly gentleman dressed in a dark suit and a bowler hat. He carried a silver-tipped walking stick and draped a raincoat over his arm. Without saying another word, he breezed past them and placed his things neatly on the bed. He looked around the room, nodding his head approvingly, then turned back to them.

Jackson turned to Samantha. "A friend of yours, I presume. Your partner perhaps?" he asked. She didn't reply.

"Not quite, Mr. Daley," he said to Jackson, then looked at Samantha and smiled admiringly as she continued to stare in awe.

"And you are?" Jackson asked as he walked back into the room and stood in front of the stranger. "Wait a minute, I know you, you're the man I spoke with in the lobby earlier this morning."

"Lincoln, Percival Lincoln, retired Inspector Percival Lincoln," he said proudly. "How do you do."

"Retired inspector?" Jackson questioned.

"Yes." He reached into his suit jacket, pulled out and quickly flipped open a badge and ID. He handed it over to Jackson.

"What exactly do you want, Inspector?" Jackson asked, looking at his identification.

"Excellent question," he said, turning and seeing Samantha still standing at the door. "Uh, Ms. Taylor, I suggest you delay your retreat, at least until you hear what I have to say." Seeing an unopened complimentary bottle of water on the table, he walked over. "Ah, perfect, I'm completely winded." He opened the bottle and took a long sip. "I must admit, keeping up with the two of you is quite exhausting."

Jackson turned to Samantha. "Ms. Taylor, is that your real name, Samantha Taylor?" Jackson asked.

Samantha looked at him but didn't answer. She was too stunned. The shock of seeing Lincoln here left her speechless.

"Ms. Taylor, Mr. Daley, please, all I ask is just a moment of your time. Actually, I had intended to meet the both of you earlier this evening, but as you seemed to get along better than I'd expected I find that I had to delay my timetable to accommodate your date."

"You sent us these notes," Jackson said.

"Indeed," he said after another sip of water. Samantha watched intently as he tipped his head back slowly to swallow the water. He was just as she remembered, calm, assured and forever composed.

"Look, you have business with me personally, this doesn't include Samantha."

"Actually, your business with me, Mr. Daley, coincides with Ms. Taylor's business with me. You see, the two of you need each other to get what you each came here for."

"What?" Jackson said.

"It's called blackmail. He wants to use us," Samantha said, coolly finding her voice and speaking up for the first time since the inspector arrived.

"I wouldn't put it quite like that, Ms. Taylor. *Blackmail* is such an ugly word. I prefer to consider it a joint opportunity of sorts on both your behalfs." Lincoln said, then turned to Samantha and smiled. She shook her head, having heard it before and knowing exactly what he was up to. "I, of course, expected you to understand. Your father taught you well." Samantha visibly tensed. "Yes, your father," he said, then turned to Jackson. "I'm familiar with your father, as well, Mr. Daley. His illustrious career speaks for itself. I also knew your mother," he added specifically to Jackson.

"What do you have for me this time, a trip around the world?" Samantha said. Lincoln turned around and smiled at her.

"So you do know each other," Jackson said suspiciously.

"Mr. Lincoln and I shared a cab a few days ago. He left an envelope for me. Inside was a first-class ticket to Los Angeles and this hotel-room reservation."

"Very good, Ms. Taylor, I'm delighted you remember me so well," he said.

"What exactly do you want from us?" Samantha asked.

"Actually, it's more like what you can do for each other, if indeed you're willing to take a chance."

"What if I say no, I don't want to do this thing, whatever it is, then what?" she said, staring pointedly at the older man.

"Not at all surprising, Ms. Taylor, given your past. You don't take chances, not anymore. And declining is indeed your prerogative, of course, but it would be to your advantage to not make any hasty decisions until you've first heard my proposal. I know you and I know that you would want…"

"Get this straight—no matter what you think you know, you don't know me," she said firmly. "You never did and never will."

"That's true, I don't. I can only hope that you'll do this to help yourself and of course help Mr. Daley. Since the two of you hit it off so well, it will add credence to the performance, making it that much more realistic."

"What performance?" Jackson asked.

"Let's just get right to the point, shall we?" He sat down in a seat by the window and pulled out an envelope and set it down on the glass table, then glanced at the two opposite chairs, obviously expecting them to sit down, as well. "I have in this envelope…"

"The documents?" Jackson asked.

"No, not exactly."

"Where are they, who has them?" Jackson continued.

"Please, if you'll have a seat I'll explain." Neither Samantha nor Jackson moved an inch. "Please, I assure you, your cooperation will be beneficial to both of you. I have in this envelope information you'll need that will enable you to achieve your objectives."

"What is it?" Jackson asked.

Lincoln slid the envelope to the other side of the glass table, expecting Jackson to move forward and pick it up. When Jackson didn't walk over, he continued, "It's a code that will get you into the place where the information is located."

Neither Jackson nor Samantha moved or spoke. They each just stood and looked at the envelope suspiciously.

"Thanks, but no thanks," Samantha said, then picked up her suitcase and placed her hand on the doorknob to leave. Both men turned to her.

Percival Lincoln stood. "Ms. Taylor."

"Don't bother. Whatever you have to say I don't want to hear it. I've heard it all before, I know it by heart, the scams, the cons, the drama. I don't want any part of it, I'm out."

"This is about Robert Taylor, isn't it, Sammy?" Lincoln said openly.

"Robert Taylor," Jackson repeated in a whisper as his heart nearly stopped beating. *His mother's Robert Taylor?*

Samantha went still, then seconds later turned around. "Don't bring his name up to me!" she said through gritted teeth.

"You're still angry. I expected as much. You're so much like your mother."

"That's funny…she said that I was so much like him."

Lincoln chuckled, "You are indeed, you and your brother."

"Leave my brother out of this," she said.

"I'm afraid that's not possible, it's too late."

"What do you mean?" she asked.

"I mean that Jefferson is already involved."

Samantha shook her head, knowing better. "No, that's impossible. He retired years ago and he owns a legitimate business, an import-export business—" She stopped, realizing the possibility. Jefferson had contacted and warned her away from Eric's apartment four months ago and had been guiding her ever since. He knew about Lincoln's envelope bringing her to Los Angeles. There had to be some connection.

"Let me tell you a story," Lincoln began. "Once upon a time, on record as the highest-priced photograph, an Edward Steichen photograph was placed at private auction. Two very competitive bidders vied for the honor of the purchase. It was sold for two million pounds—that's over four million dollars. After detailed analysis, the buyer realized that it was just a clever fake. He went to the authorities, but as stated in the contract he signed, he'd purchased an original copy. Mortified by his obvious error, he's been trying to retaliate ever since."

"So you're saying that someone is after Jefferson because of something he did years ago?"

"No, something your father did years ago."

"I hate to break up this family reunion, but you and I have business, Mr. Lincoln."

Lincoln turned to Jackson. "Yes, of course, Mr. Daley…"

Samantha turned back to the door. She wasn't sure how much to believe, if any of it. She knew that Jefferson was involved in something and needed her help. But without actually talking to him there was no way to know what to believe.

A sudden sinking feeling churned in her stomach as the idea that someone was after her brother made her fearful. There was no way she could walk away when he needed her. But not knowing the full story gave her pause. If this didn't work out or she messed up, the consequences would be just as final.

This wasn't for amateurs. Real lives were at stake. Her

brother's freedom and hers were at stake. Then the answer became clear as she could hear her father's words reverberate in her mind: family is forever. The decision made, the game was on, and as her father's daughter she would play right up there with the big boys.

She turned around, seeing Jackson and Lincoln now involved in a heated discussion. She didn't know Jackson's involvement or even if he was involved. He might or might not be. All she knew was that she needed to watch her back until she could get in touch with Jefferson. And if Jackson was part of it, he was on his own, but if he wasn't she needed to protect him, too.

The battle between the two men continued as she watched the testosterone-generated posturing. It could all be an act, she warned her heart as Jackson's fury openly raged. "You lie, and if you weren't an old man, I'd…" Jackson warned fiercely as apparently his mother was his soft spot and Lincoln had hit it hard.

Chapter 8

"On the contrary, it's the truth," Lincoln assured him calmly. "The woman you held on a pedestal conned with the best. She worked with Robert Taylor's crew. Thirty-two years ago, after they pulled one last job, she walked away with a great deal of money, money that helped Daley Communications fend off a corporate takeover, I believe. She turned her life around and no one faulted her for that. But the money didn't belong to her."

Jackson was speechless. What Lincoln said basically confirmed what the copied documents in the envelope stated. Inside was a copy of his mother's mug shot and her prison rap sheet listing a number of minor offenses. There was also a certified document showing that his mother bought her way into the Daley family with scammed money, with the complete knowledge of his father.

"So where do you fit in all this?" Samantha asked as to Lincoln's motives.

"I want to see a wrong corrected," he said.

"I'll bet," she said facetiously.

"As the story goes, Robert Taylor took the fall for Mr. Daley's mother. She profited and walked away scot free with the cash, leaving you and your mother with nothing while she lived in the lap of luxury."

Samantha turned to Jackson. The burning glint in her eyes revealed her pain. The hurt she felt boiled inside. Growing up was hard. With her father in jail, her mother working menial jobs to support them and Jefferson on the streets, she'd barely survived. Now to find out that someone had stolen from them hit her like a dagger straight to the heart.

"So why is Jackson here? Talk to his mother," she said to Lincoln, holding in the pain of the moment.

"My mother died six months ago."

Samantha looked at Jackson tensely then turned to Lincoln. "Okay, if what you say is true then it's personal. Jackson's family owes my family. What do you get out of all this, a finder's fee?" she asked.

"Nothing substantial, I assure you, except the pleasure of seeing justice served," Lincoln told her. "But I'm afraid there is a slight complication."

"What complication?" Jackson asked.

"The person in possession of the information is an old friend of yours, Ms. Taylor," Lincoln said.

"Who?" she asked.

"Eric Hamilton."

She went still. "Eric's here?"

Lincoln nodded.

"Who's Eric Hamilton?" Jackson asked.

"Mr. Hamilton is a small-time con man with visions of grandeur, far exceeding his ability, I'm afraid. I suspect that he involved himself with you, Ms. Taylor, in hopes of ultimately connecting with your brother. If I'm not mistaken, he actually used Ms. Taylor's brother's name, which pointed the police in your direction."

"He wanted me to make contact with my father. Dad is…" She paused. "Was the only one who knew how to contact Jefferson," she said, having already realized the same thing months ago.

"That's exactly correct, Ms. Taylor," Lincoln said, obviously impressed that she already knew that. "And since Eric didn't know that your father had died, he hoped you knew how to contact Jefferson."

"Where is Eric now?" she asked.

"Eric was commissioned to con Marcus Daley."

Jackson looked up, hearing his father's name mentioned. "Whatever it is, I'll warn them off," Jackson said.

"I'm afraid it's not that simple. The documents I forwarded to you are only copies. Mr. Hamilton has the original documents, or rather, his commissioned partner has."

"Who's his partner?" Jackson asked.

"If they succeed," Lincoln said, "and it appears they will, his partner will position himself to take control of Daley Communications."

"What?" Jackson said, astonished. He knew that his father was working a deal with George Cooperman, but he had no idea exactly what it entailed and how potentially damaging it was.

"Ah, now you see the connection. Mr. Hamilton's partner is George Cooperman," Lincoln said.

Both Samantha and Jackson stood silent, dumbfounded by realizations that had just changed their worlds.

"So make no mistake, it's not always about the money," Lincoln said. "You're here because you're desperate, both of you, and I'm your only option. You want the documents to save your company, and you want to help your brother and to get your life back. I can't give these things to you, but I can show you how to get them."

"You want us to steal them, don't you?" Jackson said.

"I will not be blackmailed into committing a crime for you or anyone else," Samantha said adamantly.

"This isn't blackmail," Lincoln affirmed. "You want something and I want something. It's a simple transaction."

"It's still blackmail," she repeated.

"I beg to differ," Lincoln said more adamantly.

"Semantics," she responded. "Call it whatever you want, it's still the same thing."

"Look, the two of you can go at this for the next ten years, but it all boils down to the same thing in the end," Jackson said. He turned to Samantha. Her eyes, still angry, bored into his. "We don't have a choice, we have to do this."

"You have to do this, not me. I'll take my chances alone," she said.

"Alone, Ms. Taylor," Lincoln said. "I believe you've been alone for the past four months. How far did it get you? You had no idea where Eric was until I told you. Make no mistake, there isn't anyone to help you. Your father's dead and your brother can't even help himself. I'm your only option," Lincoln repeated then turned to Jackson.

"And, Mr. Daley, warning your father will only alienate him further. He'd never believe you, considering your past relationship. He'll simply see it as another ploy by you to gain control of the business. Eric is using him. He'll take the business without your father even knowing it, and everything your grandfather and mother worked for will be gone."

"Don't bring my mother into this."

"Mr. Daley, no matter how much you try to deny it, she was a con woman. Yes, she changed and sometimes people do. But the fact remains, she had a past. Mr. Hamilton is a threat to both of you. He will succeed if you don't work together to stop him."

Jackson turned around and walked away, considering.

Samantha took a step to follow but stopped, thinking better of the idea. He needed time to process all this. It was a shock to learn that his mother had been a con woman who'd stolen her crew's money and that his father was being conned into relinquishing the family business and there was nothing he could do about it at the moment.

"How exactly do you know all this?" Samantha asked.

"I work for George Cooperman," Lincoln said.

"And you're going to betray him, just like that?"

"As I said earlier, justice must be served."

"Whose justice?" Jackson asked, turning around.

"Since you want justice and you work for him, you can get this information yourself, you don't need us," Samantha added.

"On the contrary, you, Ms. Taylor, know how to break into a computer system, and your business contacts, Mr. Daley, can get you far closer than I can."

"And you want nothing in return?" Jackson asked.

"The satisfaction of helping you both, of course."

"Of course," Jackson said, not believing him.

"Like hell, nobody does anything for nothing," Samantha said pointedly.

"Very good, Ms. Taylor. Apparently your father taught you very well. I do want something, but that will come in the end. After you've gotten what you came for." Lincoln stood and picked up his hat and coat from the bed. He draped the coat over his arm, walked to the door, then turned back to them. "I suggest you examine what I left you in the envelope. It might be of some assistance." Both Samantha and Jackson looked at the envelope on the table, then back to Lincoln as he opened the door and walked out.

"I don't believe him," Jackson said.

"Neither do I, but that doesn't matter now, does it?"

"Samantha, what he said about my mother taking money from your family…"

"That was a lifetime ago, ancient history. You're not responsible for the sins of your mother any more than I'm responsible for the sins of my father."

"So, it's true about your father, Robert Taylor?"

"Yes," she said. "It's true." She saw his reaction, the same reaction she always got as soon as someone found out that her father was a professional con man. Scorn, contempt, pity, they were all there. "My father was a con man and I spent most of my childhood running. I was—" She stopped suddenly.

Jackson saw the pain in her eyes. He knew that there was something more but she wouldn't say. It was none of his business, but earlier that evening, intentional or not, they had made a connection and this situation now cemented it.

"Tell me everything you know about Eric Hamilton," Jackson said after a few minutes of silence. She didn't respond. "Samantha," he called out.

She jolted from her thoughts, turning to him as if she'd forgotten that he was still even in the room.

"Tell me about Eric," he repeated.

"There's nothing to tell."

"Obviously there is!" he said more forcefully. "Look, you know more about this than I do. Tell me what you know."

"You need to talk to your father." She slowly walked over to the suitcase still sitting by the door.

"Where are you going?"

"I didn't sign up for this—for you."

"You can't run," Jackson said forcefully.

"Watch me." She grabbed her bag and reached for the doorknob.

"Wait," he called out. "Hold on." She opened the door. "Samantha, listen, you just said that you've run all your life. Isn't it time to stop?" She paused, hearing him move closer behind her. "I don't know what happened in your family with your father and I don't know what's going on between you and this Eric person, but I do know that the woman I was with at the inn had stopped running. She was in control of her life."

He gently took the suitcase from her. "All of this, this con stuff, everything is new to me. I don't know what my mother was into. My father must have known. They never talked to me about any of this. You have some insight. I don't know how much to believe, but you at least know something of your family's past. Help me. Talk to me."

"You don't understand. I've long ago given up on my father. And I don't talk about my family."

"And your brother, have you given up on him, too?"

Samantha went still.

"If I'm not mistaken, Eric is after him, too, isn't he?"

"I need to get out of here!" she said, opening the door.

"And go where?"

"I don't know, somewhere, anywhere away from here. I need to get away from all this." She took a step out the door.

"Wait, hear me out. Stop running, Samantha, help me, help yourself. Lincoln was right about one thing, we need each other."

Samantha went still. She knew he was right. She had grown up running. It was natural. And the one time when she'd stopped and lived a normal life Eric took that away from her. Now he was after her brother to take it away from him and she wasn't going to let him, not again.

Jackson came up and stood by her side in the doorway.

"Okay," she said softly. "But there are too many things going on. We need to figure this out, but not here."

Jackson, still holding the door open, took her suitcase. "I agree, let's go."

"Where?" she asked.

"Does it matter as long as it's away from here?"

"Wait," she said as she walked back into the room. She picked up the envelope from the glass table and put it into her purse. She nodded to him, and he nodded back. He led the way down the deserted hotel hall and she followed, wondering just how far she could go with him and whether going all the way would completely devastate her in the end.

Chapter 9

They arrived in darkness beneath a cloud-covered sky, but even then she could see the beauty of his home. Silhouetted beyond the narrow driveway, the entrance, surrounded by spiked palm trees and sweet-scented scrubs, dipped down, shadowing itself at the front of the house as a smoked-glass exposed entrance stood regal, large and comfortable. She heard the sound of surf lapping on sand as she got out of the car. "So this is what a California beach house looks like," she said.

"Yes," he said, breaking the stony silence during their long drive to his home. He led the way to the front door carrying her suitcase. He opened the door and waited as she passed. The sweet salted breeze mingled with his spicy cologne and sent her senses into overdrive. An instant flash of memories of bungalow number twelve drifted through her mind. Jillian's words came to light: "Having a man around every now and then is a good thing." She walked into the darkness of the foyer as automatic sensor lights slowly brightened.

"This is yours?" she asked, looking around.

"Yes," he answered, placing her bag by the staircase and turning to the small panel against the wall. Tiny lights blinked as a steady, slow-paced beep hummed. He pressed a few buttons, ending the hum, then turned on the living-room lights and pressed a third button. Instantly, a succession of lights turned on all over the house and soft jazz began playing.

"Nice," she said, impressed by the computerized system.

"I'm glad you approve. Can I get you something to drink or maybe something to eat or—"

"No," she said quietly, interrupting him before he finished. "I'm fine, thanks."

Then, just as he was about to continue, the phone rang, startling the quiet surrounding them. They both turned to look at the phone lying on the coffee table, then turned back to each other.

"Where is the, uh…" she began.

"The powder room is down the hall, second door on the left, and the kitchen is at the end of the hall, just in case you change your mind about something to eat or drink," he said as the phone rang a second time.

"Thanks, I'm gonna…" she said, turning.

"Sure," he responded as it rang a third time.

Samantha nodded and walked toward the powder room hearing his slow, even footsteps as he walked into the living room. As she stepped inside, she heard him pick up the phone and answer.

She closed the door and placed her purse on the counter, then turned on the cold water full blast. Her nerves had eaten at her from the beginning. Now they were frayed to near nonexistence. The cool, calm exterior she professed belied the doubt and turmoil churning inside. This was not her calling, yet here she was. Doing a favor and doing a deed and praying every step of the way that she wasn't going to make matters worse.

Not sure she was up to the challenge, she tried to steady her resolve, determined to see this situation through. She dipped her hands in the water. The sudden chill awakened her senses. Like the snap of a whip she was back in the resumed role.

She dried her hands on the towel and braced them on the counter, knowing that the next few days would either make or break her. Her head bowed, she closed her eyes and considered, just for an instant, walking away. After all, this wasn't her mess. Her only connection was Jefferson, and of course, Eric.

Sure, she wanted to get even with him for the stupid con he'd pulled on her, putting half of New York on her back, but getting even with a jerk and saving somebody's life were two different things. This wasn't her fight and there was no real reason she should even be here.

But when Jefferson asked for her help, there was no way she could turn him down, even with her own life circling the drain like the water in the sink now. She couldn't say no. She opened her eyes, turned off the water and looked up at her reflection in the gilded mirror and grimaced. Everything was happening so fast. First Jefferson, then the plane ride, then Jackson and now Inspector Lincoln.

Her hands shook even as she thought about it. She was in way over her head. She reached into her purse and grabbed the phone Jefferson sent to her at Oz. She opened it and called, but there was no answer. Not trusting her voice to leave a succinct message, she began writing a brief but detailed text message as her thoughts flew in every direction.

This wasn't working for her. No more games, no more cryptic messages from strangers, no more surprises. She needed to talk to her brother now. This, whatever it was, was bigger than she thought. The simple favor he asked had gotten complicated and it had involved far more than she had anticipated.

When she finished, she grabbed her purse and opened the door. Hearing that Jackson was still on the phone in the living room, she turned in the opposite direction toward the kitchen.

Reaching the doorway, she saw that the lights were already on. She peeked inside. A warm glow illuminated the large kitchen, bathing it with recessed lighting in the ceiling and from a hidden source above the countertops. Everything was beautifully designed, with every modern convenience; she looked around, wondering exactly how often Jackson actually used the gourmet appliances.

Walking farther in, she continued around the marble-topped center island and traced a path into the adjacent den. Manly, yes, definitely, she decided. Built-in dark-wood wall panels surrounded a fireplace on one end of the room with two large wing chairs comfortably placed on either side. Books, awards and sports paraphernalia were neatly displayed and tucked into the bookcase openings.

On the other side of the room was a large-flat screen television, seemingly suspended from the ceiling. Two overstuffed sofas were angled with a coffee table between that seemed to serve more as a desk area since there was a laptop, files and several stacks of paper on top.

She turned and went back to the kitchen. Setting her purse down, she opened it and pulled out the envelope from Lincoln and placed it on the table, then walked over to the sliding glass doors. Unlocking and opening the door and stepping outside, she felt a gentle breeze caress her face and body as a warm glow illuminated the outside. She stood on the deck a moment and inhaled the salted air, letting the sweet breeze blow all remaining doubts away; at that moment, she knew she was doing the right thing.

Walking to the railing, she noticed a gate leading down to a path that led directly to the beach below. Inspired, she removed her high-heel sandals, opened the gate and headed to the warm sand below.

"Where have you been? I've been trying to contact you all day and half the night," Marcus began, obviously on a rampage. "Did he contact you yet?"

"Hello, Dad, I'm fine, thanks," Jackson remarked sarcastically.

"You obviously have no idea how important this is. Did he contact you yet?"

"Yes, we spoke."

"Good," Marcus said, the angst in his voice immediately shifting from panicky tension to eager anticipation. "When will you get the originals?"

"It's a bit more complicated than that," Jackson confessed, moving back to the foyer and seeing that Samantha was heading toward the kitchen.

"What do you mean, more complicated? Does he have the originals or not?"

"Apparently, he's working with someone who does." Jackson paused, deciding not to tell his father about Eric just yet.

"He's lying."

"I don't think so."

"Fine, we'll deal with that later. How much do they want?"

"I don't know yet."

"What did he say?"

"He said that Mom worked as a con woman years ago and that you knew about it." Marcus went silent. "He also confirmed that the money was used to help Daley Communications when my grandfather went into the red. Is it true?"

"Truth, as it were, unlike beauty, is in the eye of the

beholder. First of all, it was your mother's money, make no mistake about it. If some idiot dupe was gullible enough to just hand over his money to her, it's fair game. So don't go feeling sorry for the fool who fell for her plot. They got exactly what they deserved.

"Secondly, I was the one who was against it from the beginning. I didn't want to take the money, so take that holier-than-thou attitude someplace else. I suggested to your grandfather to sell the radio stations and buy television. But he didn't listen. I wanted to sell the company."

"Like you do now?"

"Whatever it takes, however much it costs, get the originals," Marcus demanded, not answering the question.

"You realize, of course, the information is still out there. If he found it, someone else eventually will, too. This is only the beginning," he said, walking down the hall toward the kitchen.

"We'll ride that out if or when the time comes," Marcus said. "In the meantime, do whatever you have to do to get those originals. Take as much time away as you need, just do it. This information can't come out, not now. There's too much at stake." Jackson didn't answer. His thoughts lingered on a sudden gentle breeze.

"Did you hear me?" Marcus asked.

"Yes, I heard you," he said automatically, still focused on Samantha.

"Then take care of it."

After hanging up, he stood there a moment, realizing that whatever respect he had for his father had long since vanished. The rivalry that replaced it had built an impenetrable wall that thickened as the days passed, in as much as it seemed that neither he nor his father wanted to move past that point.

They had become comfortable in the place where anger was born. After his mother's death, the wall had gotten higher, wider and thicker. And each subsequent conversation with his father was like a hangman's noose. Strangled and asphyxiated by words left said and unsaid.

Jackson walked to the kitchen and looked around. Samantha's purse was on the table along with the envelope from Lincoln. He walked over, picked up the envelope, then put it back on the table and turned to the outside deck. The illuminated motion sensors on the deck had been activated. He slid the glass door aside and stepped out. He opened the gate and went down to the beach.

It was well past midnight; the moon with its sharp white edges crested and closed brilliantly in the night sky as stars dotted the heavens. The sight was breathtaking. He looked out and saw a solitary figure standing at the water's edge. He walked over to where Samantha stood facing the view. Side by side they stood, both lost in their own thoughts.

Samantha, looking up at the stillness of the moment, was humbled as the heavens displayed their flawless perfection. Black as coal with the moon shining the radiant brilliance of day and the stars each separate and dazzling united to fill the sky with a beyond the imaginable spectacle. "What a show. This place is magnificent." She said, knowing he was by her side even without turning to him.

Jackson looked up, nodding. "Awesome, isn't it?"

She smiled sadly. "Sometimes I forget to look up and appreciate what's right in front of me. Sometimes I'm so focused on looking back at the dramas of my life that I miss the important things."

Jackson listened, knowing that Samantha had just let her guard down. "I've always heard that the smog and pollution are the reasons we have such beautiful skies."

"I guess we all have to take the good with the bad," she said more to herself than to him.

"You're right, we do," he answered anyway. "I call this my own private slice of heaven. I come out here in the middle of the night and just sit and gaze up, appreciating."

They drifted into an easy silence.

"I received an envelope a few days ago," Jackson began. "Inside, among other damaging documents, was a copy of a personal check my mother wrote to my grandfather twenty years ago. It was for half a million dollars. That money saved Daley Communications. I suspect that's the key reason that my parents married. She got credibility and the Daley family got much-needed cash at a time when sharks were circling. She bought her way in. It was never about love." He stopped as emotion gripped him. The helplessness of her plight, hidden for years, had hastened her illness and accelerated her death. "She carried this secret all her life," he added, still choked up.

"It was her choice."

"No, she didn't have a choice."

"So, what, you're after revenge now?" she asked.

"Isn't that why you're here? Revenge?"

"Partly, yes," she said.

"Partly? What's the other part?" he questioned, sounding suspicious.

"I'm not working with Lincoln, if that's what you think."

He didn't respond.

"I have my own drama to deal with," she added.

"Eric?"

"Among other things," she said cryptically.

"Okay, this is the second time you've alluded to something more going on. If you know something, tell me."

"There's nothing to tell," she shot back instantly, turning to his hard, unwavering stare. "Look, we each have separate problems and it seems that at some point they intercepted.

Lincoln seems to be the key to helping both of us. He has something you want and he has something I want. I say we do what we have to to get the job done."

"And then you walk away."

"That's the plan."

He stepped in closer. "Was making love to me this afternoon also part of the plan?"

"Did I trick you into making love?" she asked, looking up into his eyes.

"No."

"Then how could I have planned it?"

"Samantha, if there's something you need to tell me, some secret you're keeping, hiding…"

"Everybody has secrets, Jackson. It's how we live with them that makes us who we are."

"No, that's what makes you who *you* are, not me," he whipped back.

They stood face-to-face, inches apart, looking into each other's eyes. She held her tongue as an unwavering intensity passed between them, and neither budged or gave an inch. The warm breeze surrounded them, the ocean waves continued to crest and the sky continued to darken, yet they stood steadfast in unresolved restraint.

Jackson smiled at her tenacity.

Samantha smiled at his control.

"I'm sorry, I didn't anticipate…" He paused. "I didn't expect to like you so much, so quickly."

"That's okay, I didn't expect to like you so much, so quickly, either."

Then a sudden burst of laughter caused them to turn away. A young bikini-clad woman, being chased and tickled by a young man, ran down the beach past them.

"It's late," she said.

"Yes, it is, shall we?" he offered, stepping aside.

She nodded. Side by side, they headed back to the beach house in silence. As soon as they walked into the kitchen, they immediately noticed the envelope from Lincoln still sitting on the table. Jackson picked it up and opened it.

There was a key, a disc and a folded piece of paper inside. He handed the disc to Samantha, then opened and read the paper. Seconds later, he handed her the paper, too. She read the note, then looked at the disc again. He motioned toward the laptop computer on the coffee table in the den. They went in and sat down on one of the sofas. He turned on the computer and she inserted the disc into the tray. After a few seconds a computer program showed on the screen. "Do you recognize this program?" he asked.

"No, not really," she answered as she opened the main file and looked through the listed files. "But my first guess is that it's a high-end copying program," she continued scrolling through files. Each one listed offered a download and requested a password.

"Does this help?" he asked, handing her the paper with the password.

"No."

"Then I guess we need to download it."

"I'd caution against that. There are so many viruses and hackers around. To indiscriminately download something like this is like playing Russian roulette. All your files and your entire system could be pirated out, or worse, transferred to a separate system."

"So what do we do with it?"

"I'll check it out on my computer."

"What's the difference?"

"My computer will instantly overload a pirate program and redirect the data to a third system of my choosing. If this contains a virus or highjack, it'll default and clear all the data and return to the original in-box."

"Okay, where is your computer?"

"I'll have to get it. What about the key?" she asked, pointing to the key sitting on the table beside the computer. "I have no idea where it might go. It's not for any computer I've ever seen."

"It looks like an elevator key. I have one just like it. But we can figure that out later. It's late, so why don't we continue this tomorrow. You can get your computer then."

She nodded her agreement, then removed the disc and turned off the system. Jackson led the way back through to the front of the house, then upstairs, down the short hall to a closed door. "You can have this room." He opened the door and turned on the light. She walked inside and saw a huge, welcoming bed. He walked over and placed her suitcase on the covered bench at the foot of the canopy.

"Do you need anything?"

"No, I'm fine, thank you," she said as she moved to touch the soft pillow.

"Good night," he said.

She turned and smiled. "Good night."

He closed the door behind him. She sat down slowly, then grabbed her purse and checked her phone for messages There were none. She removed her clothes, washed up and fell into bed. Moments later, exhausted from the strenuous day, she was fast asleep.

Across town, George Cooperman sat out on his terrace of the expansive estate in a velour jogging suit smoking his expensive Cuban cigar. As usual, he was on top of the world and in complete control.

It was dark, well after midnight, but he needed to know the

results of his planning. He took a deep drag of his cigar, savored the bitter sting of tobacco in his mouth, then blew it out in one long, single exhale. A gentle breeze blew through, carrying the smoke into the darkness. He smiled, pleased with himself.

The grand jury had convened and the state and federal prosecutors had presented their evidence. Each count was met by his high-priced attorney's calm, even response. He'd done an excellent job, worthy of an Oscar. Of course, his retainer was somewhere north of a million dollars each year, but well worth every penny. Now all George had to do was be completely exonerated, and that required cunning.

He took several short puffs and blew out again, idly watching the smoke fade. This was his third indictment. His second, a year ago, was a two-year suspended sentence but it had still taken its toll on him. He hated to lose, and while he was away, his business had suffered and his partners, worthless as they were, had grown antsy. But most of all, his personal funds, although staggeringly extensive by above-average accounts, had been nearly depleted. Although he had millions readily available, he didn't like dipping into his private slush fund. Traces could be tracked and his Cayman Islands nest egg could be exposed.

He had, under court order, relinquished his passport, and his offshore interests were weakening. He needed to wire cash to his account without notice and that was impossible to do with the federal and state governments watching him. So, for obvious reasons, he needed a resolution.

And by all accounts, everything was going exactly as he'd planned. In less than a week he would be cleared of all charges and be in possession of exactly what he wanted, revenge on the one company that rivaled his own and had refused his offer. He smiled again as a greedy chuckle bubbled up. This was going to be so sweet.

He stood and walked.

The pleasure of the night was his enjoyment. His property had few rivals. But then again he wasn't a typical businessman. He'd gotten what he had through cunning and brains, something few seemed to possess these days. Long forgotten, most businessmen became lazy as soon as they made a few dollars, but not he. One dollar made him want more, just as one million dollars made him want a million more. And no one was going to take a single penny from him. Not without a fight.

So in one fell swoop he was going to get everything he deserved. He rounded the perimeter of his estate, then noticed headlights approaching as he stood on the slope beside the tennis courts. The long path leading up to his driveway gave him plenty of time to walk around and meet the driver. The car stopped just as he arrived. A single figure got out and approached. He smiled, taking another deep drag of his cigar after lighting the butt again.

The man encumbered by his languished leg walked over slowly. George looked at him eagerly. "How did it go? Did they buy it?"

"Yes, as expected," Lincoln said evenly. "Ms. Taylor received the envelope. She arrived earlier. She and young Mr. Daley are willing to do exactly what you want. But then, they have no choice."

"Good, splendid," George said, not at all surprised by the news. A firm believer in precise planning, he knew that they'd have no alternative. "And our other friend?" he asked.

"Eric…" Lincoln began until George cleared his throat and glared at him. Lincoln nodded. George Cooperman was shrewd. Always the third party, he never personally took care of any business such as this. He always used at least two middlemen as go-betweens. That way few knew that he was involved. And he always declined to know the full names of the people involved, using only surnames; the less he knew, the less likely he would be exposed and implicated if anything went wrong.

"I beg your pardon," Lincoln said. "Mr. Hamilton doesn't have a choice, either. He knows that. He'll do what I say or go to jail."

"Splendid, splendid," George repeated with a broad smile, anticipating the final payoff. "Keep me informed. I don't want any mistakes this late in the game. I've come too far to have this wash out because of ineptness," he said tightly, then turned and walked away.

Lincoln felt the sting but held his tongue. "One more thing you might want to be aware of," he began. "There was a slight variation to the plan. It seems Mr. Daley and Ms. Taylor have become friends and not exactly the adversaries you expected them to be."

"What do you mean?" George said, turning.

"They spent the day together, I suspect intimately."

"Explain," George prompted.

"After they arrived, he went to his place and she went to the hotel. Then an hour later he went to the hotel and got her. They spent the morning at Perry's Inn off the Pacific Coast Highway. Afterward, they got a room."

"You're right, that is interesting. Apparently, I underestimated her charms. She's more like her father than I expected. That won't happen again," he mused more to himself than to Lincoln. "You told her about Rachel Daley, how she stole the money from her family, leaving them destitute?"

"Yes."

"And her reaction?"

"She was upset obviously, but not as angry as we assumed she'd be."

George stepped aside, mulling over the new information as he rolled his cigar between his lips. "An unlikely union, that's unfortunate. It would certainly make things easier if they weren't together. I have other plans for young Mr. Daley. See what you can do," he ordered.

"I can introduce Mr. Hamilton. That might separate them or at least create some suspicion on his part. I suspect that Ms. Taylor might still be blinded by her anger, but she may possibly still have feelings for him."

"Fine, see that it's done. The National Association of Black-Owned Broadcasters awards dinner is in less than a week. I want this cleaned up and finished by then," George said firmly, then walked away without waiting for a response.

Lincoln stood watching him go, and then he looked up at the massiveness of the palatial mansion in front of him. George was a man not given to timidity. He was bold and brash and demanding and didn't take no for an answer. He'd set his sights on controlling Daley Communications a long time ago but had been refused each time. Now he was the closest he'd ever been to achieving his goal. The smug anticipatory glee in his eyes was familiar.

He had seen it a hundred times in his business. The knowing smugness always preceded the inevitable downfall. And Lincoln, with his extensive credentials, didn't want to be anywhere around when that happened.

He turned and walked back to his car. He got in awkwardly, still pained by his leg but not as much as by his pride. The fact that he now worked for George Cooperman as his head of security showed just how far he had sunk. Once a prominent New York detective, he'd been discharged by the force because of a single error. He gritted his teeth, still seething at the cause of his discharge.

Jefferson Taylor at his prime had been nearly untouchable; he, Lincoln, was the only man to ever come close to getting him. After weeks of surveillance, Lincoln had finally caught a break and gotten wind of a con, Jefferson's last con before his self-proclaimed retirement.

Lincoln decided to get Jefferson before he got out. He had everything arranged and planned out to the last detail. As soon as the con was finished, he was going to bring Jefferson in. There was no way he could get out of it, but Jefferson did and in the process made a complete fool of him.

Lincoln grimaced. There were rules and he had broken the first one. Emotion had gotten in the way and made him sloppy and smug. The plan failed and Jefferson got away clean. Lincoln's superiors needed a scapegoat and he was it. He'd lost both his job and his credibility. That mistake had plagued him for the last few years. But in a few days he intended to right that wrong.

He was going after Jefferson and thanks to his sister, Samantha, he would finally succeed. He knew that Jefferson couldn't resist helping his sister in her hour of need. He smiled, remembering that creed the Taylors all had: family is forever. That would be their downfall, there was no question about it. That's why he needed Samantha to believe that her brother was unreachable, so that he could come and save her just as he'd planned.

Of course, Cooperman had no idea of his personal plans. He had his own agenda. All Cooperman knew was that he was finally getting the only company that refused him and ending the six-month investigation into his business practices. As far as he was concerned, Jackson and Samantha would be caught breaking into his office and planting information to frame him just like he told the federal judge.

Cooperman used people for personal gain. So Lincoln decided to use Cooperman, too. He didn't care who it was and who got in his way. He wanted Jefferson and he intended to get him this time.

Chapter 10

"Hello?" Samantha called out timidly, looking around the expansive kitchen, breakfast nook and family room. Earlier, she'd taken the opportunity to peek into the other rooms of the magnificent three-story house. It was everything she ever imagined a multimillion-dollar beachfront home would look like, and more.

With rooms the size of Grand Central Station, all with soaring cathedral ceilings, hardwood floors, magnificent ocean views from floor-to-ceiling windows, Persian carpets and expensive antique furnishings, it was the most spectacular house she'd ever seen. She couldn't imagine living in a place like this, let alone owning it.

"Jackson?" she called out again, but finally realized that she was alone. The smell of coffee made her stomach rumble. She poured a cup and walked over to the sliding glass doors. She opened one panel and stepped out onto the large deck.

She walked out farther and stood at the railing, looking around the crescent-shaped white-sand beach. The daylight view was just as breathtaking and spectacular as the one the night before.

A fine morning haze covered the entire area as the crisp blue horizon merged and faded into the sky. Dizzying, it looked like one tremendous wash of gentle blue water on a magnificent canvas.

She looked at her watch. She'd slept for seven hours, practically unheard of for her. She usually existed on just four to five hours of sleep. Anything more and she was groggy and useless. But the good night's sleep had cleared her head and completely relaxed her. She woke up remembering what had happened the night before. After a quick shower, she got dressed, repacked her bag and set it by the closed door, leaving the room exactly as she'd found it.

Now she stood on the deck of what had to be a more-than-million-dollar house, waiting for…what? Did she really need Jackson to find Eric? Lincoln had implied as much, but she didn't believe much of what he'd said, particularly about her brother.

She called Jefferson and left another message. Then she called her aunt Emily in Oz. She left a message asking about Rachel Daley. If anyone knew, she might. She was in a unique position to know just about everything there was to know about everything.

She hated dragging Emily into this drama but she had no choice since she hadn't heard from Jefferson. She had a dozen questions and it seemed that answers were in limited supply. So until Emily called back with word, she needed to do some digging on her own.

"Okay," she muttered to herself, "let's see." She had to remember and think about every word Lincoln had said. True or not, everything he'd said was important, especially about Eric. She nodded, affirming her resolve. The conning part made sense. She remembered that he was completely fixated on her contacting her brother and finding out his whereabouts. That part made perfect sense.

Using Jefferson's name made sense, too. Eric, delusional as usual, apparently considered himself just as good as Jefferson, so of course he would want to find him and prove it.

But it was Jackson's mother that confused her. She'd never heard of a woman being with her father's crew, but then she wasn't even born when her father was in his prime. What little she knew of his life she'd found out from her brother.

Her mother, who'd known all about his life, of course, had never said anything about Rachel. Samantha's mind wandered to her childhood, then to Eric and then to Jackson and the time they had spent together. She looked out at the horizon, admiring the beauty of the day again. She needed to think clearly, but images of Jackson still clouded her mind. Thank God he wasn't here. Then it hit her, the envelope. She turned to go back into the house but stopped.

"Well, hello there."

Samantha gasped as her mouth dropped open. She was stunned to see a beautiful woman standing in the doorway behind her. She wore an expensive mauve pantsuit that accented the rich chestnut of her skin and light brown hair. Dark designer sunglasses were perched on her nose and she smiled, as bright as the diamond earrings, necklace and bracelet that sparkled all around her. "Hi," she said again, pleasantly.

"Oh, jeez, he's married," Samantha muttered louder than she intended.

The young woman smiled wide hearing the remark and walked farther out onto the deck to stand by Samantha's side. She looked out at the surf and took a deep breath.

"Beautiful day, isn't it?"

"Yes, it's a gorgeous day," Samantha said finally, finding her voice firm and even.

"And you are?" the woman asked, smiling almost gleefully as she turned to face Samantha.

Samantha tensed. This wasn't how she expected her morning to begin. The last thing she wanted was a confrontation with an angry girlfriend or, even worse, an irate wife. "Just leaving," Samantha said completely automatically without panicking.

"How did you get in?"

"Look, this is my entire fault," Samantha began. "I just wanted to see the view from this vantage point. So I just came up here on my own. No one even knows I'm here or else I wouldn't have presumed to impose on anyone's privacy like this."

"So without an invitation, you just walked up here from the beach. I find that hard to believe."

"I'm sorry to hear that," Samantha countered.

"That's called breaking and entering in most places."

"Interesting," Samantha replied nonchalantly.

"You don't seem concerned."

"You'd be surprised what motivation can do."

The woman chuckled softly as if from a private joke. "Actually, I wouldn't, but getting back to the subject at hand, are you saying that you don't know the owner of the house?"

"Yes and no. We've spoken from time to time."

"I see, so you do know Jackson?"

"Indirectly."

"Is he here?"

"You might want to look around and check for yourself. In the meantime, I need to get going."

"You know, you look familiar. Have we met before?"

"I have one of those familiar faces."

"Do you live around here?"

"Sometimes."

"Do you work at the radio station?" she asked.

Samantha smiled noncommittally, then glanced at her watch. "It's getting late and I really need to get going."

The woman nodded coolly. "I understand. Shall I tell Jackson that you stopped by?"

"I'm sure you will either way," she looked over to the surf as if one last time, then began to walk toward the steps she remembered that led to the beach.

"You know, you don't have to leave on my account. And for the record, I don't believe a word you said. But then again, you didn't actually say anything, confirming or denying, did you?" the woman said.

"What part didn't you believe?" Samantha asked innocently, turning to her.

"Would it help if I told you that I was Jackson's sister and not his girlfriend or wife?" She removed her dark sunglasses showing the same incredible eyes as Jackson.

Samantha smiled.

"Why don't we start again?" She held her hand out. "Hi, I'm Jessica Daley, Jackson's sister, and you are?"

"Just leaving," she said again, as if to repeat the last ten-minute conversation.

"And you are?" she said again, this time with her hand held out to shake.

"Samantha Lee," Samantha said finally, shaking hands.

"A good friend of Jackson's, I assume?"

"The jury's still out on that one," Samantha replied.

"I find that hard to believe," Jessie said, then smiled and chuckled. "If my brother's history is any indication, you must be a very good friend as far as he's concerned."

"What makes you say that?"

"You obviously stayed over, and since no one ever stays over…" She trailed off.

"Is that a rule?"

"It is around here."

"Well, as I said, the jury's still out."

Jessie smiled brighter. "You're good, I like you already."

"I beg your pardon?" Samantha asked.

"You've managed to answer every one of my questions in the most beautifully unanswered detail I've ever heard. That must be a family talent or something."

"Yeah, it must be, or something."

Jessie burst out laughing. "And you're obviously not from California," she said between muted chuckles.

"What makes you say that?" Samantha asked.

"Two reasons. Californians, native or newly transplanted, never take the time to actually stand and watch the surf unless they have a serious problem. We usually just take it for granted that the tide will come in and then go out."

"And the other reason?" she asked.

"We can't wait to talk about ourselves. Everything from birth to yesterday's meal, which usually includes an eight-by-ten head shot and a résumé."

"Sorry to disappoint," Samantha said.

"On the contrary, it's good to finally meet you."

"Finally?"

Jessie smiled before answering, "Of course."

Samantha looked at her curiously. She wasn't sure what to make of Jessica Daley. She definitely wasn't like her brother. She seemed too street savvy and far more knowledgeable in game playing than Jackson, although they did have those same remarkable eyes.

"I'm not sure I know what you mean."

"Don't worry about it," she said, then paused. "You know,

you're just the perfect type I can see him with. He's about as evasive as you are, although not as good at it, I must say."

"There's a compliment in there somewhere, right?"

Jessie laughed again. "Yeah, there is. Come on, I smelled coffee on the way out. I could use a cup of caffeine after talking with you, I'm exhausted."

Predawn, at reckless speeds, Jackson drove the razor-sharp turns of the highway with controlled ease. Seldom had he used the full 660 horsepower of his racer, but this morning he raced against himself. Reminiscent of his youth, he battled himself and lost as the canyons of Malibu continued to whiz by.

The wind whipped the collar of his polo shirt but didn't disturb his dark sunglasses. He'd been driving on mental automatic again, his thoughts miles away, back at his house with a woman sleeping in a guest room two doors from his own.

Early, on impulse, he crept into the room and just stood and watched her sleep. She was beautiful, blissful and delicate. The urge to crawl in next to her was so strong that he had to leave his own house to fight for control. That's how far she'd gotten to him.

Whoever she really was and whatever she was doing, she'd gotten under his skin and even now he couldn't stop thinking about her. He was completely distracted and had stayed up most of the night, not thinking about Lincoln and his accusations or about his father, but about Samantha. Since he'd met her, his thoughts always came back to center on her.

He remembered waking up alone in bungalow number twelve. He immediately went out looking for her. The urgent desperation of his search surprised him. He wanted to find her, he needed to find her. The fantasy they'd joked about had become real and he didn't want it to end. The mystery of her life beckoned him and at the time he didn't care what she'd done. All he wanted was her. Then at the front desk a note had been left for him.

He'd excitedly opened it, only to find that he'd been contacted by the same man who sent him the envelope containing the damaging documents. No one knew he was at the inn except Samantha. Suddenly his heart had hardened and his spirit fell. It seemed that he had let her into his life and she had betrayed him.

Now here he was, driving away from the one woman he wanted to be with. He turned on his signal and steered off the coastal highway into a small pier parking lot. A gathering of parked cars and people mingled in and out of the specialty stores, carrying packages, laughing and talking. He noticed a man and woman holding hands as they stood at the railing with intertwined pinkies, looking out at the ocean.

His thoughts instantly went to Samantha. She had gotten to him and he couldn't shake her loose.

He got out of the car and walked down to the far end of the pier. Older men dressed for a day of fishing stood at the rails, poles at the ready, talking and joking about life, past, present and future. He stood on the side and looked down at the deep blue water cresting beneath him. The pier far out into the breakers was the perfect place to think. The sound of children at play, laughter, seagulls and waves lent themselves to the serenity of thought. So his mind drifted.

The pending battle with his father for control of Daley Communications had made their already strained relationship even more fragile, so there was no way he could confirm anything Lincoln had claimed, yet when he showed his father the copied documents that had been sent to him, he wasn't at all surprised.

As he was growing up, his mother never talked about her

past or her family. As far back as he could remember, he had only one set of grandparents, his father's.

So what did he actually know to be true?

The answer came, frank and simple—nothing. His mother was dead, he was sure that Jessie was just as much in the dark as he was and there was no way his father would talk about it. So the only other people who could shed some light were Lincoln, whom he didn't trust and had no idea how to contact, and Samantha, the woman sleeping in his house.

He looked up at the sky and watched a red balloon bounce and float on the delicate breeze. The playful dance reminded him of the past few days. Wayward and out of control, he was afloat on thin air, without a clue as to what was really happening.

"Enough of this," he said aloud. He needed to get back home and confront Samantha. He wanted some answers and she was the only one who could provide them. He hurried back to his car and drove down the coastal highway. As soon as he pulled into his driveway, he saw a familiar bright lipstick-red convertible Lexus parked in the second space. His sister was here.

Hurrying inside, he checked the living room and kitchen and was just about to retrace his steps when he heard laughter and then talking coming from outside.

"Good morning," Jackson said slowly, seeing Samantha and his sister out on the deck drinking coffee and talking. He walked over to his sister and kissed her cheek. "Hey, what are you doing here this early?"

"Good question," Jessie said brightly. "We were supposed to get together this morning for breakfast at the inn. So since you didn't show and I have never been stood up, I decided to drive up the coast and see you. I'm glad I did," she said, turning to Samantha. "Samantha and I are having a wonderful conversation."

"Is that right?" Jackson looked at Samantha. His expression showed slight concern. He'd never told her about his sister or that he didn't want Jessie involved.

Samantha smiled sweetly and something in her eyes instantly laid his fears to rest. Jackson immediately understood that she hadn't told Jessie anything about what was actually going on. Relieved, he walked over and kissed Samantha on the lips casually, as if it was the most natural thing in the world. "So what exactly have you two ladies been chatting about?"

Jessie opened her mouth, then closed it. This was the first time she'd ever seen her brother show any type of public affection. "The weather," she finally said, still slightly stunned by his uncharacteristic demonstration.

"The weather?" he asked, then looked at Samantha.

"The weather," she confirmed.

Knowing that there was more to their conversation than just weather, he decided to drop it for the time being. He wrapped his arm around Samantha possessively.

"So," Jessie said, hoping to finally get a few answers, "you two are together now, I gather?"

"Sometimes, then sometimes not so much," Samantha said, still evasive.

Jackson smiled. Apparently, Samantha had taken his sister on the same no-direct-answer that she'd taken him on for nearly two days.

"I don't suppose you'd like to elaborate on that answer?" she asked her brother.

"Nah." He turned to Samantha, leaned down and kissed her briefly. "That pretty much sums it up."

"Oh, you two are impossible."

"Now, where have I heard that before?" Jackson asked as Samantha smiled at what appeared to be a private joke.

"Okay, awkward moment, I get the hint, I can see that you two want to be alone and I have an appointment in two hours, which gives me just enough time to do a little shopping beforehand." She walked over to Samantha and air kissed her cheek. "It was a pleasure finally meeting you and don't forget we have a lunch date next week."

Samantha nodded and agreed happily, knowing that she wouldn't be there.

Then Jessie grasped Jackson's arm and asked him to walk her to her car. He did, nodding to Samantha as he left.

As brother and sister are prone to do, they teased and joked about her shopping until they reached her car. Then Jessie changed the subject.

"The press has gotten wind of something."

"What?"

"I don't know," she said. "I had dinner with my friend, Paul Garfield, the reporter for the *L.A. Chronicle*. He told me that rumor has it there's something in the wind involving Dad and George Cooperman. And since we already know that the federal government is looking at George for tax fraud and illegal business practices, this isn't exactly the best time for Dad to buddy around with him."

"Was Paul specific?"

"No. But he did mention that they're looking at all avenues, including George's family and close friends."

"Who exactly?" Jackson asked.

"I don't know and he wouldn't say. I faked disinterest, so I didn't press him for details. He wanted an exclusive. I dissuaded his interest, of course, but to tell you the truth, I don't think he's that far off the mark. There's definitely something more going on with Dad and George," she stated. "What do you know about his cable company deal?"

"Not much. Have you talked to Dad?" Jackson asked.

"Yeah, but you know Dad is stubborn. Talking to him was like talking to a brick wall. I got nowhere. All he can see is dollar signs. He doesn't have a clue."

"What else did Paul say?"

"One of his sources told him that the government knows that George is sitting on a numbered account worth billions in the Cayman Islands."

"That's not surprising," Jackson said. "The government has been after him for years on tax fraud. They can't prove anything because the bulk of his cash is offshore. If they could get their hands on his account that's jail time."

"Exactly," Jessie said. "But Dad's renewed friendship with him has him way over his head. And with Mom not around to veto his plans, Daley Communications will most likely be caught up in George's drama, and that's the last thing we can let happen. We need to protect him from himself."

"Don't worry, I'm already on it," he said.

"What can I do to help?" Jessie asked.

"Nothing right now, but I'll let you know."

Jessie eyed her brother suspiciously. He was definitely hiding something, too, but coming from a family of secrets she expected nothing less.

Jackson smiled and hugged his sister. Underestimating Jessica had always been their father's downfall. He always said that she was just like their mother. He just had no idea how much. She was brilliant in business and an unmovable competitor in anything she wanted. God help the man who tried to use her, and thank God she was on his side.

"You know, of course, that she's hiding something," Jessie said honestly, changing the subject again but not taking Jackson off guard.

"Yeah, I know," Jackson admitted freely, knowing that Samantha was the subject now.

"Anything I should be concerned about?"

"No, she doesn't know it yet, but she's on our side."

"Good, 'cause I like her."

"Do you?"

"Yes, she's cool, relaxed, even if she can't answer a straight question to save her life. She's quick to think on her feet, protecting you instantly. I like that about her, too." She nodded. "She's natural and unpretentious, not like those brain-dead starlets and Beverly Hills brats you used to bring around and pass off as dates. Your taste has finally improved."

"By all means, Jessie, tell me what you really think," he joked as she playfully punched his muscled arm, nearly breaking a nail in the process.

"She'll be good for you."

"Did she tell you that?"

"No, call it sister's intuition. You might consider keeping her around."

"I don't know if I can. She's a free spirit."

"I could tell, and I could also tell that whoever hurt her in the past did a hell of a job. She's angry and scared."

"You got all that from a twenty-minute conversation? Who's the psychology major here, you or me?"

"It wasn't what she said so much as what she didn't say."

"Meaning?" he asked.

"It's in her eyes. Oh, she hides it well enough, but when she's off guard, which apparently is seldom, she's really hurting. I was making another pot of coffee and I looked and saw it in her face. She covers it well with jokes and evasiveness, but she's scared."

Jackson turned and looked back up at the house. His sister had noticed something in the few minutes they'd been together that he hadn't seen in almost two days.

"Keep her around. Like I said, she's good for you."

"I'll see what I can do." Jackson opened the car door and Jessie climbed in.

"Make sure you do that," Jessie said as she put on her sunglasses. "You know what, I think that Mom would have adored Samantha. I just know it. That's it, there's something about her that reminds me of Mom. Isn't that odd?"

Jackson didn't answer.

"She likes you and you, dear brother, obviously like her."

"She told you that?" he asked as she turned the key and started the engine.

"Again, didn't have to, neither one of you did, it's all over your faces. I'll let you know if I hear anything else. Oh, I almost forgot the other reason I stopped by. Dad called and said that your phone was turned off again. He needs to speak with you and he wants us over to the house for dinner this evening. He said that it was important."

"I'll bet," Jackson said skeptically. "I think I'll pass."

"He's celebrating."

"What?"

"I don't know, guess we'll have to find out when we get there this evening."

"Send my regards."

"Come on, you wouldn't let me face dinner with Dad alone. Why don't you bring Samantha? He'd enjoy meeting her."

Jackson turned and looked up at the house again and smiled. It would be interesting having Samantha out for the evening. "Okay, I'll see you later."

Jessie nodded, stepped on the pedal and pulled off quicker than he would have liked, her arm raised up high, waving goodbye.

Giving brother and sister privacy and time to talk, Samantha waited a few minutes, then went upstairs and grabbed her suitcase. She was coming down when Jackson walked back into the house. He looked at Samantha with her suitcase in her hand. "Leaving me so soon?" he asked.

"It was bound to happen," she joked, then continued walking down the stairs. "Thanks for everything," she said, expecting him to allow her to pass.

"We need to talk."

"Look, about Eric and whatever he has that you want. I'll take care of it and make sure you get your papers, okay?" she said, then stepped around him.

"No," Jackson said, holding his hand out to her.

She stopped walking since he hadn't moved from the doorway. "No is not an option," she said. "Thank you for everything. But I need to go now."

"Hear me out first and if you still want to go and do things on your own, then fine, I won't stop you. Just hear me out, okay?"

She looked up into those glorious eyes and considered his offer. Listening wouldn't hurt. So she nodded as he took her suitcase and put it back on the landing to go upstairs. "Come on, we can talk over an early lunch." He stepped out of the way and let her pass.

Chapter 11

An hour and a half later, after the lunch dishes had been cleared, they sat out on a restaurant terrace talking about nothing in particular. "Shall we go?" he offered. She agreed. They headed back toward his car, but she asked that they walk awhile. He agreed. Like lovers on a movie screen, shoes in hand, they walked along the water's edge.

"Thanks for not mentioning anything to my sister. I'm not quite ready for her to find out about this yet." Samantha nodded her reply. "She likes you," Jackson continued. Samantha smiled, then looked away across the water's surface, watching the sparkle of sunlight dance. "She thinks that I should keep you around." She still didn't respond. Jackson looked close, trying to get a sense of what his sister had mentioned. But Samantha was too guarded around him. Like an exceptional poker player she gave nothing away.

"Samantha," Jackson said. She turned back to him as he

stopped walking and removed his sunglasses. His eyes pierced right through her. "I need straight answers."

"All right," she said.

"Tell me about Eric Hamilton," Jackson requested simply. Samantha looked at him, slightly surprised. Eric's name coming from his mouth seemed odd, yet it appeared that for Jackson he was the center of everything. It was only natural for Jackson to want to know more about him.

"What do you want to know?" she asked.

"Everything," he said.

"Eric Hamilton is a con man, short cons mostly, not a very good one at times. But then again, he conned me and that should have been close to impossible to do," Samantha said.

"But it wasn't."

"No, it wasn't."

"Because you trusted him?" he asked.

She nodded once, affirming his answer. "That's the whole idea of a confidence man, he needs you to trust him."

"But he also got into your heart then betrayed you." She nodded again. "And now?" he asked, prompting her further. She looked confused by his question. "Does he still have your heart?" She didn't answer, yet the piercing glare in her eyes spoke volumes. "How long have you known him?" he continued.

Samantha hesitated. This was hard to talk about even to her closest friend, Jillian. But she did and now here again she was about to lay open her soul to a relative stranger. "We were together for about six months, before he moved on. We met outside my father's attorney's office. My father is—was in prison," she said boldly, expecting to shock his affluent sensibilities. But to her surprise he didn't even flinch.

"I went to the lawyer's to collect his belongings. As I left the office someone grabbed me from behind and ran off with my purse. Eric showed up out of nowhere. He ran after the guy and chased him down the street. I lost sight of them when they turned the corner a few blocks down. Eventually Eric came back. My purse had been ripped apart and the cash was gone but everything else was there.

"I recognized him from where we worked. He was a salesman. I was suspicious at first but he assured me that he hadn't followed me to the lawyer's office from work. In hindsight I guess I should have gone with my first instinct. But it felt good to talk about my father openly with someone." She looked over to Jackson, then quickly back toward the water.

"Let me guess. It was no coincidence that he showed up when he did and saved you. He arranged it all," Jackson surmised.

Samantha looked over at him, smiled and half chuckled. "Very good. You're catching on quickly. It was all a setup from the beginning. But oddly enough, he still wasn't sure if I was the right woman."

"So he needed to make sure that you were really Robert Taylor's daughter."

"I guess so."

"Why?"

"He tried to get me to contact my brother."

"Why?"

"I don't know really. I guess it might have had something to do with the fact that he used my brother's name to do a con."

"A con, what kind of con?" Jackson asked.

"A biz-op. It's something like a business opportunity with a twist. He sold fraudulent investments in mutual funds. Targeting desperate marks, he offered to take illegal money and wash it legit, then invest it with a marked return, for a percentage, of course."

"Why just desperate marks?"

"Felons or anyone with something to lose wouldn't

complain. When you're already doing something illegal it's kind of a moot point, they're just as guilty. It would be like the pot calling the kettle black, my mother always said."

"Isn't that dangerous?"

"Yes, extremely."

"I can't believe this actually goes on," Jackson said.

"Wealthy businesses con workers every day and it's all legit. They raid pensions and line their pockets with million-dollar investment funds, and when they're found out they get platinum parachutes and retire wealthy while the employees suffer. Just because you wear a suit every day and carry a briefcase doesn't make you honorable. The biggest con men in history are more than likely politicians and corporate executives. We just don't know about it because it's more acceptable."

Jackson nodded his understanding. "So if this con was working for him, why did he move on?"

"Apparently, it fell apart somewhere along the line, so he took the money and ran, leaving me holding the empty bag."

"People are looking for you?" he asked. She nodded. "Do you know who?"

"Yes, the police want to ask me questions, and some of his marks think I know where he is. Also, Eric took money from the computer company where we worked. They think that I helped him. He also conned some others. They're looking for him, too."

"How long ago was this?"

"Four months, two weeks, four days, and about four hours, East Coast time."

"You just walked away from your life just like that."

"What was I supposed to do, take the fall for him?"

"That's not what I meant."

She sighed heavily, "I know, and yes, I just walked away. You do what you have to do to survive."

"What about your family?"

"My mother died a while ago. My father and brother, well, you already know."

"Friends, lovers?"

"I don't do attachments easily, something about moving around a lot when I was younger I guess. I never had time to make friends then, and now, well…as soon as I tell someone about my family they look at you differently."

"Is that how Eric got close to you, you told him and he wasn't fazed?" She nodded. "So you gave him a chance and he betrayed you." She nodded again. "And after that one time you just walked away." Another nod. "Did you ever think about giving someone else a chance, opening up to someone else?"

"What would be the point?"

"You could stop running."

She opened her mouth, then closed it and looked at him, hearing his words and feeling the emotion. His eyes betrayed him. He was getting too close and she couldn't let him. She knew that she'd be walking away again.

"So you've been hiding for over four months?"

"It's not too hard if you know how."

"Your father taught you?"

"More like my brother, hide in plain sight."

"He's a con man, too, right?"

Samantha nodded and smiled brightly. It was the first ray of joyful emotion Jackson had seen all morning. "Retired. Jefferson, when he worked, was beyond your average con man. He was a master."

"He can't be so good if he's hiding, too."

She looked at him. "Don't believe everything you hear."

"He's not hiding?" Jackson asked. Samantha just smiled.

"You know this for a fact?" She smiled even brighter. "Can you contact him?"

"I already tried. He hasn't called me back, but he's around."

"Good, I think we could use all the help we can get. So since you know how to contact him I suggest you try again." She didn't reply but instead stared off, looking over his shoulder. "Samantha," he said. "Samantha," he repeated.

"There he is," she said, nodding upward at the television above the bar area. On the screen, George Cooperman stood in front of several microphones with two of his attorneys, smiling and professing his innocence after his grand jury appearance.

Jackson turned around and looked at the image. "Lincoln said that your father was doing business with him."

"Yeah."

"That's pretty strange, isn't it? I mean, besides the fact that he's trying to take over your company, he's being indicted and you're still doing business with him?"

"I'm not, but my father is. Apparently, business makes strange bedfellows."

"Why does he want your company?"

"George is an investment banker. He gobbles things up for a living. Daley Communications has huge potential and he's wanted it for over twenty years." The camera angle changed.

"Grant," she said, looking over his shoulder and changing the subject again. She was surprised to see his familiar face on television. She had no idea that he was connected to the Cooperman case.

Jackson turned back to the television. There was a close-up of Grant Andrews on the screen. He was listed as being a key prosecutor in the federal case against George Cooperman. "You know him?"

"That's Grant Andrews, my brother's best friend."

Jackson turned to her, surprised. "Your brother, you mean the retired con man has a federal prosecutor as a best friend?" he asked. She nodded. "How is that possible? He's a federal agent of the court. How can he and your brother be best friends?"

"They grew up together and family is forever, remember? They were something else when they were younger, completely inseparable. You never saw one without the other. Everybody used to say that they should make a fifty-two-dollar bill just for them, Jefferson and Grant."

"But then they went their separate ways, right?"

"I'm sorry you got dragged into all this," she responded without answering.

"Neither one of us have much of a choice."

"No, that's not what I mean. Eric, his thing with your father, you're not a part of the after-midnight world."

"You're not, either," he confirmed.

She smiled. "No, maybe not directly, but at least I know how it works."

"Your father?"

She nodded. "And my brother."

"You really admire him."

"Yes, I do."

"Even after everything he's done?"

"Yes, even after everything he's done."

"But what he does, what he did is still all part of who he is."

"True, I love my father and my brother, Jackson. That won't change, just as much as you love your father and your mother and what they did and do won't change anything for you."

"Tell me about it, this after-midnight world."

"That could take a very long time."

"Give me the Cliffs Notes version. I think I'm gonna need a crash course if we're going to do what Lincoln wants."

They walked back to the car and for the next forty minutes

Samantha talked about cons, swindles and scams. Jackson was enlightened by the different names and the historical tradition that thrived today.

Then they drove back to his place and sat out on the deck, continuing the in-depth conversation. When she finished telling him the basics, Jackson was stunned. "There's a whole world out there that I know nothing about."

"Not true. As I said, the con is done on all levels, government, big business, even on the inner-city and suburban playgrounds."

"You're right."

"The games never change, just the players."

"So what's Jefferson like?"

"A lot like you, actually."

"How so?"

"Jefferson is talented, intelligent, patient, polished and a bit egotistical," she said, smiling, "but in a good way."

"And that's a lot like me?" Jackson asked.

"Oh, yeah, definitely."

After a brief silence Samantha looked back at Jackson. She could see him processing the information she'd told him. "What Lincoln said about your mother, do you think that she was really part of any of this?"

"I don't know. She never talked about her past. And my father refuses to even consider talking about it. It's like there's some deep dark secret. Actually, I guess you probably would know better than I." She paused. "You're rich, right?"

"I have money, yes," he affirmed.

"Money, big money, sometimes comes from dirty hands. The old-money billionaires of today had ancestors who did questionable things to secure a future. Money doesn't know it's dirty, but people do and most often than not they don't care."

"You're right," he conceded.

"But if it's any help, as a child I didn't ever remember anyone mentioning a woman. But she, your mother, would have been around before I was even born."

"Rachel, my mother's name was Rachel Love," Jackson said. "She died six months ago."

"I'm sorry."

"It was cancer," he said. "She was a good woman."

Samantha nodded. "I'm sure she was."

"She didn't steal any money," he said adamantly. Samantha nodded again. Jackson looked into her eyes. "She didn't."

"She was from back East, New York, I think. I don't know for sure…as I said, she never talked much about her past or her family, so everything is sketchy. I think I remember her talking about a sister, but that was a long time ago, I wouldn't even know where to begin to look. I don't even have a name or address or anything else."

"She moved here to L.A. for a reason, obviously."

"I don't know. I do know that she met my father here."

"Your father, what does he do?"

"You have no idea, do you?"

"About what?" she looked at him blankly. "I met your sister and she seems nice. I suppose the rest of your family can't be that bad."

"My father is CEO of Daley Communications. We own over eighty-five radio stations across the country. My grandfather founded and built the business more than sixty years ago. It's grown from there into a broadcasting empire. When he died he gave the reins to my mother, not my father."

"Your mother? What about his own son?" Jackson didn't answer. "Bet that went over well," she said dryly.

"You can only imagine. Later, when my mother died, she left me the majority of her shares."

"Passed over twice."

"Yeah."

"So much for the perfect family portrait."

"At the moment the company has its hands in a lot of baskets. Money is moving around fast, too fast. We're hemorrhaging and completely vulnerable to takeover."

"And the perfect mark," she said.

"Apparently," Jackson said.

"If your father is the CEO, doesn't he realize this?"

"I'm sure he does. My father and I don't see eye to eye. He's contesting my mother's will, and since Cooperman Enterprises has always wanted Daley Communications this is the perfect time to make a play. My father has a deal on the table now that would join the two companies."

"With George Cooperman recently indicted for tax evasion and fraud, why would you connect the two companies?"

"Good question."

"Is your father trying to save her company or lose it?"

"To tell you the truth, I don't really know."

"Is there anything you can do to stop him?" she asked.

"Not at the moment. But in a week I hope to be voted in as CEO. Unfortunately, my father's deal might go through before then. Daley Communications is not run by a board of directors. The essential decisions are made by three—my father, my sister and me. If George Cooperman joins with my father in this cable partnership, he'll automatically get on the board. He can easily buy out my father's shares and literally take over the company or at least permanently damage it, if not even worse."

"This just keeps getting better and better, an internal power struggle and a hungry suitor. It's no wonder you don't have con men lined up for miles. But the question now is, how is Eric involved with your father?"

"He's negotiating the cable company buy."

"What cable company buy?"

"That's how George is buying his way in. He has a small cable company on the market and my father has put a bid in for it."

"What about money, didn't you say that your company was cutting back on expenditures?"

"My guess is that my father's offering majority stock as collateral. He's also using a professional mediator to handle the negotiation details. My sister mentioned a financier acting as a middleman since my father doesn't trust Cooperman completely."

"That would probably be Eric and it sounds like he's doing the bogus escrow scam."

"You mean these cons actually have formal names?"

"The three-card monte, the fiddle game, the pigeon drop, pig in a poke, the wire, the pyramid, glasses drop and about a dozen others, not to mention the modern variations."

Jackson shook his head. "So what's the bogus escrow?"

"The con goes after men in financial trouble, offering to help for a small percentage of the end result or a small finder's fee. As a third party he acts like a kind of escrow service where there's a business deal and the two parties don't trust each other. The third party holds funds in escrow until both parties are satisfied with the deal. Usually when an escrow goes through, the mediator takes a percentage and everyone's happy. In this case Eric will probably convince them to invest the money for a better return and then just claim that the investment tanked and keep it all."

"Yeah, I get the whole escrow thing—what's the after-midnight part?" he asked citing her terminology.

"If Eric is acting as the third party and your father and this other man, Cooperman, are as mistrustful as you say, then he's probably made each man a lucrative side offer to con the other man. But in reality he'll probably be conning both and taking everything."

"That's great. I guess there's no honor among thieves."

"The con wouldn't work if a mark doesn't want something for nothing and there's always an out, a moment when he decides to walk away or not. Remember, the con only works if you're dealing with men who are already greedy. Sorry," she said, realizing that she was referring to his father as one of the marks.

"No, I guess you're right," he said.

"Greed is the key. You can't con someone who isn't interested in getting something for nothing," she said, subtly pointing out that his father wasn't exactly an innocent in all this.

"How can I stop this?"

"You can't, but maybe with a little help *we* can. You see, the ultimate con is to scam a con man, and that's what we need to do—scam Eric, George and Lincoln before they con your father."

"How? They're holding all the cards."

"Not all of them. They don't know that we know the game. And as my father always said, to con a hunter you need to know his game."

"So we need to see this scam from every direction."

She smiled. "Exactly. Spoken like a true professional. But first we need information. The key is to know as much as possible, who the mark is, their weaknesses and their strengths and of course what they ultimately want."

"Eric wants the money and George wants my company."

"What about Lincoln, what does he want?" she asked.

"Good question, he's a wild card. So I say we confront George directly," Jackson said. "A frontal attack."

"He'll just deny everything and without proof you have

nothing. No, the trick is to let him think that he's getting exactly what he wants, then beat him at his own game."

"That won't be easy, will it?"

"It never is, but we have one very important advantage," she said, smiling. "George doesn't know that we know. And even if Lincoln is setting us up, we can be one step ahead. The question is, where would he keep this information?"

"His office, his company is the most secure place on the planet. Seeing him is like trying to get into Fort Knox."

"Okay, we need to get to Cooperman, then."

"That might be difficult. I'm not exactly his favorite person at the moment," he said. She looked at him, questioning. "It's a personal matter, but I'll see what I can do."

"In the meantime, I'll see if I can figure out the disc Lincoln gave us and then do some online research. Cooperman's just been all over the news with this boardroom scandal and the grand jury testimony. It shouldn't be too hard to get information on him. But finding Eric is going to be difficult."

"Why do we need him?"

"He's the weak link. We need to know exactly what he's planning."

"He's not going to just tell you, even if we do find him."

She smiled. "Actually, he would. Eric has an enormous ego. The art of the con is to play to greed. Ego is his Achilles' heel and paranoia is his weakness. He'll talk. The hard thing will be to shut him up afterward. These original documents that Eric has about your company, could they damage you personally?"

"No, but they could embarrass the family. They're more about my mother's past, her criminal record and so on."

"Do you have any idea how Eric might have gotten them in the first place?"

"No, as a matter of fact, I didn't even think about it. I was so focused on getting them back that I never questioned how he got them."

"Maybe you should. Who would be hurt more if they were released to the public?"

"It would be an embarrassment to the family and the company, but if I were to choose a person, I'd say my mother, or better yet her memory. One of the documents shows that she had been paying blackmail money for over twenty years. Someone found out about her police record and held it over her head."

"I doubt it was Eric or Cooperman," Samantha said.

"What about Inspector Lincoln?"

"Sounds possible."

They paused a moment to let the numerous questions and answers settle in their minds. "Can we really do this?" Jackson asked.

"We don't have a choice. Lincoln's right about one thing, neither one of us can do it alone."

"So you'll stay?" he asked.

"Yes, until this is finished."

"Good. One more question," Jackson said, then paused. "About Eric. Did you love him?"

"No," she said without qualms or hesitation.

"Did he love you?"

"I doubt it."

"There's a chance you'll see him again, soon."

"Probably."

"And you can handle that?" he asked.

She snickered. "Definitely," she said firmly.

"Yet you were together?" he asked nonjudgmentally.

"Yes, we were," she said, then paused, feeling the need to justify her actions. "People are together for a number of reasons. You and I are obvious proof of that. Love had nothing to do with Eric and me."

He smiled wide, enjoying a private thought. The possibility of love, once seeming so foreign, was now an interesting prospect. He was attracted to Samantha, that much was obvious, and he enjoyed being with her, but love, he considered temptingly, there were still too many things he didn't know about her. So how do you love someone and not completely trust them?

"What?" she asked, seeing his expression.

"Nothing, just considering."

She looked at him, puzzled by the remark.

He smiled, completely assured. "One more thing. There's a dinner party this evening that I need to attend. Would you join me?"

Chapter 12

Tall, arching trees, building-high hedges and mammoth gate entrances lined the nearly restricted path. The golden community was security gated and set aside from the usual Hollywood prestige and grandeur. Seemingly forbidden to most, the narrow streets twisted and turned in an erratic way, jolting and jarring in different directions at any given moment. At times a mass of luxury cars lined the tapered sideways, evidence of a party or celebration. Then the streets would be bare, devoid of life and hidden in secrecy.

"So, where exactly are we?"

"Somewhere between Bel-Air and Beverly Hills."

"So this is the infamous Beverly Hills," Samantha said, impressed by the splendor of the glamorous terrain. "Who would have thought that it's actually hills?" she joked.

Jackson smiled and glanced over to her as he drove farther up into the quiet hills of Los Angeles.

Easily maneuvering the winding curves, Jackson still wasn't sure what he was doing—all he knew was that he wanted to be doing it with Samantha. They had come to an arrangement of sorts. And for the time being, it was fine with him.

After their long talk that afternoon they went shopping. Granted, it was his first experience shopping with a woman, but it was delightful and he couldn't remember having so much fun. They'd gone into numerous boutiques looking for just the right look, not too sexy and not too conservative. The final outcome consisted of several new outfits, from business wear to formal dining wear and several in between.

This evening she'd chosen to wear his favorite. It looked breathtaking on her and the moment he saw her coming down the stairs with the complete ensemble he was captivated. He walked over, took her hand and kissed her lovingly. "You look sensational, breathtaking."

"Thank you, Jackson, you don't look so bad yourself," she said, smiling at the perfect way his suit fit his body. Walking down the stairs a moment earlier she very nearly tripped when she spotted him at the landing waiting for her. His dark suit and crisp white shirt with a light-colored tie made him look debonair and just too sexy.

They each spared a second to take a breath, and then she held a gold necklace out to him. She stepped back and turned around, revealing the dramatic sight of her bare back plunging to a glimpse of the tiny tattoo he loved so well. She grasped the loosely curled hair resting on her shoulders and held it up, exposing her neck for his convenience.

He stood motionless for an instant, awed by the sight of her. Then he stepped in and slipped the necklace over her head, holding the two ends to clasp together. After two fumbled and failed attempts, he focused and finally succeeded in fastening the necklace around her neck.

"You take my breath away," he whispered in quiet desperation as she released her hair and he placed his hands on her shoulders, nudging her back to lean closer to his body. She closed her eyes as she instantly felt the hardness of his arousal. His hands lowered to her small waist. Her head was bowed low as she turned to face him again.

"Do you have any idea what you've done to me, Samantha Lee Taylor?"

She smiled, looking up at him, expecting him to say something trivial to lighten the mood. But seeing the intense emotion in his eyes, she stopped smiling. She knew the look; it was the same reflecting in her mirror. But she also knew that she needed to be the one to stay the course. "Jackson, when this is over…" she began.

"No, I don't want to hear that."

"You have to, we have to. This was a fantasy, remember? We made this whole thing up."

"This isn't a fantasy anymore and you know it. That ended a long time ago, a lifetime ago. There's something more and I can't just drop it. When we're together everything feels so right. You feel it, I feel it."

"Jackson, it's just a physical thing, we're attracted to each other and when we're together our bodies—" She stopped, realizing that she couldn't finish her statement.

"No, don't trivialize this. I can see it in your eyes. When we look at each other it's real. You've been running all your life, Sammy. Stop now. Don't run away from me, too."

Emotion overtook her.

She wrapped her arms around his neck and held him tight to her body. His arms wrapped around her and they stood embracing for what seemed like forever. Her mind swirled dizzyingly as his words seeped into her heart. He was right but she couldn't listen. Hearing any more would definitely have weakened her resistance. She'd waited all her life to feel this way, but she knew what she had to do. She stepped back and looked up into his heavenly eyes.

He licked his suddenly dry lips and the simple action sent a bolt of fire through her body, then into her stomach. She reached up and kissed him with all the passion she felt building inside. Tongues teased and intertwined as the breathless embrace demanded more. The hardness of his body pressed to hers, adding to the fire that needed no fuel.

Always just below the surface, they knew the desire would erupt. Through playful jesting while shopping, to quiet talks on the deck and wanton glances across the room, it was always there pulling them to one conclusion.

The kiss faded to a gentleness of touch as she rested her head on his chest and he held her close. "Not the best timing," she said.

"Probably not," he agreed.

"We'd better leave," she said as she leaned away and looked up at him. He nodded, took a deep breath and straightened the golden necklace around her neck, letting the back of his hand brush the soft swell of her breasts. She secured her purse and turned to the door. Jackson watched a second as the thought of losing her when this was over cut through his heart.

Then he steeled himself. Assuredly, that wasn't going to happen, he promised himself, then smiled as the idea of marriage came to mind. He wanted Samantha in his life forever, and no one, not even she, was going to end this.

"Hey, planet earth to Jackson, you okay over there?" Samantha asked, still admiring the array of houses seemingly planted among the lush greenery of Beverly Hills.

"Yeah, I'm fine. I'm sorry, what did you ask me?" Jackson said as the thoughts faded.

"So where is this restaurant we're going to for dinner?" she asked as they rounded a corner and passed through a security-gated street. Private and remote, it was tucked neatly away behind a mass of overgrown hedges. Jackson nodded at the guard on duty as he continued driving.

"It's not a restaurant. Dinner's at my father's home."

"You didn't mention that this was dinner at the family abode. Any suggestions on how we're going to explain my presence to your father?" Samantha asked.

"I'll tell him you're my friend."

"What kind of friend?" she asked curiously, playfully.

"A very close friend," he added.

"Will he buy that?" she asked.

He nodded. "Yes, and since you've already met Jessie, the evening ought to be a breeze. It'll just be the four of us, unless Jessie decides to bring Paul along."

"Who's Paul, her husband?"

"No, he's a friend, although he'd love to be married to Jess. As a matter of fact, he's proposed about a half-dozen times already that I know of."

"And she turns him down?"

He nodded.

"Good for her," Samantha said decisively.

"Why's that? Don't tell me that you've got something against marriage."

"No, marriage is fine, just not for everyone."

"Is it for you?" he asked.

"I'm not sure yet, I'll let you know when I find out. I do know that I'm not the stand-by-her-man kind of woman. My mother did that all her life and she was left with heartache and pain. That's not me. What about you, ever think about taking the walk down the aisle?"

"The thought had crossed my mind at one point," he said, but didn't mention that it crossed his mind only after she had entered his life.

Samantha didn't respond. Somehow, she just didn't feel like the levity of joking anymore. The thought of Jackson considering marriage with another woman stilled her to silence. She knew, of course, that what they had was transitory at best, but still, the thought of him being with someone else didn't sit well.

For the first time in her life she was falling in love and it was with someone she could never have. Their worlds were miles apart and nothing could change that. She could pretend for a while, her father had given her that talent, but when it came to the real thing, she knew she'd never measure up.

A sadness stirred in her. Looking away, she saw a blur of green as the car zipped through the silent streets. She knew that she would walk away after all this was over. That was the plan. Correct the wrong, then return to her life. Jackson would return to his life and everything would be as it should, except she knew that it wouldn't. She'd gotten too close to Jackson, an obvious amateur mistake.

He had gotten through and she was falling for him and every time she kissed him she was falling deeper and deeper. But her heart wouldn't be denied. Her feelings were real, but she knew that she had to walk away from him for his sake.

"This little fantasy of ours took an unexpected turn," Jackson said, interrupting her thoughts as if they were his own.

"Yeah, I guess it did."

"Regrets?" he asked, glancing over at her.

"No, you?" she said quickly.

"Never."

"Good, I'm glad." She went silent again until he took a final turn. "This is your home?" she asked as they approached massive iron security gates and a forbidding entrance surrounded by ivy-covered stone walls.

"No," he said, "this is my father's home. I live at the beach."

He pushed a button on the front panel of his car and the gates opened automatically.

"You know what I mean. You grew up here?"

"Yes, but it's not as impressive as you might think."

"Wow, not exactly the hood, is it?"

"My family's affluent, you already knew that."

"Obviously," she said as he drove his car up the path leading to the stately home, then parked alongside a Bentley, a Benz and two BMWs and his father's midnight-blue Enzo Ferrari. Then he spotted his sister's car and smiled. Thankfully she was already here, as she was the designated referee whenever he and his father were in the same room.

As soon as he got out, his cell phone rang. He answered. "Yeah," he said seeing that it was his sister calling. "I'm right outside," he said.

"Dad's got company in case you haven't already noticed by the mini car showroom as you drove up," Jessie said quietly into the receiver.

"I noticed," Jackson said, not at all surprised that his father would have one of his young ladies with him for the evening. "Another one of his family dinners I assume."

"Even better than that. Tonight he's entertaining George Cooperman, his latest wife Darla, and of course Shauna and his latest conquest, Pamela Frasier, and a few others. Their deal went through, we're celebrating!" Jessie added.

"Thanks for the warning," Jackson said, then closed the phone ending the conversation.

He walked around to the passenger side of the car and opened the door, helping Samantha out of the car. She noticed his annoyed expression instantly. "What's up?"

"My father has invited a few new friends to his usual family dinner," Jackson said tightly.

"Okay," she said, not getting his point.

"Looks like you'll be meeting George Cooperman sooner than you thought. He's here," Jackson said through gritted teeth.

Samantha smiled, understanding his statement. "In that case, this ought to be a very interesting evening," she said, then paused, seeing Jackson's fierce expression. She touched his arm. "Jackson, wait." He stopped and turned to her. "Jefferson once told me that acting like you don't have a clue is sometimes the hardest part of the game. Remember, George can't know that we know what he's up to or it's over before it begins. We have to pretend nothing has happened, like we don't know anything, or else he's already won."

He nodded tensely.

"Jackson, if you find yourself getting angry, walk away or find me. If he doesn't buy this, it's over."

He nodded again, this time more accepting. Then they climbed the steps and walked inside. She felt a familiar rush. The game was about to begin.

Marcus met them as they entered the oversize foyer. His eyes nearly bulged from the sockets at seeing Jackson walk in with Samantha on his arm.

Dressed in the designer chiffon halter-style dress, high heels and a glamorous hairstyle, she looked like a movie star straight off the red carpet.

"Dad," Jackson said, shaking his hand, "what's the celebration?"

"Patience, you'll see," Marcus said smugly, his eyes flaring with hardened intensity. "Afterwards we need to talk." Then his attention turned. Ignoring his son, his focus was solely on Samantha. "I didn't realize you were bringing someone this evening."

"Samantha graciously accepted my invitation at the last minute. I hope that's not a problem."

Jackson smiled as Marcus directed his attention to the woman standing by his side. His eyes widened and his entire demeanor transformed to a lecherous smile. "Of course not, the more the merrier. Good evening, my dear, welcome to my home, and you are?" he asked, taking her hand gently while completely enamored.

"Dad," Jackson said, "this is a friend of mine, Samantha Lee. Samantha, this is my father, Marcus Daley."

Samantha instantly turned on the charm. She smiled graciously as Marcus continued to hold on to her hand. He squeezed gently, adding a punctuated interest as he moved closer to kiss her cheek. The otherwise cool welcome to his son was long forgotten as poise and grace flowed out like water.

Samantha went into action. She chose a slight accent, giving her vernacular and cadence a sophisticated character. "It's a pleasure and an honor to finally meet you, Mr. Daley. I'm a huge fan of yours."

"Please, call me Marcus," he gushed as Jackson's jaw dropped slightly. Without the slightest hesitation, Samantha had slipped into a perfect British accent.

"Marcus," she said sweetly as she held on to his hand a second longer than necessary, "I must say, your photos don't do you justice," she added, knowing that Marcus would appreciate the compliment. He did.

"Come in, come in," Marcus said, overly attentive to her plunging neckline. "Well, now, Jackson, you've been holding out on me. Where have you been hiding this lovely young lady? I see why you were reluctant to leave town. You, my dear—" he took the opportunity to let his eyes drift down her body "—are breathtaking."

"Thank you, Marcus," she flirted easily. "I can see where Jackson gets his charm and attractiveness."

Marcus chuckled. "So you're British?" Marcus asked.

"Really, I hadn't noticed," Samantha said jokingly.

Marcus laughed aloud. "Priceless, you are simply priceless. It's a shame you met Jackson first or you and I might have become great friends."

"More's the pity."

Jackson smiled, knowing his father's preference for women more than half his age and Samantha with her abundant charisma and now British accent had won him over instantly. But he also knew enough about Samantha to know that her flirtation was all show. Two seconds in the door and she already had him eating out of her hand. Marcus, completely ignoring Jackson, talked to Samantha a few minutes more.

"Tell me, how did you two meet?"

"Quite by accident actually. I leaned over and kissed him while on an airplane."

Marcus roared with laugher. "I love it. I love it. And as I said, we might have become great friends." He turned to Jackson incidentally. "Watch out, boy, I might just edge you out. Come, I'd like to introduce you to some of my closer friends."

Marcus extended his elbow and Samantha instantly tucked her arm into his as he led her into the living room. Jackson smiled, shook his head and followed.

As soon as he reached the living room, Marcus paused. He'd obviously forgotten his assurances to George that Jackson would arrive alone, giving him and his daughter the perfect opportunity to get reacquainted. Uncertain of his next move at seeing George standing at the fireplace with his wife Darla, he turned to Jackson standing on the other side of Samantha. Marcus froze midstep.

"Are you ready for this?" she whispered to Jackson.

"As I'll ever be," he answered.

"Then let's go get him."

George and Darla turned and looked up, seeing them

enter, surprised by the sight of Samantha evidently with Jackson. George eyed Samantha suspiciously as he stared angrily at Marcus for misleading him. He'd been assured by Marcus that Jackson was still very much enamored with his daughter, Shauna.

Jackson glanced at Jessie, who smiled, obviously entertained by the moment. Paul, her friend, stood to the side talking with another couple as several others mingled. Samantha walked over to George and Darla smiling. "Hi, I'm Samantha Lee, a friend of the family."

George paused a brief moment to spare a glace to Marcus, who looked slightly shell-shocked, then introduced himself, his wife and his daughter seated beside Jessie. They all shook hands as Samantha noticed George reach into his pocket and wipe his hands on his handkerchief.

Seeing Jackson enter, Shauna stood, glared at him, and walked over to her father's side. Jackson looked at Samantha—she understood. Apparently he and Shauna had a history. Bewildered and confused, Shauna shook Samantha's hand timidly and looked at her father for confirmation, then to Jackson who stood across the room still speaking with his father.

Pleasantries continued as another young woman seated with Jessie stood and walked over. She was introduced as Marcus's latest acquaintance, hopeful D-list actress and rising television star, Pamela Frasier.

After graciously acknowledging Pamela, Samantha turned to Jessie, who had also walked over. They hugged warmly as if old friends, giving added credence to the friend-of-the-family story. "You look fantastic," Samantha said to Jessie, hoping that she wouldn't blow her cover story. Instead, surprisingly, to her delight she added to the performance and even seemed to delight in seeing her again.

"Thanks, girl, you look great yourself. I love your hair down like that. The last time I saw you it looked shorter, but it seems like ages ago. You know that we still have lunch scheduled next week."

"I'm there," Samantha promised.

George excused himself and walked over to Marcus and Jackson.

"Okay now, where did you get that dress? It's fantastic. Turn around, let me see the back," Jessie added.

Samantha turned, spotting Jackson glance at her from across the room as he talked with his father and George Cooperman, who hadn't taken his eyes off her since she'd walked in. Jackson looked furious. Knowing that Shauna would witness the interaction, Samantha winked at Jackson, prompting his expression to ease as he smiled and winked back.

"Oh, I love it, I love it," Pamela gushed joyfully with her slight Brooklyn accent.

"It is gorgeous," Darla chimed in as Shauna stood mute, not liking the obvious competition for attention. "I'd love to get one. Where did you find it?"

Samantha talked easily about her excursion to the boutiques, leaving out Jackson's presence, of course. Then she talked and joked easily with Jessie, giving the impression of a long well-developed friendship. She played the role and they accepted. The brief girlfriendlike conversation was apparently all that George needed to be assured that Samantha was indeed a close family friend and not in competition with his daughter for Jackson's affections.

Having saved a potentially awkward situation, Samantha and Jessie gathered Darla and began talking about the latest clothing designs. Pamela sizzled over to Marcus and entwined her arm with his possessively, poking her silicone breasts into his arm in an obvious attempt to reclaim her position.

The doorbell rang, and several more guests arrived. As they intermingled, dispersed in the living-room den and out on the terrace, they sipped champagne and ate hors d'oeuvres from silver platters circulated by waiters. The small intimate dinner party had turned into a major event.

George found his way over to Samantha. As he'd been staring at her since she arrived, she'd expected as much. "A friend of the family, eh?" George said, walking over after making sure that both his wife and daughter were preoccupied in the garden with several other guests.

"Yes, our two families go back a ways," she said.

"Oh, I see," he said, nodding his understanding. "Samantha Lee," he began. "That's a beautiful name for a very beautiful woman."

"Thank you, Mr. Cooperman," she replied, lightly stroking his arm for added effect.

"Are you here visiting or are you a resident now?"

"I'm just passing through on my way home."

"England, I presume. Is it Leeds or London proper?" he asked, showing his astute knowledge of accents.

"You have a very good ear, Mr. Cooperman."

"Thank you. In fact, I was just in your country a few weeks ago. I picked up a little something for my office."

"Really, pity we didn't meet earlier," she said openly. "Could have showed you around. There are some interesting out-of-the-way places you might have enjoyed."

"Yes," George said with interest. "Pity."

"Maybe next time," she said as his eyes sparked.

They continued talking, mainly about his business, his wealth, his ingenuity, his success and his money. Then he finally got around to what she had expected. "So, Ms. Lee, what exactly do you do?"

"I consult."

"On business matters, perhaps?" he asked.

"Business, oh, no, hardly, I wouldn't know where to even begin," she said, playing the part well. "I'm much more imaginative."

"For instance," he asked quickly, sounding excited, "what do you consult on?" George asked.

"A number of things, but for you, Mr. Cooperman, I think—" she paused and smiled "—art." She remembered that the quick search on the Internet had been a wealth of information. She knew from her research that he collected art and fancied himself an art connoisseur, patronizing local artists and galleries, and most importantly, he loved anything British.

"Intriguing," George said, stepping closer. She smiled.

"Tell me, what do you think of this piece?" he asked about a small painting on the near wall behind her.

Samantha looked over, smiling. "It's enjoyable."

"Is that your professional opinion?" he asked.

"Well, in my professional opinion," she began, then took a closer look at the small painting. "For what it is, it's under-dramatized. The artist is too timid. He used pastel oils, which gives the piece an ethereal effect. Consequently, the piece comes off weak and inadequate. Although there are definite traces of a bolder and more brazen brushstroke, I think the painting falls flat."

George's face brightened as he eased closer, blocking the rest of the room with his large body. "I quite agree."

"Perhaps too Norman Rockwell's Saturday Evening Post where the outrage of Picasso might have worked better." She laughed noncommittally. He joined in for no apparent reason.

"Do you like art, Mr. Cooperman?"

"Yes, I collect art, as a matter of fact."

"Fascinating. I'd love to see your collection," she said pleasantly.

"That can definitely be arranged."

"I'd be delighted."

"Splendid, perhaps you might come by my office one afternoon and—" he paused "—consult. I'd love to get your opinion of some of the art I recently purchased. A new piece arrived for my office just last week. I think you might enjoy seeing what I have to offer."

Samantha smiled. This was just the invitation she was expecting. "That would be wonderful." George reached into his pocket and handed her his personal business card. She read the information, then smiled up at him. "How about tomorrow afternoon?" she asked.

George stepped back and looked around, and saw that his wife had just entered the room again. "Perfect," he said happily. "I look forward to your consultation."

"As do I," she said sweetly, seeing Paul also walking toward them. "So tell me more about your business," she offered, changing the subject as Darla approached.

George instantly began to describe in detail the pressures of his company and the new pressure of the federal indictment. A few minutes later Samantha excused herself as George went back to bragging to Paul about the deal he'd recently struck with his ex-partner, sending the man into bankruptcy and making himself a large fortune, and how he'd just testified to a federal grand jury of no wrongdoing. Boastful and arrogant, he continued his loud bragging.

Small groups spread throughout the lower level. Jackson eventually wandered over to stand beside Samantha. "Enjoying yourself?"

"Immensely."

"I noticed you speaking with George."

"Yes, we—" she began but was interrupted.

"Excuse me, may I have everyone's attention?" Marcus

began. The room quieted down as everyone looked to the center where he stood. "Well, now that almost everyone is here, I'd like to make a little announcement. Actually, George and I would like to make a little announcement. George?" Marcus offered, motioning for George to join him.

"Yes, of course," George said, stepping to the center of the room beside Marcus. They shook hands and smiled, pleased, then turned to the assembled guests.

"As you all know," Marcus said. "Daley Communications has gone through several challenges in the past few months. The death of my wife and the leadership role I've assumed have given me a renewed insight. I have reorganized our executive offices and the changes will be continuing in the near future. I have also taken steps to ensure our visibility in the current market by initiating a new division.

"My father started this company and I intend to keep it firmly rooted in Daley family beliefs. And those beliefs are solely my beliefs. So without further ado, I'd like to announce that I have just finalized negotiations on the purchase of a small cable company owned by George Cooperman. The official announcement will take place in a few days, but I wanted to share this with my close friends and family. George and I are looking forward to a long profitable partnership together."

Surprised and joyful oohs, aahs and applause rang out instantly as Darla, Shauna and Pamela hurried to Marcus's and George's sides.

"That's wonderful, dear," Darla said to George as she kissed him, then wiped the red smear from his cheek.

"Congratulations, darling," Pamela said, following Darla's lead, kissing Marcus generously, leaving her own colorful stain to wipe away.

Paul walked over and shook Marcus's and George's hands as did Jackson and Samantha. Jessie hugged and kissed her father's cheek and then one by one the other guest congratulated them in turn.

George and Marcus smiled happily, excited by the new venture. The conversation circled around them as hopeful praise was gathered.

Jessie moved to stand beside Jackson. "How about that?" she said quietly. "He actually did it."

"The question is, how?" Jackson said. "He doesn't have the money to front something like that."

"Sounds like a Faustian bargain to me."

"Exactly. Unfortunately, paying the devil is probably going to destroy the company."

Chapter 13

Moments later, the group was ushered into the formal dining room, which looked to be the size of a small football stadium. Hardwood floors shined to a high gloss reflected the crystal chandeliers hanging from narrow beams outlined by smoked-glass windows overhead. Three long tables were set in the center of the room with small handwritten name tags.

Marcus stood at the head of the long center table and surveyed the seating arrangements, Jessie by his side, Paul beside her, Samantha next, then another guest and finally Darla next to her husband, who sat at the opposite end. Beside him was an empty seat, then another guest, Shauna, Jackson and Pamela between him and Marcus.

As soon as they all sat down, hired waiters instantly appeared, each carrying two bottles of champagne. The wine and celebratory champagne glasses were filled and the traditional birthday toast was presented by Jackson. Short and thoughtful, after which a round of applause began, Marcus's ten-minute speech was on new beginnings and new directions.

Afterward, George presented a toast praising Marcus, their new business relationship and hopes for the future.

Shauna beamed victoriously as Samantha smiled and nodded, acknowledging Jackson's wink. Jessie toasted her father's love and devotion as Paul toasted Marcus's long standing in the business community.

A fresh green salad was served after Pamela led an awkward, pointless conversation on the possibility of birthdays on other planets since they have either longer or shorter days and years. A brief nod from Marcus appointed Jessie to take over the hostess duties, keeping everyone involved and entertained.

The salad course finished, the entrée was placed in front of them. Exceptionally prepared by five-star chef Andre Pree, the food looked incredible. When all the plates were served, Andre emerged from the kitchen and personally explained each of the five selections. Midway through his presentation the doorbell rang. He finished quickly and disappeared back into the kitchen.

Moments later Samantha saw Eric Hamilton enter the dining room carrying a wrapped gift and a briefcase. His suave entrance was as cool and calculating as ever.

Obviously not at all surprised to see her, he smiled around the table, then turned his attention to Marcus as the host. "There he is, come in, come in, we'd almost given you up for lost," Marcus said, standing and shaking Eric's hand heartily.

Eric walked over and shook George's hand, and then Marcus introduced Eric as a private investment broker and an indispensable business associate. Never missing a beat, Eric smiled and nodded pleasantly but kept his attention focused on Marcus and George. Marcus, the ever-diligent host, made further introductions as Eric nodded amiably with the women and shook hands with the men. His eyes darted to Samantha from time to time, as if he was fearful of her reaction, but once introduced to her and receiving no perceivable regard he was assured of her silence and noticeably relaxed.

He was in character, of course, personable and charming, barely distinguishable from the man she once knew. Bearded now, with nerdy tortoiseshell eyeglasses and a near-bald haircut, he folded his tall wiry frame into the empty seat beside Shauna. But instead of joining in the conversation about global warming, he sat looking from face to face as if to visually memorize each person's mannerisms.

He was quickly served and ate with ravishing purpose, never once freeing his cloth napkin from the neatly rolled ring beside his plate. Samantha smiled at the oversight. Although it could possibly be perceived as an eccentric flaw, she knew it was the same old Eric. The quips and witticisms of conversation surrounded him, yet he focused solely on his roast chicken and baby vegetables enveloped in a crispy phyllo shell. He poked and prodded the flaky pastry, then devoured the inside, leaving the empty shell bare. Typical.

Samantha noticed that Jackson had glanced at her several times. He of course knew the history between the two and noted her detached behavior. She caught his eye and winked slyly. Almost simultaneously she added an interesting yet witty remark to the conversation that made everyone chuckle. She smiled and shook her head as Eric laughed louder and longer. *What in the world did she ever see in him?* she wondered.

She observed the two men across from her. They were separated by Shauna, who now seemed to be in seventh heaven, but her preference was obviously for Jackson. She constantly made witty remarks to engage him in conversation. He was polite but his focus was never drawn to her.

Jackson exuded class. His manly body was far from the lankiness of Eric's. Jackson, with his reserved calm and elegant coolness, walked with a kind of confident swagger that exuded power and purpose, whereas Eric seemed to meander along from one situation to another. As Jackson was naturally suave, Eric was on a treadmill, never keeping up. Jackson was the real thing.

After dinner Jessie and Paul, along with several of the other guests, excused themselves with previous engagements. Marcus, Jackson, George and Eric were talking business as Darla and Pamela toured the house and Shauna and Samantha sat outside on the terrace.

"So how are you a friend of the family exactly?" Shauna finally asked, seeing that there was more to the simple relationship than was stated.

"Through Rachel," Samantha said. Shauna looked at her, slightly confused. "Rachel Daley, Jessie and Jackson's mother," she explained.

"Oh, right, of course."

"And you?" Samantha asked innocently.

"Jackson and I were to be married last year."

"Congratulations, how nice for you," Samantha said without skipping a beat, although her insides twisted into a knot as she realized that this was the woman Jackson meant when he'd said earlier that he'd considered marriage at one time. "Jackson is a wonderful man," Samantha added, refusing to appear fazed by the targeted emotional blow.

"But I called it off. I just wasn't ready at the time, but now…" she said evenly.

"I see," Samantha said, understanding Shauna's remark as a warning to back off. Shauna nodded pointedly, obviously reclaiming her man.

A few minutes later Eric walked outside and stood by

Shauna attentively. The three of them talked generally, about the weather and travel, until Shauna excused herself when her phone rang.

"Samantha," Eric said, moving closer.

"Eric," she replied, glaring into his dark eyes with a syrupy sweet smile that made him nervous.

He quickly glanced around, making sure that the other guests were reasonably preoccupied, then leaned in with a gentle whisper, "Thanks for not blowing this for me." He smiled smugly, seemingly assured of her silence. "Look at you," he said boldly admiring what he saw. His eyes slimed down her body like a boa constrictor, covering every inch in seconds. "Who would have guessed? I think being with me had a good effect on you after all."

She glared at him, stunned by his outrageous assumption. "You have got to be kidding me," she said loudly, drawing attention from George and Darla, who were sitting just inside the terrace door.

"Keep your voice down," Eric shushed her, and moving farther away from the doorway and taking her arm with him. "What do you mean?" he asked innocently, smiling happily as if the past four months hadn't happened.

"Eric, it wasn't that we just lost touch, or that you didn't call me after a date. You stole money from the job, pissed off heaven knows who else, had the police after me for questioning and then left the mess for me. You conned me."

"Look, I never thought they'd come after you. I owed money and I needed to get my hands on fast cash. I was desperate."

"Oh, please, so is that why you switched computers and left a signature a mile wide leading back to me?" she hissed quietly. He turned away, looking off into the landscaped darkness. "I can't believe you, you're pathetic."

"And you look incredible," he said, changing the subject.

"Avoidance was always your issue."

"No, seriously," he said, smiling the innocent boyish grin that she remembered and had once adored. "You really look incredible. So this is what was under all those frumpy sweatshirts and baggy pants. If I'd known that I might have stepped up."

Her glare hardened. She was too furious to answer.

"So what exactly are you doing here?" he asked.

"Same as you, Eric, enjoying the evening," she said.

"Come on, you expect me to believe that? You don't do the con, that's your brother's gig. You told me that you hated this stuff. You followed me here."

"Careful, Eric, your paranoia is showing," she said.

"I knew it, I knew it," he repeated softening his voice raised louder the second time. "You still want me," he reached up to gently stroke her face. "You still love me, don't you?"

She quickly leaned back, then slapped his hand away from her. He smiled. "Oh, please, I got over you a long time ago. Get over yourself. I learn from my mistakes. You should, too. And speaking of mistakes, what's the con this time?" she asked, knowing that his ego wouldn't let him keep quiet. Bragging was what he did best.

"You expect me to tell you?"

"Why not?" she offered. "I couldn't care less about the mark, you know that."

He considered her remark, then glanced around quickly with dark shifty eyes and leaned in conspiratorially and whispered, "Initially it was just a simple escrow thing, but now it's a bit more complicated."

"How so? Who's the mark?" she asked.

He smiled happily, "Marcus Daley," he said proudly. "Impressed?"

"I'll let you know."

"Check it out," he continued. "He needs cash to float this

new company he wants and I'm set up as a moneyman. I fed him a twenty-thousand-dollar convincer a few days ago. Tonight I'm dropping off fifty thousand dollars in cash from a supposed moneymaking investment. He's buying it hook, line and sinker. I'm—"

"Where did you get the front money?"

"Silent partners."

"Who are they?"

"Nobody you'd know. Anyway, tonight I'm about to close another deal. Now, in another few days I'll up the stakes to a million dollars. He'll give me the cash thinking I'll triple his money. Then I just walk away."

"What about your partners?"

"I keep the whole million. They're after something bigger."

"What?"

"They want the whole store, Daley Communications."

Samantha smiled. She was right. "The company?"

He nodded.

"What happens to Marcus and his family?" she asked with concern.

"Don't tell me you're attached," Eric said.

"Not at all. A mark's just a mark, you know that."

"Yeah, well, that's not my problem."

"So let me get this straight. You're helping a couple of thugs steal someone else's company for a million-dollar payoff."

Eric nodded proudly. His stupidity astounded her at times, and this was one of those times.

"Eric, disappearing with someone's money isn't the same as not getting caught. The whole idea is for the mark not to know he's been conned."

"See, I knew you wouldn't get it. Check it out, Marcus wants sole control of his company, but to get it he needs financial backing. With his lacking the ready funds, enter me, I help him make some quick cash." She nodded. "But he needs more, right?"

She nodded again as it hit her. "He's gonna leverage the company to someone, your partner perhaps."

"Exactly. He leverages his business and it defaults."

"And the company belongs to your partners."

"Exactly. And I walk away with a cool million. Believe me, Marcus will be so stressed out about losing his company that he won't even think about the million he gave me."

"I must say, Eric, I underestimated you. So what's going on beneath the surface? Can you trust your partners?"

"One of them just claimed bankruptcy to avoid paying federal taxes. He sat before a federal grand judge and testified that he's broke. Perjury is a criminal offense, not to mention fraud. I'm talking jail time. So he can't touch me. I have leverage on him. I get caught, I talk," he said proudly.

"Impressive," she said, choosing not to mention the obvious holes throughout his scheme.

Eric smiled boastfully. "You know, I actually thought you might blow this for me when I first saw you, but then I remembered that you are your father's daughter, aren't you? You know the game. You wouldn't do that to me."

She smirked. "That would be presumptuous of you."

He looked affronted as his cocky, confident expression changed to that of instant alarm. "Okay, I get it, hell hath no fury like a woman scorned. All right, fine, whatever. Not one of my finer moments, I admit it. Is that what you want, an apology? Fine, I'm sorry. So what do you want to keep quiet, two percent of the take, five percent?"

"The complete lack of veracity aside, your obliviousness fascinates me. Look beyond the obvious, Eric. Will there actually be a take?" She smiled, seeing his sudden concern. "Two, five or ten percent of nothing is nothing."

"Now look who's pathetic," he said mockingly. "Don't make this more difficult than it is."

"Me?" she said innocently. "Not at all. I'm just here for the show."

"You're obviously going to make this personal."

"You still seem to think that all this is about you."

"Isn't it?" he asked, completely assured. "Isn't that why you followed me?"

"I told you, I didn't follow you, I was invited."

He looked over to Jackson and nodded. "By him or someone else?"

She smiled. "Still paranoid, I see."

He reached his arm out comfortably across the railing letting his fingers stroke her hand. "Look, for the record, I didn't mean to leave like that, but the score was falling apart and I needed to cut and run. I knew you wouldn't go with me, so I left."

"Yes, you did," she said. "But a word of warning. I'm not the one you should be worried about."

"What does that mean?" She smiled her answer as Pamela laughed loud and long, drawing both their attention. Eric noticed Jackson coming toward them. "Look, we need to talk, but obviously not here," he said. "I'll meet you later. Where are you staying?"

"This is California, Eric. On the beach of course."

"The beach?"

She laughed.

After seeing Jessie and Paul off, Jackson came back inside and looked around for Samantha. He found her outside on the terrace taking with Shauna and Eric. He intended to join them. Just as he walked toward the open terrace doors his father called to him.

"Jackson," Marcus said. "May I speak with you?"

Jackson turned, and saw his father waiting at his office door for him. He glanced outside at Samantha and Eric, then turned and followed as his father led the way inside his office. As soon as he closed the door, Marcus began. "Bet you didn't think I could do it?" he gloated boldly, then snickered. "I was brilliant."

"Did it ever occur to you that George handed you this company for a reason?"

"I never would have expected resentment from you. I gave you the opportunity to join me, but you declined. As soon as the board sees this deal they'll have no choice but to instate me as permanent CEO."

"It's not about being CEO or this cable company, it was about Daley Communications. If this deal goes through we'll lose it. George's reputation—"

"Means absolutely nothing. Now, what's going on with retrieving those originals? This has dragged on too long. If this information is leaked just days before the National Association of Black-Owned Broadcasters awards dinner I'll be a laughingstock."

"I'm handling it. It's just going to take some time."

"That's what you said three days ago. If I didn't know any better I'd say that you were sabotaging this for me on purpose," Marcus said cagily. He looked at his son closely for any sign of guilt. Jackson's stern expression remained the same. "Pay him," Marcus demanded. "Get this finished. Your mother's mess is not going to screw this up for me."

Jackson winced angrily but remained calm, remembering Samantha's words of caution. He sat down as his father offered him a cigar. He declined and waited patiently as Marcus lit his.

"You knew about this, didn't you?"

Marcus took a deep drag of his cigar, then exhaled and

blew out a long stream of smoke. "No, not exactly. Your mother, yes, of course, but that part of her life was behind us. It was a long time ago. Neither of us asked questions."

Jackson shook his head. "I don't get it. Why didn't you just divorce years ago?"

"The business," he answered simply.

"You stayed together for the business?"

"Yes."

"That's a switch. Usually, it's for the children."

Marcus chose not to reply to the obvious.

"So you knew who she was, what she was," Jackson said.

"That was before we met. The company was failing, we needed—"

"Yeah, I know," Jackson said, cutting him off. "The money she stole from someone else. She gave it to you and that saved the business."

"You need to understand our position, your grandfather was an icon to the general public, he still is. They considered us the perfect family. We are now the icon. People look up to us. We accepted the role, you accepted the role."

"You're right, we *are* the perfect family, the perfect illusion. Don't you get it? None of this is real, none of this is really worth it. Look around, it's all meaningless. Look around, all these things you love so much mean nothing if you're alone at the end of the day. Mom knew it, but you don't get it. Love is the only reality."

Marcus applauded sarcastically. Jackson stood and walked to the door.

"Wait," Marcus said. Jackson stopped, then turned around to his father again. "Jackson, I called you in here for another reason. There's a meeting I'd like you to sit in on tomorrow morning. I want you in with this next venture I'm planning."

"What next venture?"

"As you know, George and I have confirmed our deal for the cable company. Eric's handling the finances and final details. He's also putting together another venture for me."

"Eric?"

"Yes, I trust him completely. He's good at what he does."

"How can you completely trust a man you just met? You don't know anything about him."

"I know enough."

"Dad," Jackson began, tempted to reveal all, but he knew that his father wouldn't believe him.

"Look, I know you don't think I know what I'm doing," Marcus said, "but I do. I made over three hundred thousand dollars on a simple investment last week, no gamble, no risk. This cable company purchase will expand Daley Communications."

The muscle in Jackson's jaw tightened. The reason they were in the red was because of several bad investments Marcus had talked the board into accepting. Jackson was just about to reply, when the office door banged open. Pamela, slightly tipsy from several glasses of champagne, poked her head in, giggling. Jackson turned and walked back over to the door.

"I'll see you tomorrow," Marcus said.

Jackson nodded and left.

He was on his way to the terrace again when Shauna came up beside him quickly before he got too far. She'd been waiting outside the office door.

"It's good to see you again, Jackson," she spoke up quickly, then continued, more demurely, "I've missed you, being with you, I mean, our little talks and other things."

"Shauna…" Jackson began, still walking toward the terrace.

"No, wait, before you say anything," she said, grasping his arm and holding him still. "Listen, please, hear me out first, okay?" She kept her hand comfortably on his arm. "I've changed. I understand what you were saying back then and

I've changed. I really have. I'm no longer that selfish self-centered woman you knew a year ago. I'm different. I'm in the program, two months clean."

"Good for you, Shauna. I'm really happy for you."

She reached out and took his hand to gain his full attention. "Jackson, I still want you in my life."

"Shauna," he began again.

"No, don't say anything now." She looked around, seeing her father nodding and smiling at them. "I'd like to stop by later. Maybe we can talk."

"That's not a good idea."

"Think about it, okay?" she said gently. "We still have deep feelings for each other. I can see it in your eyes."

"It's not you, Shauna."

"Who?" she asked quickly, then followed his line of vision, seeing Samantha outside talking. "Oh, you mean her. You can't be serious. She's so far out of our league, she needn't even try."

"Again, I'm happy for you, Shauna," he said, then looked away again. Eric and Samantha were still standing outside on the terrace talking. "Excuse me," he said to Shauna as he removed her hand from his arm and walked away, leaving her behind.

Samantha was laughing.

"Am I interrupting something?" Jackson said, seeing Eric standing too close to Samantha. Eric visibly jumped at hearing Jackson's voice right behind him.

"Not at all," Samantha answered, still smiling. "Eric was just telling me about the beach."

"Is that right?" Jackson said, walking over to stand on the other side of Samantha. Shauna came out seconds later and stared at Jackson and Samantha, then stood beside Jackson as Eric stammered and stuttered and began a two-minute monologue about Caribbean beaches.

"Jackson has a beautiful home in Malibu right on the beach. Speaking of which, Jackson," Shauna said, turning her body directly to him, "did you finish remodeling your home yet? It's such a beautiful location."

"Yes, about a year ago, but then, you knew that."

"Oh, that's right," Shauna said, smiling innocently. "I must have forgotten. But you were still working on your bedroom, if I remember correctly. Did you consider any of the suggestions I made the last time I was there?"

"I had a design firm come in," Jackson said.

"Oh, the one I told you about?" she asked hopefully.

"No, Jessie gave me a few names."

"How did it turn out?" Eric asked, hacking his way back into the conversation.

"I like it," Samantha said speaking up instantly while lying easily, having never seen his bedroom. "I think the openness and the bold design suit you, but then I guess I told you that before." She smiled, looking at Jackson, then at Shauna. The implication was easily discernible: She'd recently been in Jackson's remodeled bedroom.

Jackson returned her smile. "That's right, you did."

Eric and Shauna seemed irritated by her remark.

"I'm getting chilly," Shauna said to Jackson, waiting for him to offer her his jacket or escort her inside. When he didn't, Eric spoke up and escorted her back into the house.

"Interesting woman," Samantha said, obviously referring to Shauna and her very noticeable fixation on Jackson.

"So that's Eric Hamilton," Jackson said, evening the score as he sized up the man who'd once had Samantha's heart.

As neither responded to the other's comment, they fell into a comfortable silence, standing side by side at the railing looking out at the captivating bird's-eye view of Los Angeles. Breathtaking, the lights below shone as brightly and brilliantly in the distance as the stars twinkled above.

Like gems on a swath of midnight velvet, the gleam of lights sparkled everywhere she looked. She turned and looked up, observing every architectural detail of her surroundings.

The house was old style, made of a grayish stone and ivory cast marble. It looked more like a movie set from an old black-and-white film with its grand entrance, rounded staircase and huge twenty-five-foot ceilings. Each room that she'd been in looked exaggerated and pretentious. Even the terrace was overdone. Surrounded by dozens of ornamental trees, expertly manicured bushes and a flower garden that looked more like a showcase for a garden center, the fanciful home was beyond belief.

Grand to the point of near ostentation, the Beverly Hills mansion sat high on a lofty perch overlooking the city below.

"This house is really incredible," Samantha said to Jackson.

"It's big," he corrected gently.

"And you grew up here, right?"

He nodded.

"How many bedrooms does it have?"

"Twelve, not including the guesthouse and the two one-bedroom apartments over the garage."

"Wow, that is huge. Where does this path lead?" she asked, pointing into the darkness, then beyond as landscaped lighting led down into the garden and curved out of sight.

"The steps lead to the lower patio, then to the infinity pool, the basketball court and the cabanas. There's another path that curves to the side and leads to the guesthouse, then to the indoor pool and exercise room."

"It must have been nice growing up here, having all this."

"They're just things, meaningless things." Jackson looked out into the darkness of the huge landscaped patio and yard. His thoughts centered on years past. "My mother loved this place," he began. "She picked out every piece of furniture, every set of china and oversaw every stitch of fabric sewed. All that's gone now. My father completely remodeled after she died. I don't come here much anymore."

"Why not?" she asked.

"Every time I come here it reminds me of her. This was her sanctuary. Everything in here was once a part of her. She worked so hard on this place. Now everything's gone."

"The memories we keep forever," she said.

He nodded.

"You miss her a lot?" Samantha asked quietly.

"Yeah, I wish you could have met her," Jackson said, then paused, hearing his father's latest acquaintance giggle riotously. They both turned, and saw her wiggling a suggestive dance as Marcus applauded. "In more ways than one."

She looked up at the back of the house. Every light was on, making the massive estate look like a virtual palace. "So which of the twelve bedrooms is yours?" she asked.

"*Was* mine," he corrected, then looked up at the structure and pointed. "That one over there in the corner, second floor by the old oak tree."

"Convenient, so you could sneak out of the house by shimmying down the drainpipe and climbing down the tree," she joked.

"No," he said, then took her hand to change the subject. "Tell me you're not still going when this is over."

"Live and let go, right?"

"Would you consider staying?" he asked.

She slipped her hand from his. "I should never have let it happen, we're getting too close." She turned away and looked out at the pristine landscape. "Yes, Jackson, I'm leaving as soon as all this is over."

He touched her shoulder, then slowly let his hand drift down her bare back. The touch relit the fire always simmering. "Might you reconsider?"

"I can't," she said, turning to him and looking into his eyes. "When this is over, I'm gone." She walked away quickly, knowing that if she stayed she'd surely change her mind.

Jackson looked after her as she walked back into the house, passing Marcus as he came outside.

Marcus walked over to the railing surrounding the terrace and patio. Jackson watched as his father observed Samantha eagerly. "Interesting young woman," he said, standing by Jackson's side.

Jackson glanced at Samantha as she stood by Pamela, who was laughing hysterically at nothing in particular. "I think so."

"Where'd you find her?"

"We found each other."

"I expected you to come alone," Marcus said, implying his persistent interest in having Shauna in his life. "Ms. Lee is nice enough, I'm sure. And no doubt she is beautiful and whatever her assets, I'll be the first to encourage you to take full advantage of them, but this is business. Have her on the side, set her up someplace out of the way, all that's fine. As a mistress she's perfect, but you need someone of quality."

"Someone like Shauna Cooperman, I assume."

"Someone *exactly* like Shauna Cooperman," Marcus said.

"Good night, Dad, thanks for dinner," Jackson said before walking away.

"Jackson," Marcus called out. Jackson turned to him. "Understand, we need this. I did it. Now it's your turn."

Chapter 14

Jackson and Samantha drove back to the beach in relative silence, each deep in thought, considering the evening. Samantha stared straight ahead as her mind whirled in the mists of doubt and confusion. The crystal-clear precision she'd once had had faded. She was losing her perspective. Her emotions had gotten tangled with her reasoning, and seeing Eric had only muddied the waters. It wasn't that she wanted him back but that she saw more clearly the man she did want: Jackson. Her feelings for him had escalated. She wanted to be with him now more than ever. But she knew she couldn't be. And the pain of that realization tore at her.

Never let your emotions get involved. She remembered Jefferson saying that over and over again. Unfortunately, she had and they were. Now she needed to breathe through the hesitation and clear her mind. There was no way she could tell Jackson what was really going on without him hating her, so silence was best and distance was even better. She had gotten too close and had lost her focus, Now she needed to step away if she was going to finish this and make it right.

She nodded then in the quiet darkness. Distance, she decided ardently, yes, distance. But her smile faded as quickly as it came. How do you distance a breaking heart? She was an amateur in more ways than one.

"Are you okay?" Jackson asked softly as he glanced at her, then back to the highway.

"Yes," she said quickly. "Just a little tired." How could she finish this and walk away when all she wanted to do was be swallowed up in his arms?

Moments later, Jackson pulled into his driveway and turned off the ignition. "Thanks for coming with me," he said, still sitting in the car.

She nodded, afraid her voice would give her away. Then she opened the door and got out. He followed her to the front door and opened it. She walked inside and immediately headed toward the stairs. He followed, and she paused. "Thank you for this evening, Jackson, I had a good time," she said, turning to him as he stood too close behind her.

"You're welcome. Samantha, we—"

"Don't worry, everything will work out perfectly. You'll have your company and life back just as it was."

"What if I don't want it back the way it was? Samantha, we—"

"Good night," she said quickly before he continued, then turned to walk away. Knowing this moment would come, she decided that a swift retreat was her best option. Anything more would tear her apart as the memory of their time together stayed in her thoughts all evening. She wanted him. Her body ached for him. But her heart couldn't handle walking away forever. She teetered on the verge of falling in love. Foreign but sure, she knew that the emotion would never let her go.

Jackson grabbed her arm before she climbed the stairs. She turned. Their eyes met and everything they felt poured out. In a nonverbal nuance, their hearts met. He pulled her into his arms and for a brief moment they were connected on a higher level. Staring, hearts pounding, their breath mingling they were as one.

She bit at her lower lip nervously as he licked his own lips. Slow and seductive, the intimate acts pushed them beyond the tease. He leaned in closer. She met him halfway. They stopped, afraid that if they kissed it would be their undoing.

"We can't do this," she whispered in heartfelt remorse, then leaned away.

"Samantha..." he began.

"We can't do this," she repeated. "I can't do this."

"You're all I think about," he said, then smiled miserably. "My once very comfortable world is falling apart all around me, and all I can think about is being with you. Your eyes, your mouth, your smile—you haunt me. And I don't know what to do about it. I don't understand it. My family's reputation, my business, my life, everything I know, everything I am, nothing matters when I see you..." His voice trailed off to a faint whisper.

"Jackson, don't do this."

"All I want to do is touch you, love you, make love to you."

Her insides melted. "Jackson," she uttered and looked away. Looking into his eyes was tearing her apart inside. "I...I feel...if we...if you only knew." She shook her head. "Live and let go, remember? That's what we said, that's what we promised," she stated firmly and eased from his hold and turned back to the stairs.

"That was before," he said.

"We can't change it now."

"We can do anything we want."

"Jackson," she said, "it's complicated."

"No, it's not complicated, it's just us and whatever we want it to be. Just let go, Samantha. Whatever it is you're holding on to, let go and take a chance with me." She didn't respond but continued walking. "Is this about seeing Eric again?" he asked, knowing that it wasn't and that the remark would stop her in her tracks.

"No, of course not," she said adamantly.

"Then let me love you," he whispered. Her heart stopped and the raging torment inside erupted. How do you fight love? He had her and she was helpless to refuse.

"Turn around," he said.

She didn't move.

"Turn around," he repeated.

She did.

Looking into his eyes she saw the same heartfelt emotion surging inside her. A battle raged. But the reassurance of her actions gave her strength. "I'm doing this for you. You'll understand later," she said, then hurried up the stairs for distance.

Jackson watched her go. He stood at the bottom of the stairs debating whether or not to go after her, then decided against it as her last words echoed in his thoughts. *I'm doing this for you. You'll understand later.* The meaning was unclear but the feeling behind it wasn't. She wanted him as much as he wanted her, but something held her back.

He needed Samantha to trust him. But he had no idea how to reach her. Frustrated, he moved to the sliding glass doors leading onto the deck. Opening them, he walked outside and stood at the rail looking out at the ocean view. The night was still. The full moon had crested above and the water glistened below as waves splashed against the surf.

She'd come into his life wearing stiletto heels and Chanel

perfume, and just like that, in a sudden splash, everything he thought he knew was different. Tame and safe she certainly wasn't, and he liked it.

Sure of himself for the moment, he walked back into the darkened living room and stood looking around at nothing in particular. He turned on the fireplace, then walked over to the wet bar and poured himself a glass of brandy. In almost slow motion he replaced the decanter stopper, then picked up the glass and unconsciously swirled it beneath his nose. Instantly the vibrant, pungent aroma of the amber liquid pierced his nostrils, sending a rush of life back into him.

I'm doing this for you. You'll understand later.

Surrounded by darkness, he turned around and stared up at the illuminated upstairs. He took a slow easy sip of the brandy, feeling the heated lava burn down his throat. After another halfhearted sip he walked over to the sofa and sat down, holding the glass up to stare into the cracked and fractured hues of the amber liquid reflecting the gas-fired logs.

His life was just as fractured as the crystal goblet he held. He relaxed back on the sofa, letting his neck arch to stare up at the high ceiling above. The evening played out in his mind like a slow-moving picture show. For obvious reasons his father had chosen to turn a simple family dinner into a business opportunity. It was apparent that his whole evening was just an excuse to reintroduce him to George and to hopefully stir interest in Shauna. Neither worked, to his father's chagrin.

Jackson smiled.

His father hadn't expected him to bring Samantha. And she was too good to be true, taking him completely by surprise. As a matter of fact, she'd taken everyone by surprise. Seeing Eric's face when he walked in and saw her was worth the evening's annoyance. Jackson glanced up at the second floor again.

Samantha and Eric had talked privately on the terrace for some time before he interrupted them. He wondered what they'd talked about. He loosened his tie and took another sip of brandy as a tiny sliver of suspicion crept through. Just as he raised his glass to take another sip, car lights beaming through the front window caught his attention.

Curious as to who would be visiting this late, he placed his drink on the coffee table and went to open the door. As soon as he opened it, Shauna turned around.

"Hi," she said, smiling. "I didn't think you were at home yet." He glanced behind her seeing that she'd parked right next to him. She licked her ruby-red lips as she tossed her long auburn hair over her shoulder nervously.

"Shauna, what are you doing here? It's late."

"I could say that I was doing some shopping at a boutique near here and thought I'd stop by to say hello, but we'd both know that would be a lie."

"Shauna, this really isn't a—"

"Look, before you say anything about tonight, I know things were messed up before and we…" She paused and looked around, then behind him into the house. "May I come in at least?"

"Uh, sure," Jackson said, stepping aside. A sweet whisper of perfume drifted behind her as she passed. Jackson closed the door and followed her.

She walked through the foyer, catching a brief glance at her passing image in the large gilded mirror. She smiled, satisfied with the results. She'd changed clothes and it had taken her an hour to choose the perfect outfit. Something that looked casual enough to be elegant, and elegant enough to be casual. Her navy blue silk suit with matching stiletto sandals and purse was the perfect choice.

Impeccably cut and tailored, the silk designer suit fit her body perfectly. The skirt was short, showing her long legs, and the jacket was cut low, exposing her bountiful surgically enhanced overflow. Blue was Jackson's favorite color, and with her red hair and golden-blond highlights she was irresistible.

She walked into the living room and stopped, looking around. It had been a long time, but it was just as she remembered. Jackson stood waiting for her to continue. When she didn't, he moved closer. "Shauna?"

She took a deep breath and turned to face him. "Jackson, all I'm saying is that I know things weren't real great between us. I know our fathers wanted us to be together and I tried, but… Look, maybe some of that was my fault. I wasn't ready. But I've changed, things are different."

"Shauna, that was a long time ago. It's late and we—"

"No, wait, before you say anything, hear me out. I want you in my life, Jackson," she said, walking to stand in front of him. She reached up and fingered the loose tie still open at his neck. "Whatever or whoever you have going on right now doesn't matter. The only thing that matters is that I want you back. We could be good together. And when our fathers combine the companies, it will be ours."

"Shauna, this isn't gonna happen."

"What isn't?" she asked, unbuttoning her jacket and opening it to expose the fact that she wasn't wearing a bra and her gainful endowment nearly overflowed. She looked up into his eyes, seeing that he hadn't looked at her offered attributes but was instead focused on her eyes. "All I'm saying is that I miss you and after this evening, I know that you've missed me, too. The feelings are still there, Jackson. I saw the love in your eyes. You want me. Here I am. We could go right back to what we had before."

She tipped up to kiss him. Then as he leaned his head back she realized they weren't alone. She stopped and glared over his shoulder at Samantha standing in the doorway smiling. Jackson turned to see what caught her attention.

"Samantha," Jackson said.

"I'm sorry, I didn't realize you had company," Samantha said standing in the doorway like a deer in oncoming headlights.

Shauna's eyes burned with fire and surprise. "Samantha, I didn't realize you'd be here."

An awkward silence permeated the room as Shauna casually walked back over to the sofa and sat down, obviously expecting Samantha to leave the room. "If you'll excuse me," Samantha said as she turned and went back upstairs.

Shauna watched as Samantha climbed the stairs to the second floor. "Jackson, I'd like a drink please. Tequila."

"Aren't you still doing the program?" he asked.

She shot a hard stare. "I don't need that anymore." Seeing that Jackson hadn't moved, she walked over and poured herself a tall drink. She took a sip, then turned back to him. "So, she lives here now, this friend of your family?"

"For the moment," Jackson said, moving and handing her her purse from the table.

"If she's such a friend of the family, why isn't she staying with your sister? That would make more sense, wouldn't it?" Jackson didn't answer. "Or maybe she's just a friend of yours. What exactly do you know about her? I mean, she just shows up out of nowhere and attaches herself to your life. She says she's a friend of your mother's. What exactly does that even mean? For all you know, she could be—"

"I'm sure you didn't drive all the way over here just to get involved in my personal life and things that don't concern you. What I do and whom I see doesn't concern you."

"Jackson, I'm only trying to look out for you."

"Don't," he said firmly, ending any further discussion.

"Now, if you don't mind, it's late. And I'm right in the middle of something important."

Having been put mildly in her place Shauna huffed and slammed the drink on the coffee table, spilling it. "Fine," she sulked, buttoning her jacket, then crossing her arms over her chest. "I suppose this something important has something to do with Samantha." Jackson didn't answer. "If you want me to leave just say so," she said.

"Good night Shauna," Jackson said.

"Fine," Shauna snapped again as she snatched her purse from his hands angrily, stormed to the foyer and slammed out the front door.

Samantha leaned back on the other side of the closed bedroom door. A few minutes later she heard the front door slam. Going back downstairs had been a mistake.

She walked over and sat on the side of the bed. She was so far in over her head that drowning would be a welcome relief. She stood up and paced the floor a few times, wondering what to do next. Her thoughts scattered in every direction. What if she got caught, what if she couldn't do it, what if…? She sat on the side of the bed again and grabbed her cell phone from her purse. She needed answers and only one person could give them to her.

To her surprise, as soon as she picked up it, it began vibrating. She looked at the display and opened it quickly.

"Jefferson?"

"Sammy, are you okay?" he asked, hearing the stress in her voice. "I got your messages," he said. "Sorry I couldn't get back to you sooner."

"I can't do this blind," she said in a near panic.

"Slow down," he said patiently. "Tell me what happened."

"I need answers, Jefferson," she said. "And don't give me that *I don't want you any more involved than you have to be* logic. I don't buy it. I'm already involved, so it's too late for that. I want to know everything. Who exactly is Percival Lincoln and what does he really want?"

Jefferson sighed heavily. He'd hoped to avoid all this. Samantha was the only good thing in his life and dragging her into the middle of this situation was a mistake, but it was too late now. "Technically, Inspector Percival Lincoln is a retired fraud squad detective."

"So he's legit?"

"Yes, but as I said, he's retired and it seems like he's trying to pull his own con game. Now he's a personal consultant, primarily for George Cooperman. But the real truth is as a cop he has been after me for years. He helped put Dad away years ago and has been obsessed with our family ever since."

"What does he want?"

"He wants me."

"But you're retired," she said.

"He doesn't think so. And he'd like nothing better than to be the one to bring me in. You see, my retiring kind of messes up that whole conquering-hero, never-failed scenario."

"But why now?" she asked.

"Your friend Eric did a con in New York and used my name. Lincoln got wind of it and caught him, thinking that it was me. Now he's using you, Jackson and Eric to get to me. Plus, he has a thing on the side."

"So it doesn't matter who gets hurt in the process as long as he gets you."

"Pretty much," Jefferson said.

"He's going to just keep coming after you, isn't he? Your leaving the life means nothing."

"No, not much. Some people would rather I just keep doing it. It's easier that way. I walked away while I was still on top.

No arrests, no convictions, that doesn't sit well for some people. So they kind of make it their life's work to come after me."

"That's just crazy. It sounds like a bad remake of *Les Misérables* with Jean Valjean and Inspector Javert."

"Life is crazy, you know that. But make no mistake, Samantha, Lincoln is for real. He's cunning and deceptive and he's a brilliant strategist. He'll back you into a corner to get what he wants."

"So this changes everything."

"Not at all. His being here was predictable."

"What do you mean? He's after you now?"

"It's public record that he caught Eric Hamilton just after he left New York. He recruited him to work this con with the promise of going free and keeping whatever he gets. All he wants is me, but he won't be able to resist putting Eric away, too, and anyone else," he said slowly.

"That means me, too, right?" she asked, shuddering.

"No, never. I won't let that happen, ever."

"But it's not up to you, is it?" she said. "Is it?"

"Samantha…" Jefferson began to reassure her.

"They're working together and he's going to double-cross Eric."

"More than likely."

"Where exactly do I fit into all this?"

"Eric apparently told him about you, so he's used the opportunity to come after me. He knows I'd never walk away and leave you out there alone."

"He expected you to help me, didn't he?"

"Yes. He planned on it."

"And here you are, just as he planned."

"Yep."

"He's waiting for you, to arrest you, right?"

"I suspect that he's going to pull me in as working with Eric on this con with Marcus Daley."

"That can't happen."

"It won't."

"What about Jackson? Lincoln said that his mother—"

"Paula worked with Dad."

"So it's true. She took the cash and ran out, leaving us broke. All those years Mom struggled to raise me when Dad walked out on us and went back to the life."

"Sammy, it was more complicated. We'll talk when I see you."

"No, now, tell me now."

Jefferson sighed heavily. "Okay, as I said, it was more complicated."

"How? He left me, you both did."

"I never left you, Sammy, and neither did Dad. I was always by your side just like Dad. He was—"

"Don't talk to me about him. There's no defense for what he did. He walked out on us and left us with nothing."

"There was money. Your mother just didn't want to touch it. Dad had an account for her, but she never went near it. He told me about it. So the money that Rachel took was her money. She earned it, it was hers."

"I don't understand. He walked out on us, I remember. He left us, he left me."

"Sammy, he didn't leave willingly. He didn't want to go, he had to."

She stoned her emotions. For so long, she'd wanted to believe that it was all a mistake, that her father had always loved her. "So why did he leave?"

Jefferson paused. "Your mother asked him to."

"That's ridiculous, she'd never do that, she loved him too much."

"But she loved you just as much."

"What?"

"When you were ten she found out that Dad used you in one of his cons. I'm sure you don't remember. It was all just a game to you, but when your mom found out, she was furious. She divorced Dad and made him promise never to contact either one of you again."

"What?" she said, totally stunned by the confession.

"He went back into the life. That's when Lincoln caught him. Dad made me promise never to tell you why he left. He didn't want you angry with your mom and coming to him. He knew this life was wrong and he already had one child in the game. He didn't want you there, too. He was protecting you and so was your mother."

Samantha started crying. As far back as she could remember she'd loved and hated her father for walking out and leaving them. Now to learn that it was all because he was protecting her…

"Samantha," Jefferson said softly. She didn't answer. "Samantha," he repeated.

"I can't believe this," she sobbed. "It was all my fault. I told Mom what we did that day, how we played the game with the man and his wife. I thought she'd be proud of me."

"It wasn't your fault, lollipop. You didn't know. We were all just protecting you."

Jefferson went silent for a moment. "Samantha Lee," he began, using the rarity of her full name. "I never expected any of this to happen, for you to get involved. I promised Dad that I would never allow you near any of this, but I needed someone I could trust and someone who knew how to get into Cooperman's computer."

"So that's the whole job. What's in the computer?"

"Files to help Rachel and Grant."

"I should have known, family is forever. You needed to help Rachel and Grant and getting Cooperman can do it."

"Can you still do this?" he asked.

"Yes, and I'll make you proud."

"I know you will. Did you get everything you need?"

"I have a bit more to work to do," she said, "but I'll be ready when the time comes."

"Good. I'll check on you in the morning. Till then relax and enjoy the night. It's almost over."

Closing the phone, she hung up. The tears, still moist on her face, reminded her of everything she'd ever hoped for. Family is forever. Everyone had protected her and now it was time for her to give back. Putting her drama with Eric aside, she dried her tears and collected herself, focusing on what she needed to do, protect Jefferson from Lincoln and protect Jackson from Cooperman. Their futures rested on her and she wasn't about to fail them.

Chapter 15

Ten minutes later she went back downstairs, not at all surprised to see Jackson waiting for her. She saw that he was sitting on the sofa in the living room with a glass, just staring into the fireplace. Her heart pounded with each step she took. She came down slowly, holding on to the banister with each descending step. He looked up at her approach. Looking around, she walked over to the sofa.

"She's gone," he assured her.

"I didn't mean to interrupt."

"Don't worry about it."

"I get the distinct feeling that she doesn't care for me much," she said sarcastically.

"Shauna doesn't care for a lot of people, least of all herself. Would you like some brandy?" he offered.

"No, thank you," she said, then sat down on the other end

of the sofa and curled up, tucking her feet beneath her. "Jackson, make no mistake. When this is over I am leaving."

He nodded once with a knowing smile that seemed to suggest differently.

"And us, together," she said, "this attraction, isn't going to change that. We're attracted to each other, yes, we made love, yes, but this is business, too. Each of us has something to lose and I don't intend to let that happen."

He nodded again. "What did Eric say?"

"He told me what he planned to do."

"Just like that?" he asked.

"Eric has an ego equal only to the size of his paranoia. Push the right buttons and he'll tell you everything."

"And you pushed the right buttons?"

"Yes. As I said, he's paranoid, so I fed the paranoia."

Jackson looked at her as if for the first time. He realized that she had skills beyond what even he had imagined. She apparently knew what she was doing. Getting information from Eric was the last thing he had expected. But she had done it. "What's his plan?"

She outlined exactly what Eric had said, detailing each move. He asked questions and she answered to the best of her knowledge. "Sounds too easy," he finally said.

"Most cons are. With easy you never see it coming."

"How can he guarantee that George will keep his end of the bargain?"

"That's the sad part. He actually thinks that he's got it all figured out. But he's forgotten one very important part."

"What's that?"

"Greed."

"What?"

"All three men want something out of this. Eric wants the money and probably the credibility of pulling off this con.

Cooperman is greedy, he wants it all. He's obviously not going to stop at just getting a piece of the company, he's gonna want it all. Everything in his past points to that."

"And Lincoln, what does he want?"

"I don't know," she lied, deciding not to tell him about her conversation with Jefferson. "But it certainly isn't the justice he claims. He's definitely a wild card in all this."

"They'll all double-cross each other?" Jackson said.

She nodded. "More than likely. Awkward and clumsy gets you caught. The perfect con has two things—a contingency plan and a clean exit. Eric doesn't think that far ahead. Sometimes it's not all about the score."

"Because everybody has an angle to work," Jackson said. "That sounds so cynical."

"But true."

"How exactly does it happen, a con I mean?"

"A mark is chosen, a seemingly respectable businessman with deep pockets, someone easily susceptible to greed. He's lured into thinking that he's getting something for nothing. Tempted, he usually take the bait. The con man earns trust with a small test of faith, a convincer, a small bit of cash to prove that whatever is failsafe. Then a bigger test is played, and they lose. Afterward there's the blow off and the con walks away."

"What about the mark, when he goes to the police?"

"It's called beefed. And no, seldom do marks talk. Embarrassment, ego, whatever, no one wants to admit they've been greedy and conned no matter how much is involved. It's all about credibility. You can't complain to the police that you gave someone money, particularly if sometimes that money shouldn't even exist."

"And your father and brother were good."

"They were more into the high-end long cons, particularly

my brother. But yes, they were good, very good. They weren't called con artists for no reason. It's like an art form. You have to think on your feet while persuading in such a way as to give the illusion that it isn't your idea.

"My brother was the ultimate chameleon. His setups were always precise, he researched and covered all the angles, his game was clever and he always walked away clean with no one having the slightest clue that they were even conned."

"That sounds so impossible."

"He's the perfect strategist."

"Except the last time," Jackson said. "You don't believe Lincoln, do you, about your brother not retiring?"

"No."

"Then where is he?"

"Let's just say that the cards haven't all been played just yet," she said, smiling happily.

Jackson shook his head. "You're not a poker player, are you?"

"Actually I am, and a very good poker player at that. I learned from the best."

"You obviously don't bluff well, I can see right through you."

"We're not paying poker, are we?"

Jackson smiled. "Dealer's choice?"

"You're on."

He got up and went into the family room off the kitchen and returned with two decks of cards.

"Two decks?" she questioned, seeing him open the two separate packages.

"To make it more interesting, of course," he said.

"Of course."

He dropped the empty packages and jokers on the far side of the table, then shuffled the cards as he sat down. He continued thoroughly shuffling the decks. When he was satisfied he placed the decks on the coffee table for her to cut. Brand new and slippery, cards were awkwardly dropping off the table and flying into the air.

"Oops, sorry," she said. He helped her gather and collect the mess. "What are we playing, Texas hold 'em, five card stud, draw…?" she asked, completing the cut.

"How about strip?" he asked, confidently smiling.

"I think you have an unfair advantage, you have more clothes on."

"I'll be happy to even the playing field."

"No, I'll take my chances," she said nicely.

He dealt out five cards and the game began. She lost the first hand and removed a high-heel shoe. She lost the second game and the other shoe. By the third game Jackson was feeling extremely confident. He dealt himself a pair of jacks and a high ten. Eagerly anticipating Samantha's disrobement he placed his cards down on the table with a smug smile.

She placed her cards down. She had two queens and a jack.

He removed his jacket.

Seven hands later she'd collected both shoes, both socks, shirt, belt and pants. "You look chilly," she said, smiling innocently as he dealt again.

"Don't try to distract me. What do you have?"

Still fully dressed, she laid down her third full house in a row. Her pleasant smile drew his gasp.

"That's impossible," he said, putting his small pair down on the table. "I deal and you get three full-house hands in a row, that's impossible."

"Are you accusing me of cheating at cards just to see you naked?"

Jackson smiled. "The thought had crossed my mind."

She smiled innocently. "Shorts, please."

He stood up, grabbed a throw pillow from the sofa and positioned it securely in front of himself as he pulled down and
removed his shorts.

"You can't be embarrassed. It's not like I've never seen you
naked before."

He sat down and shuffled the cards, making sure that they
could not be tampered with. He set them down in front of her
and waited for her inevitably clumsy cut. But this time her cut
was perfect. It was too perfect. With one hand she cut the cards
while chuckling at his stunned expression. He was astonished. She'd been playing him from the beginning.

"Nice tie," she said, indicating that she intended to have
his tie on the next hand.

The hand played out. He won. Knowing that she'd manipulated the outcome of each hand, he assumed that she'd lost
on purpose. Samantha stood up and slipped her hands beneath
her evening dress and removed her lace panties, adding them
to the pile of clothes already on the floor.

The game had taken a seductive slant.

"You deal this time," he said, sliding the cards over to her.

She picked them up and began a recitation of shuffling and
hand manipulations that would have amazed the kings of Las
Vegas. Jackson sat back, astonished by her skill. "Winner take
all," she said as she dealt. He nodded his agreement. As each
card was dispersed, their eyes stayed focused on each other.
She finished dealing and set the pile down between them.

He picked up his cards, assessed them and pulled two out
for replacements. With one finger she slid two cards from the
top of the deck across the table to him. He picked them up
and placed them in his hand.

"No cards for you?" he asked.

"I'll play what I have."

Knowing that she must have dealt herself a winning hand,

he placed his cards facedown on the table and stood up reaching out to her. She took his hand and stood in front of him, then took his protruding pillow and tossed it back onto the sofa. The result of their poker game on his body was evident.

"I know another game," he said as his mouth came to hers, kissing her completely and feeling her return embrace. She wrapped her arms around his body, feeling his firm muscles. She rested her hands on his buttocks, and his kiss deepened, devouring her as his tongue intertwined with hers.

With ease he released the one hindrance between them, letting her evening dress fall to the Persian carpet on the hardwood floors. They stood naked and open, each giving the other what they needed.

He kissed her neck and shoulders, then trailed kisses down to her breasts. Pert and taut, they beckoned to him and he greedily captured each, one with his hand and the other with his mouth. As he suckled, his fingers tweaked the small nipple to a pout. She gasped and his other hand held her rear and pressed her to his face.

As he knelt down before her, his hands came up to her waist adoringly. He held her still as he closed his eyes and rested the side of his face on the flat of her stomach. She reached down to caress him. In that place, in that position, they stayed for a time.

"I can't let you go," he whispered.

"You have to," she said, looking down while stroking the tips of his earlobes. He looked up at her. "But we have tonight."

He shook his head. "Not good enough."

"It's all we have." She sat down on the sofa, pulling him toward her. They kissed, promising a sweet surrender. "Do you have any…"

"Yes, upstairs in my bedroom." He stood and took her hand. Together they walked up to the second floor. She turned and stopped at the guest bedroom as he continued to the master bedroom. He turned, puzzled. "Would you like to join me in the master bedroom?" he asked.

"No," she said. Jackson looked stunned as she smiled. "Would you like to join me in the guest bedroom?"

He smiled, nodding. "I'll be right there," he promised.

Samantha opened the guest-bedroom doors and walked over to the bed. She pulled the covers back and eased between the cool sheets. Her naked body quivered more from anticipation of Jackson's arrival than the slight chill of the cotton. She closed her eyes and laid her head back, hoping to remember every second of this evening.

Moments later, Jackson came in. She opened her eyes. He smiled and the butterflies in her stomach danced a new dance. The sight of his naked body thrilled her. Every inch of him was divine, he was simply magnificent.

His body was artistically chiseled as every muscle defined strength and power. Tight abs rippled at his stomach as cast-iron biceps and triceps encircled his arms. He held a bottle of champagne and two glasses in one hand and several condoms in the other. A quick shiver sped through her again as an open smile welcomed him.

Jackson stopped and just stood there looking at her. Seeing her lying in the bed waiting for him felt so right. There was no way he intended to let her walk out of his life, not now, not ever. "You look so beautiful lying there like that," he said.

She chuckled. "Hey, I'm lying here butt naked. You don't have to flatter me, I'm pretty much a sure thing at this point."

Jackson laughed. "What am I going to do with you?"

"I have a few ideas," she joked.

"Do you?" he asked playfully. She nodded. Jackson licked his lips. He knew that he wanted this, he wanted her, every night for the rest of his life. "Do you have any idea what you do to me, Samantha Lee Taylor?"

She held out her hand to him. "Come here, tell me," she whispered.

Jackson walked over, took her hand and sat down on the side of the bed, tossing the condoms beside them.

He stroked her face lovingly, gently, with the barest touch of adoring affection. "When we made love the first time…" he began.

"In bungalow number twelve," she interrupted.

He nodded. "It was a fantasy."

She nodded. "That's what we said."

"We were wrong, there was nothing fantasy about it. It was real, just like it's real now."

"Jackson…"

"We connected, Samantha, I know it and you know it."

"Jackson…"

"And here we are again."

"Yes, here we are again," she repeated, pulling the covers back for him. He slid beneath the sheets beside her. She cuddled in his arms, holding him, not wanting to ever let go. His body instantly folded around her. She closed her eyes tight and tried to burn the memory of this moment into her mind, the sight, the smell, the taste, the feel and the sounds.

"I dream of having you in my arms like this."

She smiled happily. "I like the sound of that."

"It's true."

"I know," she whispered as she molded her body to his even more, then kissed and nibbled the underside of his neck. Hearing a low rumbled groan from his throat, she raked her teeth at the same spot, then kissed it. She looked up and saw his eyes close as he licked his lips and exhaled hard. The sensation struck a nerve, so she continued masterfully.

Submissively, he yielded to her whim, giving her full control to play his body as she desired. The sensation was exhilarating for both of them, as she desired all of him and she played all of him. Touching his body thrilled her. Controlling his body thrilled her more. Moments later she sat up, tossing the covers back, exposing all of him to her continued play.

She eased up to sit on top of him, straddling his hips without connecting their bodies, and prepared to play some more. She felt his hands as he held her thighs when she rested her palms on his chest for balance. He began rubbing her thighs and hips and waist and shoulders, massaging and caressing her. She leaned over to kiss him but was taken by surprise as he grasped her hips and arched her higher so that her breasts gently touched the tips of his lips.

He opened his mouth, welcoming the offered nipple. Kissing, licking and sucking, he enjoyed the hovering delight. Samantha moaned, then gasped and started to move back but he held her in place. To equal the pleasure he grasped the other nipple and executed a second mind-blowing assault.

Perked and primed, he teased her as she looked on, watching his tongue flatten over her nipple to lick her like a lollipop, then gently circle and draw her into the warmth of his mouth. With fervor and vigor he suckled every delicious inch of her breasts as she watched. The sight and unexpected thrill took her breath away.

Then in an instant he sat up, placing her squarely on his lap. She wrapped her arms around his neck, gathering him as he edged her closer by wrapping his arms around her waist and hips. Face-to-face, they kissed and caressed with unyielding hunger.

Reaching over, she grabbed a condom packet from where he'd tossed them on the bed earlier. She opened one and pulled it out, then with the finesse of a seductress covered him.

Then she arched up again and slowly came down onto his hardness, long, thick and firm. She moaned as he filled her completely. She inhaled quickly, sizzling as her nails bit into his shoulders and the sweet sensation of engulfing him burned thick and hot inside her. She arched her hips up, releasing him. Then holding tight, she eased back down. Repeating the formula again and again, in and out, she filled the refilled. Up and down, back and forth she led them closer and closer to the pinnacle of pleasure.

He kissed hard and long, devouring her with unrestrained passion, ravaging her mouth, her neck, her shoulder, then captured her offered breasts again. Near her climax she leaned and arched her body back, feeling her release coming. Sitting up straight she rocked her hips on top of him as his hands covered her breasts and his thumbs tantalized and teased her nipples.

The pace quickened and the inundated ravaging, ceaseless in its fervor, intensified. The swell of passion escalated as she rocked her hips back and forth on top of him, each time teasing the bud of her pleasure and stoking his hunger. He lifted her hips, aiding the fierceness and power of each thrust. Passion surged in near-abandoned zeal. Locked together their bodies molded and their rapture soared. Then in a crushing, blinding, piercing crest they came as one, each holding on to the other.

She called out to him, and he answered.

Breathless and gasping, she dropped her head to his shoulder as her body contracted and the throbbing spikes of climactic ecstasy took her again and again. She moaned her release as he arched his hips and came again. Then sated, weak and drained, she collapsed against his body. His arms encircled her, holding her tight.

"I'll never let you go," he whispered breathlessly, lying back and taking her with him.

Samantha was too exhausted to argue, so she nodded and closed her eyes until once again they joined and reached the pinnacle of pleasure.

Chapter 16

The next morning, Samantha went for a walk on the beach. The fine white sand sparkled like crystals in the glorious sunrise as huge boulders and jagged rocks dotted the even terrain. She climbed a planted rock and sat high, gazing out at the western horizon. Her thoughts were just as distorted as the view in front of her. Juxtaposed, the ocean belied its true nature. Calm, gentle waves lapped lovingly over the beach as turbulence raged farther out in the distance.

At a mere twenty feet tall, the crashing waves tumbled and churned, troubling the breakers as the early-morning surfers tried desperately to tame the beast with their feeble boards. She watched as they paddled desperately in hopes of catching the wild creature, only to be devoured over and over again by its power.

At what point do you admit defeat and surrender, giving in to the stronger power of a force beyond yourself. Her heart had found its wholeness, and her spirit had been quenched, but to what avail? In the end she would still lose him.

She slid down from her perch and headed north toward a pier in the far distance. Like a protruding javelin, it jutted out into the water awkwardly, breaking the unending line of beach that looked as if it led to nowhere. It seemed appropriate.

As she walked, the peace and serenity of the water's edge eased her thoughts and lulled the vivid memories of the night before. It was just sex, she confirmed to herself silently once more. Just like the last time at the inn, it was merely a physical attraction between two consenting adults, a hormonal release of pheromones through pent-up tension, and just a physical urge manifested through lust. It was just sex.

But it wasn't. And no matter how she tried to deny it, classify it, reclassify it and spin it as anything else, she knew that it wasn't just attraction, tension, lust or sex. It was more, much more. They had connected and forged a bond the first time at the inn, and now, last night, the connection was complete.

Joyfully, a tiny part of her breathed easily; at long last she knew what it felt like to belong, to rest her heart in safe keeping. It was what she had longed to feel her whole life. It was the same joy her mother had felt with her father. And like her mother she would hold strong, the inevitable singe of heartache without reservation or regrets.

All her life she had been neither here nor there, neither in nor out, always looking, searching to belong somewhere to someone. But now, finding her heart meant losing it, as well.

They had made love, a feeling deeper and stronger than the simplest act of lustful sex. Indeed, semantics to some but to her the difference between having sex and making love was the sympatico feeling and an unwavering connection that she knew she felt and sensed Jackson felt, as well. No matter how she justified it, she came up with the same end result—it was already too late. She was in love with Jackson.

The transcendent feeling of her mindless walk had led her two miles down the beach to the pier she and Jackson had visited the day before. The same café where they'd sat and eaten lunch was open for breakfast. She got in line and purchased piping-hot chocolate croissants and beignets. Carrying them in a vented bakery box tied with string, she headed back to Jackson's beach house, hopeful of finding pleasure for as long as she could.

A quarter mile from his home her cell phone rang. She looked at the phone number. She answered instantly. "Hello."

"Good morning. You okay?" he asked as soon as she picked up.

"No, yes, I have no idea," Samantha answered, welcoming a familiar voice.

Jefferson chuckled. "That means you're doing a great job. We didn't talk about the party last night. How was your evening?"

"You knew about Marcus's private little birthday party, didn't you?"

"It's all in the research, lollipop," Jefferson said. "Marcus has a family thing every year, although I didn't expect the guest list to be so extensive. I assume you met Cooperman."

"Yes, I did."

"Any thoughts to substantiate?" Jefferson asked.

"He's a joke and basically an overpompous, self-absorbed jerk with a touch of mysophobia and OCD."

"Fear of germs and an obsessive-compulsive disorder, that's an interesting mix. I'd heard that, of course, but couldn't get verification."

"Consider it verified. Also, he's a dirty old man."

"Yeah, he has a thing for young women. As a matter of fact, Darla, his child bride du jour, is five years younger than his daughter."

"Shauna, I met her, too, she's a real delight."

"Don't underestimate her. Granted, she's in and out of rehab so much they've installed a swing door just for her, but she also has a thing with Jackson Daley," Jefferson said.

Samantha smiled. "Had a thing, past tense. I know. Eric was also there."

"And?" Jefferson asked.

"I handled it. And in typical Eric fashion, he told me everything."

"Good. Then you know what to do?"

"Yes, Cooperman already propositioned me."

"No doubt."

"I'm meeting him this afternoon in his office."

"That'll be perfect. Do you have everything you need?"

"Yes, I'm ready," she said, slightly nervous.

"Sammy, don't worry, you'll do fine. It's just a computer job. I wouldn't have asked you to do this if it wasn't important and if I didn't think you could pull it off, you know that. You're the only one I trust to do this."

"I know and I won't let you down. I'll get what you need."

"Thank you," he said, then heard the hesitation in the silence. "What?" Jefferson asked.

Samantha sighed heavily without answering him.

"Jackson?" he asked, already knowing the answer.

"I don't know what to do about him."

"Samantha, you're not conning him. You're helping him and you're saving his company."

"He's not going to see it that way. When this is over he'll be furious that I lied to him from the beginning."

"Again, Sammy, you're not conning him for selfish gain. This is all to help him. He'll see that. Trust me."

"Okay," she said. "I will."

"I'll see you later."

"'Bye," she closed the phone and put it in her pocket. She looked around. The privacy of the beach was perfect. It was still early and few people were out—just a few surfers and joggers—but the majority of the area was deserted.

She thought about what Jefferson had said. He had faith in her and was depending on her to finish this and she was definitely going to. Everyone had been protecting her. Now it was her chance to protect her family.

Assured of her resolve, she continued walking back toward the beach house. Then about fifty feet away she stopped as a familiar figure dashed out from between the buildings headed in her direction. He was dressed in a muted baby-blue sweat suit and a baseball cap pulled low over his eyes; Samantha instantly knew it was Eric. No one else would dare wear something like that.

"Damn, girl, I been running up and down this beach for the last two hours." Eric's breathless uttering didn't faze her. He slowed, then stopped running and leaned over to place his hands on his knees and catch his breath. She continued walking at her pace. As an automatic reflex he placed two fingers on his neck to gauge his heart rate. "Whoa, girl, wait up," he said, hurrying to catch up with her again as she continued walking. "Look, we need to talk," he said, rasping clumsily between each word.

She didn't answer.

He pulled out the ever-present pack of Newport cigarettes, hit it a few times against his hand, easing out a slim tobacco stick. He pulled out matches, lit the cigarette, then took a deep breath and coughed.

The absurdity of a health nut smoking two packs of cigarettes a day was completely lost on him. He walked alongside, puffing and coughing equally from the short jog and the smoke.

"You know, I forgot how beautiful you are. I couldn't take

my eyes off you last night," he continued as he looked her up and down. The sight of her now, dressed in the plunging bikini top and low-cut shorts sent an instant sexual charge through his body as his eyes took particular note of the chained waist belt dangling free from her hips. His attention finally drifted upward to her profile. "You know, I was thinking about it last night after you left. We should get together, you know, clean slate and all. You know I missed you, still do, truth be told. We had some good times, didn't we?"

"Un-huh, the last time was the best," she said facetiously.

"You need to get over that," he said, still following her step for step.

She stopped. "Oh, get over it," she said as if a lightbulb had just turned on over her head. "You mean, get over it. So exactly what are you suggesting I get over? Get over not having a normal life? Get over people coming after me? Get over looking over my shoulder for the last four months? Exactly what part am I supposed to get over?"

"Hey, that wasn't all me, some of that might have been you and you know your brother."

"Are you kidding?"

"Look, all I'm saying is don't mess this up for me," he warned.

"You are so far out of your league," she said, shaking her head pitifully. "You have no idea what's really going on, do you?" The paranoid, confused expression on his face made her chuckle. "Like I said, I'm the last person you need to worry about." She turned to walk away.

"Come on," he said, holding her arm securely, keeping her beside him. "We were good together," he said wishfully. "You know that I still love you." He leaned in closer.

"Oh, please, Eric, that boat has so sailed and sunk. What do you want?"

Seeing that he was getting nowhere with his available

charm and current course, he changed tactics. "To get our business straight."

"We don't have any business." She glared at him evenly.

"So what did you mean when you said that I needed to worry about someone else?"

"Just what I said, you don't need to be concerned about me."

"Like who? Who exactly are you talking about?"

"Ask your partner."

"What does he have to do with any of this?" She didn't answer. "Look, I can dump him and we can walk away from this with at least ten million dollars, enough for a new life together. The down payment alone can set us up for life. And I'm handling the whole thing, he trusts me."

"But do you trust him?"

Eric's face shadowed instantly. "You mean a double cross?" he asked with obvious concern.

"Look out for number one, remember?"

"Yeah, I remember," he said. "So what's up with you and homeboy? Got a taste for some rich blue blood now?" Eric motioned to Jackson's house. He leaned back and glared at her. "Does he know about your father and your brother and the family business?"

"You are so pathetic," she answered.

He smiled menacingly, presuming he had the upper hand. "Fine, whatever, just don't interfere with me and I won't interfere with you. And whoever you have working with you…"

She smiled, causing him to reconsider his last thought. "Sammy," he said, using her nickname as he grabbed hold of her arm and held firm, "you know how I feel about you, I still love you." He stepped closer, still thinking that emotion might soften her determination.

She winched back as if disgusted by the sight of him. She

twisted her arm back, pulling his in an unnatural position, forcing him to crumple to his knees and release her.

"Remember what I said—don't interfere with me," he warned, extinguishing the spent cigarette butt in the white sand as he stood up again.

She looked down at the remains, then at his silly smile. "Remember what I said. I'm not the person you need to worry about." His face darkened again. She turned her back, smiling, happier than she had a right to be. Suddenly, she realized that she didn't need to get revenge on Eric. He was already too far gone in his own world. Nothing she could do could hurt him any more than his self-deluded ego and panicked paranoia. She chuckled. The joke was on him and he didn't even know it.

Jackson woke up alone. The sheets, long cooled, were neatly smoothed out beside him. He sat up slowly, looked around the room, hazily realizing that he was still in the guest bedroom. He lay back contently, closing his eyes and smiling. The scent of her perfume lingered on the sheets and instantly brought back sweet memories of their night together.

Like glittering sparks on diamonds, they shone with the resilience of a long-awaited fantasy come true. Samantha had been amazing. And together they had experienced a night of passion and ecstasy beyond his wildest imagination. They had talked and laughed and made love and finally fallen asleep in each other's arms.

As the blissful recollections faded, Jackson stirred once again, this time realizing that Samantha hadn't just gone to the bathroom or to get a quick bite to eat. He sat up more purposefully this time as the awareness occurred to him, she was gone. His first thought was of their last time together. She'd left him at the inn the same way, that time intending not to see him again.

He got up quickly and looked around. Calling out to her, he discovered she wasn't in the guest bedroom, on the second floor or in the house. He went back upstairs, grabbed a quick shower, dressed and went back downstairs. As soon as he entered the kitchen a second time he noticed that the sliding glass door was unlocked and the gate at the top of the steps leading down to the beach was slightly open.

He walked out on the deck and looked around. The sky was overcast, with gentle rays of morning sun beaming against the dust of dawn as it faded beyond the horizon. A warm breeze blew readily across the sand, stirring the last remnants of the night before. The beach was nearly empty, only a few people out this time of morning. Looking down at the beach and across to the water's edge, he spotted her immediately and was instantly aroused by the sight.

She was dressed in low-cropped-cut shorts that exposed the flat firmness of her stomach and the sweetheart roundness of her rear. The scant bikini top covering her in only two strategic places sent blood flowing straight to his groin, stirring renewed passion inside him. He smiled, thinking of the numerous things he could do as memories of their intimacy just hours earlier still burned hot.

Sexually they were perfection. He yearned for her in ways he never knew possible, and the intensity of his hunger seemed unquenchable. The slightest touch of her hand or a brief glance from her sent his body surging. The simple lustful fantasy that they'd started days ago had transformed into something stronger, and the fierce power of the renewed desire scared him. She had gotten to him and he had willfully opened his heart to her.

The physical was mind blowing, yes, to be sure, but the woman behind the body was more than he had ever hoped to find. She was smart and savvy, with an intoxicating mix of brains and sensuality that kept him wanting more.

With a box in one hand and sandals in the other she danced playfully against the water's edge. Just as Jackson moved to join her he watched as a man came running up to her, turning her attention to him.

Concern hit him but caution stilled him.

The man's back was to him, so his identity wasn't clear, but he could see the hardened glare in her eyes.

He wasn't sure what he was witnessing but it was obvious that they weren't strangers. Their body language showed an intimate familiarity as they pulled close in what looked like a conspirators' promise. The stray shreds of doubt that had played with Jackson from time to time solidified into real apprehension. The idea that something else was going on sent a spike into his heart.

He knew that Samantha was the consummate artist, showing only what she wanted him to see and know and nothing more. But now, somehow more real, the doubts resurfaced as he watched. The stranger talked and she apparently listened. When she began to walk away, the man reached out and grabbed her arm, drawing her back against his body. Jackson tensed, unconsciously making a move toward the gate leading to the steps down to the beach, then to her.

As he opened the gate he watched as she jerked back and twisted upward, freeing her arm and pulling him off guard. Nearly falling off balance, the man stumbled back, fell to his knees, then regained control. The simple act gave Jackson the hope of trust. He watched as she stepped back and crossed her arms over her chest, appearing to mentally close off all interest. The man moved in closer. Samantha stood her ground. His gestures widened with added animation, and whatever he was saying gave her pause. With full attention, she listened.

Although Jackson had no idea who the man was, he suspected that it was Eric. Her aloof body language revealed her disinterest, yet she stayed and listened. Jackson grimaced.

The small voice in his head cautioned. There was more to this than he knew.

Finally their conversation seemed to be over.

Samantha backed away slowly, turned and headed back toward the house, her head down, unassumingly distracted. He, the man on the beach, stood staring as she walked away. Then he glanced up, and saw Jackson on the deck for the first time. Their eyes held across the distance as Samantha unknowingly walked between them.

A knowing challenge had been met. The man stood staring a moment longer, then backed up, lighting another cigarette. Tossing the match, he slowly, eventually, turned and walked away. With one glance back he began trotting, then running full speed.

Samantha approached, her head still down, buried in thought. She climbed the wooden steps and opened the top gate stepping onto the deck and seeing Jackson standing there for the first time. Beguiling as usual, she smiled, betraying nothing. He realized at that moment that he was being played.

"Good morning," she said, her voice seductively low, with a sweet-as-sugar innocent expression.

"Good morning," Jackson answered firmly.

Samantha looked him up and down, smiling. "You look great," she said playfully. Always perfectly neat in either a tailored business suit or casual slacks and polo shirt, this morning he was casually unkempt. Faded tight jeans and a gleaming white shirt, completely unbuttoned, with rolled-up sleeves, gave him a daring, debonair look of suave mischief. She liked it.

"So do you," he responded truthfully. She smiled appreciatively. "Where'd you go?" he asked.

"For a walk."

"Anywhere in particular?"

She nodded. "Down to the café on the pier."

"That's quite a walk."

"It wasn't too bad. I picked up some chocolate croissants and powdered beignets. But you're in charge of making coffee. I'm lousy at it. I have been told that I make the worst coffee in the world, somewhere between Ellie Mae Clampett and Lisa Douglas."

"Somehow I doubt that you're incapable of anything."

"You'd be surprised," she said, smiling.

"Would I?" he asked as the fire in his eyes burned.

She looked at him curiously. "Are you okay?" she asked, questioning his aloof manner. "You seem, I don't know, kind of different this morning."

"You think so?" he asked.

She nodded, then placed the stringed box on the glass table and undid the sturdy bow. As she opened the box she inhaled deeply. "Mmm, I think they're still warm," she picked at a piece of chocolate croissant, pulling the soft flaky dough easily apart. She bit into it, then after licking her finger turned and saw him standing there staring at her. "You want some of this?" she offered suggestively.

Jackson's mouth was too dry to answer as the anger of her obvious betrayal seethed to a low boil. He grabbed her waist and drew her hard against his body, connecting intimately through jeans and shorts. He gazed into her eyes. A fathomless stare searched for confirmation of her betrayal, deceit or guilt, but found none.

The smoldering heat between them quickly escalated as the joys of previous encounters pressed hard into their thoughts. He held her there in silent anticipation. Then he kissed her hard and long. Tongues playfully, lustfully, joyfully intertwined and devoured.

He backed her up against the railing and she pressed into him as they stood in the open for all to see, a passion full grown, a desire beyond boldness. Her breasts scarcely covered pressed hard against his bare chest as her arms encircled his neck, holding firm. His hands dropped to her rear, lifting, and she rose up against him as he held her firmly in place. She wrapped her legs around his waist as she tucked herself protectively within the openness of his shirt.

He slipped his hand between their bodies. Her nipples instantly hardened. Within seconds her bikini top fell to the wooden floor as the intimacy of the position intensified.

His kisses hardened as he held her tighter, trying desperately to suffocate the pain in his heart. She held on tight, matching passion with passion, feeling herself being completely swept away by their seduction. He kissed her neck, her shoulder and her chest.

"Are you sure you're okay?" she asked again, breathlessly, through his onslaught of vigorous kisses feeling the strong-willed uninhibited power of his passion.

He didn't respond. With intensity he kissed her mouth again. The consuming need to punish her betrayal forced control. He was hurt and his pride was wounded. How could she betray his trust? The power of his will continued, but behind that the compulsion to love her began to surge.

"Jackson," she stammered. The near-blind excitement of his actions and the relentless onslaught of his passion persisted full force. "Jackson," she repeated louder. "Jackson." The concerned hesitation in her voice finally seeped into him.

Then without warning he stopped, the kisses ended. Breathless, she rested her head on his shoulder as he closed his eyes and looked down. He released her, letting her flow effortlessly down the front of his body. "Jackson, what is it? What's wrong?" she asked.

He opened his eyes, looked at her pink toes, then looked away again, shamed by his actions. He removed his shirt and wrapped it around her, shaking his head as remorse took him. "I'm sorry," he whispered.

She slipped her arms through the sleeves of his shirt and placed her hands on his cheek and smiled. "For what?" she asked, looking up to see his face.

He licked his lips. She tasted like chocolate. Then Samantha, still holding the piece of croissant between her fingers, offered it to him. Jackson opened his mouth and she gently placed it on his tongue. He chewed, savoring the melted thick chocolate and warm doughy treat.

"Who are you exactly, Samantha Lee Taylor?" he asked in a faded whisper.

She looked him straight in the eye and with unwavering love smiled and answered honestly, "For the time being, I'm yours, Jackson, Jackson Daley."

"I like that answer," he said.

"Me, too." She smiled happily. "Are you okay?"

He nodded.

"Are we okay?"

He nodded again.

"Good, you do the coffee thing while I wash up. I'm all sandy from the walk," she quickly kissed his cheek, grabbed the bakery box and hurried inside.

Jackson stood watching her go, then turned back to the ocean view. He looked out at nothing in particular, then held his head low. His actions were unforgivable, he knew that. And had he not exerted restraint... He paused as a sorrowful pain gripped his heart, and the thought made him shudder. What was he doing? Being with Samantha was like playing with fire. He had no idea if or when he'd get burnt.

The phone rang. He walked into the kitchen and grabbed it on the second ring.

"Trust can be a curious thing," the man said.

"Who is this?" Jackson asked.

"Inspector Lincoln," he said.

"What do you want?" Jackson asked, skipping the pleasantries as she stepped back out onto the deck.

"Has Ms. Taylor figured out the code yet?"

"No, I don't think so."

"Perhaps she just hasn't bothered to tell you."

Jackson didn't respond. "At any rate, when you're ready, I'll have Mr. Hamilton's computer available. All you have to do is use the information and get the files you need."

"Yeah," Jackson said.

"I want to caution you. Don't be fooled by Ms. Taylor's air of dainty femininity. She's attractive and seductive indeed—just remember that she is her father's daughter, cunning and calculating. Can the fruit truly fall far from the tree? She will use you as a means to an end. Giving her body to you is all part of the process."

Jackson turned, looking around and realizing that Lincoln had to be near and must have observed their open embrace.

"No need looking around now, Mr. Daley," Lincoln continued. "Her partner is long gone."

"Eric?"

"Who else? But I'm sure that you suspected as much. You watched her talking with him on the beach moments ago, didn't you? Did she perhaps enlighten you, perchance mention their little tête-à-tête, include you in their plans possibly?" He paused, giving Jackson a moment to consider the question. "Of course not," Lincoln finally concluded. "That's because they're playing you for a fool."

"And I'm supposed to trust you?"

"As I said earlier, trust is a curious thing. At times we find ourselves collaborating with the most unlikely of comrades to get what we want."

"And who are you collaborating with?" Jackson asked.

"Justice," Lincoln said simply and hung up.

Jackson placed the phone on the outside table and looked through the sliding glass door. He could see the bakery box sitting on the kitchen table exactly where Samantha had placed it.

He leaned back against the railing. Doubt had begun to creep in again. He knew that he couldn't trust Lincoln, but now he questioned whether or not he could trust Samantha. Seeing her with Eric dissuaded no fears. Eric planned to con his father and help Cooperman take control of his company.

What was Samantha's part? Confuse him, distract him, seduce him? All three had been done efficiently and completely.

Lincoln was right about one thing—trust was a curious thing. He picked up the phone and called his father's office, agreeing to meet. They needed to talk. It was time to clear the air and end this.

Lincoln watched as Jackson walked back into the house. He was sure that he'd planted the seed of doubt and hopefully Eric had made some headway. Jackson looked and sounded furious at seeing Samantha with Eric, that much he was sure.

He placed his binoculars back in the case and waited.

Time and patience had always been his friend. He picked up the bottled water and took a sip, enjoying the cool liquid as it poured down his throat. He looked at his watch. It was almost time.

"Hey, why the hell did you park this far away? I had to, like, climb Mount Everest to get up here," Eric said breathlessly as he approached. He tossed his spent cigarette butt down and leaned over against his knees to catch his breath. This California air was killing him. He couldn't wait to get out of here.

"How did it go?"

Eric walked over to where Lincoln stood and looked down at the million-dollar homes enviously. "Damn, I'm gonna get me one of those, right there on the beach. Man, those houses are tight. Ten million dollars ought to do me up just right. Think I'll hit Hawaii, Fiji, or maybe Tahiti. What do you think, Link, my man?"

"Yeah, I get it, anyplace that ends in the letter *i*. What about the file transfer, didn't you get the majority shares yet?"

"Yep, they were sitting there in the computer first thing this morning. And you know what I was thinking? Yo, I could just print those babies out, sign them and bam, just like that, Daley Communications would be mine, it's that's easy."

Lincoln turned to him menacingly.

Eric smiled. "Yo, Link, man, I was just joking, homes. Can't you take a joke?" Lincoln's expression didn't change. "All right, yeah, whatever, the files with the transfer of shares arrived. As soon as I get my money I'll forward them to your friend."

"Excellent. And what about your meeting on the beach?"

"Yeah, I told her what you said but I don't think she bought me."

"Perhaps you weren't convincing enough."

"Yo, what was I supposed to do? I told her I wanted her back, that I still loved her. It's not my fault she's got a thing for blue blood down there. Bump her. We don't need her anyway. I already have Marcus biting at the bit to get this deal done."

"Separating them is part of the deal."

"Why?"

"Because that's what we were asked to do."

"Why?"

"It doesn't matter why, you just need to do it. You bragged that you were irresistible to her, you said you could handle this."

"I can. Just give me some time."

"We don't have time. This has to be finished soon."

"All right, I'll take care of it. Maybe you should get some young chicky to work on blue blood while I work on her." He looked at his watch. "Yo, it's getting late, I need to jet. I'm meeting Marcus in a few and I still need to get back and change clothes. Today is the big payday." He slapped his hands together and chuckled happily. "Let's go."

Lincoln didn't move.

"Hello," Eric said, waving his hand in front of Lincoln's face, seemingly in hopes of breaking a hypnotic spell. Lincoln grabbed his wrist and for the second time that morning twisted it and sent him to his knees.

"Don't ever do that again," Lincoln warned.

Eric jumped up defensively. "What's up, old man? What's wrong with you? I suggest you keep your hands off me. I'm doing you a favor, not the other way around. You'd better check yourself next time. I don't want to have to hurt you." He reached into his pocket and pulled out another cigarette.

"Don't ever do that again," Lincoln repeated.

"Yeah, whatever. Can we leave now?" Eric headed to the car. He lit the cigarette and tossed the match. He leaned on the car looking at Lincoln as he watched the blue blood's house. He had a feeling that Samantha was right. He needed to watch his back.

Lincoln looked at his watch. It was time. He reached into his pocket and pulled out his cell phone. He dialed a number and waited.

"Well?" George asked as soon as he picked up.

"It's unconfirmed but we've made progress."

"Is that all?"

"Yes."

"So when is this going to happen?"

"It's impossible to approximate the precise time. I can only make a logical assumption and calculate the probability. To that end, I'd say Friday evening right before the awards ceremony. They'll assume we'll be distracted. It should give them the perfect time to go in."

George sighed heavily. He despised listening to Lincoln's excessive blustering. "Are you sure of that?"

"There's no guarantee. I can only plan and calculate. But Friday evening would be the perfect opportunity to go in."

"That's in two days. Make sure you have everyone in position. I don't want any mistakes. What about the program file, can they read it?"

"Yes, I've tracked it."

"And the elevator key?"

"Everything's ready."

"Perfect."

"I'll be away from the office, so make sure you have this on file. I want to see every single second."

"Of course."

They hung up. Lincoln pulled out his binoculars and focused them on Jackson's driveway. His car was still there. He nodded. So far, so good. He turned and saw Eric sitting on the hood of his car. He grimaced. In two days he'd have him locked up behind bars right next to Jefferson and his sister.

"Are you going out?" Samantha said, seeing that Jackson had changed his clothes, now wearing more conservatively sedate business attire.

"Yeah, I need to go in to the office and take care of some business," he said, grabbing his briefcase from the table.

"Want some company?" she asked, already knowing that he wouldn't.

"No, that's okay, you just relax, enjoy the beach. I'll be back later."

She nodded as he opened the door and strolled to his car. Gut instinct told her that something had happened. She walked over to the window and watched him drive off. The heartbreak of purposely driving a stake into her own heart didn't make it less painful. She knew that Jackson had been on the deck and that he had watched as she talked to Eric. She knew that he would be distant and hurt and she needed that to separate herself from his life. She couldn't do it, but she hoped he could.

Slowly and deliberately, she turned away from the car long gone, and went back upstairs. It was time to get to work. She had a lot to do in a short time. She opened her laptop computer and went to work.

Her mind drifted a few times but for the most part she stayed focused. She had been able to dissect the disc Lincoln had left them. Embedded within the disc was a tracer program with a five-mile radius that was designed to keep track of the program's access, and a timed deletion program virus. It was difficult at first to locate and identify, but she finally detected them and altered their effectiveness. Then for the past few evenings she'd been rescripting that program and altering its code.

Four hours into the morning she finished, then looked up. It was time to get started. She made two phone calls.

Chapter 17

The highway traffic back into the city was dense as Jackson whizzed by, speeding in and out like an overwound zigzag toy. Every so often he'd glance up in the rearview mirror, seeing the car he'd just sped by quickly fade in his wake. Two near accidents and still he continued undaunted. Doubt ate at him all the while he drove. On complete automatic, he headed to Daley Communications, but his thoughts stayed back at his house.

Seeing Samantha on the beach with Eric had staggered him. Even though it seemed that she wasn't particularly receptive, the fact remained Eric had tracked her down and she had stayed and listened. The thought of it now twisted Jackson's insides. Leaving was the only thing he could think to do. He didn't like it. And the fact that she never even bothered to mention the encounter was disconcerting.

Then the phone call from Lincoln insinuating a liaison

between Samantha and Eric only made it worse. For some reason Lincoln wanted him not to trust Samantha. And that interested him. As Samantha suspected, it was obvious that Lincoln had an ulterior motive.

Jackson parked his car near the front entrance of Daley Communications and strolled inside. Greeting several co-workers on the way to the twenty-fifth floor, he continued to his office. His secretary handed him his messages and apologized for not having his schedule up-to-date, then informed him that his first appointment had already arrived and was waiting in his office.

"What appointment?" Jackson asked.

His secretary immediately looked concerned. "Shauna Cooperman. She said that it was a personal matter and wanted to wait in your office." Jackson's face darkened. "Shall I call security?" she asked immediately.

Jackson, already aggravated, shook his head. "No, just get my father on the phone. Tell him I'd like a word with him this morning," he said as he started to his office door.

"Actually, he called earlier. It's one of the messages you have there, and I also left a notation on your computer. He got your message earlier. He'd like to see you today but won't be available until later this afternoon."

Jackson nodded. The day, having started off wonderfully, had quickly plummeted. First Eric and Samantha, then Lincoln and now his father. "Let me know when he's available." She nodded and he went into his office.

As soon as he walked in he found Shauna sitting at his desk reading through his mail and several interoffice notices left on his desk. He tensed instantly. Dealing with her was the last thing he needed.

"What do you want, Shauna? I have a busy day ahead."

"Too busy to see me?" she asked sweetly, then stood and

walked around to the opposite side and sat down as he took the vacant seat behind his desk. Jackson's annoyed expression remained the same. "Despite what you think about me, Jackson, I still care about you and I still wish you well."

"I'm glad to hear that," he said and tossed the mail she'd been going through to the side, then began flipping through the messages from his secretary. "But whatever it is, Shauna, make it quick. As I said, I have a long, busy day." He turned on his computer and entered his code. A warning message instantly came up. Three attempts to breach his system had failed. He looked up at her. She looked away, knowing that she'd been caught snooping again.

"It was good to see you last night," Shauna said hastily. "I mean, earlier at your father's house."

"Shauna," he said firmly, having lost patience.

"Fine, I'll come to the point. I came to warn you."

"About what?" he said, continuing to go through his computer appointments and messages.

"Your family friend, Samantha Lee. She isn't who she says she is."

He stopped. "Isn't she? Who is she, then?"

Shauna smiled happily having gained his undivided attention. "She's a fake."

"And you know this how?"

"I had my father's security check her out after last night."

"You did what?"

"Jackson, I told you, I still love you and I know that a part of you still loves me. I couldn't just sit by and let her hurt you."

"First of all, Shauna, this wasn't a love thing, never was. If anything, it was infatuation on your part. Secondly, you and I have been through this before. I don't appreciate you prying or snooping into my life or investigating my friends."

"But what I found out—"

"Lastly, I don't care."

"She's a con woman and she's out to get your money."

"Really?" he said nonchalantly.

"Yes, there was something about her that just didn't suit me so I had her checked out."

"You realize, of course, that she's not here to suit you."

"That's not the point. She lied about her name and everything else."

"What?" he asked.

"Her name isn't Samantha Lee, it's Samantha Taylor, and her father is a con man from Boston. She lived in New York up until a few months ago. Her company fired her for undisclosed reasons."

"How did you get all this information if all you knew was that her name was Samantha Lee?"

"Her fingerprints."

"Her fingerprints?" he asked.

"Yes, I got them off a glass last night. I gave the glass to one of my dad's security men and he gave it to a friend of his in the police department and he gave me the information this morning."

"So let me get this straight, you stole a glass from my father's house to spy on someone without cause other than she didn't suit you?"

"I have plenty of reasons. She's going after you."

"That's not your concern."

"I guess you didn't hear me—she's going after you."

"Goodbye, Shauna," he said, standing.

"I'm trying to help you," Shauna insisted.

"Goodbye, Shauna," Jackson repeated.

"Fine, I was only trying to help you not make a fool of yourself." She stood and headed to the office door. "Samantha Taylor is going to take you for everything you've got and I don't give a damn. Let her," Shauna spat out.

"One more thing," Jackson said calmly. Shauna turned around, glaring. "I'd appreciate it if you'd stay off my computer and out of my office and that includes lying to my secretary." She turned and stomped out without a word.

Jackson exhaled and relaxed back in his seat. Shauna's revelations didn't faze him, but the fact that Samantha's fingerprints were in police files did. If she was as she said, just the daughter and sister of possible felons, then why would the police have her prints? Before he could consider the question fully, his phone rang and his day began.

Shauna, refusing to be outdone, took the elevator to the next floor down. There was no way a thief was going to steal what she had worked so hard to keep. Jackson didn't know it yet but she was about to save his neck whether he liked it or not. And in the end she was sure that he would appreciate her help. Walking into the public relations suite, she looked around for Jessie's office. The place had changed since she'd been there last. Remodeled, she was happy to see.

"Hi, may I help you?" an assistant asked nicely, looking up from her desk.

"No, thank you, dear," Shauna said condescendingly as she continued to look around. A few minutes into her search she found what she was looking for. She knocked on the door and waited. "Come in."

Jessie looked up and saw Shauna Cooperman standing in her doorway. She instantly knew that her day would be going downhill. Although Jessie's expression remained calm and even, Shauna was the last person she wanted to deal with this morning. "Shauna, how unexpected, what can I do for you today?"

"Jessica, we need to talk."

"Of course, would you like to set up an appointment? I'm on my way out in a few minutes."

"No, we need to talk now. It's about Jackson. He's in trouble and you need to speak with him." She crossed the room and sat down quickly. Moments later she began her tale. She relayed Samantha's real name and her affiliations with unsavory characters. Five minutes later she finished, then waited for Jessie's predictable outrage. Curiously, there was none.

"Is that it?" Jessie asked.

"Isn't that enough?" Jessie didn't reply. "I have to say that I'm a bit stunned by your reaction, or rather your lack of reaction. I just sat here and told you that this woman is after your brother and you have nothing to say about it."

"Shauna, there are a lot of women after my brother. Exactly what proof do you have that Samantha is after Jackson for financial gain?"

"Hello, weren't you listening, isn't it obvious?" she asked rhetorically. "She's living in his house and I'm sure she's doing everything imaginable to con him."

"Shauna, please, reel it in, I don't have time for this. I have a million things to do today, the awards ceremony is in two days, and I have a few dozen last-minute details to finalize."

"What, are you kidding me?" she began in near hysterics. "Jackson is in trouble and you're not going to do anything because you're too busy?"

"Other than the fact that Jackson is a grown man and is capable of taking care of himself, his personal life is none of my business. And I'm sure that whatever arrangement he and Samantha have is perfectly legal and legitimate. As for her staying at the beach, they're both consenting adults and unless what they're doing goes public there's nothing I'm going to do."

"What is wrong with you two? You're both crazy. I just told Jackson the same thing and he was just as blasé." She went on to repeat what she'd just said with added inflection and two decibels louder.

"Shauna, calm down," Jessica sighed loudly.

She and Shauna had never traveled in the same circles for obvious reasons, but she knew of her even before her brother dated her. Shauna was six years older than her, but she had the mental capacity of a sixteen-year-old. She was rich and pretty and slightly anorexic, drank like a fish and fit the typical Beverly Hills stereotype perfectly, as her spoiled, stubborn, bratty behavior had given her a well-deserved reputation.

"How can you be so cavalier? It's your brother and she's gonna take him away."

"Take him away where?" Jessie asked, patronizing her angst. "Look, Shauna, we appreciate your interest but I assure you your fears are groundless. Nothing is going to happen to Jackson."

"How can you be so sure? Jackson has no idea what she's up to. He doesn't even know who she really is, and to make matters worse he doesn't want to know."

"I'm sure you've misunderstood," Jessica said, losing patience with Shauna and the conversation.

"Samantha is—" Shauna nearly shouted.

"Samantha is fine, Shauna," Jessie interrupted.

"See, you're not even listening to me. Samantha Lee isn't even her real name, at least not her full name. Her name is Taylor, Samantha Taylor, and her family are all con artists. She's trying to scam Jackson."

Jessica's interest piqued but her face remained stony and uninterested. "Shauna, if it will make you feel any better I'll talk to Jackson myself as soon as I get back this afternoon. I'll let him know your concerns, okay?"

"That's not good enough," she demanded. "You need to go over there and tell him to get rid of her...*now.*"

"I can't do that. As I said, his personal life is his business. And besides the fact that you actually got her fingerprints without her knowledge or consent, I don't see any proof of any wrongdoing."

"What kind of sister are you? You're just gonna stand by and let some con artist hoochie-momma take Jackson?" she screamed, then held her hands to it as if her head were splitting apart. "This is so not happening." She gathered her purse and sunglasses. "Fine, I'll take care of this myself. You want proof, I'll get you proof." She stomped out and the room fell silent instantly.

Jessica relaxed back in her chair. The sudden stillness in her office gave her pause. Shauna had caused such a ruckus that she'd completely forgotten the peace and quiet of the feng shi atmosphere she worked so hard to maintain. She closed her eyes and breathed deeply, calming her now tense and aggravated nerves. Shauna was lethal to anyone with an IQ over fifty.

Moments later, she cleared her head and turned back to her computer screen. The letter she'd been working on when Shauna came barging in followed by her assistant needed to be worded carefully. Her father's new venture, along with Jackson's possible chairmanship, had her working double time. She had a million calls to answer and a dozen press releases to review.

She typed in a few lines, then stopped, deleting and retyping. Unfortunately, Shauna's ranting had stayed with her. Shaking her head to lose interest and to refocus on the task at hand, she typed a few more words, then stopped completely.

She grabbed the phone and called Jackson's office line. His assistant took a message. Next, Jessica called his cell phone and again left a message. She looked at her watch, then at the screen. There was no contest. She grabbed her purse and informed her assistant that she was on her way to her appointment and could be reached on her cell. She exited the building just in time to see Eric carrying his ever-present briefcase and following Shauna into the restaurant across the street.

A black limo pulled up and the door opened. She got inside. "Was that who I think it was?" Jefferson asked.

"Yep, an interesting couple, I think."

"We might have to consider doing an intervention."

"For which one?" she asked. He chuckled as she leaned over and kissed his cheek. "Nice to see you again."

They looked over at the hotel bar again. Eric was already inside. Jefferson shook his head. "It can't be this easy. It's hardly worth the trouble."

"That's what happens when you retire from the game."

Jefferson smiled. "Tell me about your brother and my sister."

Jessica sat back against the soft leather and recapped the past few days from her perspective.

His business finished with Marcus for the moment, Eric's day was clear and he was in a great mood. Things were going perfectly. The only thing that concerned him was what Samantha had said earlier. He was sure she knew more about what was going on than she seemed to want to admit.

But now even that didn't bother him. He had a ten-million-dollar certified check and his laptop computer had the majority share for complete ownership of Daley Communications. He was on cloud nine.

He chuckled happily. Seeing Samantha last night and then again this morning had got him thinking. Maybe he was wrong in leaving her to take the fall before. Maybe she was a greater asset than he expected. He smiled leisurely, letting his thoughts wrap around her body. She looked fantastic last night, and then this morning she was breathtaking.

But she was a wild card. He wasn't sure what she was up to, but she was definitely up to something. Maybe it was

Jackson that had her all screwed up. His influence on her was obviously something Eric needed to watch. He was just about to call her when he spotted Shauna Cooperman cross the street. An idea occurred to him. His smile broadened.

He already had Daley in his pocket, so conning Cooperman should be a breeze. And the way to get to him was through his devoted daughter. Eric watched her hurry out of the building and then walk across the street to the restaurant. He followed.

Once inside, he looked around quickly. Not seeing her, he assumed that she'd gone into the restroom and decided to have a seat at the bar since it had the perfect vantage point leading to the front door of the main lobby. He walked over and grabbed a seat. The place nearly empty, the bartender looked up from his racing form and came over.

"What will it be?" he asked, wiping the already clean bar counter with a pristine white cloth.

"Yeah, let me have a—" Eric said, then glanced at the draft choices and stopped short.

The bartender stared at him. "What?" he asked, placing a small square napkin in front of him and looked around, trying to see what he saw.

"Hold on," Eric said, smiling. "I'll take whatever she's drinking and give the beautiful lady another one on me with my compliments."

The bartender glanced down the bar, and saw the woman who'd just walked in. She ordered and downed a straight tequila shot in two seconds, then asked for another. "Original," he muttered and dutifully poured two shots. He gave one to Eric and placed another in front of Shauna. She looked up, her eyes clear and focused. The bartender relayed the message. Eric nodded and smiled as she turned her head.

He got up and walked over and set his briefcase on the floor in front of the bar stool.

"Did I ask for company?" she said tightly.

"No, but you looked like you could use a friend."

"Go away before I have to call my security."

"That's not nice, Shauna."

She turned and stared at his face, finally recognizing him. "I know you, don't I."

"We met last night at Marcus Daley's dinner party."

She sucked her teeth loudly. "Please, don't remind me."

"What's wrong?" he asked sympathetically.

"You were there, you saw it."

"Saw what?"

She sucked her teeth again, obviously annoyed by his lack of coherence. "Her, them, together."

"Oh, yeah, I saw that," he lied easily, having no idea what she was talking about.

"She just threw herself at him and he just let her."

"Disgusting, wasn't it?" he agreed.

"Tell me about it. So what are you doing here?" she asked, getting more comfortable by leaning her elbow on the bar counter.

"No, you tell me more, what happened?"

"I don't even want to think about it," she said as Eric ordered another round.

"No. I can help, tell me what happened."

The drinks came and came and came. Surprisingly Shauna remained as if she'd been drinking water. Eric, on the other hand, was seeing double and talking with a definite slur. He had no idea what he'd been saying for the past thirty minutes, but whatever it was got Shauna's attention.

"What do you mean you could still love her?" she shrieked.

Eric's head pounded like a jackhammer as his head swam and spun in circles. What the hell did he just say?

"You," he corrected quickly. "You, I could love you."

Shauna smiled coyly, accepting his tangled words as a tequila-induced confusion. "But I told you, I still love him and I know if that hoochie-momma would get her fat butt out of the way we could be good together. Wait," she said, "that's it. I've been talking to the wrong people," she ordered another round to celebrate.

"What?" Eric asked as his head floated completely off his shoulders, but he finally understood that Shauna wanted Jackson, and Jessie was in her way. At least he thought that's what she meant. He still wasn't perfectly clear.

"So why don't I go after Jessie and give you a clear shot at Jackson?" he slurred.

"Are you nuts?"

"Huh?"

"Never mind," she said, sucking her teeth. "I know what to do now." The drinks arrived.

Shauna picked hers up, took a deep breath and downed it in one gulp. Then she turned and looked at Eric, expecting him to follow her lead. He wasn't there. She looked around the bar, then down. He was on the floor of the bar staring at her shoes.

"What are you doing down there?" she asked.

That was the last thing he remembered, or at least he thought he did. His head fogged completely as someone helped him up.

Chapter 18

Meeting after meeting consumed most of Jackson's morning, keeping him thankfully busy because stopping to think only frustrated him. Samantha meeting Eric on the beach and Shauna's revelations scattered around in his head all day.

At two o'clock his father called him into his office.

"You wanted to see me?" Jackson asked.

"Yes, have you seen the overnight projected ratings?" Marcus, standing, dropped a few pages on his desk. "You need to get back on air. And what's going on with that other situation, did you get it taken care of?"

Jackson didn't expect to have his father bombard him with questions as soon as he entered his office. "No, not yet," he said.

"Look, we've got to get this finished."

"I know."

"You don't look too upset," Marcus said, seeing Jackson's distracted yet calm demeanor.

"I've just got other things on my mind."

"What's more important than getting this situation cleaned up? You obviously have no idea how damaging it can be. Your mother's dead but this scandal can still damage us."

"Tell me about the Cooperman deal."

"What?" Marcus asked.

"The deal with Cooperman, from last night," Jackson specified.

"Well, it's about time you finally came around. Good, we can reassess the particulars. Cooperman will be thrilled, and Shauna, no doubt, will be ecstatic."

"I'm just curious about the details. I assume George initiated the deal."

"No, actually Eric suggested it."

"I see. How exactly did you meet Eric?"

"I know what you're thinking. I might have been set up for some kind of scam. But you're wrong. An old colleague introduced us, someone I trust, and believe me, he's definitely on the up-and-up. He checked into Eric's background and did a thorough search. He came up clean."

"Who's the old friend?" Jackson asked.

"Percy Lincoln."

Jackson's mouth went dry. "Percival Lincoln?"

"Yeah."

"How do you know him?"

"He was a friend of your mother's from back East. She introduced us years ago."

As if a lightbulb had just turned on, Jackson instantly knew Lincoln's motivation. He'd been blackmailing his mother. That's how he had copies of the checks. And as a cop he'd easily pulled her files and kept them. That's why none of this ever came out. There was never anything on record because he had the files.

"They're conning you, Dad," Jackson said. Marcus laughed. Jackson looked confused. "Did you hear me?"

"Yeah, I heard you."

"And?"

Marcus chuckled again, shaking his head. "Remarkable, Eric told me that you'd say that."

"He what?"

"Jackson, I tried to offer you an olive branch and you throw it in my face. I wanted you in on this deal with me. I told Eric as much. But he told me that it would never happen and it appears that he was right."

"Dad, listen to me, Eric Hamilton is a con man. He's conning you, and this deal you think you're doing, it's all a scam…"

"Jackson, please, this is just pathetic. Be a man. Let it go. I won. I just gave Eric Hamilton ten million dollars in investment money this morning. At a fifty percent return, I'm looking at a five-million-dollar investment at one-tenth the price. I intend to approach the board with a firm deal in hand."

"It's not going to happen."

Marcus chuckled again. "Fine, let's play your game. Why should I believe you?"

"Because you're my father and I'm trying to protect you and it's the truth. You have a friend on the police force. Have him look up Eric Hamilton and Percival Lincoln."

Marcus frowned. "My father thought so little of me and my business skills that he handed over the family company to your mother. Yeah, it's true, everything in that file is true. She had a police record, she conned people for a living. Then her faith was just as rewarding as she continued the insult by leaving the company to you. But all that's changed. It's my turn. This cable venture is all mine and my abilities will be recognized. Now, if you don't mind I need to get back to work. I have a lot to do. In twenty-four hours I'll have the money for the down payment on Cooperman's cable company and then all bets are off. I won't need the shares to buy in."

"What shares?"

"My shares and your mother's shares."

"That's the majority. Even if Jess and I put ours together it wouldn't add up. You leveraged them?"

"Of course. Where else was I supposed to get the funds to put this deal in motion? But it doesn't matter now since I'll get the cash from Eric."

"I can't believe this."

"Believe it," Marcus said proudly.

"You don't understand. You have no idea what you've done. You just gave away ten million dollars to a con man who will be turning over escrowed majority shares to George Cooperman."

"Don't be ridiculous, he'd never."

"Wouldn't he?"

"Fine, if you're so sure that this is all a scam, then marry Shauna," Marcus said quickly. "He'd never do that if you married his daughter."

Jackson looked at his father and shook his head, then walked out.

After Jackson left, Marcus sat at his desk contemplating the conversation. A small prickly feeling churned in his stomach. Ten minutes later he picked up the phone and called his friend at city hall.

Jackson left wordlessly, knowing that he still had to save his father, the company, even from himself. As soon as he got to the office door Jessie called to him. "I'm glad you're here, we need to talk." They walked into his office and she took a seat across from his desk.

"Okay," Jackson said as he looked at his watch and sat down. "This can't take long. I need to take care of a few things this afternoon. What's up?"

"That's exactly what I want to know from you. What's going on?"

"What do you mean?" he asked evasively.

"Shauna stopped by my office earlier."

"You, too, huh?"

"She seems to think you have a problem on your hands."

"You mean other than her?"

"Yeah, Samantha." She paused, watching the muscle in his neck twitch. "You know that I make it a point not to interfere in your personal life, but if there is something I need to know—"

"What do you think about Samantha?"

Jessie smiled. "She's nice, funny, smart and much too good for you," she said jokingly. "She's also hiding something and so are you."

Jackson knew that he couldn't keep anything from his sister for too long. She was too perceptive and had a nose for the truth. "What are you doing this evening?" he asked.

"I have a couple of parties to attend, why?"

"I'd like you to stop by my house later."

"I can do that. Any particular reason?"

"Yeah, we need to clear the air. There's something you should know."

"Tell me now," she said.

"No, I need to clear up a few things first."

"All right, I'll be there this evening," she said, standing and walking to the door. "I can't wait."

Chapter 19

This was it.

Samantha looked skyward at the massive structure in front of her. Cooperman Enterprises looked like any ordinary office building, except it was bigger and grander with a well-defined hint of superiority. Climbing above the clouds, the building seemed to go on forever as huge smoke-coated windows surrounded the street level, blocking any hint of visibility.

She entered the main lobby, then walked directly to the security desk and announced her name. The guard made a phone call confirming her appointment. After a few minutes he nodded, then hung up and asked her to follow him. She did. They walked to the bank of elevators down a wide marble hall. He stopped at the last elevator, inserted a familiar-looking key and the elevator doors opened instantly.

He held them open as she got on. He followed and inserted the same key. The penthouse light illuminated. "Mr. Cooperman's assistant will meet you," he said, then turned and got off just as the elevator doors closed.

As the elevator climbed to the penthouse, Samantha used the time to calm her nerves. She took a deep breath and exhaled slowly. But still, every nerve in her body was on edge. She adjusted her jacket and casually released the first button on her camisole, exposing the soft swell of her breasts.

Seconds later the doors opened and a prim angular man stood smiling, backlit by white lights. "Please follow me, Mr. Cooperman is expecting you," he said softly. She nodded and followed him down a brilliantly lit white marble hall to a sparkling glass door beyond which everything was even whiter, gleaming as intensely as the sun. She winced at the brilliance. Then as soon as she entered the private suite she smelled the distinct odor and sneezed.

George's assistant turned to her instantly, seemingly bemused. He knocked on the door and opened it. She walked in. "George, may I call you George?" she asked. He nodded. "George," Samantha said, clearing her throat as she was escorted into his office by his assistant. George was seated at his desk typing on his laptop computer. Samantha smiled broader, focusing on the desk in the center of the room. Perfect timing, at least she didn't have to get him to turn it on.

George stood up, greeting her. Dressed in a formal business suit, he straightened his tie, readjusted his buttoned vest and grabbed his jacket, putting it on as he approached.

"Ms. Lee," George said, walking toward her nodding to dismiss his assistant. "I'm delighted you called this morning. I was just thinking about you." He quickly assessed her, glancing briefly at her face, then down to her tailored pantsuit and the lacy silk camisole beneath. His smile looked overwhelmingly pleased.

"Really? What a coincidence, I was just thinking about you, too." Clearing her throat once more, she looked around admiringly as George beamed. "Excuse me, I think I'm a bit nervous meeting you again." The flattery worked like a charm. George was overjoyed by the effect he presumably had on her.

"No need to be nervous, my dear, we're all friends here. Perhaps a glass of water?"

She looked around to see if he had a water pitcher, but he didn't. "Oh, no, don't bother, I'm sure I'll be fine in a few minutes." She walked farther in and looked around the huge white room. "George, thank you so much for sending the limo to pick me up, that was so sweet."

"You're very welcome, no trouble at all."

"Want to hear a secret?" she asked. He nodded eagerly. "I love the beach, but I must confess I love the city even more— the shopping, the theater and the museums, I love them. There's an exciting energy in the city that you just can't deny. I think it kind of recharges me."

George nodded, looking amazed. "I completely agree. As a matter of fact, I said something quite similar in an interview years ago."

"Is that right?"

"It looks like we have something in common."

"I'm sure we have quite a bit in common, George," she said sweetly.

"Yes, of course. So tell me, you and Jackson—"

"Oh, my, George," she gushed excitedly, "your office is absolutely stunning." She walked over to his white antique desk while slyly reaching into her jacket. "This is absolutely divine, French eighteenth century original, is it not?" she asked, already knowing the answer, having just read about him and his penchant for expensive things, particularly expensive and white, on the Internet.

"Good eye. Yes, it is. I purchased this piece at an auction a few years ago. As soon as I heard about it I had to have it," he said suggestively.

"I can see why, it's incredible. I've never seen a desk like this in white. It's breathtaking. How is it possible?"

"It's a bleached-blond oak, quite rare, there's only three left in the entire world."

"Remarkable."

"This desk cost just over half a million dollars," he said proudly, "but well worth the investment."

"Wow," she said, then cleared her throat again. "I can definitely see that. It's marvelous. May I?" she asked, preparing to walk around to the back.

"Of course," he said happily. "Please, sit, get comfortable."

She opened her jacket, drawing his eyes instantly to the form-fitting camisole, then sat down in the large white chair and gently touched the pallid wood surface. "Oh, wow, it feels so smooth." She laid her cheek on the hard wood and inhaled. Her eyes shifted quickly as she felt the underside of the desk, then spread her arms wide, seemingly to accidentally connect with his laptop-computer ports.

"You have incredible taste, George," she said, standing up and looking across the room. An abstract painting on the wall across the room caught her attention. "That is beautiful," she gasped as her hand was busily attaching a small amplifier to his computer output.

George smiled and chuckled. "Thank you, my dear. That is an original Saunders."

"Saunders, I've never heard of him. Is he a local artist?" The receiver in place, she removed her jacket and dropped it to cover the small amplifier wire attached to his computer. She coughed a few times to cover the clicking sounds.

"Are you sure you're all right? Perhaps water?"

"No, no, I'm fine, really, just a tickle." She coughed again, prompting George to casually step away.

Yet true to form, George gushed about his taste in art, the price and how he was able to get it cheap by intimidating the seller. They walked over to the painting together. She examined it in detail, listening to his continued boasting.

When he finally finished, she turned and looked around the room, walking around admiringly. George followed, continuing to boast as she stopped to admire each piece.

"Come, have a seat with me." She smiled as she led him to the Italian leather sofa across the room from his desk. "We should consult."

"Yes, indeed, I'm looking forward to it."

She sat down, clearing her throat. George sat down beside her just as her cell phone beeped twice. She excused herself and looked at the number, then pressed a few buttons and turned back to him. "I must say, George," she began, then cleared her throat again and coughed. He leaned back slightly. "It was such a pleasure meeting you last night. I, of course, have read all about you in magazines. Your career, your business savvy, you are my idol. And of course, meeting you in person was a dream come true for me."

George smiled and instantly began a two-minute biographical monologue and a self-accolade. She seemed completely enthralled, ignoring her cell phone as it beeped again.

George, a megalomaniac, impressed by her admiration of him, inched closer and suggested they have an early dinner at his private club. She was about to answer but instead began coughing uncontrollably. George moved away as she requested a glass of water. He stood, hurried to his desk and called his assistant to bring in a glass of water quickly.

She followed him, sitting down at his desk again. He backed away, giving her space. His assistant rushed in with the glass of water. He attempted to hand it to George, who in turn motioned for him to give the water directly to Samantha. Just as the assistant gave it to her she dropped it, splashing water all over the antique desk.

"Oh, no, I'm so sorry," she exclaimed, moving his computer away quickly as George and his assistant secured the drenched papers and files. She began coughing again.

"Get more water," George ordered his assistant, who instantly hurried out again.

"Oh, can I get mineral water possibly?" she asked as the coughing fit continued.

"Of course, of course," he said anxiously, then reached over the desk to call his assistant again just as Samantha coughed near his hand. George instantly withdrew his hand, looking at it as if it were contaminated. "I'll go hurry it up," he said, rushing to the office door, opening it just as his assistant attempted to knock with another glass of water. A brief conversation sent the assistant hurrying away to find mineral water, with George right behind him, wiping his hands with a handkerchief.

Samantha, finally in the office alone, went to work. With her jacket for cover she quickly entered several keystrokes, completing her program's retrieval. Then she disconnected the device and removed the computer hookup. It was done.

She quickly sat back just as seconds later George came bursting through the door, flying back across the room toward her. Her heart nearly stopped as she began coughing for real. She looked up, fearful that she had somehow overlooked a security device and she'd been caught. But to her relief George only rushed over to hand her the glass of mineral water. Her hands shook as she took the water and sipped it. Then, finally in control, she exhaled slowly.

"I'm so sorry, George, this is so embarrassing."

"Not at all, dear, not at all," he said, having backed away, retreating to the far side of the desk as far away from her as possible lest she cough on him again.

"Maybe we should just do this another time," she suggested, knowing that she needed to leave quickly.

"Yes, yes, that would probably be best, of course."

"Could I have a rain check on that early dinner, too?" she asked.

"Yes, anytime, just give me a call." He began pulling a handkerchief from his pocket. "Once you're over your cough," he added, walking to his office door.

She grabbed her jacket and gathered her purse from the sofa, then hurried to the door. "Thank you, George, I'll call you soon," she said, reaching out to take his large hand. He withdrew slightly, nervous as their hands touched, but she didn't let go.

"Absolutely, I look forward to it," he said, now anxious to get rid of her, knowing that he had no intention of seeing her again with or without the cough.

She squeezed his hand softly. "Thank you, George, it was good meeting you. Goodbye."

"Likewise, goodbye," he said as he wiped his hand, looking past her for his assistant. She walked out as his assistant rushed in past her with several cans of disinfectant spray.

As soon as she left the suite she removed the small device from her pocket and slipped it into her purse. The deed was done. She walked to the elevators and pressed the button. She realized that she'd been holding her breath the whole time since she'd left his office. Her heart was beating like she'd just run a mile in thirty seconds. She pressed the elevator button again and looked back at the suite entrance.

The door opened. Her pulse raced and her heart lurched. She expected George to come barreling out to stop her. But it was only one of his assistants carrying another can of disinfectant. He politely nodded and smiled and hurried by. She returned his silent greeting as the elevator arrived.

Once inside she looked up and watched impatiently as the numbers descended to the lobby. On the second floor the elevator stopped. Seconds later as the doors opened, she looked out nervously, expecting the worst. But instead, a familiar face greeted her.

Inwardly she smiled her relief, but knowing of course not to show any outward recognition while working, she nodded and stepped aside. Carrying a laptop-computer case, he stepped onto the elevator and stood beside her. They both looked forward as the doors closed and the elevator began moving again.

"How'd it go?" Jefferson asked softly.

"Perfect, just as expected," she said just as softly.

"Good, are you ready to finish this?" he asked just as the elevator arrived on the ground floor. There was a slight pause.

"Definitely," she said as the doors opened. They exited the elevator and walked in opposite directions from each other. Once outside she walked around the corner and caught a cab back to Jackson's beach house.

Chapter 20

With the long day behind him, Jackson arrived home late and exhausted. After his early-morning conversation with Shauna, the rest of the day—back-to-back meetings and a pointless talk with his father—was a blur. All he could think about was Samantha and Eric on the beach. The thought of her in cahoots with him made him sick. He knew that he should have confronted her earlier, but he couldn't. He needed time to think.

He dropped his briefcase on the foyer table and, walking into the living room, saw a house of cards precariously placed on the coffee table. Four tiers high, it looked as if it would fall and collapse at his feet at any minute. He sat down, picked up two cards and cautiously added them to the towering assembly.

The house of cards didn't move an inch. Apparently it was stronger than he thought. He picked up another two cards, and then hearing laughter he looked up and unconsciously grimaced. Samantha was here and he knew that he had to confront her. He stood, tossed the two cards back down on the pile, then followed the sound of laughter coming from the kitchen.

Samantha sat at the center counter with two laptop computers in front of her, connected through a series of cords and wires. She typed on one as she focused her attention on the other's screen. She looked up quickly and smiled. "Hi, welcome home. How was your day?"

"We need to talk," he said, walking over to her.

"Okay, sure," she answered without looking at the laptop screen. Her fingers busily pressed a series of keys, paused, then pressed several more keys. The screen blinked and then a long list of file names appeared. She stopped and turned to give him her full attention.

"What's all that?" he asked, looking over her shoulder at one of the screens.

She pressed another key, exiting the longer list and bringing up another list. She focused on the screen and pressed a key, then answered, "These are George Cooperman's files from his personal computer."

"What? How did you get George Cooperman's personal computer files, break into his office and steal them?"

"Of course not," she said stiffly. "I told you before, I'm not a criminal."

"So, you figured out the program Lincoln gave us?"

"The program was faulty, essentially useless."

"So how'd you get the files?"

"The same way he did."

"What do you mean?"

She turned back to the computer, hit several keys, paused, then hit a few more. The screen cleared, then blinked to a new screen, and the Daley Communication logo appeared. "How did you do that?" he asked.

She pressed another button and files appeared. "I didn't.

These files were already in George Cooperman's personal computer."

"What? How did he get them?"

"As far as I can figure, he somehow got access to your mother's company files and had them transferred to his personal laptop."

"How?"

"Any number of ways. If you had computer system problems, your company might have called in tech support from the outside. Cooperman might have bought them off beforehand. All he'd have to do is copy what he saw and then get paid."

"Wait a minute, you mean to tell me that anybody can just sign onto another personal computer and copy their files?"

"It's possible."

Jackson walked away from the counter and stood in the center of the kitchen. "When my mother died six months back, we needed to get into her personal computer files. We had an outside consultant come in."

"That's a possibility."

He turned, "So just anybody can do this."

"No, of course not." Then she paused to qualify the statement. "Well, not just anybody. You'd have to know quite a lot about computers. Remember, I'm a computer engineer, I specialize in software programming and detection. Once I got Cooperman's WEP key I—"

"Hold it, what's a WEP key?"

"Simply put, it's a single computer's password encrypted key. If you know the WEP you can get into that system from anywhere. Every computer has its own WEP."

"So it's like a password?"

"Like a password, yes, but much more detailed. The WEP is composed of ten digits, both numbers and letters. Ordinarily it secures a computer against outside systems pirates. In this case it was used against you, so I used it the same way and it opened the system to me. So to get these files, Cooperman's files, I simply had to redesign and tweak a retrieval and master copy program I'd already created."

"Simple, right?" he mocked.

"No, not quite. It took a while, all morning and most of the afternoon to get it set up just right. I also needed to embed another program to count down to expulsion in about—" She paused and looked at her watch. "Twenty-six hours."

"Then you just walked into George's office while he was sitting there and copied the files from his personal computer."

"No, of course not, George invited me to see his new artwork last night at your father's party. So, while I was there I returned the file Lincoln gave us."

"You said that that program was faulty."

"For our benefit, yes, but not for his. Lincoln gave us the elevator key, the password and the disc to George's computer knowing that we'd figure out that he had your mother's information. He wanted us to sneak into his office and get it back. I assumed that's when we'd get caught."

"He could have blamed everything on us," he said as she nodded. Jackson looked down at the screen at the listing of his mother's files. He shook his head. "You knew about Lincoln's disc this morning?"

"Yes."

"What else haven't you told me?" he asked.

Samantha didn't answer. Instead she turned and cleared the screen of Daley Communications information and went back to Cooperman's files, knowing that it was better not to elaborate on the afternoon's events.

"Lincoln knows my father and introduced him to Eric," Jackson said. "He told me this afternoon,"

She stopped searching the screens, leaned back and looked at Jackson. "That's interesting."

"And my father has no idea what's going on. He actually thinks that he's getting something out of all this. I tried to tell him but Lincoln was right, he didn't believe me. He believed two con men over his own son."

"Jackson," Samantha said, "don't worry, we'll get everything back, I promise."

"And how are you going to do that, Samantha? Call him, meet with him on the beach again?" He observed that she had no outward reaction. Their eyes hardened as they glared at each other.

"If you have something to say, Jackson, just say it."

"Yeah, okay, I saw the two of you out there this morning."

"I know. I wanted you to see us."

"Why?"

She paused and considered how much to tell him. "Seeing Eric and me together was the easiest way to…"

"Get your point across that you're leaving," he said, finishing her sentence.

"Yeah, something like that. I guess it didn't work as well as I assumed it would."

"It worked well enough. I was furious until just now when I looked into your eyes." She immediately looked away. "No amount of manipulation can change that."

"You have no idea—"

"You're right," he interrupted, "but I will, in time."

"You are one stubborn man."

He smiled for the first time that day. "Now tell me about you and Eric."

"There's nothing much to tell. I've wanted revenge for months, but now, seeing him, it just doesn't seem worth it. I don't really care what happens to him."

"I'm afraid that I can't be that objective. You see, my father gave him ten million dollars this morning to invest in some bogus scheme in hopes of making a fifty percent return. He also signed over his and my mother's company shared as collateral. That means it's over. We've lost. I tried all afternoon to contain this, but I couldn't."

"About that—"

"Tell me something, do you have a police record?"

"No," she said truthfully.

"But your fingerprints are on record, aren't they?"

"Are you referring to the IAFIS?"

"The what?"

"The Integrated Automated Fingerprint Identification System. It's a national fingerprint bank and criminal history system maintained by the FBI. Yes, my fingerprints are on file. How did you know that?"

"Why are they on file?"

"Sorry to disappoint you, Jackson, but they're not on file with the police for a criminal history. I do computer work for them from time to time. You checked out my fingerprints?" she asked.

"No," he said, looking away. "Someone else did, but that's not the point."

"Shauna," she guessed correctly. "So I guess she told you the rest."

"What rest?"

"You know, Jackson, if I were going to con you I would already have done it. I don't need your money and I don't want your money. I was doing all this as a favor."

"A favor for whom?" he asked.

"Rachel," she said just as the telephone rang.

"What?" Jackson said, stunned by her answer.

"Get the phone," she instructed.

It rang a second and third time. "What do you mean you're doing a favor for Rachel?" The phone rang a fourth time. He picked it up, listened and then hung up. "I need to go," she nodded wordlessly, focusing on the computer screen again. "This isn't over. We'll talk about this when I get back," he said, then immediately left.

Samantha watched him walk out, then turned back to the computer screen. She needed to finish looking for the files.

George Cooperman sat in his office as Lincoln entered.

"When is this thing going to happen?" he asked impatiently.

"I spoke with Mr. Hamilton this morning. Everything was on schedule. Marcus should have given him a ten-million-dollar certified check early this afternoon."

"Excellent." He smiled, nodding his head approvingly, "And the signed majority shares?"

"According to Mr. Hamilton, they were transferred first thing this morning."

George nodded happily as he opened his personal laptop and glanced at the pirated files he'd acquired. It was the best five thousand dollars that he'd ever spent. He went into the search engine and looked for new files. There were none. He continued looking. "What about the break-in here? When will that happen?"

"I don't know exactly. Soon, I would imagine. Marcus must realize by now that Mr. Hamilton's missing."

"Make sure that he's on a plane out of here. I don't want any last-minute problems. He got his money. Make sure he won't cause any trouble for us." Lincoln nodded. George continued searching for the files from Eric.

"I haven't heard from him, he must already be gone."

"I still don't like the fact that you gave them the system code and the elevator key. Damn it, where are those files?"

"We need to catch them in the act, but you can't personally be involved. That way there will be no question of your innocence and that Marcus put them up to stealing from you and planting evidence."

"Has the code been figured out yet?"

"No."

"Maybe this Ms. Taylor isn't as smart as you said she is."

"I don't know what's taking so long. I'll contact them again this evening."

"See that you do. I'm scheduled to appear before the grand jury again in two days. I want this new evidence presented then. I need to be completely exonerated," he said as he continued searching. "Wait a minute. There's something wrong. The files aren't here anymore. Find Mr. Hamilton. I think he just tried to double-cross me."

Lincoln nodded, stood, then left. As soon as he got to his office he used one of his disposable cell phones and called Eric but got no answer. He frowned. It was late and he should have been there by now. The thought occurred to him that Eric had taken the money and the shares and run as he'd joked earlier, but Lincoln knew better. Still, he needed to find him.

He took the service elevator down and left the building. He got in his car and tried calling Eric again. Vowing to strangle him upon his next opportunity, he shifted gears to drive off. Seconds later, he watched from his parking spot across the street as several police and unmarked cars arrived at the building. He turned on his blinker and drove away.

Eric quickly covered his face lest the bright lights melt him to ash. His head was on fire and his brains were charcoal briquettes. Breathing hurt. Thinking hurt. So speaking or opening his eyes was totally out of the question.

"So you gonna help me or what?"

The voice was too loud and too obnoxious.

"Shh," he mustered with great difficulty. The sound seemed to add to the sizzle as his brain fried.

"What? Don't hush me, you promised to help me, so what are you going to do?"

He was in bed, that much he surmised, and by the close feel of the sheets he was naked. The question was, where was he and who the hell was screaming at him. He began to doze off again when the fire was stoked and his head reignited into a full blaze.

"Eric, do you hear me talking to you? I know you hear me. Answer me. What are you going to do, are you going to help me or what?"

The loud noise needed to stop, but he had no idea how to turn it off. He didn't know any prayers to say, so he said the only one he could think of.

"What the hell are you talking about, now I lay me down to sleep? Are you crazy or something? I bring you home with me this afternoon and you can't even get it up to show me what you got and that's all you can say is some children's prayer. What's wrong with you?"

"Please stop," he said, his voice trembling in angst.

"What?"

"Stop," he begged slightly louder. "Just shut up."

"What? Oh, no, you didn't just tell me to shut up in my house. Get your butt up out of my bed and get out, now." She watched as Eric's smile widened and he began to snore. "Fine, I'll do it myself, it was time for you to leave anyway." She stomped out of the bedroom.

Eric smiled and slept in peace. Whatever banshee he'd just defeated he was proud of himself. But for a dream, or rather a nightmare, it felt awfully real. The thought eased his mind and nearly extinguished the fire burning in his head.

The next time he woke up he was butt naked on the pavement on Hollywood Boulevard and being forcefully helped into a car by two police officers.

Chapter 21

"You knew about Lincoln and Eric from the beginning, right?" Samantha asked.

Jefferson nodded.

"So why didn't you just stop them before now?"

"I got there too late. By that time Eric had already set you up and you were walking right into it."

"That's when you called me at his apartment?"

"Yes." He looked over at the screen. "Is everything ready?"

She nodded.

"Okay, let's get started. Jackson should be on his way to the office and Jessie will need this."

"He's not going to be happy about this."

"The final outcome is all that matters. Daley Communications will be safe and he'll have control and that's what Rachel wanted."

"I've been manipulating him from day one."

"He'll understand that everything you did was to protect him, Jessie and Rachel. Trust me, I know what I'm doing. I've been doing this a long time."

Samantha nodded. She did trust her brother.

"You're in love with him, aren't you?" he asked, smiling happily.

Samantha smiled back and looked at Jefferson as he took her hand. "Is it that obvious?" she asked.

"Only to your brother and possibly the rest of the world," he said.

"I know, very unprofessional. I remember the golden rule, never make it personal and never fall for your mark."

"First of all, lollipop, you're not a professional and Jackson was never a mark, and secondly, everything you did was because of love, for him, for me and for Dad."

"He won't see it that way."

"He will, just give him a chance and don't run."

The doorbell rang. Both Samantha and Jefferson turned.

"Are we expecting someone else?" she asked. He shook his head.

"Then I guess I'd better get the door," she said.

Samantha opened the front door. Shauna was standing there. "Shauna," she said, "this isn't a good time."

"I want to speak with Jackson now."

"He's not here, you just missed him."

"No games, Samantha Lee Taylor," Shauna said nastily. "Yeah, that's right, I know your real name and what you are. So just run along and tell him I'm here. I left my sunglasses the last time." She pushed past Samantha and walked in and dropped a pair of sunglasses on the foyer table. After pausing a second to glance in the living room, she turned back to Samantha. "Where is he?"

"I told you, he's not here. And I would think that you

could afford more than one pair of sunglasses," Samantha said, then picked up the sunglasses on the foyer table and handed them to her. She ignored them and continued looking around.

"Jackson," Shauna called out, then waited. "Jackson, it's Shauna, I need to talk to you now." She began climbing the stairs, then stopped when she heard the sound of water running in the kitchen. She smirked at Samantha, turned, and headed toward the back of the house. "Jackson, we need to—" She stopped, seeing Jefferson at the sink wiping a glass clean. "Who are you?"

Jefferson smiled as Samantha and Shauna entered the kitchen. "Where's Jackson?" Shauna asked.

"As I told you, he's not here," Samantha said.

"But you are and you have a friend here, too. That's interesting." She looked Jefferson up and down admiringly as she walked over to him. "Shauna Cooperman, and you are?"

"Pleased to meet you, Shauna," Jefferson said without introducing himself.

"We're right in the middle of something right now," Samantha said.

"I bet you are," Shauna answered, smiling, assuming that she had something on Samantha.

"I'll tell Jackson that you stopped by."

"Don't bother, I'll tell him myself," she said, not taking her eyes off Jefferson.

Shauna turned to Samantha. "You are so busted."

"Goodbye, Shauna. Don't forget your sunglasses."

"What did you say your name was?" she asked Jefferson.

"I didn't," he said, smiling.

Shauna nodded slyly, smiled and walked back to the front door. Samantha followed. "Here, don't forget these; I'm sure you wouldn't want to make another trip here."

Shauna took the glasses, still smiling like the Cheshire cat. "You are so busted," she said again.

As soon as the door closed she walked happily over to her car. This was even better than she had planned.

Marcus had sat in the main lobby of Cooperman Enterprises and waited for the past thirty minutes. He stood and walked over to the security desk. "Do you have any idea who I am?"

The security guard looked up from his newspaper. "Yeah, I know you. I worked at your company a few months ago. I got laid off."

"Well, things are tough all over. I'm waiting to see George Cooperman. Is he here?"

"I'll check," the guard said, then went back to reading his newspaper.

Disgusted, Marcus walked over to the bank of elevators and pressed the button to the one marked Penthouse. Nothing happened. "This isn't working," he called out down the hall. The guard ignored him. He walked back to the large semicircular desk. "I need the key."

"Sorry, no one goes up without being invited by Mr. Cooperman personally."

Marcus fumed and walked back over to the waiting area and sat down. He opened his cell phone and called Eric again. There was still no answer. He called George's private line, no answer. Furious, he stormed out.

Driving like a madman, Jackson arrived at Daley Communications in record time. He headed straight to his sister's office. Her door was already open.

"What's the emergency?"

"I got a call from a friend of mine. Eric was arrested this evening."

"Good." Jackson smiled, feeling somewhat vindicated that at least something went right today.

"He was picked up on Hollywood Boulevard passed out and drunk."

"This keeps getting better."

"Dad gave him a ten-million-dollar cashier's check. He was naked when they picked him up. No identification, no clothes, no check."

"You mean ten million dollars just disappeared?"

She nodded.

"Where's Dad?"

"I have no idea."

Jackson sat down just as Jessie's phone rang. She picked it up, nodded and smiled. "Thank you, we owe you." Whoever responded and whatever they said made her smile. She hung up.

Jackson looked at her. "Who was that?"

"A friend of the family," she said as she sat at her desk and waited, looking at the computer screen.

"Who, Paul?"

"No, Jefferson Taylor, Samantha's brother."

"Jefferson Taylor, as in Robert Taylor's son?"

"Yes."

"You know him?" he asked, stunned. "How is that possible?"

"We met a long time ago. Mom introduced us."

"Mom?" he asked. "Wait, you knew about her past, didn't you?"

Jessie nodded.

"She told you and not me?"

"She never wanted to disappoint you, Jackson. You put her on a pedestal, she was perfect as far as you were concerned."

Her computer message sounded. She opened her e-mail,

read quickly, smiled, then looked up at Jackson. He walked to her and stood over her shoulder. He read the message, and then together they opened and read through the attached files.

"He got these, how?"

"Actually, Samantha sent them."

"Samantha, but she's not a—" Jackson stopped midsentence and looked at his sister differently. "What's going on?"

"I was supposed to meet Samantha at the airport, then at the hotel. Imagine my surprise when my brother met her instead."

"You knew Samantha before? Why didn't you—"

"No, actually I'd never met Samantha until that day at your house. She's just as I imagined. Mom once told me that if I ever needed help, Jefferson would be the one to call."

"Because family is forever," Jackson quoted Samantha.

She nodded. "Even extended family. Paul told me that one of his contacts heard in the wind that George Cooperman was going to make another attempt at getting the company. I needed help."

"Why didn't you tell me?"

"It was right after Mom died and you were too busy keeping everything else together. You didn't need this, too. So I called in a favor."

"Jefferson. But he's a con artist, they both are."

"*Was* a con artist. He's very much retired. He works mostly with a friend of his now, Grant Andrews. But the story on the street is that he's either in jail or in hiding. He says it keeps him free and honest."

"Grant Andrews, the FBI prosecutor?"

"Yes."

Jackson's mouth dropped open as Jessie continued, "He was right in the middle of another case when I asked him for help. He couldn't come, so he got Samantha to come instead. And since Grant was going to need information from a computer system, she was perfect. The whole Eric thing was just a coincidence." She began printing out several pages.

"She was with him the whole time?"

"I don't know. I do know that Jefferson sent Samantha to help with the computer part and apparently she did. I can't believe she found all this." She handed him a few papers.

"What's this?"

"For your approval."

Jackson read through the paper, smiling. "Fine, perfect, but with one little change," he said, then picked up a pen and wrote it in.

"Are you sure about this?"

"One hundred percent. Where's Dad?"

"He was out earlier."

Moments later, Jackson walked into his father's office without knocking. Jessie followed. Marcus stood at his desk packing his briefcase. He looked up to see Jackson walking over to him and Jessie taking a seat. "Make it brief," he said.

"I can do better than that." He tossed an envelope on the desk. Marcus picked it up and looked at it.

"I hope these are the documents. It took you long enough."

Jackson smiled. "Open it up."

Marcus picked up his letter opener and cut through the envelope. He pulled out a pink folded paper and quickly read through it, then looked up at his son. "Is this some kind of sick joke?"

"No, your services at Daley Communications are no longer needed. You will vacate the position of CEO immediately."

"You can't do that. The board meeting—"

"Doesn't matter anymore. Jessie turned all of her shares over to me and I turned the company over to her."

"You can't—"

"It's already been done and it's perfectly legal. We even had a federal prosecutor look it over."

"Get out."

"Actually that should be my line," Jessie said, smiling.

"You think this is over? You have no idea what's going on."

"Actually, we do. You've been working with George Cooperman to sell the company from under us just as you tried to do thirty years ago. Mom stopped you then, we're stopping you now."

"This is my company. He turned it over to her."

"She was better suited."

"She was a con artist with a record. The only reason I married her was because he made me marry her to secure the deal. A deal I never wanted."

"You were selling the company."

"I'm expanding my options. And George—"

"Can't even help himself."

"What are you talking about?"

"It seems that your plan to distract me worked too well. Yes, we got the information you and George planted, but we also acquired more damaging information. There's a federal warrant sworn out for George Cooperman. I suspect he's running about now."

"What?"

"Apparently the FBI received an anonymous file containing a number of damaging documents. It seems he's been lying to a federal grand jury. That's a punishable offense— jail time."

"He'd never get—"

"He's on the run."

Marcus sat down slowly. The once-pompous man shriveled, dejected in his chair. He read through the papers again. "This isn't over."

"It is. Your number-one ally has fled. Lincoln and Eric will be picked up and charged as soon as they're caught. And since there were warrants out on both con men already, they'll be unavailable for quite some time."

Marcus looked up at his son, then at his daughter. Their mother's eyes smiled back at him.

"Tomorrow evening you will graciously accept the National Association of Black-Owned Broadcasters Lifetime Achievement Award for Mom, and then as promised you will make a special announcement. You will resign your position effective immediately as CEO and turn the reins over to your daughter, Jessica Daley."

"What?"

"You heard me, Jessica is to be the next CEO. She's more than qualified to take the lead. And just as Mom did, she will take Daley Communications further than either one of us. As stated in the letter, you will receive adequate compensation for your years of service."

"What does that mean?"

"I wouldn't worry about that right now," Jackson said as he turned to leave.

"What about you?" Marcus asked as Jackson opened the door to leave.

"I'll be around."

In a sudden fit of rage Marcus tossed his briefcase across the room. "Fine, you want it, you got it. Take it, it's yours." he stormed over to the door and opened it just as a man stood ready to knock.

He smiled and flipped an FBI badge to Marcus. He froze with his mouth open.

"Excuse me," the man said. "I'm looking for Jessica Daley. I was told I might find her here."

Marcus stepped back, still stunned, afraid that he might be

arrested. Jessie stood up and walked over. "Hi, I'm Jessica Daley. How can I help you?"

He opened and showed his badge again. "My name is Grant Andrews, I work as a prosecutor for the federal government."

"Yes, of course. Come in, what can I do for you, Mr. Andrews?"

"I was asked to return this to you." He handed her an envelope and a laptop computer. She opened the envelope, looked inside then handed it over to Jackson. "I'm afraid that all the information on the computer has been permanently lost. The hard drive is completely fried."

"Thank you," she said.

Grant nodded and smiled. "I'll pass that on."

"I'd appreciate that."

Grant nodded to Jackson, then to Marcus and left.

"What's in the envelope?" Marcus asked.

"A certified check for ten million dollars," Jackson said.

"What? How did you get it back?"

"Have to go," Jackson said as he kissed his sister's cheek. "Congratulations. You were born for this."

Chapter 22

"Are you insane?" Lincoln asked as he walked out of the police station. "Do you know how many lies I had to tell to get you released? What the hell were you thinking getting picked up for indecent exposure, obscenity and vagrancy? And couldn't you think up a better lie? Why not say you'd been robbed? Damn, you had no clothes on, no ID, they might actually have believed you."

Eric, stumbling to get the shoes on that Lincoln brought him, hurried to catch up. "What, would you prefer me to give them my real name and file a police report, too? Remember, I'm already in the system thanks to you."

"How the hell did you get this way?"

"I don't know. I think I went drinking with Shauna."

Lincoln stopped short and just stared at him as if he was nuts. "You did what? What the hell were you doing drinking with her?"

"I thought she could give me some information. You know, to con her old man."

"Fool, she drinks for a living. She's the only one I know who could actually drink a full bottle of Jack Daniel's and not feel a thing."

"We were drinking tequila shots. At least, I think we were."

"Oh, great, that's like water to her. She's been drinking since her mother died when she was ten. Believe me, Shauna Cooperman is a professional."

"I thought—"

"That's your problem, you thought, you think. Stop it. I do the thinking, remember that," he said, stabbing his finger into Eric's chest to make the point. "Do you have any idea how close you came to blowing the whole thing?"

"Look, just because you have this hard-on for Jefferson Taylor don't blame me. I was fine all by myself. I don't need you."

"But you do. Without me your butt would be rotting in a New York City jail. And need I remind you that all I have to do is press one button and all your nightmares will come true?"

Eric glared at Lincoln. There was nothing to say.

"Where's the check?"

"In my briefcase."

"Where's the briefcase?"

"Uh, I was in Shauna Cooperman's bedroom. It's there."

Lincoln stopped walking again. "Where?"

"In her bedroom, that's were the witch took my clothes and my things."

"Damn," Lincoln said.

"What?" Eric asked.

"Hurry up, maybe we can still get there before they do."

Moments later they drove up to witness firsthand the complete efficiency of the FBI. George Cooperman's home had already been seized and cordoned off, and three huge trucks were backed up in the driveway as agents loaded boxes of evidence.

"There goes ten million dollars," Lincoln said.

"We got to get out of here," Eric said.

Jackson drove home.

As soon as he pulled into his driveway, Shauna got out of her car. She smiled. This was just too good to be true. She closed the door and walked over to meet him.

"Your family friend has company. Don't say I didn't warn you. Now you've got another con man in there with her."

"What are you talking about, Shauna?"

"Her family are all con artists. Thieves," she spat out. "They actually steal other people's money for a living."

"Con artists aren't thieves."

"What are you talking about? She's a thief. You have a woman you don't even know living in your house and you're talking about the differences between thieves and con men. I don't believe this."

"Shauna, none of this is your business."

"I can't believe what I'm hearing, you're going to actually stand there and defend her, you don't even know her. She's apparently lied to you from the beginning. But she can't get out of this one. He's in there with her."

Jackson thought about Eric instantly. "Goodbye, Shauna."

"Fine, don't believe me, see for yourself. Know this, I'll be home when you're ready to come crawling back."

Jackson walked in and looked around. Samantha was just as he'd left her, still sitting at the counter with her laptops in front of her. She looked up. "Hi," she said. "You just missed your friend."

"Hi. I know, I ran into her just as she was leaving. She told me that I had company."

"You do."

"She said that you were here with a man."

"That would be me." A man spoke up, entering the kitchen from the deck.

Jackson saw a familiar man standing in the doorway between the kitchen and the deck. "And you are?"

"Jackson, this is my brother, Jefferson Taylor."

Jackson looked at him strangely. "I remember you. You're the bartender in the airport lounge in Chicago."

"Good memory."

Jackson went still as the realization in his eyes hardened sternly. He turned to Samantha, shaking his head. "You knew all this from the beginning. You're one of them, a professional con artist, and this was a con all along, wasn't it?"

"Yes," she said softly.

Jefferson looked at her oddly. "Think of it more as an intervention for the greater good," he said.

"I've heard that before. Justice, right? Your friend Percival Lincoln said the same thing. So it was you and your brother working together the whole time, a family con."

"Yes, but…" she said, taking a step to go to him.

"Don't," he said, interrupting, taking a step back.

"Jackson…" she called after him.

"I think you said it all." They stood staring into each other's eyes.

"If you'll excuse me," Jefferson said, "I need to make sure that Eric and Lincoln get a well-deserved send-off." He leaned over and kissed Samantha's forehead. "I'll see you later." She nodded. He turned to Jackson and nodded.

Jackson held out his hand. "I guess I owe you thanks."

"I've heard a lot about you. It was good to finally meet you. And for the record, you don't owe me anything."

Jefferson nodded and left as Jackson turned to Samantha. "One last thing. Was any of this real?"

Samantha remembered what Jefferson had said. "No, it was just as you said, a con from the very beginning."

He smiled. "And I fell for it."

"Hook, line and sinker," she said as she continued packing up the two laptop computers.

"And making love to me, that was part of it?"

She didn't respond.

"I guess that's my answer, and now you leave."

"I told you I'd leave when this was over."

"To con someone else?"

"That's what I do. You said it, I'm a professional."

"You were right. I guess I get to walk away wiser and wishing that I hadn't gotten up this morning. It was a nice fantasy." He walked out of the kitchen.

"Yes, it was," she said and she finished packing. She picked up her bag and walked out. It was over.

Chapter 23

Samantha looked around. A mass of humanity swarmed in every direction, another reason why she hated airports. So why her brother had insisted she meet him here was beyond her. She continued looking around. Then she spotted him smiling at her from across the path. She walked over. "Hey there," she said as she kissed his cheek.

"You're late," Jefferson said.

"I know, sorry, I had to pick up my ticket," she said, smiling. "What in the world are we doing here of all places? You know how much I detest airports."

"Tell me you're not taking a train all the way across the country." She smiled nicely. "What am I going to do with you? Come on, we have a seat right over there."

Samantha turned. Grant was sitting at a coffee bar sipping from a small cup. They walked over. Grant stood, smiling.

"Hey, you, how are you?" she said. "I saw you on television last night. You looked great. Looks like that anonymous file someone sent you really sealed your case against George Cooperman."

"Hey, lollipop," Grant said, kissing Samantha on the forehead, then winking. "Thanks."

They all sat down at the small table. A waiter brought over another cup of espresso and an herbal tea.

"Don't mention it," she said. "So what's this surprise you have for me?"

Grant looked at his watch. "It's time." Just then a small commotion aroused interest as several airport security teams hurried to the area. The crowd parted and two men were being led away in handcuffs. They walked right by the small coffee shop. Samantha, Jefferson and Grant smiled as Lincoln glared at them. Eric, too busy demanding his rights and his attorney while professing his innocence, never even looked around and saw them.

"To the victor, the spoils." Jefferson toasted with his small cup.

"Ah, thank you." She smiled. "What a perfect gift. That really felt good." She hugged both men.

"Well, that's it for me, I have a ton of paperwork to do back at the office." Grant stood and leaned down to Samantha. "Thanks again, Sammy, without you..."

"Family is for forever. 'Bye, good luck."

Jefferson and Grant shook hands. "I have something you might be interested in doing for us," Grant said to Jefferson. "I'll call you in the next few days."

"So, how does it feel to end your first and only con?" Jefferson said.

"Good," she said, smiling. "No, it feels great!" She threw her arms around Jefferson and hugged him fiercely. "The thrill and excitement were exhilarating. What a rush."

"Whoa, whoa, don't get too used to it. Dad said that you were never to come out after midnight."

"I know, and I won't."

"Good."

"What I do, what I did is dangerous. But like Dad, I never conned anyone who wasn't already a thief and a crook."

"I know."

"So how did you leave it last night?"

"What do you mean?"

"With Jackson. Why would you allow him to believe that you were a professional con artist?"

"So I could walk away."

"You never walk away from love. Nothing is that important."

"You did, Dad did."

"And look where it got us."

"He's better off with someone else."

"That would be his decision, not yours."

"I helped."

"Are you sure about this?"

"I'm sure."

"When's your train?" he asked.

"In four hours. And your flight?"

"Soon, as a matter of fact," he said, finishing the last of his espresso. "I'd better get going."

"But we didn't get to spend any real time together," she said sadly. "I'm missing you already."

"No, you miss him. You should have gone back."

"To what end? His world is way too different from ours. I would never fit in."

"You don't have to. But that's your decision. Are you headed back to Boston, to Oz?"

She nodded. "Yeah, for a little bit. I want to take some time to chill out. Then who knows where."

"Good." He pulled out and handed her a business card. "Take this."

"What is it?" She looked at the card, recognizing the name instantly. "Dad's attorney?"

"You have an inheritance to pick up in New York first and probably a lot of shopping to do while you're there now that you're off the hook for Eric's crime."

"What?"

"I figure, let's see, over about fifteen years of sound investments, and after taxes, of course, I'd say you were looking at somewhere north of nine million dollars."

"Are you kidding me?" she asked, astonished.

Jefferson stood and kissed her forehead. "Take care and be good," he warned in that brotherly way that always made her smile.

"I will."

She watched as he walked down the corridor and disappeared into the crowd. He turned once and waved. She nodded and waved back just before heading in the opposite direction.

Opening the cell phone, she called her friend Jillian. "Whatever you're doing put it on hold. Meet me in New York in a few days, we have some serious shopping and celebrating to do."

Chapter 24

The awards ceremony was, as expected, long and tedious, but his mother's presentation was beautiful. His father, the consummate actor, took the stage, accepted her award along with Jessie and formally announced his retirement and Jessie's secession to CEO.

The assembled guests were stunned, having suspected that he would announce he would be taking the reins of Daley Communications permanently. Afterward, the press and media swamped them as Jessie took the lead. She was brilliant, as usual.

After a long, slow drive home, with keys in hand, Jackson walked up the path to his home. The door was slightly open. He entered and stopped at the alarm system. To his surprise it had already been turned off. He walked through the house looking into each room, not sure what or who to expect.

He went into the kitchen and saw that the sliding glass door was open. He walked out onto the deck hoping to see Samantha standing outside. She wasn't. But someone else was. He walked outside and stood at the railing.

"Nice place you have here," Jefferson said as he sat perched on the railing looking out at the sunset. "I have a view just like it on the Côte d'Azur. The water's a bit bluer or greener in France, mind you, but this is pleasant nonetheless. I don't get down there too often. I like the city too well. There's something about Piccadilly Circus that excites me. Maybe it's the statue of Eros."

"What are you doing here, Jefferson? I thought this was over," Jackson said as he looked out at the sun setting in the west.

"Eros, the god of love, the son of Aphrodite, but more importantly he represented the sum of all instincts for self-preservation." Jefferson looked over to Jackson for the first time.

"Where is she?" he asked as he sat down beside Jefferson and looked out at the waves cresting against the sand.

"I can see why she loves it here," Jefferson said. "It's peaceful, makes me want to head over to France before going home."

"London, right?" he guessed, remembering Samantha's perfect accent at his father's place.

"Sometimes. Have you ever been to London?"

"Yeah, a bit crowded but it's nice."

"I agree," Jefferson said.

"So what you do, I mean, did," Jackson corrected, "you don't do that anymore?"

"I retired some time ago."

"And now you work for the government?" Jackson asked.

"At times," Jefferson said evasively.

"What exactly do you do for them?"

"I acquire information and handle tricky situations."

Jackson looked puzzled, then began chuckling. "You con people for the government," he guessed.

Jefferson smiled and looked away. Jackson nodded, not expecting a more formal answer one way or the other. "And this whole thing was to get Cooperman. So when Lincoln said that you were in a European jail, that was just a cover story to keep you off the radar?"

"Let's just say that he was misinformed."

"So the bad guy is actually a good guy," Jackson said. "Samantha knew about all this."

"She knows some. Enough…" Jefferson said.

They lapsed into silence.

"I love her," Jackson finally said.

"Of course you do."

"I need her, I want her in my life."

"Understandably," Jefferson agreed.

"So, are you going to tell me where she is?"

"What if she doesn't want you?"

"She does," Jackson said with complete assurance.

"What if she doesn't love you?"

"She does."

"You're so sure?" Jefferson asked, turning to him.

The two men sat face-to-face, glaring eye to eye.

"Avoiding questions is a family trait. But I'm only going to ask you this one more time," Jackson challenged sternly. The cut in his eyes was fierce. Yet Jefferson broke and smiled nonetheless.

"She's on her way back to Oz."

"Where?"

"Far be it for me to tell a man how to run his life, and I know we don't know each other and trust is a totally different issue, but Samantha is my sister and she's, well…" He paused. "Don't confuse her with me and my life and what I used to do."

"I never did."

"You didn't believe her?"

"No, of course not."

"Then why did you let her go?"

"I couldn't hold her if she didn't want to be with me. But now I know that she was still trying to save me by leaving."

"Jessie was right, you two are impossible."

Jefferson looked at Jackson and smiled. "As I said, she's on her way to Oz. After that I have no idea."

"What's Oz, where is it and how do I get there?"

"Okay, I'm tempted to say follow the Yellow Brick Road, but…" He chuckled. Jackson didn't find it funny. "Boston." Jefferson reached into his pocket and pulled out an address.

"When did she leave?"

Jefferson looked at his watch. "Six hours ago."

"Damn, she's already there."

Jefferson chuckled again. "I thought you didn't believe her."

"What do you mean?"

"She never lied to you, Jackson. She hates flying, she panics every time. Right about now I'd say she was someplace in the Midwest. But I'd hurry if I were you. You have about four or five more days to catch up with her." Jackson looked at him, confused. "She took a train back to Boston after a quick stop in New York."

"Thanks," Jackson said as he stood and walked away.

"Don't mention it," Jefferson said, still sitting.

"Hey," Jackson called out. Jefferson turned just as Jackson tossed him the keys to his house and car. "No wild parties, please."

Jefferson laughed. "Trust me."

Jackson laughed as he hurried upstairs to pack. He filled a suitcase, called and filed a flight plan, then ordered his private plane fueled. He was on his way to Oz, whatever, or whoever, that was.

Epilogue

"Yo, Sammy, welcome back."

Samantha smiled brightly as she wrapped her arms around Deacon and he engulfed her completely. "Thanks, it's good to be back. I have something for you," she said, handing him a brown paper bag.

"Now we're talking." He took the bag, opened it and inhaled, smiling. "Perfect timing as always."

She looked around. "Where's everybody? This place is like a ghost town."

"Shift's about to change."

"Oh, right," she said, looking at her new gold watch, then realizing that within minutes, dozens of cabs would come rolling into the garage. "I'm gonna head over to the office. Is Emily here?"

"Yep, she's there, drilling the new cabbie and giving her the safe-driving speech."

Samantha nodded, knowing that lecture by heart. She saw Darnell walk by with a huge black eye. He didn't speak, just hurried in the opposite direction. She turned back to Deacon. "What was all that about?"

"Oh, that's right, you weren't here for the fireworks and live entertainment. Darnell's wife came into the garage unexpectantly and caught him pushing up on one of the office clerks. She made her point with a left hook to his right eye, then nearly tore the garage apart going after him."

"Ouch," Samantha said, openly laughing. "Beautiful, I love it, I just wish I'd been here to see it."

"Yeah, you would have loved it. The sound of him screaming echoed in the garage for two days." He chuckled. She laughed.

"That must have been a sight."

"Oh, yeah, cell phones came out like paparazzi cameras. There're still some pretty good action pictures on the wall outside the office and there's a video floating around somewhere," Deacon added.

They both laughed this time.

"I guess life goes on," she said as Darnell walked by again, this time not even looking at her.

"It does indeed," he said. "By the way, there was someone looking for you earlier."

"Who?" she asked, concerned as dread of those words sank into her soul.

Deacon looked around and smiled. "I don't see him now. I'm sure he'll be back soon."

"Okay, see you later," she said with caution, then headed to the office. Then, prompted by curiosity, she stopped at the employee board where she saw six eight-by-ten glossy prints of Darnell ducking from his wife as she landed her fist on his face. She chuckled again at the justice of life, then continued to the office. She knocked on the already open door.

Emily was sitting at the desk discussing the ramifications of safe driving with a new cabbie. Relieved to be interrupted, the new cabdriver jumped up and excused herself as soon as Samantha walked in.

"Hey, baby," Emily said, standing and hugging Samantha warmly. "When did you get here?"

"A few minutes ago."

"You all right?"

"Yes, just fine, Auntie Em."

"Listen, love, I'd love to chat and catch up and Lord knows I have a hundred questions, but I got to get these cabs rolling out of here. You know they can't do a thing without me. I'll be right back."

Samantha sat down at the dispatch desk and watched as dozens of cabs suddenly came rolling in. Emily was out in the garage, pointing and collecting fare bags. She had her life back and everything was as it should be except...

She rested her forehead in her palm and placed her elbow on the desk. She was miserable. Love was hell. "Is this where I turn in my fare packet?"

The voice was familiar but out of place. She turned and saw Jackson standing behind her, smiling. Confused at first, she stood trying to understand how her imagination had come to life. "Jackson?" He smiled and nodded, seeing her stunned expression. "What are you doing here?"

He walked farther into the office. "Someone told me that Oz was a good place to hang out, but your auntie Em said that if I intended to be around here waiting for you for the next week or so I might as well make it worth her while. She gave me a cab."

Samantha laughed, knowing the rule. "Wait a minute, you've been here a week. What happened?" she said, suddenly concerned. "Did something go wrong? I saw Eric and Lincoln get arrested myself, and Grant called to say that George's files were a gold mine. His attorney is begging for a deal."

"No, everything's fine."

"So why are you here?" she asked again.

"You didn't really think that that was it, did you?"

"Yeah, that was the general idea."

"Then you were wrong. I told you before I wasn't going to let you walk away from me, from this, from us."

"Jackson…" She paused to breathe. "What we did, what I did…"

"None of that matters. You saved me. You saved my family, my company, my life. I need you. Good or bad, con or not."

"But that's not how it works, you walk out before they do. So…" she said, taking a step to walk around him.

"No," he said firmly. "You've been pushing me away from day one, only this time I'm not leaving."

"You don't have to. I'm leaving, remember?"

"Then I'll find you again."

"Look, get it through your head. We're over."

"On the contrary, we've just begun. I'm not letting you go that easily. I love you and you love me."

Tears welled in her eyes. She'd seen the look in his eyes before. It was the complete assurance of fact.

"Stop running," he said softly.

"I can't, I have to."

"No, you don't, not anymore. Run to me." He opened his arms wide to her. "I love you, Samantha Lee Taylor, and I know you love me. So since you for some strange reason refuse to stay and be with me, I've come to be with you. See?" He raised his cash bag with the cab company logo on it. "I even found a new job."

Tears slowly crawled down her face. "You're the CEO of

Daley Communications. I sent the paperwork myself. You can't just walk away from that. It's what you've always wanted."

"No, you're what I've always wanted."

"But the company…"

"Is fine, I transferred my stock on loan to Jessie, she's CEO. Dad made it official at the awards ceremony last week."

"Jackson, your world and my world are as far apart as—"

"Mars and Venus?" he asked.

"Something like that." She smiled. "You need a woman in your life from a good family, someone who can stand by your side without you ever being ashamed."

He reached out and pulled her into his arms. "I have that and so much more. You said it yourself, family is forever. Thank you for helping us."

She nodded. "You're welcome."

"I love you," he said.

"I love you, too," she responded.

They kissed, long and leisurely, sealing the love they shared until the sound of applause rang out. They looked around the garage, seeing that through the office window they were suddenly the center of attention as everybody laughed and whistled their approval.

"Okay, okay, break it up in here, we have a business to run," Emily said as she walked in.

"This is for you," Jackson said, handing her the money bag. "And this—" he pulled out a stunning diamond ring and slipped it onto her ring finger "—is for you."

Emily hugged them both, then chased them out of her office. "Where to now?" he asked.

"I don't know, how about a nice long vacation? I've been running away for so long that it'll be nice to stay in one place and relax for a week or so."

"That sounds like a great idea. Do you have any particular place in mind?"

"No. Switzerland, Africa, anywhere is fine as long as we're together."

"Well, I know this little inn out on the West Coast. It has great little rooms and it's right by the ocean. I already reserved bungalow number twelve."

They kissed again as they walked out.

Dear Reader

I hope you enjoyed reading *Love After All*. It was great fun writing it and even more fun researching. The art of the con was a lot more diverse that I expected but to do it justice I wanted to show all sides of this world as it is sometimes intricately woven through families for generations. I wanted to explore family dynamics and relationships and show that sometimes the things we do or choose to do affect more than ourselves.

Samantha Lee Taylor and Jackson Daily had family dramas that nearly destroyed them. Both characters denied who they really were, which only made it natural for them to deny what they really felt. Finally accepting helped them to open to love and realize that they were meant for each other and that their love was meant to be.

As always, thank you for taking this ride with me. I hope you found it as thrilling and exciting as I did.

My next release is a young adult novel for the Harlequin

Kimani TRU line entitled *Push Pause* and is scheduled to be released October 2007. So gather your daughters and sons and enjoy. Afterwards, Mamma Lou steps up to guide a friend in *Following Love*, coming in December 2007.

Please feel free to write and let me know what you think. I always enjoy hearing from readers. Please send your comments to conorfleet@aol.com or Celeste O. Norfleet, P.O. Box 7346, Woodbridge, VA 22195-7346. Don't forget to check out my Web site at www.celesteonorfleet.com.

"Robyn Amos dishes up a fast-paced, delectable love story…!"
—*Romantic Times BOOKreviews*

BESTSELLING AUTHOR

AMOS ROBYN

Promise ME

After taking a break from a demanding career and a controlling fiancé, Cara Williams was ready to return to her niche in the computer field. It looked like clear sailing—until AJ Gray came on the scene. As the powerful president of Captial Computer Consulting, AJ offered Cara the expertise she needed—even as his kisses triggered her worst fears and her deepest desires.

Coming the first week of March,
wherever books are sold.

ARABESQUE®

www.kimanipress.com

KPRA0070307

An emotional story of family and forgiveness...

National bestselling author

Phillip Thomas Duck

PLAYING WITH
DESTINY

As brothers, Colin and Courtney Sheffield know
their lives will always be connected. But their mistakes,
and those of their absent father before them, have tangled
them in a web of bitterness and regret neither can shake.

As painful secrets threaten to shatter their futures,
both must deal with the emotional complexities
of true brotherhood.

"Duck writes with a voice that is unique,
entertaining and compelling."
—Robert Fleming, author of *Havoc After Dark*

*Available the first week of March,
wherever books are sold.*

sepia™

www.kimanipress.com   KPPTD0390307

Enjoy the early *Hideaway* stories
with a special Kimani Press release...

HIDEAWAY LEGACY

Two full-length novels

ROCHELLE
ALERS

Essence Bestselling Author

A collectors-size trade volume containing
HEAVEN SENT and HARVEST MOON—
two emotional novels from the author's
acclaimed *Hideaway Legacy*.

"Fans of the romantic suspense of Iris Johansen,
Linda Howard and Catherine Coulter will enjoy the first
installment of the *Hideaway Sons and Brothers* trilogy,
part of the continuing saga of the *Hideaway Legacy*."
—*Library Journal* on *No Compromise*

Available the first week of March
wherever books are sold.

KIMANI PRESS™
www.kimanipress.com

KORA0650307R

Everybody's guilty of something…

ONE NIGHT WITH YOU

National bestselling author

Gwynne Forster

Determined to restore his reputation after
losing a bitter court battle, Reid Maguire needs
Judge Kendra Rutherford to set things right.
But the sexy judge is making it hard for him to
keep his priorities straight—and soon they're
both guilty of losing their hearts….

"Like fine wine, Gwynne Forster's
storytelling skills get better over time."
—*Essence* bestselling author Donna Hill

*Available the first week of March,
wherever books are sold.*

KIMANI
ROMANCE

www.kimanipress.com   KPGF0080307

A sexy new novel from acclaimed author

Ann Christopher

Just About
SEX

Attorney Alex Greene is determined to expose celebrity
sex therapist Simone Beaupre as a fraud. It seems
34-years-young Simone is still a virgin! But when
Alex actually meets the good doctor, his campaign
turns from prosecution…to seduction!

"Christopher has a gift for storytelling."
—*Romantic Times BOOKreviews*

Available the first week of March, wherever books are sold.

KIMANI
ROMANCE ™

National bestselling author
FRANCINE CRAFT

The Way
You Make Me Feel

The diva who had amnesia…

Suffering from amnesia, singer Stevie Simms
finds refuge in Damien Steele's home. As they
become lovers, Damien's frozen heart thaws
and Steve starts to recover. But someone is
trying to kill Stevie—if only she could
remember who!

*Available the first week of March,
wherever books are sold.*

KIMANI
ROMANCE